CALLING ELDRITCH HAYES

TORI LEWIS

Copyright 2024 © Tori Lewis
www.authortorilewis.com
All rights reserved.
The characters and events portrayed in this book are fictitious. Any similarity to real persons, living or dead, is coincidental and not intended by the author.

No part of this book may be reproduced, or stored in a retrieval system, or transmitted in any form or by any means, electronic, mechanical, photocopying, recording, or otherwise, without express written permission of the publisher.

Cover design by Tori Lewis
Formatting by Kalayna Blanch

Edited by Holly Sadowski, Fox & Muse Editing and Consulting
www.foxandmuseediting.com
&
Taneet Grewal
www.writingsformydaughters.com

ISBN: 979-8-218-38519-4
Imprint: Chapter 4 Publishing LLC
www.chapter4publishing.com

For those who believe, in spite of the pain.
And for Charlie, who will forever be my Eldritch Hayes.

CONTENT WARNING

This book contains depictions of addiction, general gore and horror, and attempted suicide. If you are struggling with thoughts of suicide or self-harm, please call or text 988. Help is available 24 hours a day, seven days a week.

The world is a better place with you in it.

www.988lifeline.org

THE OFFICIAL PLAYLIST

"Guitar Man" — Bread
"(They Long to Be) Close to You" — the Carpenters
"Make it With You" — Bread
"Tequila Sunrise" — The Eagles
"If" — Bread
"The Best of My Love" — The Eagles
"It Don't Matter to Me" — Bread
"I Can't Let Go" — The Hollies
"Merry Christmas, Darling" — the Carpenters
"Just One Look" — The Hollies
"The Air That I Breathe" — The Hollies
"Bus Stop" — The Hollies
"Solitaire" — the Carpenters
"Yesterday Once More" — the Carpenters
"Baby I'm-a Want You" — Bread
"Down On My Knees" — Bread
"Everything I Own" — Bread
"One of These Nights" — The Eagles

Listen Now on Spotify!

PROLOGUE

It starts small—it always does. Floorboards creaking in the middle of the night, the car keys that were hung by the front door finding their way to the kitchen counter, the overall sense of unease, the feeling of being watched.

Then it progresses. The footsteps in the attic, the slamming doors, the whispers, the shadow that moves just out the corner of your eye. Sometimes, it's gradual enough that you start to ask the question all people who experience such things ask: *Am I going crazy?* It is in these moments where we begin to write such activity off as our overactive imaginations.

Keys on the counter. *I forgot I placed them there.*

Creaking floorboards and footsteps overhead. *Just the house settling.*

A slamming door. *A gust of wind. I did feel a draft earlier.*

We find this behavior comforting. As the peculiar activity in the house continues at a moderate pace, we continue to rationalize. But to continue is one thing—to escalate is another. When you enter the kitchen to find not only are your keys inexplicably on the counter for the fourth time this week, but every cabinet door has been flung open and all four dining chairs are stacked in the center of the table, all thoughts of rationalization finally give way to the unspoken truth that has been gnawing at the back of your mind:

Something is in here.

At this point, we have two choices: push the truth back down and live in denial or come to terms with the phenomenon and seek a solution. For those who choose the latter, the first step seems an obvious one: identify the presence in question. In the town of Sommerset, South Carolina, a name will be spoken, a number given, from one person who has previously taken this first step to the next person in need.

Step one: ...

PART I

CHAPTER ONE

"Eldritch!" a chipper voice calls from behind the counter, coffee in hand. Eldritch makes his apologies to the handful of patrons he squeezes past on his way to the front of the shop. "One coffee—two sugars, one cream—as usual," she smiles, handing over the beverage in question.

"Thanks, Kelly." His voice is quiet. Eldritch has always been soft spoken, but he knows Kelly hears him above the din of the bustling café.

"Anytime."

She winks, he nods, placing a few bucks in the tip jar before turning to leave.

The whispers that follow as he turns his back don't bother him anymore. It's hard to go anywhere in this town without hearing the hushed murmurings of "That's Eldritch Hayes," the second they think he's no longer within earshot. For the most part, people are terrible judges of what constitutes *within earshot*. Eldritch almost always hears.

The door of The Grind slams behind him as he exits, caught by an unexpected gust of wind. It's unseasonably cold for this time of year. The temperature fell below freezing last night—quite unusual for the first week of November—and a light sheen of frost still lingers across the town. Closing his eyes, Eldritch breathes deep, the crisp air filling his lungs with a bite. He exhales, eyes opening in time to watch his breath materialize—a faint cloud of white—before fading into nothingness.

"For what is your life? It is even a vapor that appears for a little time and then vanishes away." The loud cry of a train whistle pulls him from his reverie. Eldritch takes a tentative sip of his coffee, careful not to burn himself, and decides it is far too early in the morning for such thoughts.

He continues down Main Street, face downcast to block the wind; at least, this is what he tells himself in the moment. Truth be told, Eldritch's face is always downcast—a habit he developed as a child. There are two reasons for this behavior. First of all, it is easier to pass by unrecognized when people can't see your face. Secondly, when you're not looking at people, you can't see them...or whatever might be attached to them. The latter is the main reason why Eldritch goes through life the way he does: unattached, uninvolved.

From a young age, it was clear he wasn't an ordinary child. He's heard the story of his birth more times than he can count; the story of how the whispers began the moment he emerged from the womb with a birth caul—or "veil," as is the more common term in these parts—covering his face. The old wives' tale cast a long shadow over newborn Eldritch, and he quickly became the talk of the hospital for the duration of his stay.

Even after the thin layer of placenta was removed from around his head, the attending nurses could be heard chattering amongst themselves, "He had a veil over his face. That means he can see spirits!"

For a while, it seemed like that's all it was: superstition and idle chatter. But at the age of four, his ability reared its head and could no longer be ignored. He began speaking of people and events that he should've had no knowledge or memory of; relatives, long deceased, his parents insisted had never been discussed in front of him. Once, while visiting his great-grandmother, he kept referring to "Old Rocking Man" and would point to the rocking chair in the corner of the sitting room. Four-year-old Eldritch could not understand why his parents continued to badger him about the old man in question, confused as to why they couldn't just talk to the man himself. Eventually, an exasperated Eldritch huffed out a name: Papa Reuben. His great-grandmother informed him, years later, that Reuben Sholly built that house in 1802 and was found dead at the age of 82 in that exact rocking chair.

Similar moments occurred on a regular basis. Sometimes, three to four times a week; sometimes, three to four times a day. When he was six, Eldritch and his parents happened by the pastor of the church they attended while out for a Sunday stroll. Reverend Len Holland was a stern man; tall, rotund, and imposing. Pentecostal Holiness to his core, he had a reputation for his fiery sermons and dramatic presentation of The Word. While the adults engaged in conversation about the weather and the tragic state of this Godless world, Eldritch noticed a man approaching. Charlie Haskell, who attended their church, was of small build, middle aged, and always donned the customary denim and plaid of Sommerset's working class. Nothing about his appearance on that particular day was

notably peculiar except for the dark circles under his eyes—
dark circles which touted that special brand of weariness that
could be felt bone-deep. The man's behavior, however, spoke
otherwise. His movements were erratic; arms fidgeting, head
jerking from one side to the other. Eldritch saw this draw the
attention of Reverend Holland who muttered a disapproving,
"Looks like Charlie fell off the wagon again," to Mr. Hayes.

As Charlie came nearer to their location by the town
gazebo, Eldritch was overcome with a feeling of extreme
unease. The little hairs on the back of his neck stood on end,
and he recoiled from the man, launching himself toward his
mother. It was then that an inhuman sound escaped Charlie's
lips—a gravelly chuckle that seemed more akin to a growl than
a laugh—as he passed by. Reverend Holland tried to get
Charlie's attention, but the man continued on his way,
twitching as he went, as if he hadn't heard the preacher
shouting his name.

In that moment, the fear Eldritch felt gave way to another
sensation: recognition. Although he couldn't explain it at the
time, Eldritch instinctively knew the being the pastor kept
referring to as "Charlie" was, in fact, not Charlie at all. It was
such an obvious thing to the small boy that he was confused
as to why Reverend Holland kept calling the man by the wrong
name. In an attempt to help the mistaken pastor, Eldritch
called out, "Amaymon!"

The man froze, and Reverend Holland seemed at a loss for
words, staring at Eldritch, eyes wide, mouth agape. Later that
day, Eldritch overheard his parents talking and learned that he
didn't just see the occasional ghost, but he was sensitive to the
presence of other spirits. Eldritch could see demons.

This simple fact, which would define the course of his life
from that moment on, is the reason Eldritch crosses the street

where he does on his way to work every morning: at the only stop light in town, right before he reaches Gordon's ABC Packaging store. It's no one's fault the liquor store is located across the street from Hayes Hardware, where Eldritch has worked since he was nineteen. He has been sober for seven years now, but that doesn't stop him from clutching his coffee a little tighter when he catches the three red dots out the corner of his eye.

Eldritch chugs the last of his coffee and tosses the cup in the trash can by the back entrance of the hardware store before pulling open the heavy, metal door just enough to squeeze inside. The abrupt, mechanical stamp of the timecard machine echoes down the concrete corridor, signaling the start of the workday.

"Man, it's cold out!"

Eldritch jumps in surprise and looks over his shoulder to find his coworker, Amir, snickering at his reaction. Amir pushes himself away from the doorjamb he'd been leaning against, shaking his head as he makes his way toward Eldritch.

"Sorry about that. Didn't mean to scare you. Sometimes I forget how jumpy you can be."

"It's fine," Eldritch offers with a tight-lipped smile as the younger man delivers a light punch to his left shoulder. Eldritch appreciates the casual familiarity of their exchange, cognizant of the fact that Amir is the closest thing he has ever had to a friend.

They walk side by side down the corridor, Amir talking on and on about what all needs to be done today and the shipment they'll be getting in around nine o'clock.

"So that guy who's flipping the Birch-Rainey house is coming in later. Most of the stuff on that truck will go straight to him: lumber, paint, a lot of custom pieces too. Your uncle has that deal with the historical people, so everything that guy needs has to come through us—the major stuff, at least."

Eldritch is familiar with this deal. Hayes Hardware has been serving the town of Sommerset for over ninety years. But five years ago, his Uncle Calvin made a lucrative decision that put sales at an all-time high: joining forces with Restore South Carolina. One of the many things the town is known for is its abundance of historical homes. Thanks to the prevalence of cable TV and its endless slew of remodeling shows, the idea of the "fixer upper" has hit the midlands by storm. However, all renovations within the town limits must be given the green light by Sommerset's own historical society, Restore SC, before they begin. Part of getting that green light is agreeing to use Hayes Hardware for all renovating supplies.

Eldritch knows it was a genius move. It helps keep the "little man" in business, and renovators benefit from the knowledge of people who grew up in this town and understand and appreciate the history of these homes. But when you're Eldritch Hayes, even something as symbiotic and beneficial as this has its downside: a barrage of new faces and the chance they're bringing more into this family-owned hardware store than meets the average eye. That's why he stays in the back, stocking, pricing, keeping to himself.

Eldritch feels the shift in his own demeanor, and he knows Amir can sense it too.

"Hey, it'll be fine," Amir assures him. "I'll handle the driver and sign for the stuff. You just help with the unloading. Good?"

"Good," Eldritch nods in agreement as Amir turns to head toward the storefront. "Oh, Amir!" he calls out before his friend disappears around the corner.

"Yeah, what's up?"

"What time will the guy—the contractor—be by to pick up his stuff?"

"Eleven-ish? Sometime before lunch, I think."

Eldritch hesitates, thinking of how to phrase his question, "Will I need to—?"

"No," Amir interjects, and Eldritch is relieved he doesn't have to voice his fear aloud. "No, I got him."

"Good. Thanks."

When Amir doesn't turn to leave, Eldritch knows what's coming and braces himself.

"You know, this month's poker game is at Sam's tomorrow night. Just thought I'd offer."

Eldritch has received this offer once a month for the last six years and has yet to accept, but Amir remains undeterred. The thought does not move Eldritch to accept the invitation, but it makes him smile, nonetheless.

"Thanks, but I still don't think it's a good idea."

Amir shrugs, "You're only a social outcast by choice, Eldritch."

"Is that so?" Eldritch laughs. Amir's attempts at psychoanalyzing him never fail to entertain.

"Yeah, it's so. Trust me, I know. You're talking to the only Arab boy in town!" he bellows, stretching his arms wide and bowing with a dramatic flourish.

"That can't be true!" Eldritch calls back as he turns to walk away.

"It better be!" Amir counters. "I need something to make me feel special! We can't all see ghosts, Eldritch!"

The first hour of work passes quickly for Eldritch. He spends most of his time reorganizing the warehouse and sweeping up shards of glass after Lanny-Ray knocks over four pallets of lightbulbs. Calvin has strict rules in place regarding Lanny-Ray's use of the forklift, but Lanny-Ray tends to disregard all of Calvin's rules, especially ones related to him operating heavy machinery. He insists that he can do as he pleases because he's been here since the store opened 93 years ago. No one argues with him because they're not entirely sure he's lying.

Nine o'clock rolls around, and the Birch-Rainey delivery is right on time. Amir intercepts the driver at the loading dock, and Eldritch makes a point to busy himself inside to avoid having to interact with the stranger. Only when the semi is in gear and rumbling toward the street does Eldritch join Amir on the dock to help with the inventory, which includes two full pallets of paint, numerous boxes of hardwood flooring, rolls upon rolls of insulation, and several custom, hand-carved pieces of gingerbread trim and decorative brackets for the old Victorian home.

In its prime, the Birch-Rainey house stood sentry over Sommerset, poised as gatekeeper to the sleepy town center. A stately, southern interpretation of the Queen Anne architectural style, its bright, white paint and ornate trim gave it an air of sophistication and elegance that proclaimed the wealth of the Rainey family to all who beheld it in the late nineteenth century.

But that was then. Now, it stands derelict; its weatherworn roof sagging from a century of neglect, the once white paint all but stripped away to reveal sickly, gray boards faded by the elements, windows shattered and boarded up with cheap plywood, the elaborate trim and frieze splintered and broken. What stands there now is a fractured, empty shell; that sort of dilapidated remnant of a world long since passed which calls to mind images of chain-rattling ghosts wandering halls of withered opulence. Yet, despite its haggard appearance, Eldritch harbors a deep-rooted fondness for the old house. As he stares at the shipment, grateful someone has decided to give the home a second chance, fragmented memories drift to the forefront of his mind—memories of blood-stained confessions whispered into a sacred space beneath a towering, grand staircase; and although he knows it's a phantom sensation brought on by this nostalgic interlude, the scar in his left palm begins to throb.

"It's got to be haunted." Amir's sudden comment pulls Eldritch from his thoughts, putting an end to the illusion, and he glances over at his friend who has resumed checking the invoice.

"Being old doesn't automatically make a house haunted." Eldritch pushes the pallet jack under one pallet of paint and begins to haul it inside.

"Yeah, but…look at it. If ever there was a haunted house in this town, that's it."

"It's not haunted, Amir. Trust me."

Amir's head snaps up from his clipboard, eyebrows jumping up to meet his hairline. "You've been inside?"

Eldritch sighs and knows there's no point in putting off the inevitable. "Once. A long time ago. Back in high school."

"And?"

"And there's nothing in there. It's not haunted."

"Oh," Amir mumbles, and Eldritch can tell he's more than a little disappointed at the revelation. "Well, you're the expert."

Eldritch chuckles and continues inside with the pallet of paint as his Uncle Calvin rounds the corner.

"That the Birch-Rainey delivery?"

"Yessir. Amir has the paperwork," Eldritch replies, depositing the pallet and heading back outside for the second one.

Calvin inspects the contents of the shipment as Eldritch and Amir bring it inside, letting out a whistle as the last pallet is hauled indoors. "That's a lot of paint."

"It's a lot of house."

Calvin laughs, clapping a strong hand on his nephew's shoulder. "That it is, Eldritch. That it is. Oh, Amir's probably going to ask you if it's haunted, by the way."

Eldritch snorts in response and turns toward the storefront to see what products need restocking.

"Just out of curiosity—" his uncle calls after him.

"It's not."

A crash from the front of the building echoes down the hallway, and the three men rush to find the source of the sound, splitting up amid the aisles of the store. Eldritch rounds the work boot display on the end cap of aisle two to find Lanny-Ray sprawled out on the concrete floor, tangled in a web of multicolor, incandescent, plug-in Christmas lights. Beside him, the aluminum step ladder—which Lanny-Ray is also forbidden to use—lies on its side, overturned.

"Lanny-Ray! What the he—?"

"Language, Amir," Calvin chastises as they rush to Lanny-Ray's side, seconds behind Eldritch. "Are you hurt? What happened?"

"I'm alright, I'm alright," Lanny-Ray insists. He tries to lift himself from the floor but lets out a sharp cry and crumples to the ground once more, clutching his right arm.

"Yeah, you look it," Calvin mutters and motions for Eldritch to help him lift the injured man to his feet. "Can you stand?"

"*Of course*, I can stand! I don't need your coddling!" But despite his protests, Lanny-Ray doesn't pull away, leaning on the two men as they help him to a chair near the register. "My arm hurts," he grits out once he's seated.

"Can you move it?" Eldritch asks, worry creeping into his tone.

"Not really. Hurts when I try to."

"Right. We need to get him to the hospital," resolves Calvin.

Amir nods, pulling his keys from his pocket. "I'll drive him, Cal. Let me go pull my car around front," he offers, hurrying off through the back of the store.

Calvin turns back to the elderly man, who is now cradling his right arm against his chest, and voices the question Eldritch knows he's been holding in since spotting the old codger on the ground. "What were you doing on the ladder, Lanny-Ray?"

"I was trying to get them Christmas lights up! It's already November. Down at the Home Depot, they've had 'em up since before Halloween!"

"I told you Amir was going to do that this afternoon. You know you're not supposed to be up on that ladder, Lanny-Ray!" Calvin's face is turning red, and Eldritch knows he needs to intervene before things get out of hand and Lanny-Ray ends up at the emergency room with *two* broken arms.

"Hey, hey, Lanny-Ray, we'll get those Christmas lights up today. Don't you worry. And look, Amir just pulled up out front, so let's get you to the hospital. That's the most important thing right now, okay?" Eldritch reassures the old man as he lifts him from his seat, making a point to lock eyes with Calvin as he utters the last few words.

The jingling of the overhead bell as the front door is pushed open fails to drown out the deep sigh Calvin exhales—

a sound Eldritch knows is a response to his pointed comment. Once outside, they escort Lanny-Ray to Amir's car, where the latter is waiting with the passenger door open. After the torturous affair of getting the old man into the seat, Lanny-Ray looks up at Eldritch and speaks, his voice raw with emotion.

"Make sure you're the one who gets them lights up. That one there probably don't even know what Christmas is," he half-whispers with a jerk of his head in Amir's direction.

"Wow. And to think I offered to drive you to the hospital," Amir deadpans with a shake of his head and slams the passenger door shut. "I deserve a raise after this," he says with a forced smile to Calvin, who rolls his eyes in response.

"Just try not to kill him before you reach the emergency room."

"No promises!" Amir shouts, voice dripping with false enthusiasm, as he climbs into the driver's seat and shuts the door.

Moments later, the car disappears down Main Street, and Eldritch and Calvin find themselves back inside, staring at Lanny-Ray's Christmas light fiasco.

"What time is it?" Asks Calvin.

Eldritch glances down at his watch. "Twenty-five after."

"Twenty-five after what?"

"Twenty-five after ten. Why?"

"Oh great. I'm supposed to meet with Harry about the new Restore SC project they're about to approve."

"When's the meeting?"

"In five minutes! I have to run. You mind getting all this cleaned up?" he asks, motioning toward Lanny-Ray's mess, as he heads for the door.

"I can do that, but—w-wait, wait, Uncle Cal!"

CALLING ELDRITCH HAYES

Calvin comes to a stop, one hand on the door, and turns back to face his nephew.

"When will you be back?" Eldritch asks, eyes wide with fear. He hears the desperation in his own voice—hears how small he sounds—and he hates it. He knows Calvin hates it too; the look on his face gives him away, and Eldritch wonders what thoughts are cycling through his uncle's mind. Calvin is the only person left who truly knows—knows what the fear and crippling anxiety do to Eldritch, knows how the prospect of encountering strangers alone can reduce this grown man to a small child in an instant. So many people call Eldritch's ability a gift, but Calvin doesn't. Calvin never has—a fact for which Eldritch has always been grateful.

"I won't be gone long. I promise."

"But the contractor—"

"He said he would be here around eleven, and he's *always* late. Always."

Eldritch does his best to push the fear away, to purge it from his mind, to force the bile back down his throat, and stop the tears from forming in his eyes.

"You better hurry. You're going to be late," is his only response.

Calvin hesitates and opens his mouth to speak, but the South Carolina Gamecocks' fight song—Calvin's ringtone—cuts through the moment. "That's Harry," he says, looking down at the screen, "I have to go." He answers his phone and rushes out the door, assuring the man on the other end of the call that he's on his way. The bell jingles, and the door slams shut. Eldritch flinches at the sound.

He looks around the empty storefront and down at the Christmas lights strewn about the concrete floor and tangled in the overturned ladder. Maybe, if he busies himself with this task and then starts restocking the drill bits on aisle six, time will fly by. Maybe the meeting won't last long at all, and Uncle Cal will be back in time to deal with the contractor. Maybe he's just overreacting, and nothing will happen while everyone is away.

Maybe.

Eldritch takes a shuddering breath and kneels down to start untangling the lights from the step ladder. Upon finishing that, he contemplates hanging them up like he promised Lanny-Ray but decides against it considering he's alone in the store, and no one is there to rush *him* to the hospital should he fall and break a limb of his own; so the ladder and lights are put away, and Eldritch heads to the back warehouse to retrieve the box of drill bits.

Eldritch enjoys stocking shelves; enjoys the repetition and finds it meditative. He's nearly done restocking the Milwaukee black oxide bits when the front bell jingles. Looking down at his watch, Eldritch sees that it's five 'til and decides Uncle Cal must be back. He sets the drill bits on the floor and walks toward the front, ready to hear all about the new Restore SC project.

"How'd it go?" he asks but stops dead in his tracks. Uncle Cal is not back. Instead, Eldritch finds himself face to face with a man he has never met before, and then…darkness—an overwhelming, all-consuming darkness. He supposes anyone else in this situation would be able to describe the man: his clothes, his hair, his height. But for Eldritch, there is no man anymore; he has been swallowed up by a black, undulating shape that looms overhead—a great shadow, tall and imposing.

The shape speaks, but all Eldritch hears is the sound of his blood rushing to his ears and the frantic beating of his heart. Seconds later, the stench hits him: decay, spoiled meat, a hint of sulfur, rot. Eldritch doubles over as his stomach churns and a mix of old coffee and bile finds its way into his throat. He is vaguely aware of the shape reaching out for him, and he pulls away, arms flailing in an attempt to protect himself. The shape withdraws, but Eldritch wastes no time in fleeing. He turns heel and dashes through the store, kicking over the half empty box of drill bits in his retreat, and locks himself in the employee bathroom.

The sound of footsteps reaches his ears as the shadow approaches the door, and Eldritch presses his back against the opposite wall. Then comes the knocking—a forceful, relentless knocking that has him flinching and the door rattling with every strike. There is a brief reprieve when the attention moves to the handle, which jiggles for several seconds before it stills and the knocking resumes. The smell of rot assaults his senses once more, and the last thing Eldritch remembers before blacking out is the sound of inhuman laughter as his head hits the concrete floor.

CHAPTER TWO

Gran-Gran's house was located two hours away, in a small town just outside Charleston. Eldritch's mother had told him countless stories of her childhood—a childhood spent running around Gran-Gran's marshy property, climbing trees, and scratching at the redbugs that never failed to burrow their way into her skin after a day of hanging around in the Spanish moss. The bedtime stories his mother would tell painted such a wonderful picture of Gran-Gran's house. In his mind, it was a magical place, full of fun and adventure he couldn't wait to experience for himself.

Eldritch was four years old the first time his parents took him to visit his great-grandmother's house in the Lowcountry.

The house was old. Eldritch knew this upon arrival, without his parents saying a word.

The house had voices. Eldritch could hear them the second he climbed out of the family's wood-paneled station wagon.

The house had faces in the windows. Eldritch could see them, and he waved to them as his mother helped him along the brick pathway that led to the front porch.

"Who are you waving at, sweetie?" she asked, with a grin.

"All the people."

"You see all those people, huh, darlin'?" came a sugary sweet voice from the porch. Gran-Gran stood, arms open wide, ready to envelop the small boy.

"He has quite the imagination," Louise explained to her grandmother. Gran-Gran hummed and tossed a wink Eldritch's way before sweeping him up in her arms.

After dinner, the family gathered in the sitting room to unwind and reminisce about "old times." Eldritch's parents laughed every time Gran-Gran told a funny story about little Louise scraping her knees or falling out of the large oak tree behind the house, only to hop back up and climb it again. Eldritch liked hearing these stories. He liked hearing his parents and Gran-Gran laugh at these stories; but for the life of him, he couldn't figure out why the old man in the corner never laughed with them.

The more he thought about it, the more Eldritch realized he'd never even seen this man until now. He wasn't there to greet them when they first arrived. He hadn't joined them for dinner. Eldritch didn't even know his name; but there he sat, rocking back and forth in the old rocking chair in the corner of the room, staring at Eldritch with pale, unblinking eyes.

Eldritch extended a hand in the old man's direction: reaching, pointing. The old man continued to rock, continued to stare, but said nothing. Unsatisfied with the lack of response, Eldritch offered up a soft, "hi." The old man remained silent, but brought a wrinkled, crooked finger to his lips—a gesture Eldritch knew meant "shhh." The sound of his parents' laughter drew his attention away from the old man for a moment, and it was clear to Eldritch no one had witnessed his interaction with the curious houseguest. He turned to face the old man again, but all he found was an empty chair in the corner. It rocked two or three more times on its own before stilling.

Sleep eluded Eldritch that night. The stifling heat of the Charleston summer made it impossible to get comfortable, and the humidity hung like a thick fog in the air. He stared at the ceiling above his bed for hours, drenched in sweat, as sleep remained a stranger. In the wee hours of the morning, Eldritch's mind switched over to the only other thing he could think about besides the heat, and he began to list every detail he remembered about the old rocking man.

"Old man, rocking back and forth. Black coat. Shirt up around his neck—couldn't see his skin except for his face. Old face, lots of wrinkles. Eyes were far away. Pointy nose. Skinny lips, almost no lips. Crooked finger, scary. Boney, like a skeleton. He wouldn't talk to me. Told me to 'shush.'"

After a while, Eldritch grew restless and rose from his bed. The room was sweltering, sticky, and his pajamas clung to his skin. A slight breeze filtered through the window on the other side of the room, and Eldritch knew he would feel a lot better if he could stick his head outside for a little while. He pushed back the thin curtains and leaned out the open window. His room was on the second floor, and the ground was a long way down. His parents were very firm when they told him to stay away from the window because he could get hurt if he fell, but it was just too hot. Eldritch knew to be careful.

The breeze was cool on his skin, and the relief was immediate. After taking a few deep breaths, he opened his eyes and looked around at the world outside his window. The moon was high and full, and a thin layer of fog stretched out along the ground. Eldritch thought of werewolves and laughed to himself. As his eyes fell on the large oak tree behind the house, however, the laughter died in his throat.

There were people in the tree—three of them—in the same tree his mother climbed as a child, but there was something very wrong about the way they swayed side by side, suspended from one thick, low hanging branch. Eldritch knew this was not what his mother meant when she said she used to play in the oak tree all day.

Despite the heat, a chill ran through his body, and Eldritch ran back to his bed, burying himself beneath the covers. When his mother came to wake him five hours later, she found him in a pool of sweat, curled up in the fetal position beneath the comforter. He hadn't moved since 3:00 a.m. Eldritch didn't mention the tree people to his parents, despite his mother's constant litany of, "What's wrong, baby boy?" over grits and eggs.

After breakfast, Louise was adamant about showing Eldritch around the grounds of her grandmother's property so he could see firsthand where his mother spent the majority of her childhood. With his tiny hand in hers, they wandered the well-worn grass trails that snaked about the five-acre lot, amidst a sea of colorful plants and blooms: azaleas in every shade imaginable, massive beds of various irises and daylilies, and the creeping vines of bright, yellow Carolina Jessamine wrapped around every trellis and fence post. Louise told tales of days spent rolling about in the sweetgrass, jumping over the small bubbling creek that ran alongside the woods at the edge of the property, and of course, there was the tree.

"Here it is, Eldritch. The tree I was telling you about. I used to climb this thing from sunup to sundown. I can't even count how many times I hurt myself falling out of it," laughed Louise.

Eldritch did not laugh. As his mother spoke fondly of the old oak and recounted every memory as it came to mind, Eldritch found himself unable to concentrate on her words. There were many sounds drifting along the Lowcountry breeze, all familiar to the small boy. There was the rustling of leaves, the chirping of birds, the singing of cicadas, the melodic speech of his mother, but there was also another sound—a sound Eldritch couldn't seem to place.

Closing his eyes, he tried his best to pinpoint the strange sound and focused on it until the leaves, the birds, the bugs, and his mother's voice all faded into one indistinct hum in the background. He could hear it now, more clearly than he could before. It was a creaking sound.

Creak.

It was familiar somehow.

Creak.

It made him think of the tire swing in the backyard at home.

Creak.

A long, low, steady creak, like something was tied to the tree and swaying in the wind.

Creak.

Then he remembered what he had seen the night before. Eldritch's eyes snapped open, and there they were, right in front of him: three bodies dangling from the large limb of the giant oak. They were so close. If he reached out, he could touch their muddy, bare feet as they twitched and struggled, gasping for air with the rope tight around their necks. Eldritch dared to look at one of the faces, and the unseeing eyes looked back at him. He watched as the mouth of a dark-skinned man opened wide and unleashed a harrowing wail of agony and despair. Eldritch opened his mouth to release a terrified scream of his own, but fear had gripped him, and no sound would come. His jaw locked, and his muscles froze, forcing him to stare at the shrieking man, time standing still as he beheld the horror before him.

He heard someone calling his name.

"Eldritch! Eldritch!"

The dangling man continued to wail.

"Eldritch! Honey, look at me!"

But he *was* looking. Did the man know Eldritch's name? Who was calling him?

A persistent shaking of his shoulders jostled him from his stupor, and Eldritch could see his mother kneeling in front of him, eyes wide with alarm, tears streaking her face. "Baby, what happened?! Are you okay?! Don't scare me like that!"

He met her gaze and, having gained control of his muscles once more, asked with a trembling voice, "Don't you hear him?" and with that, he sprinted back toward the house, as fast as his tiny legs would carry him. He had been seeing things for as long as he could remember, but the image of the bodies dangling from the branch of that mossy oak, howling in anguish, was the first thing that ever scared him. This was Eldritch's first encounter with the dark side of his gift—a laceration that would never truly heal.

When he reached the house, his legs were weary from overexertion, and his lungs burned within his chest with every heaving breath; yet he flew past his father and Gran-Gran on the porch and made it to the sitting room before collapsing on the floor beside the old rocking chair. He could hear the hushed voices of Gran-Gran and his parents in another room.

Eldritch didn't know how to explain what he was feeling to his family. His mother hadn't seemed bothered by the people in the tree, and Eldritch didn't want them to get mad at him for running away when he was supposed to stay by his mother's side. Before long, the tears began to fall, and Eldritch wept freely into the hardwood planks of the sitting room floor.

Minutes passed—or maybe hours, Eldritch was unsure—but as his tears began to dry, he felt a hand on his head, patting his mop of brown hair, threading slender fingers through the strands. Thinking one of his parents had come to comfort him, Eldritch lifted his eyes to find the source of the ministrations. To his surprise, it was neither his parents nor Gran-Gran petting his head but rather, the old man in the rocking chair from yesterday.

In a soft, gentle voice, he whispered to the boy, "There, there. Don't you cry. Papa Reuben is right here."

Eldritch considered the man—the kindness in his eyes, the tenderness of his actions—and decided he wasn't scary in the least. The old man offered up a friendly smile as Eldritch sat up to face him.

It was then that his parents and Gran-Gran joined him in the sitting room, and his father approached the rocking chair to have a seat. Eldritch gasped and tried to protest, but before he could voice his concern, the old man was gone—vanished into thin air before his very eyes.

"Old man," he said, finger pointed at the chair.

"What was that, bud?" his father asked.

"Old rocking man. He patted my head."

The three adults looked at one another, each of them wearing the same expression: eyebrows drawn together, mouths turn downward.

"Eldritch, baby, did you see something?" Gran-Gran—her voice soft and sweet as honey—asked after several seconds of silence.

The little boy sighed with exhaustion and nodded. "Faces in the windows…people hanging from the tree…old man in the rocking chair," he trailed off, pointing toward the seat his father occupied.

Gran-Gran brought a trembling hand to her mouth. "Louise, it was only a matter of time," she whispered to her granddaughter.

"What old man, baby?" his mother asked, eyes wide as she looked from her grandmother to her son.

His father cleared his throat, twisting in his seat; scanning the back and arms of the chair as he questioned his son further. "Eldritch, I need you to tell us the truth. Did you see someone in this chair?"

"Yes. He was right there."

"Who was there, honey? Who was it?" his mother begged.

Although frustrated and overwhelmed, Eldritch managed to recall the old man's name, and cried out, "Papa Reuben!"

Gran-Gran rose from her seat on the sofa and left the room without a word, returning moments later with something in her hand—a small, stiff piece of paper. Eldritch watched as she handed it to his mother and instructed her to turn it over. Louise did as she was told and read the words inscribed on the back.

"Reuben Sholly, 1802."

With a gasp, his mother released the paper, and it fell, landing face-up a couple of feet away from Eldritch on the floor. He saw now that it was a drawing—an old drawing, weathered and faded with time—and reaching out a tiny hand, he grabbed it to take a closer look. The subject of the drawing was a man, and Eldritch recognized him in an instant.

"Papa Reuben," he said with a smile, holding the portrait up to his parents and Gran-Gran, unaware in that moment his life was forever changed.

CHAPTER THREE

He can hear a voice calling him, shouting his name over and over—a deep voice, filled with worry and panic. *Dad?* Eldritch concentrates on the voice and tries his best to claw his way back to consciousness.

"Eldritch! Come on, kid!" the familiar voice shouts again, pitch rising in distress, bordering on hysterical.

I'm trying.

He's lying on his back on a hard, cool surface—that much he can tell. For a moment, he thinks of the slabs at the morgue and panic washes over him, but then he realizes his head is being cradled by two firm hands, shaking him and patting his cheeks. *They don't do that at the morgue.*

"Eldritch! Please, don't do this to me!" The voice returns, dragging him back through the fog of unconsciousness.

Dad? Is that you?

"Kiddo, wake up! Wake up, Eldritch!"

No. Dad's gone. They both are.

It is not his father's voice, but it is familiar all the same, and in a rush it all comes back to him: the voice, the store, the man, *the shadow*. He remembers running and locking himself in the bathroom. He remembers the shadow chasing after him, pounding on the door; then there was the laugh, and darkness followed. He blacked out; hit is head on the floor when he fell, and now, it seems, someone has found him in this state and is desperately trying to wake him up.

"ELDRITCH!"

"Uncle Cal?" he manages.

"Yes! Yes, I'm here! I'm here."

Eldritch hears the panic in his uncle's voice subside; feels the tension drain from the hands holding his head and face. He fights for control of his senses and forces his blurry eyes to meet the watery gaze of his uncle. Calvin gives him a tight smile, and Eldritch knows the man is trying his best to hide just how worried he is.

"Uncle Cal," he repeats as he moves to sit up.

"Easy, easy," Calvin chides as he helps lift his nephew into a sitting position, fingers pressing lightly against the back of Eldritch's head, checking for damage. "Well, you're not bleeding. Probably going to have a nice-sized knot though. You going to tell me what happened? 'Cause in all honesty, I've had enough of people falling and busting themselves up today."

The answer Eldritch offers is a simple one: "He was early."

Calvin's face falls. Eldritch doesn't elaborate, knowing full well his uncle understands.

"He was early, and you weren't back."

"I know. Eldritch, I'm so sorry." Calvin's hands are back on his head, cradling his face, forcing his nephew to meet his eye.

"I heard the bell. I thought it was you, but he was there. He—I looked at him once. Just once, just one loo—oh, God—!" Eldritch is overcome by a wave of nausea and frees himself from his uncle's grasp. He fumbles to his knees and manages to scramble the few feet across the floor to the toilet in time to retch into the bowl. This morning's coffee and a generous helping of yellow bile are purged from his quivering body until it has nothing left to give. He dry heaves a few more times before flushing the contents away and dropping back against a nearby wall.

"You could have a concussion," Calvin says as he rises to his feet. "You throwing up like that could mean a concussion."

"It's not that," counters Eldritch, leaning his head back against the wood paneled wall a little too hard. "Ow."

"What then?"

Eldritch answers with a question of his own, "Where is he?"

"Up front, at the counter. I told him to wait there, and I'd be back once I sorted you out." Calvin's hands are on his hips, a clear sign he's about to reassume his authoritative position and order his nephew—his *employee*—about. "Go home, Eldritch."

"That's a no," Eldritch drawls, with a slight lift of his chin in defiance.

"Better yet, go to the doctor. Get yourself checked out."

"That's a *definite* no. I'll be fine once *it's* gone," he assures his uncle with a wave of his hand.

The two men lock eyes, Eldritch refusing to back down. The silence stretches on and soon becomes uncomfortable. Calvin is the first to cave.

"He was worried about you, you know."

The comment confuses a minorly concussed Eldritch for a moment. "Who?"

"Mark. The guy. The contractor. Said you walked up, freaked out, made like something was wrong with you, then you took off running. He ran after you because he was worried. Tried to check on you but you locked yourself in here."

"That wasn't him. I mean it was *him*. It just…wasn't."

Calvin says nothing, and Eldritch appreciates the space his uncle gives him—the space to catch his breath, to gather his thoughts before unburdening himself. He knows Uncle Cal is always willing to help shoulder the burden, even if it just means listening.

"I felt it—I *saw* it—the second I laid eyes on that guy. It was dark, Uncle Cal. Darker than anything I've ever—I passed out, for God's sake! I threw up! That's new, that's not normal. There's something in him, and it is so evil it incapacitated me. And it *laughed!* I haven't been that scared since…" his voice falters, frustrated by his inability to explain the horror.

"Is it a demon?" his uncle asks, tone neutral, unfazed by the paranormal nature of their discussion.

"Yeah. But I was too distracted. I couldn't tell you anything else about it," Eldritch admits, his voice small and tinged with shame.

"You wait here. I'll take care of Mark and let him know you're ok. I'll say it was food poisoning and…I don't know, low blood pressure or something."

CALLING ELDRITCH HAYES

Eldritch hauls himself up on shaky legs, putting most of his weight against the wall for balance. "He needs to know. That thing has a hold on him, Uncle Cal."

"Right. Okay. So should I slide that bit of information in before or after I ring him up?" It's classic, Calvin Hayes wry humor, and Eldritch can't help but smile.

"After. Get your money first."

Calvin turns to leave but hesitates with one hand on the doorknob. "Are you sure you're alright?"

"I will be," assures Eldritch, letting go of the wall and standing to his full height.

Calvin nods, "I'll let you know when he's gone," and closing the bathroom door behind him, leaves Eldritch alone once more.

"You won't have to," whispers Eldritch to the empty room.

Twenty minutes later, he's back up front, picking up the drill bits he scattered across the floor during his retreat and making sure everything in the store is stocked, orderly, and ready to be perused by their loyal customer base. After breaking for lunch, he finds himself climbing atop Lanny-Ray's adversary, the aluminum stepladder, to hang the Christmas lights when Calvin emerges from his office.

"Nope! No way. Get down. You're not getting up on that thing with a head injury." Calvin strides over to the ladder, holds it steady with one hand and motions at the floor to better emphasize his point with the other.

"I'm fine, Uncle Cal. And it's hardly a head injury," Eldritch grumbles, irritated at being treated like he's fragile or weak; but he sees the resolve in his uncle's eyes and relents, descending the ladder as commanded. "But if I don't get these Christmas lights up, Lanny-Ray's gonna pitch a fit." It's more of a joke than a warning; an attempt to relieve the current strain on their rapport.

"Lanny-Ray's gonna be out for a few days," calls Amir as he enters the storefront from the back entrance and joins the two men at the base of the ladder.

"Oh, look: Amir's back. *He* can hang the Christmas lights," Calvin says, taking the lights from Eldritch's hands, and passing them off to Amir. "It's that bad?"

"Broken arm. Lucky for us, it's his *right* arm, so he literally can't do any work—or destroy anything—for quite some time."

"I Suwannee," Calvin sighs, rubbing a calloused hand over his face. "Fine. Look, I got some phone calls to make. Can y'all hold down the fort for about an hour or so?" Eldritch and Amir nod as Calvin makes his way back to his office, calling over his shoulder, "Amir, take care of the customers and try to get those lights up. Oh, and Eldritch," he turns before shutting his door, face stern and eyes narrowed at his nephew, "I better not see you up on that ladder!"

Eldritch shakes his head with a groan and looks over at Amir, who is staring at him, an inquisitive eyebrow cocked in curiosity.

"What was that about?"

"It's a long story."

―――――――

It's already dark when Eldritch walks out the back door with Amir. They say their goodbyes, and Amir lists off all the things Eldritch shouldn't do in case he has a concussion. The genuine concern from his friend makes it a little harder to regret filling him in on the events that transpired that morning—which he'd begrudgingly done while holding the ladder as Amir hung the Christmas lights. In true Amir fashion, his immediate response had been, "Man, you're lucky Cal has a key to that bathroom," followed by a skeptical, "Are you sure it was a demon and not one of the ghosts that totally live in that creepy house?"

That pulled a full-bodied laugh out of Eldritch as he further insisted the Birch-Rainey house was not haunted.

"You got plans tomorrow?" Amir asks, opening his car door.

"Do I ever? I offered to come in and work, but he said you two could handle it."

"You never work Saturdays. No point in you coming in."

Eldritch used to work six days a week, Monday through Saturday, from the time he was nineteen up until about six years ago when Calvin hired Amir. His uncle insisted Amir wanted more hours and that Eldritch needed more time off to rest, and he cut out Eldritch's Saturday shifts all together. Before clocking out this evening, Eldritch offered to come in and work on his day off, but Calvin shot him down. Eldritch hates feeling useless and doesn't want Amir to think he isn't doing his share of the work.

"Yeah, but with Lanny-Ray out, I just don't like the idea of y'all being short staffed and me sitting at home," he sighs.

Amir laughs in response, "Trust me, Lanny-Ray being out is more of a help than a hindrance. We'll be more than alright. Besides, we get most of our strangers in on Saturdays. You're better off at home."

Eldritch nods, and Amir gives him a warm smile before climbing into his decade-old Altima. He watches Amir drive off, taking a right out of the store's parking lot and speeding off down Main Street. Eldritch follows the same path on foot, by way of the sidewalk that runs throughout the downtown area. After the events of this morning, he can't help but steal a glance at the liquor store across the street, and his hands twitch at his sides. Mind wandering against his will, Eldritch pictures the rows of bottles lining the cramped space and is reluctant to admit how good a drink sounds right now—just a few fingers of whisky to calm his nerves. But he knows thoughts like this are poison and reminds himself that seven years of sobriety isn't something he can just toss aside for one moment's respite. Taking a deep breath, he diverts his eyes and begins the five-minute walk back to his house, concentrating on his breathing and running through the usual steps that are supposed to help when he feels his mouth go dry and the tremor return to his hand. *God grant me the serenity to accept the things I cannot change—No.* Eldritch cuts the prayer short in his mind, deciding it's far less complicated to recite the lyrics to "Guitar Man" by Bread instead.

As the front door shuts behind him, he breathes a sigh of relief, inhaling the familiar scent of his childhood home; the only home Eldritch has ever known. He has lived in this house all 41 years of his life, aside from a brief period in which he tried attending college in the early 2000s. Gene and Louise Hayes bought the house in 1980, just a couple years before Eldritch was born. The house itself was built in 1924 and had more than enough room for the family they intended to make. Although it needed a lot of work at the time, the newlyweds couldn't pass up the amazing deal. Gene was always very handy, and his father owned the hardware store, so they purchased the home—Gene seeing to every renovation and repair himself.

This house has been Eldritch's safe space for as long as he can remember. Even when the dark side of his ability overwhelmed him, it was here that Eldritch could rest and find solace with the two people he loved most in this world. But now, returning home at the end of the day is a bittersweet experience. The relief he feels locking the door behind him is colored with sadness, because now, Eldritch lives here alone. For many years, the sound of his dad's record player blasting mellow classics from the '70s and his mother's exclamations of "No she did *not*," while gossiping on the kitchen phone with a friend, were always there to greet him. Now, the melodies of his father's records are silent until Eldritch switches on the console himself, and the phone in the kitchen no longer works—the landline having been disconnected ten years ago. There is only silence, and the sharp pang he feels because of that has not lessened these last eight years.

Deciding what he really needs right now is a shower, Eldritch climbs the steps of the narrow staircase that leads to the second-story bathroom. He flips on the faucet and lets the water heat up while shedding his clothes, leaving them in a pile on the bathroom floor. The ceramic tile is cold on his feet, causing goosebumps to form on his arms and legs after his socks are removed. The vanity mirror opposite the shower begins to fog up as Eldritch gives his reflection a once over. *Same old me*, he thinks, bringing a hand up to his chin and feeling the days old stubble that dusts his jaw. His brown eyes are a little bloodshot from earlier, his face a tad gaunt, but overall, the same old Eldritch stares back at him until the steam from the shower shrouds his image completely.

Eldritch has always preferred his showers just shy of scalding, and today is no exception. The hot water bears down on his skin, burning the tension from his shoulders and neck. He dips his head under the spray and runs his hands through his hair when he's hit with a jolt of pain as they make contact with the knot on the back of his head. Eldritch touches it again, assessing how bad the injury is, as his mind drifts back to what transpired that morning.

Eldritch has faced many spirits in his lifetime, both malicious and benign. He has seen countless poltergeists and demons, but nothing of this caliber. What he encountered today was, without doubt, the strongest and most malevolent spirit he has ever happened upon—an ancient, powerful force. The visceral reaction his body had to the presence disturbs Eldritch to no end. The level of terror that overcame him, the fact that he was rendered unconscious and made physically ill, shakes him to his core.

It caught me off guard. I wasn't expecting it.

Eldritch determines the sheer surprise of the encounter was a major factor in the intensity of his reaction. Had he been more prepared, he would have had greater control of his senses and frame of mind; however, despite this rationalization, the power and force of this entity cannot be denied.

Picking up the bodywash resting on the corner of the tub, Eldritch remembers what his uncle said to him after finding him passed out in the bathroom.

"He was worried about you, you know. Mark. The guy. The contractor."

Throughout this entire ordeal, Eldritch had yet to consider the man who was at the center of it all: Mark, the contractor. Mark, the innocent man who was playing host to one of the foulest spirits to ever roam the earth and who was, most likely, oblivious to that fact. Sure, Eldritch told Calvin the man needed to know, but he knew his uncle would never broach that subject with a paying customer, nor did Eldritch expect him to. If he wants the man informed of his situation, Eldritch will have to do it himself.

A whirlwind of thoughts plagues his tired brain as he continues washing his body and hair—thoughts that boil down to two definitive and opposing resolutions. On one hand, Eldritch feels the contractor needs to know just how precarious his situation is—that he be made aware of his predicament and advised on how to seek help. On the other hand, Eldritch wants absolutely nothing to do with any of it. He doesn't know this man; he doesn't owe him anything. Had it not been for an ability he never asked for or wanted in the first place, he wouldn't even be privy to the knowledge of this man's demonic possession.

In the end, the ferocity of his initial encounter with the spirit becomes the deciding factor, and self-preservation wins out in Eldritch's mind. He feels sorry for the man—for *Mark*—but he can't run the risk of putting himself in that situation again. Resolved on this course of action, Eldritch rinses the last of the soap suds from his body and shuts the water off.

Dried and dressed in his old, plaid pajama pants and a threadbare College of Charleston t-shirt, Eldritch descends the stairs, taking a left where they split at the bottom. The soft patter of his bare feet echoes through the empty house as he crosses the back den to the antiquated kitchen to determine which frozen TV dinner he'll be choking down this evening. Jerking open the freezer door, he surveys his limited options and settles on some generic grocery store brand Salisbury steak, mashed potatoes, and green beans. He removes it from the box, slits the film on top, and pops it in the microwave for four and a half minutes, as instructed.

While he waits for his food, Eldritch wanders about the house, making his way through the formal dining room— which hasn't been used in years—over to the old, upright piano in the sitting room. Looking for anything to help him pass the time before the microwave beeps, he flips open the lid and hammers out a few notes on the keys. It's a familiar tune, one he plays out of habit more than anything else: the intro to the Carpenters' "(They Long to Be) Close to You," his mother's favorite song. When he reaches the moment where she could always be counted on to chime in with the lyrics to the first verse, he slams the lid shut and returns to the kitchen just as the microwave counts down to zero.

    Careful not to burn himself, Eldritch retrieves the container, peels back the film, gives the food a good stir, and pops it back in the microwave for another four minutes. This time, instead of pacing around the house, he walks into the back den and over to the large Magnavox record console—his father's most prized possession. He opens the cabinet doors and sifts through his father's old vinyl collection, as if he doesn't know every record by heart at this point. Each album comes with its own set of memories, and every song can be linked to a specific moment in his life. From the excitement of family game nights to mundane evenings spent winding down and discussing the events of the day, The Eagles, the Carpenters, The Hollies, and most of all, Bread, were always present. To think, when he became a teenager, he teased his parents about their outdated music collection, yet now, he refuses to listen to anything else.

    Settling on *The Best of Bread*, he lifts the lid of the console, and places the 50-year-old album on the turntable. The needle drops and, in an instant, the nostalgic crackle and pop of white noise pours through the speakers. Eldritch ups the volume as the soothing strumming of an acoustic guitar starts, followed by the effortlessly sung lyrics of "Make It with You." He stands still for a moment, eyes closed, and lets the music wash over him; lips curling into a small smile as he thinks of his father singing along to this, his favorite album. They say time heals all wounds, but Eldritch knows that isn't true, because in this moment, when he can almost hear his father's voice ringing out alongside David Gates's, he misses him more than ever before. He flashes back to that moment in the bathroom when he struggled to regain consciousness and heard his uncle calling out to him. He thought it was his father, and waking to find he was mistaken hit him like a bullet to the chest.

The beep of the microwave interrupts his reminiscing just as the song comes to an end. Eldritch grabs his dinner and returns to the den, taking a seat on the old sofa and picking at his lackluster meal. Amir told him to avoid looking at screens, in case he was concussed, and Eldritch follows his friend's advice. Putting aside his phone and leaving the TV off, he allows the record player to serenade him with scenes of the past as it continues to play through both sides of the album.

The rest of the evening passes in relative silence, save for the droning of the record player. Eldritch dozes a little on the couch, only getting up to swap the albums out as they come to an end. By the time The Eagles finish their first set, Eldritch has been asleep for half an hour, and this time doesn't move from his spot on the couch. The house falls silent and remains that way for another hour; the soft sounds of Eldritch's breathing and the steady ticking of the clock on the mantle are all that can be heard.

When his alarm goes off at midnight, Eldritch jolts awake at the sudden onslaught of sound. He fumbles around for his phone to shut off the offending noise, breathing a sigh of relief when he finally locates it on the floor by the sofa. He rubs his eyes and gives his back and arms a good stretch before heading upstairs to change out of his pajamas and into some actual clothes. Minutes later, dressed and ready to go, he remembers to grab his heaviest winter coat from the closet at the foot of the stairs. If the frigid temperatures from this morning are anything to go by, he knows he'll be needing it. Making sure he has his phone and keys, he locks the front door behind him and heads into town on foot, ready to begin the ritual he has performed every Friday night for the last eight years.

CHAPTER FOUR

"I think it's safe to say the boy has a gift!" Reverend Holland was exceedingly animated in his argument to the Hayeses. After Eldritch had recognized Charlie was possessed by a demon, and had then identified that demon, Holland had started shouting about divine providence and Eldritch's spiritual gifts. Eldritch, being six years old, did not particularly care to listen to the pastor or discuss the impact of what he had done that afternoon in the town square. More pressing to his adolescent mind, *Mary Poppins* was going to be shown on ABC this evening. Eldritch hadn't seen that movie yet, and Reverend Holland was blocking the doors to the sitting room and the television set.

"I'm telling you, it's a gift! A gift from God himself! Just like The Word tells us, 'Your young men will see visions, and your old men will dream dreams.' This young man has had a vision into the spiritual world! He has seen the work of the enemy and has called him out by the power of God!" The reverend's presentation was a fiery one, like most of his sermons. He paced and gesticulated, raising his hands up to Heaven and crying out with fury and conviction.

Eldritch locked eyes with his father from his seat at the foot of the stairs, conveying his confusion to his father. *Why are they talking about me like this?*

"He's only a boy, Len," Gene interrupted, turning his head to face the preacher once more.

Reverend Holland leveled his gaze at Eldritch's father. "Was not Christ himself only a boy when he spoke in the temple and taught the masses The Word of his Father?"

"Yessir. But then again, Christ was twelve when he did that. Eldritch is only half that age. It's a gift, sure, but I don't know how I feel about parading my son around the altar of a church, advertising…whatever this is to a congregation full of people!"

"Reverend," Louise interjected, her tone soft and even, "why don't you give us some time to talk about it as a family, pray on it a bit, and then we can let you know where we stand on the subject?" Louise Hayes could always be counted on to use her quick thinking, judicious words, and calming manner to change the atmosphere of any room; "pouring oil on troubled waters" is what Gran-Gran called it.

Holland grew silent at Louise's words, and Eldritch watched the minister's brow furrow, his eyes narrow—features scrunching up into a harsh expression only to soften seconds later. With a nod of agreement, he shook hands with Gene and let Louise usher him to the front door. Before making his exit, he encouraged the couple to pray and seek God's counsel on the matter but assured them this was not to be taken lightly.

"Your son has a mighty gift from the Lord, and letting it go to waste would be wrong in His eyes."

Eldritch didn't miss his father's eyeroll at the minister's admonition or the look of concern on his mother's face. In fact, he was so focused on the silent exchange happening between his parents that he was startled when Reverend Holland called out his name.

"Eldritch, my boy! Come here."

He turned and looked at the minister who had a hand extended in his direction, motioning him over. Eldritch rose from his seat on the stairs and looked at both parents, uncertain. He had no idea what Reverend Holland had been talking about or why he was the subject of conversation.

"Come here for a moment. I just want to pray over you before I go," insisted the pastor. Gene nodded and walked with his son—his presence a solid reassurance at the boy's back— over to the doorway where the man of God stood with Louise. Closing his eyes and placing a large hand atop Eldritch's head, Reverend Holland began to pray over the child, speaking of prophecy and spiritual warfare against the enemy. Eldritch tried to be good and pray along with the preacher, but the hand on his head was heavy and pressing down hard, shaking him in time with the rhythm of the man's spirited cadence. It was uncomfortable, and the small boy felt guilty for not being able to concentrate on the words of the prayer.

After several long minutes, the prayer shifted, and the reverend spoke over Gene and Louise—that the wisdom of the Lord be given to these two obedient, God-fearing, servants, and that they would make the right decision regarding their son and his special gift. With a vigorous "Amen," and a hand still planted on Eldritch's mop of brown hair, Holland looked down at the child. In a low voice, he recited a passage from the book of Timothy: "'Do not neglect the gift that is in thee, which was given to thee by prophecy with the laying on of the hands of the eldership.'" With that, he nodded his farewell to the family and took his leave.

Gene shut the door and turned back to face his wife and son. "Well, then. There you have it. Either we do what he says or we're going against the will of God." He punctuated the last few words with a huff and a shake of his head.

"Gene," said Lousie, with a jerk of her head toward Eldritch, "not now." The tone of her voice shifted, excitement creeping into her sweet, southern drawl as she addressed her son. "Baby boy, it's almost seven! Didn't you want to watch *Mary Poppins*?"

Eldritch nodded in excitement as his mother took him by the hand and led him through the French doors off to the side of the living room and into the sitting room, where the TV set was located. He plopped down on the plush, shag rug, hands tucked under his chin, and waited for his mother to switch on their Quasar console television. She turned the channel knob on the wooden set a few times before the screen lit up with the Buena Vista logo, and the first few measures of the overture rang out atop a hazy, London cityscape.

"Oh, this brings back memories," his mother sighed. "That part right there—in the overture—it's from that 'Feed the Birds' song. That one's my favorite," and with a wink, she left him to enjoy the movie alone. "We have a decision to make," he heard his mother say as she joined her husband in the living room once again, shutting the doors behind her.

Eldritch could barely make out the exasperated sigh of his father over the movie's opening credits as the overture gained momentum and the sound increased. He knew he wasn't supposed to listen. He knew that anytime he was told to watch

TV or play in his room or run around outside, that meant the grownups were discussing things they didn't want him to hear—discussing *him* more often than not. Ever since that day at Gran-Gran's house a couple years ago, it seems they had more and more of these closed-door discussions about Eldritch, and this time he wanted to know what was being said. He peeked over his shoulder to see if his parents were watching him and, finding them engaged in conversation and oblivious to his movements in the next room, he reached up and turned the volume knob to the left.

The blare of the overture was reduced to a low hum, and the voices of his parents became much clearer. He kept his eyes fixed on the television set, watching as a pretty lady floated in on a cloud and powdered her nose. Dampened music still drifted from the speaker in front of him—crescendos and swells as the melody reached its zenith—but Eldritch's ears were tuned in to the conversation happening on the other side of the glass doors.

"And did you catch what he said out there? Before he invited himself over?" his father spat, voice dripping with irritation. "When you mentioned Eldritch can see all sorts of things, and he was all 'there's no such thing as ghosts—only angels and demons—for to be absent from the body is to be present with the Lord,'" Gene said in a haughty voice. Eldritch giggled to himself at his father's impression of the pompous preacher, but as he considered the words of the comment, all laughter stopped. A fog of confusion settled along the edges of his mind as he tried to understand why his father was talking about ghosts.

"How does he know?" Gene continued. "How does he know there's no such thing? He thinks he knows everything, but let me tell you right now, that little boy in that room right there, knows more about spir—!"

"Gene, try to calm down." His mother's tone was tender but effective as she ended her husband's rant mid-sentence, and Eldritch could almost hear Gran-Gran's voice in the back of his mind: "*oil on troubled waters.*"

"He's six years old, Louise," Gene's voice grew quieter. Eldritch turned his head to see his father slumped on the window seat, back bowed and head in his hands. "He's six years old, and I can't imagine the things he's seen, especially after—" but his father's voice grew muffled and indistinct, and Eldritch was finding it difficult to understand the rest of the words.

He watched as his mother crossed the room and sat beside her husband, placing a gentle hand on his back. Her voice had dropped to a low murmur, and Eldritch couldn't make out what she was saying either. Deciding it would take a little risk if he wanted to listen in on their conversation, he rose from the rug—eyes trained on his parents—and crept into the dining room. Once assured the action had gone unnoticed, he scurried across the dining room and all the way through the back den to crouch in the hallway just outside the living room where his parents sat. From his new position, unencumbered by closed doors, he could hear every word.

"One thing we need to keep in mind," he heard his mother say, "is that what our son can do—what he can *see*—*is* a gift. We know this. Take Len Holland out of the equation. You and I have always said it was a gift."

Why does everyone keep saying I have a "gift?"

"I know that. I just don't understand why it has to be *Eldritch's* gift. When it was just ghosts, it was one thing, but that out there today?" his father's voice trailed off.

CALLING ELDRITCH HAYES

Both parents were silent for several minutes, and Eldritch began to ponder their words—along with the words of Reverend Holland—finding most of what they said to be very confusing. In his mind, there was nothing special about him. He didn't have any gifts or miraculous abilities that he could think of. To be honest, Eldritch hadn't given much thought to what he had done today in the town center. He had seen Charlie, and then he had seen inside; he had seen the thing that lurked just beneath the surface. In Eldritch's young mind, it was no major feat or revelation that he was able to call the being by name; but after, he had noticed a shift in the way people were acting around him—*toward* him. He began to wonder if he had done something wrong.

"He can see these things for a reason. We don't know why just yet, but there *has* to be a reason," his mother stated, "and Reverend Holland can be a bit over the top sometimes, but I still think deep down, he means well."

"I know. He does a lot of good; I'm not denying that," his father agreed with a sigh. "I just don't want him getting so caught up in Eldritch's gift that he forgets he's just a little boy."

What gift?

"I agree," said Louise. "So, let's just take him to the prayer meeting and see what happens. If we don't like what's going on, or if Eldritch feels uncomfortable, we never go back there again. And not just to prayer meeting, to the church altogether."

Eldritch could hear the shifting of the window seat cushion and knew one of his parents was standing up. He had to get back to the sitting room before they noticed he was no longer in front of the television. As he rose from the floor and began tiptoeing back down the hallway, he heard his father say, "He saw a demon today, Louise. Inside a man. He saw it and he knew its name," and Eldritch paused just outside the doorway to the back den. "He's my little boy, and he's seeing demons," his father continued, "and I don't want that for him. I don't want him to see things like that—to see evil like that—and to be scared. I'm supposed to protect him, but I don't know how to do that anymore. How can I protect him from something I can't even see?"

In an instant, everything clicked in Eldritch's head. *Now* he understood why his insight into such matters was considered exceptional or unusual. Only *now* did the meaning behind words like *gift*, *ability*, and *special* register in his mind.

Other people can't see them.

The more Eldritch pondered this, the more it began to make sense. He thought back to that weekend at Gran-Gran's: the tree people, Papa Reuben. He remembered being confused when they had asked him over and over about why he panicked and ran from the large oak tree, as if they weren't bothered at all by the sight of the hanging bodies or the sound of the hanged man's wail. He remembered being annoyed when they had bombarded him with questions about the old man in the rocking chair. A four-year-old Eldritch couldn't comprehend why they hadn't just asked Papa Reuben those questions themselves. Sure, the old man had a bad habit of disappearing, but he always came back, and Gran-Gran had seemed to know all about him. She'd even had a portrait of him—a very old portrait…

There, hidden within the shadows of his home, over two years later, Eldritch finally understood.

Ghosts.

The men in the tree, Papa Reuben, the faces in the windows—they were all dead. The realization sent the small boy whirling. He thought of other incidents, incidents before and after those moments at Gran-Gran's. He remembered staring out the window of his kindergarten class and seeing a man crossing the highway on his bicycle. Upon reaching the other side, the man had vanished. Eldritch had thought it odd, but his teacher had called on him to answer a question about the letter T, so he'd pushed it aside and hadn't thought of it again, until now.

This brought to mind another incident from a few months ago in the antique store. His mother had taken him along with her to do some shopping, and she'd become enamored with a beautiful emerald ring. The man behind the counter had pulled it out of the case and his mother tried it on, but neither of them seemed to notice the scowling, dark haired lady standing inches from the both of them. The ring ended up being too expensive, and his mother had reluctantly handed it back to the man, and only then had the frightening lady disappeared, right in front of his eyes. He'd wanted to ask his mom about it, but she was very sad over not having the extra money for the ring, and he hadn't wanted to bother her.

He tried to think back further, as far back as he could remember. There were impressions on his mind from long ago—faces he couldn't account for—the old lady that had hovered over his crib at daycare during nap time.

She used to touch my cheek.

As dozens of memories flashed before his eyes, Eldritch began to piece together the unsettling truth that would loom over him from this moment on. He could see ghosts and other people couldn't. Still, what had happened earlier in the town square was different. He thought back on how he felt when he saw ghosts. Apart from how terrified he had been at the sight of the wailing man hanging from a rope in the tree, the other ghosts didn't seem to affect him that much. Sometimes he was startled by their sudden appearance and departure, and other times he would feel a bit of a chill, but the experience he'd had today was new.

When the thing wearing Charlie had come close to him, Eldritch had felt anxious, uncomfortable, scared. When it had looked at him, the little hairs on his arms and neck stood up. Eldritch remembered jumping back and running toward his mother as it laughed and snarled. Then something strange had happened: a name had popped into his head, and Eldritch had known, without a doubt, the name belonged to that thing.

Amaymon.

He had been right, and that's why Reverend Holland had been here, but it hadn't made sense to him until now. Now, he realized the only thing the adults had seen that entire time had been Charlie, not Amaymon. Eldritch had seen *past* Charlie somehow.

But what was that thing?

Eldritch knew that since Charlie was alive, it couldn't be a ghost. He thought on it for a few minutes before recalling his father's words from moments ago.

"He saw a demon today, Louise. Inside a man. He saw it and he knew its name."

A demon.

"I don't want him to see things like that—to see evil like that—and to be scared."

Evil.

Eldritch felt the sting of tears in his eyes as he stood stock-still in the hallway outside the living room, too preoccupied with his thoughts to bother hiding anymore. He didn't even budge when his mother spotted him and called his name.

"Eldritch?"

Gene and Louise rounded the corner to find him standing there, silent tears streaming down his face.

"What are you doing?" his mother asked.

The small boy looked up and met the concerned gaze of his parents. "What's a demon?"

CHAPTER FIVE

The frigid, night air bites his cheeks as Eldritch ambles down his front walkway and out onto the sidewalk that runs along Main Street. Most cities are just getting warmed up at ten past twelve on a Friday night, but Sommerset—like many towns of a similar size and heritage—has taken to bed. Save for the occasional car or motorcycle passing through, the town is silent, and to the casual passerby would seem all but deserted. Darkness covers the township, except for a few evenly dispersed patches of illuminated sidewalk, courtesy of the streetlights. Eldritch prefers his hometown this way: hushed, lulled under the spell of sleep.

He continues down the sidewalk, stuffing his hands into the pockets of his heavy coat to shield them from the chilly night air, and crosses Main Street in front of the antique store. The path here is darker as several of the streetlight bulbs have blown, and town maintenance hasn't gotten around to replacing them. Still, Eldritch walks on, humming the melody of "If" to fill the silence surrounding him. After a brisk four-minute walk from his house, he stops in front of Sommerset Pentecostal Holiness Church. The humming ceases as he stares up at the old brick structure, countless memories racing through his mind—many unpleasant—before taking a seat on one of the benches in the churchyard. He and his parents attended this church for many years, up until *The Incident*. Eldritch laughs to himself—the sound bitter and cold—at the thought of *The Incident*, considering there were so *many* incidents that should have driven them away from this place long before their official break with Reverend Holland.

Eldritch hasn't set foot inside this building since he was thirteen years old, but every Friday night, he sits outside and waits. This is the church his parents had attended years before he was born. They were married in this church. Eldritch was dedicated here as a baby, and here he was baptized at the age of nine. Despite the horrors that occurred within, there's still a chance they could be attached to this place; so he waits and watches, eyes scanning the deserted church grounds and the stone steps that lead to the front doors. He remembers the weight of those doors; too heavy for him to open on his own as a child. An hour passes, and all Eldritch sees are the occasional headlights from late night drivers passing through the sleepy town. With a sigh, he stands to his feet and retraces his steps back down the sidewalk toward Main Street again.

When he reaches the antique store, he rounds the corner and walks a little further until he arrives outside Kitty's Place. On the nights when his mother didn't cook dinner, they would often find themselves here, their favorite restaurant. Gene Hayes insisted you'd never find a better cheeseburger in all of South Carolina than the ones at Kitty's. Eldritch remembers the milkshakes and the sundaes they would get after finishing off their baskets of burgers and fries, and how the interior was always decorated with antiques since Kitty and her husband, Jay, also owned the antique store.

It's been a long time. I wonder if the burgers are still as good.

Eldritch avoids people as much as possible nowadays—an act of self-preservation—and sadly, Kitty's is always packed with patrons. With his parents, it wasn't so bad. As a child, Eldritch was brave enough to weather the potential storm of new faces, as long as his mother and father were by his side. By the time he reached adulthood, he had stopped visiting many of the places he once loved—Kitty's being chief among them. He puts his face up against the glass windows of the storefront and peers inside. All he sees are empty chairs, empty booths, and an unmanned counter. This is to be expected, of course, of a restaurant that closed over three hours ago; still, he searches the little, hole-in-the-wall joint for any sign of a presence.

Nothing.

After no sign presents itself at Kitty's Place, Eldritch continues down Main Street. He can see the silhouette of Hayes Hardware just ahead of him, illuminated by the waxing moon, and crosses the road just in front of the liquor store. Luckily for him, it's as dark as the rest of the town. Gordon's closes at seven, and after the day he's had, Eldritch is beyond grateful for that fact.

Leaving the main stretch behind him, he moves along down McLeary Street, looking both ways as he crosses the train tracks; more of an impulse than anything else, given the blare of the whistle would be heard miles away. As he approaches the curve in the road just beyond the tracks, the Birch Rainey house comes into view. Although it always stands out among the other homes in Sommerset, it catches Eldritch's eye for more than one reason tonight. Despite being well past one o'clock in the morning, every light in the house is on.

Eldritch watches the ramshackle structure from across the street as he continues on his journey. Glancing up at the second story, he sees the figure of a man cross in front of the window on the left side of the façade. He is startled at first, before a muted buzzing escapes the walls of the old home.

A table saw.

Mark.

The thought of the man's name has Eldritch tearing his eyes away from the house and quickening his pace. Mark is simply pulling an all-nighter at the property—Eldritch knows this—but the events from earlier bombard his mind, and he fights off another wave of nausea.

"He needs to know. That thing has a hold on him, Uncle Cal."

Eldritch had said that—had *meant* that—but he had decided to do nothing about it. The sound of the table saw fades into the distance as he moves along, putting the Birch Rainey house—and Mark—behind him.

Half a mile later, he arrives at the entrance of Sommerset Cemetery and feels the usual disappointment at the state of the grounds. Many of the graves are unkempt—weeds and highway grass growing tall amidst the headstones. He takes a left past the iron gate and heads toward the rows near the back before veering off to the right. Many would think it a curious thing that Eldritch Hayes, of all people, would venture into a graveyard after one in the morning, but few understand the nature of his gift; fewer understand the nature of the spirit world in general.

In Eldritch's experience, ghosts don't linger around their own graves. Instead, most tend to haunt something or someplace that had meaning when they were alive: their homes, places of business, churches, beloved restaurants, and in many cases, the spot where they shed their earthly bodies and stepped beyond the veil.

In the eight years he's been coming here, Eldritch has seen exactly one ghost: a woman bent over the grave of a small child, weeping. She never acknowledges his presence, never pauses her mourning or looks up from the resting place of her baby. Every time he sees her, Eldritch contemplates offering up a short prayer of comfort for the spirit, but since praying isn't something he does much of anymore, he continues about his business.

There are no lights in the cemetery—the town council deeming it an unnecessary expense because "no one in their right mind goes there at night"—so Eldritch pulls up the flashlight app on his phone. A beam of light shines out about ten feet before fading back into the palpable darkness that surrounds the well-worn path ahead. Frost is beginning to form on the thick grass beneath his boots, a pronounced crunch resonating with every step as Eldritch treads carefully to avoid any rocks or low-lying grave markers. Even without the flashlight, he could make his way around the grounds without missing a step. He has walked this path many times, is well acquainted with the dips and divots in the dirt, the juts of brick and stone. After a few paces, he reaches his destination and comes to a stop. The beam from his phone falls on two headstones, identical in shape and size, and Eldritch reads the words he has read over and over again, every week for the last several years:

Robert Eugene Hayes, III
August 13, 1958 – December 19, 2015
2 Timothy 4:7

CALLING ELDRITCH HAYES

Louise Sholly Hayes
February 26, 1958 – December 19, 2015
1 Corinthians 16:13

    This December will mark the eighth anniversary of the accident. His eyes drift over the headstones for what feels like the millionth time since it happened. Sometimes, he regrets not putting something more in the epitaphs—some pretty words to sum up who his parents were in life—but how does one do that in such a limited space? Things like "loving father, devoted husband" don't quite do Gene Hayes justice. "Wonderful wife and mother" falls tragically short of capturing the treasure that was Louise. In the end, he sifted through their favorite Bible verses, had them inscribed on their headstones, and that was that.

    He looks down and sees where a pile of leaves has gathered against the right side of his father's marker, deposited there by the harsh November wind. He reaches down and clears them away, raking them onto the walking path with his hands. Unlike many of the surrounding graves, his parents' are perfectly maintained: no trash from the highway, no high grass, no weeds creeping around the headstones—his mother couldn't stand a weed, and she could always be found crawling around the yard on her hands and knees, pulling them up by the root.

    Eldritch smiles at the image, remembers how funny it was to watch her scoot around in the grass, dragging her bucket with her. *"Never put a weed back on the ground after you've pulled it up, Eldritch. It'll just take root again and you'll have a mess! Put it in the bucket."* He misses the sound of her voice—that signature, Lowcountry drawl of hers. With the exception of Amir, everyone Eldritch has ever known has had a southern drawl, but none as sweet or pronounced as his mother's.

When his father spoke, it could be defined as "country" more than anything else. Sometimes, when his Uncle Calvin speaks, Eldritch can hear his father's voice bleed through: same accent, same tone, same southern vernacular and turns of phrase peppered throughout his speech. Calvin is eleven years Gene's junior, but the similarities are uncanny at times, filling Eldritch with equal parts comfort and sorrow whenever he's around the man.

Turning off the flashlight app and pocketing his phone, he begins to speak, surprised at how shaky and tired his voice sounds when it reaches his ears.

"Hey," he begins, despite knowing in the back of his mind that no one can hear him—that no one is listening. But he finds a strange, bittersweet solace in his conversation with the cold marble in front of him, and he continues.

"It's been really cold lately—freezing, actually. Uncle Cal said people are talking about our chances of a white Christmas this year, but you know how that goes: by Thanksgiving we'll all be in shorts again." He always starts with the weather, a southern tradition the Hayes men have upheld for generations.

"Oh! Lanny-Ray broke his arm today trying to hang up some Christmas lights at the store. I can't believe it's already time for Christmas lights. Pretty soon, it'll be…well, you know." The lump rises in his throat at the reminder that December nineteenth is just over a month away, but Eldritch swallows it down and holds back the tears he feels stinging the corners of his eyes. It never fails to amaze him how quickly the date seems to come every year, racing toward him like a runaway train; and every year, there's nothing he can do about it.

He clears his throat, "Something else happened today…something bad. Remember how I told you someone was renovating the Birch-Rainey house? Well, he—the guy, Mark, he came in to get a shipment today, and I was by myself, and—" He feels the break in his voice more than hears it, but he presses on, recounting the story in its entirety to the silent gravestones.

"And now I don't know what to do. I feel bad for the guy because he has this thing in him and doesn't have a clue. But at the same time, I can't...I can't..." Eldritch can't bring himself to admit to his parents what he decided earlier in the shower—can't let them know of his cowardice, his selfishness.

"I just wish you were here to tell me what to do."

Eldritch waits but receives no answer. The icy November wind sweeps through the cemetery and ruffles his hair as a single tear rolls down his cheek. There's no one there, no one save for Eldritch, a statue among the headstones in the pitch black of night. Before turning to leave, he reaches out and rests his hands atop both headstones. "I want you to know, I'm still looking. Every week, I look. If you're still around here somewhere, I'll find you. I have to find you, I need to—" he stops himself as a sob threatens to wrack his body, pats his mother's marker once more, and walks away. *It never gets easier*, he thinks to himself as he leaves their graves behind.

The site of the crash is less than half a mile away from the cemetery itself. There's a bend in the road right before you reach the town limits. It's hard not to imagine the scene from that night. The car was totaled, hit head-on by someone from out of state who fell asleep behind the wheel. Eldritch can almost hear the squealing of their brakes, the honking of a horn, the smashing of metal before all is silent—silent like it is now. Eldritch takes a seat on the damp ground, checks his watch, and sees that it's just after 2:00 a.m. In all the years since the ritual's inception, he has yet to pick up any sign of his parents' spirits, but every Friday night will find him here, waiting, just in case. The night grows colder around him, the wind picking up. His teeth chatter against the dropping temperature, and his nose begins to run. Still, he sits and watches, sits and waits, and all he sees are two passing cars and a large great horned owl that lights on a tree branch across from him.

 For the better part of an hour, Eldritch loses himself in the rhythmic call of the owl, staring off down the road, eyes scanning back and forth in time with its doleful cry. At length, it spots something in the field behind Eldritch and flies off in the direction of whatever poor creature it has zeroed in on. The world around him grows quiet again. Another hour passes, and Eldritch finds himself on the verge of drifting off. The rumble of an eighteen-wheeler pulls him back from the edge of unconsciousness, and he checks his watch again. It's well after four. The town will start stirring soon. Rising to his feet, he can hear the joints in his knees crack from hours of sitting idle on the hard ground. His right leg is asleep, so he shakes it a few times to get the blood flowing. Once the tingling subsides, he brushes off his pants and begins the journey back into town.

 Maybe next time, he thinks, as he does every week. *Maybe next time.*

CHAPTER SIX

Wednesday night's prayer meeting was packed. Word travels fast in a one stoplight town like Sommerset, and Reverend Holland had done his share of talking over the last few days. Eldritch sat in the front pew of the sanctuary, flanked by his parents on both sides. He tried not to fidget with the sleeves of his suit jacket, but he wasn't used to wearing it, and his nerves were getting the better of him. When Reverend Holland entered from the side door, followed by his armor bearer who carried the minister's Bible—*the Sword of the Spirit which is the Word of God*—the parishioners sprang to their feet.

Reverend Holland ascended the steps of the stage and positioned himself before the people, arms raised high toward the heavens. The armor bearer laid the Bible on the pulpit before making his way down the steps and to a pew on the other side of the church. Eldritch followed the man's path, wondering—as he often did—why the preacher needed someone to carry his Bible for him; but his attention was called away by the sound of the old piano ringing out the intro of the night's first hymn. The old instrument had been out of tune for years, but that did not deter Reverend Holland as his voice rang out over the congregation, leading them in a familiar hymn:

> Would you be free from the burden of sin?
> There's pow'r in the blood, pow'r in the blood;
> Would you o'er evil a victory win?
> There's wonderful pow'r in the blood.

Eldritch lost himself in the melody of the song, listening to the voices of his mother and father as they sang along with the rest of the congregation. When the hymn ended, Reverend Holland asked everyone to take their seats and motioned for Eldritch and his parents to join him on stage.

"Now, I know many of you have heard tales of what happened just this past Sunday afternoon," the preacher began as the Hayeses made their way out of the pew and up the steps, "and I know that is the reason the house of the Lord is packed tonight! Amen?"

The congregation confirmed his question with a fervent "amen" of their own.

"What God has shown me in this last week is nothing short of a miracle, for this child—" he gestured toward Eldritch, who was standing with his parents, beside the pastor, "has a gift unlike any I have ever seen! The wisdom and power of the Lord is upon him, and we will all bear witness to it tonight!"

The church erupted in another chorus of "hallelujahs" and "amens" at the minister's prompting. Eldritch shrank back between his parents at the abrupt shouting from the pews of worshipers, but the desire to bolt dissipated at the steady and reassuring weight of his father's hand on his shoulder. Tilting his head upward, he saw his parents exchange a look above his head. Eldritch didn't know what they were thinking, but they didn't seem sure of the situation themselves.

"Dan, Lamont, if you will?" The pastor addressed two of the deacons who had previously been standing at the back of the church. They started down the center aisle before stopping a few pews from the back and turned, speaking to someone seated in that row. The man in question stood, and fear took hold of the small boy, just as it had Sunday afternoon in the town square. He flinched and felt his father's hand squeeze his shoulder. Eldritch had to be brave—brave like his dad. He knew he had nothing to worry about because his parents were there, right beside him, and they wouldn't let anything happen to him.

Charlie slid out of the pew and joined the deacons, who positioned the man between them—Dan on the left, Lamont on the right. Eldritch watched them escort the thin, disheveled man to the altar; watched as Charlie twitched and jerked his head and arms, his movements erratic. Eldritch felt someone grab his left hand and looked over to see his mother had laced their fingers together and was holding him in a firm, unrelenting grasp. A hacking cough from Charlie drew Eldritch's attention back to the altar, where the frail, sickly man now stood, flanked by the deacons on either side, their hands gripping his upper arms.

Eldritch looked—really looked—past the visage of Charlie, looked beyond the veil to what lay inside. Once again, the familiar sensation overtook him, just as it had four days prior. The initial fear he felt gave way, and Eldritch, lifting his small hand and pointing at the being in front of him, called out with more conviction than he thought possible, "Amaymon!"

Charlie's eyes, which had been looking everywhere but in Eldritch's direction, snapped up and locked onto the six-year-old; but these were not the eyes of Charlie Haskell. These eyes were black as night, devoid of feeling and life. Time stood still, and everything became a blur—everything but Eldritch and the demon standing before him. The whole of what Eldritch recognized as distinctly Charlie had vanished: his hunched, thin form, his mussed hair, the confused, unsure expression he always wore, the tendency to shrink into the background of any crowd—all these details evaporated as Amaymon took control. The being facing him now did not shrink but commanded attention. The hunched shoulders were pulled back and the spine straight. There was no confusion in its face, only curiosity—curiosity about the small human child with the outstretched hand who possessed the power to know it and call it by name.

The black, unblinking eyes were transfixed, and Eldritch watched as it cocked its head to the left with a twitch. The motion reminded Eldritch of a dog that had just heard a strange sound and was trying to make sense of it. No sooner had the thought entered his mind than the growl reached his ear. It began as a rumble, a rumble that seemed to be coming from everywhere and nowhere all at once. Eldritch could feel it in the soles of his feet and deep in the center of his chest, like when a train would pass by the house, and he could *feel* how loud it was. The source of the sound was revealed as Amaymon threw back its head, and the reverberating growl transformed into the most inhuman of laughs. Eldritch wanted to run, but he was glued to the spot, unable to move. Amaymon punctuated the laugh with a vicious bark as its head snapped forward to face the child once more, and the thin line of its lips began to part and stretch upward into an impossibly wide, distorted mockery of a smile.

The smile grew closer, and Eldritch wasn't quick enough to understand the demon had lunged in his direction; but before he could react, he felt himself being pulled backward and lifted up into the air. In a rush, the rest of his surroundings came back to him and flooded his senses with a cacophony of movement and sound. Eldritch realized he was being hoisted up by his father; he could hear the shouts and prayers of Reverend Holland and the deacons as they descended on the corrupted form of Charlie Haskell. Dan and Lamont tried to hold it still, but the demon writhed and thrashed about in their grasp. Eldritch was moving again, wrapped securely in his father's arms as they ran from the altar with Louise following close behind.

Desperate to catch a glimpse of the scene they had just fled, Eldritch peered over his father's shoulder and saw Holland with his arms held high, Bible in one hand, calling on the power of God and the name of Jesus. Then, the pastor was speaking in a language Eldritch didn't recognize. More men rushed to the aid of the minister and deacons, and soon, Amaymon and his vessel were obscured from view by a wall of shouting parishioners who wailed in unknown tongues. The remainder of the congregation were on their feet, arms stretched toward the altar, praying and pleading the Blood of Jesus—some sang, others cried. One lady danced down the aisle and nearly crashed into Eldritch and his parents as she passed by.

His attention was drawn back to the altar as a beastly shriek resounded from amid the throng of deacons and believers. Many of them jumped backward as the demon was raised to its full height and tore itself free from the deacons' grasp. It howled and roared, cursed their God, and seemed to speak in many languages all at once—a symphony of unholy voices crying out in agony and hatred. Eldritch heard his mother scream and, whipping his head in her direction, saw her cover her ears as the demonic voice began to recite the Lord's Prayer in reverse. But as soon as the maelstrom of growls and curses reached a deafening crescendo, it stopped, and all sound in the sanctuary ceased as a hush fell over the room.

Then, in an unexpected and disturbing display, Amaymon turned its head one hundred and eighty degrees—the bones and tendons popping and cracking under the strain—until it located Eldritch, several yards behind it at the back of the church. The eerie smile returned as its eyes fell upon the child, and in a voice unlike any Eldritch had ever heard—a deep, gravelly voice that wormed its way inside his young mind and echoed with feral intensity—Amaymon addressed the small boy.

"Just. One. Look."

Most of the worshipers had scattered at this point, and Eldritch watched as an elderly man fainted in the third row at the sight of Charlie Haskell's twisted neck. Apart from the screams and cries of disbelief at the spectacle, no response was given the demon, so he spoke again, eyes burning into Eldritch:

"Just. One. Look. He will find you. Just one look, and he will know. He is coming for you, Eldritch Hayes!"

Eldritch felt his father's hand cup the back of his head, turning him away from the demon's gaze in one smooth, swift motion. With his face hidden against his father's chest, Eldritch saw nothing of the whirlwind that followed but heard it all with perfect clarity. Reverend Holland's voice rang out, clear as a bell, above the screams and cries of the congregation.

"Demon! Amaymon!"

At the tell-tale crack of bone and the horrified sounds of the parishioners, Eldritch gathered the demon had snapped its neck back around to face the minister.

"By the power of Jesus Christ," Holland continued, "and by the holy blood He shed at Calvary, I command you: Come out! Release this man, in the name of Jesus!"

He heard the sound of retching, and in that same instant, his father's grip loosened just enough for him to turn his head toward the sound to watch what followed. Charlie fell to his hands and knees before the preacher, convulsed three or four times before vomiting up a long, black substance. Like a snake coiled and ready to strike, the black secretion rose from the ground and darted down the center aisle, fleeing the altar and slithering out the door.

It was hours before the service ended and the worshipers departed for the night, many still singing praises and hallelujahs as they passed through the large wooden doors, one by one, until only Reverend Holland and the Hayeses remained. Eldritch had drifted off to sleep some time ago, but the raised voice of his father pulled him from his slumber, and Eldritch cracked open one of his little, brown eyes to see what was going on around him.

He was laid in a pew, his suit jacket folded beneath his head, a makeshift pillow between him and the hard, wooden seat. His father was standing in the center aisle, one hand balled into a fist at his side, the other aimed at Reverend Holland with its pointer finger an inch away from the pastor's face.

"See? *That* was what I was talking about when I said I didn't want my son in any danger!" spat his father. "This whole show of yours—"

"Now, look here, Gene—!" Holland tried to counter, but Gene Hayes did not relent.

"Don't interrupt me, Len! I'm not finished!" The severity of his father's tone startled Eldritch who had never before heard his father this angry. Opening both eyes a fraction more, he caught sight of Reverend Holland—the minister's mouth snapping shut at Gene's admonition.

"It went for him! You saw that, didn't you? If I had been a second slower, it could have grabbed him…"

Eldritch heard the fire drain from his father's voice, heard him choke back the tears threatening to fall. Reverend Holland's head dropped, and he buried his face in his hands.

Louise, who had been silent up until this point, rose from her seat at the end of the pew in front of Eldritch, and closed the distance between herself and the preacher. "Pastor, you weren't honest with us," she spoke, voice firm and resolute, "you told us you were going to speak to the congregation about Eldritch's gift. You said nothing about bringing Charlie Haskell and that demon into the mix. Len, look at me," she said when the minister refused to meet her eye.

He did as she commanded, lifting his sullen, red face.

"That's my little boy," she continued, "and we're still figuring out what all this is about, what all he can see and do." She lowered her voice to a harsh whisper, "And you fed him to the wolves tonight! He was in real danger, Len! You saw what it did, how it looked at him…what it said. I don't even *want* to get into what all that means." She turned her head toward her son as she referenced the words Amaymon had spoken to Eldritch—the threat of something worse to come.

Eldritch shut his eyes to keep up the ruse as his mother pinned Holland with a final, "That's all I'm going to say on the matter," and walked away. "Come on, baby boy," she said, gathering Eldritch in her arms. "I know you're awake, so you can open your eyes." He did as he was told and gave his mother a small smile at being found out.

"Are we going home now?" he asked, a yawn punctuating the question, as he laid his head on his mother's shoulder.

"Yeah, bud, we are," his father answered, heading back down the aisle toward his family. As he passed Reverend Holland, he turned toward the minister and reiterated what his wife had just said. "We're done here, Len," and with a hand on the small of his wife's back, escorted his family away from Reverend Holland and toward the exit.

As they reached the vestibule of the church, Gene and Louise came to an abrupt stop, and Eldritch lifted his head at his mother's sharp intake of breath. There, standing between them and the large, wooden doors that led outside, stood Charlie Haskell. The small, slender man was fidgeting with his hands and shifting his weight from foot to foot, but overall, he seemed much improved. His color was better, his movements weren't wild and erratic, and there was a peace about his countenance. He looked from Gene to Louise, nodding his head as he regarded each of them, and then to Eldritch, who let out a sleepy but courteous, "Hey, Mr. Charlie."

This was the real Charlie. Eldritch knew it—felt it. Whatever had been walking around in Charlie's skin earlier—*Amaymon*, his brain reminded him—was gone. His parents exchanged a sideways glance and didn't speak for several seconds, but in the end, Gene extended his hand to the sheepish man standing before them.

"Hey, Charlie. You doing alright?"

Charlie clasped Gene's hand with his own. "Yessir, Mr. Hayes. I'm doing just fine now," he answered with a deep sigh, followed by a laugh, genuine and free. "I'm doing just fine, thanks to your little boy." Charlie's attention turned to a bleary-eyed Eldritch resting in his mother's arms. "Thank you, Eldritch Hayes," he said in a voice just above a whisper. "Thank you for saving me," and with another nod to the family, and an awkward wave of his hand, Charlie exited the church.

Eldritch turned to his mother, a quizzical look on his face, "What was he talking about, Mama?"

Louise laughed through a flood of tears and gave him a tight squeeze, "He was talking about your gift, Eldritch. He was talking about your gift."

It was half past midnight when the Hayeses made their way down the stone steps, leaving Holland alone in the church behind them. The streets were deserted, and a few streetlights flickered overhead as they traveled the familiar path back to their home. Eldritch thought back to the events from earlier, and his body began to tremble in his mother's arms. It was a lot for his six-year-old mind to process, and even then, he found himself forgetting specifics of the evening. Louise snuggled him closer to her chest, and began humming "Close to You," her favorite song, into his ear. The melody echoed off the pavement and the brick storefronts around them, and Eldritch couldn't help but think how nice the town was after midnight, with just him and his parents walking together to the tune of their favorite songs.

After tucking him in, his parents assured him the thing that came out of Charlie Haskell was far, far away and couldn't lay a finger on him because he belonged to Jesus. They vowed to let him play hooky from school the next day and flipped off the lamp, but before they could rise from their spots on his bed, Eldritch asked his mother to sing him to sleep.

"Of course, baby boy, but only if you sing with me."

Eldritch nodded, and the two of them began the tune—the lyrics and melody comforting and familiar.

> Jesus loves me this I know.
> For the Bible tells me so.
> Little ones to Him belong.
> They are weak, but He is strong.
> Yes, Jesus loves me.
> Yes, Jesus loves me.
> Yes, Jesus loves me.
> For the Bible tells me so.

Both Gene and Louise kissed him on the head and, promising him everything would be brighter in the morning, left the door open, just a crack, on their way out. Eldritch could hear their voices in the hall as he lay there tucked safely in his bed, and the occasional "I mean, if he's helping people" and "If God gave him this gift" would reach his ears. Soon, their voices faded into the distance as his parents took themselves to bed, and Eldritch lay in the dark, alone.

It would take several hours for him to will himself to sleep, and when he did, his dreams were plagued with images of an oversized grin and a twisted neck, and a promise he would never forget:

Just. One. Look.

He is coming for you, Eldritch Hayes.

CHAPTER SEVEN

Eldritch's eyes snap open, and he jolts upright in bed, feeling the pounding of his heart as he places a hand over his chest. *It was just a nightmare*, he thinks to himself, and concentrates on slowing his heart rate and staving off the impending panic attack.

Thirty-five years have passed since the encounter with Amaymon, but the ominous threat spoken that night still claws its way into his subconscious every so often. *"He is coming for you, Eldritch Hayes."*

Eldritch scrubs a hand over his face and yawns, "Yeah, well, what's he waiting for?"

Rubbing the sleep from his eyes—and giving his head a good shake to help rid himself of the unwanted memory—Eldritch brings himself back to the present. Light from a sun already high in the sky filters in through the windows, and the steady bustle of small-town traffic can be heard outside on the main drag. With a stretch and a pop of his back, Eldritch reaches over to the bedside table to his right and grabs his phone, unplugging it from the charger. Checking the time and seeing it's well past eleven, he pulls the covers aside, and swings his legs over the edge of the bed. The hardwood is cold on his bare feet as he stands, and he wiggles his toes in a futile attempt to warm them.

Stretching once more for good measure, he takes note of just how chilly it is in his parents'—*my*, he corrects himself, *my*– bedroom as a shiver wracks his body. He pads across the room and grabs his housecoat from the closet, throwing it on over his pajamas. The recent cold snap has been hard on the outdated baseboard heaters which have been struggling to warm the drafty, old house.

He steals a glance at himself in the full-length mirror on the outside of the closet door and grimaces at his appearance. His hair is in absolute disarray, so he combs his fingers through the unruly mop, taming it as best he can. Nothing, however, can be done about the dark circles under his eyes.

I used to be good looking.

Back in high school and college, girls would sometimes flirt with him. He even had a girlfriend once, but nothing ever lasts when you can see what Eldritch can see. And so, dating and companionship were removed from the list of things he thought he could have—of things he thought he deserved. Eldritch knows some people still find him attractive. He's gotten used to the odd "if you'd just smile more and take better care of yourself" tossed his way by well-meaning Hayes Hardware regulars.

I could stand to put on a little weight. He has grown rather skinny over the last few years, only eating when he absolutely must. Food was always something he enjoyed with his family, and since they were ripped away from him, he cares less and less about it with every passing year.

The record player is waiting for him when he reaches the den—The Eagles still resting on the turntable after their set from the night before. The needle is dropped in the middle of the album with the expert precision of a practiced hand, and the mellow chords of "Tequila Sunrise" fill the small room as Eldritch trudges into the kitchen.

Tequila. Doesn't that sound tempting?

He pushes the thought away and focuses on what he really needs right now: coffee. But pulling open the cabinet door, Eldritch finds nothing but a half-empty package of filters staring back at him—a glaring reminder that he ran out of coffee the day before yesterday. *That's why I had to go to The Grind yesterday morning. Idiot.* He'd intended to purchase a bag of grounds when he stopped in for a coffee, but the thought had slipped his mind amidst the distractions of the busy café.

Faced with the knowledge he must now make another trip to The Grind, he shuts the cabinet with a groan and heads back up the stairs to get dressed. Coffee isn't just a luxury for Eldritch but a necessity. It's the only thing he can use to combat the horrible headaches he has a tendency to get. As a teenager, he was prescribed medication to keep them at bay, but that is no longer an option.

With it being after 11:00 a.m., he is hopeful the café will be deserted, and a quick peek into the storefront window confirms this. Eldritch has an interesting relationship with this small-town coffee shop. Although he isn't the biggest fan of stopping by in the early mornings when half the town is lined up for their pastries and lattes, he has found if you hit it at the right time, it's not too crowded—one of two advantages it has over the other establishments in town. The second, of course, being Kelly.

Kelly Walsh opened The Grind ten years ago when she moved back to Sommerset following a messy divorce, and she has worked the counter nearly every day since. Eldritch first met her in high school. Kelly should have been in the class behind him, but she was able to skip a grade, placing them in the same graduating class.

She is a kind but feisty soul, and Eldritch has always liked her. Despite everything that goes around town about him—the rumors, the snide comments, the speculation—Kelly has never regarded Eldritch with contempt or false congeniality. Even after what transpired seven years ago, when others would whisper and gossip, Kelly was there with a smile and his usual order. He rubs the tips of his fingers along the scar on his left palm, an unconscious habit triggered every time he sees her face—a face which has gotten more beautiful with time.

Her eyes light up when he pulls open the door. "Eldritch! Two days in a row. Did you run out of coffee again?" She grabs a cup and gets to work on his order without him having to say a word. Eldritch doesn't come in that often, but when he has no choice—when the coffee has run dry, and he needs a quick fix—this is where he can be found. It amazes him that despite his infrequent visits to her establishment, Kelly always remembers his drink of choice.

"Yeah. I meant to pick some up yesterday but forgot," he offers with a shy smile, rubbing the back of his head with his right hand.

"No worries," she beams at him over the coffee machine. "I'll throw in an extra bag, on the house!"

"Oh, no, Kelly." Her generosity never ceases to amaze Eldritch, but he won't let her do that. "I can pay. Two bags will be great, just let me pay for them," he pleads, reaching for his wallet; but when his hand makes contact with an empty, back pocket, he realizes he forgot to grab his wallet on his way out the door. "Oh, great," he sighs in frustration. "Hold that thought, and the coffee, I'll be back in two minutes."

"Eldritch, no. Wait—" Kelly tries to convince him it's fine, to not worry about running home, but Eldritch refuses and, thanks to the fervency of his protests, doesn't hear the sound of footsteps entering the front of the café. A chill runs through his body and the hairs on the back of his neck stand on end—the only warning he gets before the voice speaks:

"Hey, man. I can cover you."

Eldritch freezes, eyes wide and fixed on the menu behind the counter. His jaw locks tight, and everything in his body screams for him to run, but he is glued to the spot. The voice is still speaking, but the words fail to register in Eldritch's mind. They have become a muffled white noise in the distance, overtaken by an insidious drone Eldritch is certain only he can hear.

The familiar smell of rot fills his nostrils, prompting a visceral reaction as his stomach lurches in response. Eldritch steadies himself against the counter, hands clutching it in a white-knuckled grip as he fights the urge to double over when the nausea hits him—the same sensation he experienced yesterday in the hardware store. Eldritch tries to focus, tries to keep control of his senses and himself from blacking out again. He can feel how rapid and erratic his breathing is and knows he's in danger of hyperventilating.

I won't run. Not this time. Come on, Eldritch, get it together.
In through the nose, out through the mouth.
In through the nose, out through the mouth.
In through the nose, out through the mouth.

As his breathing regulates, his heartrate follows suit and, after a few moments, Eldritch is confident his fight or flight response has been held in check. The buzzing intensifies, and he can feel the entity within Mark reaching out for him.

Eldritch stands his ground and tries with all his might to push past the sinister presence and the low drone of demonic energy; tries to push past its influence and hold over him and tune back into the physical world around him.

The menu. Read the menu.

The idea pops into his mind, and he complies, zeroing in on the words printed in front of him. *Fresh Brew. Medium Roast/Dark Roast/Flavor of the Day. Hot Tea. Latte. Cappuccino. Americana. Hot Chocolate.* The words ground him and bring him back to the café—back to Kelly who is standing in front of him, on the other side of the counter, wearing a concerned expression and snapping her fingers in front of his face.

"Eldritch! Eldritch!" She is shouting now, and the snaps have turned into claps. "Eldritch!"

Eldritch feels the entity's hold on him slip at the sound of his name on her lips, and he comes back to himself and his surroundings. He manages to look Kelly in the eye and stutter out a breathless, "I'm fine, I'm fine," which he knows she doesn't buy. The initial wave of shock and fear has subsided, and the nausea has passed, but Eldritch isn't foolish enough to believe he's in the clear.

He watches as Kelly casts a worried look to the other person in the café. Closing his eyes and mustering every bit of resolve he has, Eldritch turns to face the man standing to his left. At first, there is only darkness—*the shadow*. He remembers seeing it for the first time yesterday—how terrifying it had been—and there it looms, hovering before him once more. Eldritch slams his eyes shut, fighting against his ability. *Get it together, get it together!* When he opens them again, the shadow is still there, but a whisper of what it was. It hangs around the unsuspecting man as he inches forward, approaching Eldritch like he's a wounded animal. Eldritch concentrates on his breathing again and forces himself to look at the man and not the darkness surrounding him.

"It's okay. You're okay," the man—*Mark*—addresses him, his voice steady and even. "It's Eldritch, right?"

Eldritch stares at him before realizing he's expected to respond. He blinks several times and shakes his head before answering.

"Y-yes. Yes. I'm Eldritch."

The man smiles. "Hi, Eldritch. I'm Mark. We kind of met yesterday—I don't know if you remember." Mark extends his hand, but Eldritch can't bring himself to take it, not yet; he won't let that thing touch him.

"I remember," he replies, casting his eyes downward and slipping his hands into his pockets, despite how rude it comes across. Mark doesn't seem to take offense; simply lowers his hand in response.

"I'm sorry for running, I just—I was very sick." It's a partial truth, perhaps a lie by omission, but Eldritch isn't about to hit this poor man with the facts surrounding his situation.

Mark nods his head as if he understands, though Eldritch questions whether or not he's convinced him of the lie. "I get it. It's all good. Are you sure you're okay?"

Eldritch chances another look at the man, sees the darkness swirling about him, and gives a weak smile. "I'm sure. Thank you."

Its obvious Mark has no idea what to say, and Eldritch isn't willing to provide any sort of explanation for what just happened. In his peripheral vision, he sees Kelly moving, about to make her way around the counter, but Eldritch holds up a hand to stop her.

"Don't. Just don't, Kelly. I'm fine," he insists, and she takes a step back.

An awkward silence settles over the café. Eldritch stares down at his shoes and makes a point to focus on his breathing again, still very much aware of the dark presence hovering a few feet away. He can hear it buzzing in his head, can feel it reaching out for him, and Eldritch does his best to guard his mind. After several uncomfortable minutes, the silence is interrupted by the ding of the register. Eldritch lifts his head and sees Kelly handing Mark his change, but her eyes are still focused on Eldritch. She places two bags of ground beans and Eldritch's cup of coffee on the counter in front of him as Mark puts his wallet away.

Mark walks past Eldritch and places a hand on his shoulder. The sensation knocks the breath from Eldritch's lungs as he feels the darkness graze his skin. He recoils—a reflex he fails to control—but does his best to recover, not wanting to offend Mark for the umpteenth time since their first encounter. The contractor removes his hand but says nothing, heading for the exit with a shake of his head. As the door swings closed behind Mark, Eldritch swears he hears the same laugh from yesterday morning—low, gravelly, inhuman. He tries to suppress the shiver that wracks his body, but he knows Kelly sees the slight convulsion.

Noticing her intake of breath, he rushes to the counter to grab the items she placed there for him. Kelly reaches for his left hand, and, for a moment, he contemplates letting her take it. *Take it, please. Touch me. Touch the scar and offer me whatever sweet words of wisdom you have stowed away for a broken man stumbling in the dark.* But because he's embarrassed and overwhelmed for the second morning in a row, all thoughts of touch and connection are shoved aside. His steps are swift as he collects his coffee from the counter and turns to leave. When he reaches the door, Kelly calls out to him.

"Eldritch—"

A slight turn of his head is the only indication she gets that he's listening.

"You don't have to do it all alone, you know."

He hesitates, fingers wrapped around the door handle, but it's not enough—not this time. This time, a rapid departure is all he has to offer.

The next two weeks pass as most weeks do. Eldritch wakes every morning, goes to work, and does his shift at the hardware store, where he chats with Amir and Uncle Cal. Every evening, he goes home to his empty house, eats dinner, listens to records or watches TV, and goes to bed alone. This series of events repeats like clockwork Monday through Friday, with Eldritch's ritual walk every Friday night the only variant in his activities. Though he has taken every precaution to avoid Mark, Eldritch casts a wary eye toward the Birch-Rainey house every Friday night around 1:00 a.m. when his path leads him in that direction. The first Friday night after the café incident is typical: the lights are on, the muffled sounds of sanding and sawing fill the air, and Mark's silhouette is hard at work despite the rest of the town being tucked away in bed. The second Friday is different. The lights downstairs are on, but all is silent, and there is no sign of Mark's figure in the windows. Eldritch goes out of his way to make sure Mark's truck is there, stepping into the street for a better look at the backyard. From this vantage point, he spots the silver pickup parked in the dim light of the utility pole behind the house. Satisfied, he shrugs and continues on his way. *Mark must be calling it an early night.*

When the fourth week of November rolls around, the only thing anyone is concerned about is Thanksgiving. Eldritch shuffles into work that Monday to find Uncle Calvin and Amir discussing logistics for Thursday.

"If you want to eat lunch with your family and come over later, that's fine. And bring your girlfriend. Tell me her name again."

"Larissa. For the fifteenth time."

Calvin brings a hand to his chest in mock offense. "Hey, cut me some slack, I'm elderly!"

"Hardly," snorts Amir, "besides, my parents don't really do anything for Thanksgiving, and Larissa *hates* her family, so we're pretty much free to come over whenever. Just let me know."

"Eldritch!" Calvin calls out when he notices his nephew approaching. "You're still coming over Thursday, right?"

"Would you expect me to have other plans?" he snarks, leaning against the wall beside his uncle.

"Unfortunately, no, but humor me next time and say you got a hot date," Calvin jokes with an elbow to his nephew's side. "Oh, I might need you to come by Wednesday and help me set up that smoker."

"You got it," says Eldritch, rubbing his side after his uncle's assault.

For the last few years, Calvin has been trying to up his turkey game. Last year was the air fryer, the year before that was the traditional deep fryer, and the year before that was the grill. This year, he's dead set on smoking one and purchased a fancy, overpriced smoker to do so.

"Oh, that's right!" Amir shouts, face beaming. "Two-day work week! Thanks, Thanksgiving!"

Calvin's eyeroll is impossible to miss, and Amir flashes Eldritch the triumphant smile of a man who measures success by how often he can get under the boss's skin.

When the three of them reach the front of the store, Amir unlocks the front door and flips on the "Open" sign, while Calvin pulls Eldritch down aisle three with a question about the amount of chicken wire they have in stock.

"I can't tell you the last time I ordered chicken wire, but let me check the—" Eldritch begins, but Calvin is quick to cut him off.

"Never mind the chicken wire. There's no issue with the chicken wire. The chicken wire is fine."

"Then why—?"

"Mark is coming by at some point today."

The laugh that escapes him is incredulous, and Eldritch lets his arms drop against his sides in defeat. "I just can't get away from this guy, can I?"

Calvin tilts his head. "Eldritch, did something else happen?"

"It's fine. Forget about it," he deflects. "I'll just make myself scarce. There's a lot of work needs doing in the lumberyard anyways."

He isn't wrong. Since the weather has warmed up—in true South Carolina fashion, just before Thanksgiving—Eldritch doesn't mind organizing things outside. The last few weeks were so cold, none of them wanted to deal with it, and it seems that has worked in Eldritch's favor. Now he has an excuse to stay out of the store and out of Mark's way.

"What does he need?" he asks, as Calvin starts to walk away. "Why's he coming by?"

Calvin shrugs, "He didn't say."

Eldritch schools his face, convinced it's best for everyone if smiles, nods, and lets his uncle go about his business.

For the next few hours, Eldritch confines himself to the lumberyard: restocking, checking inventory, and grating the back lot, which is a muddy mess of dips and holes thanks to Sunday's rainstorm. One o'clock rolls around, and Eldritch takes his sandwich on the loading dock. When the weather's nice, he prefers to eat outside, and the loading dock at noon is usually deserted. He's taking his first bite of the ham and cheese sandwich he made this morning when the back door opens.

"Thought I'd join you," Amir grins, pulling the metal door shut behind him. "What you got?" he asks, indicating the lunch in Eldritch's hands.

"Ham and cheese," comes the garbled answer from a mouth full of sandwich.

Amir nods in approval, "Nice. I got soup." He shakes the tomato soup in its disposable sipping cup to showcase his point. Amir takes a seat beside Eldritch on the edge of the loading dock, and the two eat in companionable silence for a few minutes. When Eldritch finishes his sandwich, he takes a swig of his water and, clearing his throat, turns to Amir.

"So, how are things inside?"

"Slow. Everyone's probably at the grocery store, fighting over yams or cranberry sauce or whatever."

Eldritch laughs at the picture Amir paints, knowing it can't be too far from the truth.

"Oh, your boy came in a little while ago."

He levels Amir with a look that shows just how much he disapproves of his choice of words and asks, "What did he need?"

"Nothing," Amir shrugs. "Just asked for you."

Eldritch tries not to let his apprehension show, tries not to let Amir know just how disturbing he finds that information. His hands begin to shake, and he clutches his water bottle tighter.

Why would he ask for me?

Amir doesn't appear to notice the shift in Eldritch's demeanor, or if he does, he doesn't comment on it. "It was weird. He walked in, asked for you, I told him you weren't around, and he just...left."

Eldritch doesn't like that one bit, but he tries to keep his cool. "Did you mention it to Cal?"

"No. He got trapped on a phone call in his office."

Eldritch breathes a sigh of relief, not wanting his uncle involved in this situation more than he already is. *He has enough on his plate.*

Amir looks down at his watch and stands, brushing off the back of his pants. "I'm going to leave you to it. Gotta call Larissa before I clock back in." He pauses with his hand on the back door and turns to look at Eldritch again, "Do we need to ban him or something? From the store? I don't like this, Eldritch."

Eldritch can't find the words to express how much his friend's concern and thoughtfulness mean to him, and all he can manage is a shake of his head and a, "No, I'll be fine," before Amir disappears inside.

With Amir gone, Eldritch can let the lie of his untroubled façade slip. He tosses his water bottle aside and buries his face in his hands. *What does he want with me?* When it comes to Mark and the entity within him, Eldritch has a multitude of questions and zero answers. He always knows what he's dealing with— *always*—but the mystery and confusion of this situation has

Eldritch on edge like never before. And now, it is no longer just a matter of running into Mark in a public space, but the man is actively seeking Eldritch out, asking for him by name.

Deciding he needs to get back to work and keep his mind occupied and focused on something—*anything*—else, Eldritch grabs his water bottle and hops down off the loading dock. He's halfway across the lumberyard when he remembers he didn't clock back in after his lunch break. With a sigh of frustration, he turns to head back to the main building…and finds himself face to face with Mark and the shadow.

"There you are."

CHAPTER EIGHT

By the time he was ten years old, Eldritch had become a strange sort of celebrity in the town. Word travelled fast after the liberation of Charlie Haskell, and in the years that followed, Reverend Holland began holding "deliverance" services once a quarter—the third Wednesday of January, April, July, and October. Church folk would invite family members, co-workers, friends—and at times, random people they'd met at a gas station or restaurant—who they felt were harboring demonic spirits in their lives. The visitors, who for the most part, were oblivious as to why they had *actually* been invited to a Wednesday night prayer meeting, were marched down the aisle to the altar and stood before a young Eldritch Hayes. Eldritch would name whatever spirits he saw attached to them, and Reverend Holland and his deacons would call down figurative fire from heaven and cast the demonic entity out.

CALLING ELDRITCH HAYES

It took a lot of convincing before Gene Hayes agreed to let his son take part in such a service after the initial Charlie episode, but after seeing how much the man had changed—how much his life had changed—because of what Eldritch was able to see, he acquiesced. There were, however, conditions to the Hayes's cooperation—rules set in place to ensure the safety of their little boy. As soon as Eldritch identified a spirit, he was to be removed from the sanctuary, swept back into one of the adjacent Sunday school rooms until the evil was conquered. The second condition ensured no one was allowed to approach or touch Eldritch unless Gene and Louise cleared it first. For four years, these stipulations were respected, and the services went off without a hitch. People were being loosened from the bonds of oppression and possession and, more importantly, Eldritch remained safe while using his gift.

Eldritch encountered more cases of spiritual oppression than anything else during these prayer meetings. Sometimes people would come forth with a haze around them—nothing that frightened the boy outright—and all that popped into his mind were words like "greed," "lust," and "anger." Those people were prayed for, Reverend Holland would speak in tongues, and sometimes the person would end up asleep on the floor. The church people called it "slain in the spirit;" the person being so overwhelmed by the power and Spirit of God that they could no longer remain upright, and fell to the ground, unconscious. When actual demonic entities were involved, things would unfold similarly to the way they had with Charlie Haskell. The little hairs on his arms and neck would stand up, and Eldritch would feel a wave of apprehension or fear before looking past the person and into the eyes of the presence within, calling its name as soon as it came to him.

Once the name passed his lips, Eldritch was hoisted up by his father and rushed to a separate room down the hall. There he would wait with his parents until the howling, cursing, and fervent praying morphed into a chorus of "hallelujah" and "praise God." Over time, that's how Eldritch came to know the coast was clear, and it was safe to return to the sanctuary; and every time he did, it was to massive applause from the congregation.

Despite the fear that wracked his body and the toll his ability began to take on his young mind—resulting in severe headaches that often made him physically ill—Eldritch put on a brave face for each deliverance service, secure in the knowledge that no matter what name he called out at that altar, his father would be there to scoop him up and carry him off to safety. Reverend Holland was very pleased with him, always patting his head and praising him for his service to the Lord. People they passed in the street would call his name and wave—people Eldritch didn't even know. Between the ages of six and ten, Eldritch felt special, Eldritch had a purpose, despite the drawbacks of his gift—drawbacks he felt were best kept to himself.

One Friday night, in the fall of 1991, the phone rang, interrupting an episode of *Family Matters*. Louise answered it in the kitchen and ended up on the call for over an hour. The next day, Gene and Louise told Eldritch there was someone who needed his help, and the three of them loaded up in their wood-paneled station wagon and traveled to the town of Cayce. Their destination was a small, brick, ranch-style home in a neighborhood called Congaree Heights. Eldritch followed behind his parents as they approached the front door, which was a sickly, faded yellow. Eldritch didn't like the color of the door, and his only thought, as his father rang the doorbell, was that someone really needed to paint it.

With the click of the lock and the grinding of metal as the handle turned, the yellow door was pulled open. A petite, middle-aged lady stood behind it, much of her appearance obscured by the door, which she seemed to use as a shield between her and the strangers on her stoop.

"Can I help you?"

Her voice was tired and frail, and the bit of her face Eldritch could see warranted the same description—the bags under her eyes coupled with her grim expression revealed a haggardness that had nothing to do with age.

"Hey there," his father began, "I'm Gene Hayes. I believe you spoke to my wife, Louise, on the phone. We're here with our son, Eldritch."

At the mention of Eldritch's name, the woman's eyebrows shot up, and she opened the door wide in invitation. "Of course! Oh my gosh! I'm so sorry. With everything that's been going on around here, I nearly forgot!" she sputtered, stepping to the side so the three of them could enter. "Come in, please!"

After closing the door behind her, she scurried around the living room, picking things up off the floor, tidying up for her guests. The house was messy—much messier than Eldritch was used to, on account of Gene Hayes being a bit of a neat freak. After tossing a handful of children's toys and sneakers into a nearby bedroom and slamming the door, the woman turned to her three visitors and introduced herself.

"I'm so sorry about that! I'm Nadine Jeffords," she panted, out of breath from her frantic cleaning, and extended her hand to Louise.

"Louise Hayes. This is my husband, Gene."

Nadine shook Gene's hand as well before looking down at the young boy standing behind his father. "And you must be Eldritch."

Eldritch nodded and gave her a small smile. Nadine smiled back, before turning to the child's parents.

"How long has he been able to see…what he can see?"

Eldritch's parents gave a brief history of his gift: when they'd first noticed it, how old he had been at the time—Eldritch had gotten used to tuning this part out over the years.

While the grownups spoke, he caught sight of another woman storming down the hallway and into the kitchen. She looked similar in age to Nadine and his mother and was dressed in an old nurse's outfit: white dress, white shoes, and a little white hat that sat atop a shock of bright red hair. But despite the uniform, her appearance was anything but professional. The dress itself was wrinkled and disheveled, the hat was crooked, and her hair was falling out of its bun and into her face. Eldritch could tell she was agitated as she flung open the cabinets and rifled through drawers, and he jumped when she started yelling.

"I know you've hidden them!!! I'll find them! They're not yours! I have a prescription for them!"

Eldritch looked up and realized his parents and Nadine were lost in conversation as if nothing out of the ordinary was happening not twenty feet from where they stood.

She's the ghost.

"So, what seems to be the problem?" asked Gene as he and the ladies moved to sit at the dining room table. "Louise told us you were experiencing some disturbances, but not much else—"

Eldritch, who was barely following their conversation at all, interrupted his father, breaking his silence at last, "There's a lady in the kitchen."

The three adults looked toward the room in question, Gene and Louise gasping as their eyes fell on the open cabinets and drawers.

Nadine fished a cigarette out of its box and brought it to her lips. "Like he said," she sighed, "there's a lady in the kitchen."

For the next half hour, Eldritch tracked the frenzied movements of the red-haired nurse as she scampered about the home. Now that he was a little older, his parents didn't hover over him as much as they used to—at least not when the subject of investigation was only a ghost—and they remained at the dining table with Nadine. Most of the activity was confined to the kitchen as the spirit carried on with her fevered search of the cabinets and drawers, digging through the contents of each, throwing things around; Eldritch flinched in his spot by the doorway every time a pot or pan hit the floor.

"I'm getting real tired of having to clean up that kitchen," grumbled Nadine, and Eldritch turned at the sound, watching as she took a long drag of her Salem Light and blew out a stream of smoke that danced in the warm light of the incandescent bulbs over the table.

"Is it just the kitchen?" asked Gene.

"For the most part. Sometimes doors open and slam. I heard a woman scream one night. That's how I figured it wasn't no man."

Eldritch stepped further into the space, following the ghost as she moved to the far side of the kitchen and ripped open the pantry door. He soon found there was no discernible pattern to her movements and had to jump out of the way to avoid being trampled by the angry specter when she doubled back, having found nothing in the pantry but Nadine's groceries—groceries which joined the rest of the mess on the floor.

Eldritch had encountered many ghosts prior to this instance. In his experience, some would interact with him—touch him, speak to him—others would act like he wasn't even there, like he was just as invisible to them as they were to the common observer. This lady seemed to do the latter, searching for some mystery item, mumbling and cursing to herself. At one point she stuck her head out the kitchen doorway and shouted down the hall, "Brady!! I swear to God! If you've flushed them, I'll kill you! I'll kill every person in this house!!" Eldritch shrunk back at the threat but didn't retreat from the kitchen. *She can't hurt me. I have to be brave.*

Her tirade in the kitchen went on for another twenty minutes, and by the end of it, the entire contents of Nadine's cabinets joined her groceries on the dingy, vinyl floor. The air grew thick and hummed with an electric intensity, making Eldritch's ears pop from the pressure, as the ghost grew angrier than ever. Then, with a scream of frustration, she grabbed the microwave on the counter, tearing the plug from the socket, and threw it across the kitchen. Eldritch sprang to safety just in time and turned to see it smash into the wall, breaking to pieces with a resounding crash.

The adults were on their feet in seconds. Gene and Louise rushed toward their son, shouting his name in alarm, while Nadine ran to inspect the damage done to her microwave and wall. Even from where Eldritch was standing, he could tell there was a large hole in the drywall, and the microwave was all but destroyed.

"Are you okay? What happened?" Louise asked, brushing his hair back and off his forehead.

"I'm fine. She got mad and threw it," Eldritch responded, pointing at the busted appliance on the floor. "She was looking for something and thinks Brady took it." He scanned the kitchen for the ghost, but there was no longer any sign of her.

"Who's Brady, bud?" Gene knelt beside his son and made sure the boy was okay after the spirit's violent display.

Eldritch shrugged, "I don't know, but I think that's why she threw the microwave. She was mad at him, not me. I don't even think she saw me standing there."

Nadine buried her face in her hands and sobbed, "I don't know who either of them are, but I can't keep doing this!"

Feeling a pang of sympathy for the woman's plight, Eldritch began picking up the items scattered on the floor, placing them back in the pantry as best he could. Gene and Louise joined in, gathering pots, pans, and dishes from where the ghost had thrown them, and stacked them on the counters. Nadine stood motionless, staring down at her battered microwave in a daze. Louise took charge of the organization, instructing her husband and son where to put each item, making certain every piece found its home in the pantry, cabinets, or drawers.

When Eldritch finished restocking the food items, he shut the pantry door just in time to see a flash of red and white pass by the kitchen doorway and down the hall.

"She's back," he announced to his parents and Nadine before following after.

He caught sight of her as she turned into a back bedroom and slammed the door. The force of the impact rattled the walls, shaking the pictures hung there, and Eldritch let out a yelp of surprise at the sound.

"Eldritch?" his mother called down the hall.

"I'm okay. She just slammed a door."

"She does that all the time," he heard Nadine tell his parents. "When she ain't wrecking my kitchen, she's slamming that door back there."

Eldritch knew he had to follow the spirit, but he hesitated—duty and fear at odds within him—before steeling his nerves and walking the length of the hallway to the bedroom she had entered. He placed a shaky hand on the brass knob—a million thoughts running through his mind about what he would find on the other side—and with a steadying breath, turned it and pushed open the door.

In the middle of the room stood the ghost, and she was looking right at Eldritch, green eyes bright and wide with fury. He froze, unable to speak, understanding then that she *could* see him but had been too preoccupied with her search to acknowledge him in the kitchen.

"I'll kill them all," she rasped in a harsh, throaty snarl, and Eldritch noticed the gun for the first time—a sort of shotgun with the barrel cut short. The spirit raised the gun toward the wall across from her and fired into the closet. The blast was deafening, and Eldritch brought his hands to his ears—a knee-jerk reaction to the thunderous bang. But the discharge of the sawed-off shotgun was too much for the small nurse to handle. It kicked with such force that the barrel flew back toward her face, and her hands clutched at the grip, squeezing the trigger in the process.

The gun went off again, this time blowing off the entire top half of the lady's head, and Eldritch saw it all: blood, brains, bits of skull and fiery red hair, all splattered across the ceiling and the vanity mirror behind her. A high-pitched scream filled his ears as he dropped to the floor, eyes shut tight, trying to purge the horrific image from his mind. Then there were hands on him, grabbing his shoulders; voices speaking to him, begging him to open his eyes. He struggled to make out the words over the piercing scream that would not cease.

"Eldritch! Look at me!"

I can't. I can't open my eyes.

"Baby boy, please!"

I can't look at it...and it's so loud.

"Eldritch, stop screaming!"

Stop screaming?

Realizing the scream was his own, he snapped his mouth shut, silencing it. The voices were still pleading with Eldritch to look at them, so he fought against the fear and opened his eyes to find the terrified faces of his parents. Unable to stop himself, he glanced into the bedroom once more, expecting to see blood-soaked walls and a headless body sprawled on the floor. But there was nothing—no blood, no body, no gun. Eldritch sat in disbelief, staring into an empty, ordinary room.

"She was a nurse," Eldritch explained to his parents and Nadine once he'd recovered from the shock of the phantom scene. "She thinks that Brady person hid something of hers, and she yelled at him. 'If you've flushed them, I'll kill you! I'll kill every person in this house!!'"

"Pills," interjected Gene, "she was looking for pills."

Nadine blushed and looked away at his words.

Eldritch continued his retelling of events, describing the moments leading up to the microwave incident and how she threw it with such ease; how he'd seen her appear out of nowhere while they were cleaning and shut herself in the back bedroom.

"And then—" Eldritch paused.

"And then what? What happened after that?" Nadine asked, but Eldritch was hesitant to continue. "Sweetie," she pressed, "sweetie, then what?"

Eldritch swallowed, his mouth and throat suddenly dry at the prospect of describing the horrible accident in the back room. "She had a gun," he began and saw his parents tense at the mention of the firearm. "It went off, and...sh-sh-she shot herself in the head."

His parents gasped, and Nadine dropped her cigarette on the table. Now that Eldritch had started, he was unable to stop, and the words spilled from his mouth. "There was blood on the walls and all over the room. Her hair was on the ceiling. Everything smelled like blood, and she was...she was—"

Louise crouched down, her face level with his. "It's okay, baby boy," she soothed, hand reaching out to stroke his hair like she always did, "we understand. You did so good, Eldritch."

The Hayeses instructed Nadine to call a minister and gave her Reverend Holland's number in case she didn't have a pastor of her own to call. She thanked them for driving all the way from Sommerset to ease her mind about the troubled spirit who once called this same house home.

"I suppose, in some way," Nadine said as she walked her guests to the door, "I feel for her. We're not too different. But I can't keep worrying about what she's going to smash next, and I want her to find some kind of peace."

Louise gave the woman a hug and encouraged her to call Reverend Holland, "He'll know what to do."

"And sometimes," Eldritch piped up, "if you just tell them to go away, they will."

Nadine nodded, shook their hands, and waved as they climbed back into their station wagon.

"How'd you know that, baby?" asked Louise as they merged onto the highway. "About telling them to leave."

"I don't know," he shrugged, "but you have to mean it."

"Now, who in the world is that?" Gene asked when they pulled into the driveway.

Someone was standing on the front porch, and Eldritch was curious as to why anyone would be paying them a visit after dark on a Saturday night. The headlights illuminated the individual waiting by the front door as their station wagon pulled further into the drive.

"It's Len," said Gene, and Eldritch craned his neck to see out the windshield from the backseat. The imposing figure of the minister, caught in a swathe of artificial light, cast a long shadow across the front of the house.

"Nadine must have called him," Louise reasoned as she unbuckled her seatbelt. "Maybe he's come up with a solution for that ghost she's dealing with."

Gene parked the car under the carport, and the three of them hopped out and headed up the steps toward the front door to greet the minister.

Eldritch noticed the stern look on the man's face and whispered to his mother, "He looks mad about something."

Eldritch never liked it when Reverend Holland was mad because that often resulted in a sermon aimed at him and his parents. But it had been years since the preacher voiced an issue with Eldritch's work, and the boy relished the fact that he'd been doing a good job. The displeasure written on Holland's face at present had Eldritch shrinking from the man and slowing his pace to fall behind his parents.

Before Gene reached the final step, Holland bellowed in a contemptuous tone, "I just had the most interesting phone call!"

I knew it. I'm in trouble again.

"So, what's this I hear about you making house calls now, Eldritch?" Reverend Holland asked, tone dripping with false curiosity. Eldritch stared at the pastor, willing his mouth to speak, but every explanation his anxious mind provided died on a tongue refusing to move.

"We got a call from a lady over in Cayce," answered Louise, and Eldritch breathed a sigh of relief at his mother's interjection. "She's been having some disturbances in her home and asked if Eldritch could come take a look."

The response seemed to further stoke the embers of Holland's ill temper, and he ground his next question out through gritted teeth and a fake smile. "And where did she hear about our boy, Eldritch, pray tell?"

"Well, she heard about *our* boy, Eldritch," said Gene, motioning between himself and his wife, "from a cousin who lives here in town."

"And who's her cousin?"

"Why does it matter?"

He heard the bite in his father's tone, the subtle shaking of his body as he fought to hold his anger in check. Eldritch understood—understood because he felt the same frustration building within himself, screaming to be unleashed.

"The problem, *Gene*," spat the preacher, "is that we can't just have any old person calling Eldritch up and expecting him to come running. This Nadine woman doesn't even live in this town, and she's certainly not a member of *my* congregation!"

"But she needs help!" Eldritch found his voice at last, rushing in to explain the situation. "It's causing a lot of problems in her house, and Ms. Nadine just needs help."

To Eldritch, the explanation was a simple one. When people were in need, you had to do your best to help them, however you could.

"What is causing problems?"

"The lady in her house. The ghost."

Holland's eyes narrowed at the boy's words. "How many times do I have to tell you?" he growled, "there's no such thing as ghosts. There are demons, and there are angels. That's it."

Eldritch didn't understand how Reverend Holland could be so wrong about such an obvious fact. Demons and ghosts were two very different things, and ghosts weren't angels either—not that Eldritch had ever encountered an angel, and he wasn't sure he wanted to, based on how they're described in the Bible. Eldritch knew the difference because of how they made him feel. When it came to demons, his body would react first, alerting him to the wrongness of the situation. The little hairs on his arms and neck would stand up and his heart would race as the fear and anxiety set in. Usually, within minutes of being in the presence of a demon, Eldritch could identify it and call it by name. With ghosts, it was much different. Eldritch never knew a ghost's name unless it spoke to him and offered it up. Sure, a couple had scared him here and there; they could be angry or sad—sometimes they threw things, like the lady today—but when in the company of a ghost, there was something missing that was always there when a demon was present: the tangible presence of evil.

"No, Reverend Holland," Eldritch clarified, "that's not true. Ghosts are different from demons and angels because—"

His rebuttal was cut short as Holland leaned down until they were eye to eye, pointed a finger in his face, and reiterated, "'To be absent from the body is to be present with the Lord.'"

"Okay," interrupted Gene, pushing Holland's finger out of Eldritch's face, "that's enough. He's got the point, Len. We've heard this sermon before. Besides, what does it matter? We were just trying to help a lady out."

"It matters because there are all manner of people out there who will want to take advantage of this boy and his spiritual gift," Holland insisted, puffing out his chest with a roll of his shoulders, "and I, as the shepherd of this flock, cannot allow that to happen. It is my job to keep the wolves away."

"Pastor," interjected Louise, "I hardly believe Nadine's a wolf out to take advantage here. She was a desperate woman who had nowhere else to turn."

"Well, I took care of Nadine the minute she called."

"What's that supposed to mean?" asked Gene, squaring off with the preacher.

"I informed her that I could not help, and that if there was a presence in her home, she must have done something to give it access. Did you know she's unchurched? She is, and I told her she needed to get right with God, find a church home, and maybe this spirit—this *demonic* spirit—will vanish once the *Holy* Spirit takes up residence in her house instead."

Eldritch didn't know how to respond to that, and from the looks on his parents' faces, neither did they. He still didn't believe Holland was right about ghosts and demons, but there was no arguing with the man. His word was gospel—a gospel second only to *the* Gospel, but there were times where Eldritch felt the man put more stock in his own words than the Word of God.

"Eldritch," Holland turned to the boy, "I don't think you understand how delicate your situation is. You have a powerful gift, and the enemy is going to try to sway you to his side. The more you go around talking about ghosts, the more you're letting Satan win. If Satan wins, I fear for you and your soul—the entire congregation does." It was subtle, but the implicit threat failed to escape Eldritch's understanding.

Either I do what he says, or he'll tell everyone I'm of the devil.

"From now on, no more unsolicited calls from people claiming they need your help. If anyone contacts you about spirits, you tell them to call me. I'll determine if their claims are legitimate, and if they're even worth your time."

Eldritch knew arguing was pointless, and nodded in resignation, fixing his eyes on the cement floor of the porch.

"I'm doing what's best for you, my boy—what God wants for you. You *have* to remain in His will, Eldritch, and it's *my* job to keep you there."

CHAPTER NINE

Surprised by Mark's sudden appearance, Eldritch recoils, stumbling backward and almost falling. Mark reaches out, but Eldritch refuses his assistance.

"Don't!" he shouts as he regains his footing, and Mark withdraws his hand at the admonition.

"You're real touchy, you know that?" Mark snaps.

If Eldritch had his wits about him, he'd take offense at the comment, but given his level of overwhelm at the demon's proximity, he can only nod and back away. Mark follows.

"Where are you going?"

Eldritch fights to catch his breath, but the spirit is too strong, and Eldritch can't get himself under control. He raises a trembling hand and extends his arm, trying to reestablish the distance between them, but Mark steps forward and closes the gap.

"I'm sorry, Mark, but I'm working. I'm right in the middle of something," he lies between labored breaths.

Mark scoffs, "No, you're not. You're on your lunch break. I saw you eating," and steps closer.

Eldritch, who had been averting his eyes as best he could, forces himself to look at Mark's face. Despite having focused on the man's features only once before, he notices how much Mark has changed since their encounter at The Grind. His face is thinner than Eldritch remembers, with pale skin stretching across his prominent cheekbones and sloping down into the caverns of his cheeks. He's lost a considerable amount of weight and, despite the aggression he's displayed this afternoon, he looks exhausted, drained, like he hasn't slept in weeks.

It's aged him.

"M-Mark, if there's anything you need, Amir or Uncle Cal can help you in the store, I just handle inventory and straighten things up."

Eldritch turns to walk off in the opposite direction but finds that over the course of their conversation, Mark has backed him into a corner. The evil permeating Mark's skin and creeping out toward him is extreme, and Eldritch feels his lunch return to his throat. He tries to swallow it back down, but his rational brain takes a backseat, and his thoughts are reduced to *danger, trapped, run*. He's panting, unable to suck in enough oxygen, and there's a tightness in his chest. *I can't breathe.* He faces Mark again, and their eyes lock.

Mark's eyes are an icy blue, but any luster they may have held before now has grown dull—dull irises adrift in a sea of bloodshot inflammation. In this moment, though intense and uncomfortable, the demon has yet to display its full power, and Eldritch can still see a piece of the man he must have been before the possession hijacked his life. There's a part of Eldritch that wants to tell Mark the truth, but it is silenced by his desperation to find a way out of this situation. As his thoughts snap back to his current predicament, fear takes the reins once more, and Eldritch feels his stomach churn. He doubles over, spilling his ham and cheese sandwich all over Mark's work boots.

Eldritch wipes his mouth on his sleeve and braces for Mark's reaction, but Mark simply looks down and takes another step forward into Eldritch's space, tracking his boots through the puddle of vomit.

"I asked around town about you," he says, with no acknowledgement of what just happened. "A lot of people in this town say you're real weird." This Mark is very different from the Mark in the coffee shop. That Mark was patient and considerate, even with the demon lurking within. This Mark is callous and demanding.

It's doing a real number on him.

Eldritch withdraws further until his back makes contact with the wall of lumber. Mark seems undeterred by the tight quarters and steps even closer.

"Mark, please. I need you to back off right now!" Eldritch raises his chin in an imitation of a boldness he does not possess. It would be more convincing if he could stop shaking, but he decides there's only one way out of this and it's not through the inventory behind him. Neither man speaks for a long time, and Eldritch balls his right hand into a fist, fully prepared to use it should the man take another step; but he doesn't. Instead, Mark blinks several times and takes three steps back. As the pain in his chest subsides, Eldritch breathes deep and wills his body to relax, fist unclenching at his side.

Mark's face softens, and he shakes his head, as if snapping out of his predatory trance. Looking down at his boots, he grimaces and tries to scrape the bits of masticated sandwich off in the gravel and dirt but only ends up adding mud to the mix. He looks at Eldritch with a weak smile that fails to reach his eyes.

"So, you're still sick? Or you got some kind of digestive issue?"

"Huh?" Eldritch is bewildered by Mark's abrupt change in subject and demeanor.

"You threw up again. You threw up that first day we met, too. You sickly or something?" He's different now—less intense, less combative.

"Sensitive stomach," he replies. *It's not a total lie.*

The dark energy is still there, in and around Mark, but it seems to have withdrawn somewhat, its grip on the man loosening a fraction, and Eldritch breathes a small sigh of relief.

"I'll give you money for a new pair of boots. Or you can just pick out a pair in the store. I didn't mean to…you know. It just came out."

"It's fine," Mark waves it off. "Nothing the garden hose can't take care of."

"We've got one. Right over there." He steps away from the wall of lumber and past Mark, half expecting to be stopped by the man or the shadow around him. When he finds he can walk away unencumbered, he quickens his pace and jogs over to the hose near the loading dock. He turns on the water and grabs the nozzle as Mark walks up, holding each foot a few inches off the ground and into the spray, one after the other.

"So, like I said," Eldritch keeps his tone light and aims for nonchalance as he shuts off the water and rolls up the hose, his back to Mark, "I'm really not the one to come to for questions. You're better off asking the guys inside." He turns around, brushing his hands off and placing them on his hips—an attempt to appear relaxed and unbothered.

"I don't need their help. I don't have any questions they can answer."

Eldritch is struck by the honesty of it. *So, he knows something is off. He has to.*

"Why do you freak out whenever I'm around?" Mark asks, the question far blunter than Eldritch anticipated.

This is not a conversation Eldritch wants to have. He wants out of this situation and away from Mark and the presence attached to him. He wishes Mark had never walked through the front door that day—wishes Uncle Cal hadn't had that meeting with Harry—he wishes a million little things had gone differently that morning, that their entire encounter had never happened. But it did happen, and Eldritch's life is devolving into a nightmare because of it. *Just get him out of here. I'll breathe easier when he's gone.*

He sighs and feigns confusion at the question, "I don't 'freak out' when you're around."

"You know you do!" Mark shouts. "Stop lying, man!"

"I'm not lying!" *I'm absolutely lying.*

"You're not...you know? Because I don't swing that way."

The insinuation baffles Eldritch. *Is he really mistaking a panic attack for a crush?* "Mark, don't be ridiculous. It has nothing to do with you." *A half-truth.*

Mark considers him for a minute and nods, seeming to accept the answer. "Well, people around here say all kinds of stuff. I wasn't sure. A lot of people said you've never been seen out with a woman."

The thought of his personal life still being the topic of town gossip disgusts him, and he can't suppress his grunt of irritation. "In my defense, Mark, I've never been seen out with anyone. I don't date. I don't socialize."

"Because of your big secret?"

Eldritch wasn't expecting that. He supposes it's too much for locals to keep their mouths shut about something like this, even if he hasn't used his gift in public since he was a kid. "What did you hear?"

Mark shrugs, "Nothing specific. 'Eldritch Hayes is an odd bird.' 'Eldritch Hayes keeps to himself because he's a little wacko.' 'Eldritch Hayes went crazy after his parents died.' 'Eldritch Hayes *sees things.*' What kind of things do you *see*, Eldritch Hayes?"

The anxiety Eldritch has felt throughout Mark's surprise visit turns to indignation in an instant, and he clenches his teeth to keep from saying something he may regret.

"Don't believe everything you hear, Mark," he grits out, trying to control his anger. "It's a small town. Small-minded people love a tall tale."

Eldritch watches Mark's features and the shadow around him darken. "You're lying," Mark snarls, his aggressive tone returning. "I thought you were a Christian."

Eldritch feels like he's getting whiplash from the constant shifts in Mark's demeanor, and he doesn't appreciate the questioning of his faith. The past few years have been tough on his relationship with the Almighty, Eldritch won't deny that, but it's not something he wants to talk about at present. Eldritch knows it isn't Mark's fault—knows the evil dwelling within him is poisoning his mind and turning him into someone he is not, but Eldritch resents the comment all the same.

"Don't presume to know anything about me, Mark! The details of my life and faith are of none of your business!" He knows he's lashing out and letting the demonic presence get the better of him, but he's beyond caring at this point. He didn't come into work today expecting to be ambushed by this evil spirit—*again*. He's tired of his safe spaces being infiltrated, he's tired of his life being turned upside down by this random guy and the demon that just happens to be using his body as a puppet. If rudeness is what it takes to protect himself, Eldritch can manage that.

Mark laughs, a dark chuckle that has Eldritch backing away. "That hit a nerve."

Eldritch doesn't know if he wants to argue or run, but before the decision is made, the back door opens—the sharp scrape of metal on concrete pulling his attention away from Mark. Amir steps out onto the loading dock and looks around until his eyes fall on Eldritch just off to the side.

"Hey, man," he calls over the short distance, "Cal said he needs you inside for something."

Eldritch nods, "Tell him I'll be there in a sec, I just gotta handle this," he says, jerking his head toward Mark.

Amir scrunches his eyebrows in confusion, "Handle what?"

Eldritch turns around to find himself alone in the lumber yard. For a moment, he's afraid he imagined the entire confrontation, until he hears the squelching of wet work boots tracking through mud. He looks up in time to catch a glimpse of Mark's back as he vanishes around the corner of the warehouse. Eldritch stares at the spot where the contractor stood moments prior and feels a stab of guilt for not doing more to help him, for not saying anything. *It's none of my business. He'd just call me crazy.*

"Eldritch?" Amir is still standing on the loading dock, holding the back door open and waiting for a response.

"Nothing," Eldritch turns and casts him a small smile to show just how normal everything in the lumber yard is.

Amir doesn't look convinced but doesn't press the matter, and Eldritch is sure to keep the phony smile plastered on his face as he climbs the steps to the loading dock.

"What does Uncle Cal need?" he asks, taking the weight of the door from Amir as they walk inside together.

"He didn't say," shrugs Amir. "Probably Thanksgiving related. Amy just called and was chewing his ear off about something. He started making a list."

"Good old Aunt Amy."

Calvin's wife, Amy, has a reputation as a perfectionist and over-planner, so there's no telling what task Eldritch is about to be assigned.

"Better not let her hear you call her that. 'Old.' She'd die. Or kill you. Actually, that's far more likely."

Eldritch is grateful for Amir's infectious humor—grateful there is someone in his life who helps take his mind off his problems and makes him enjoy a laugh every once in a while, in the most effortless way possible.

"Well, don't go telling on me. The last thing I need is a pissed off Amy on my tail. I got enough to worry about," Eldritch laughs—trying to ignore the sliver of truth that slid into his otherwise good-natured joke—and parts ways with his friend in the storefront as Amir runs to catch the ringing phone.

"Hayes Hardware. This is Amir."

The phone call fades into the background as Eldritch walks over to his uncle's office, rapping his knuckles against the open door as he enters. "You wanted to see me?"

Calvin looks up from the legal pad he's scribbling on, "Oh! Yeah, Amy called a little while ago—"

"I heard," Eldritch interrupts with a snort.

Calvin rises from his desk, tearing the front sheet from the notepad and handing it to his nephew. Eldritch swallows hard, terrified that his uncle is about to send him to the grocery store the week of Thanksgiving to fight his way through a mob of people—*and God knows what else*—to pick up whatever ingredients are written on this list.

"Amy needs a few things from the store," Calvin begins as Eldritch looks down at the paper, mind too busy running through the horrors of this undertaking to read the list, "so, I got to run down there real quick before it turns into a mad house."

The words register with Eldritch as he notices the items written in his uncle's messy scrawl are not groceries but tasks that need to be handled around the hardware store.

"If you and Amir don't mind taking care of all this before you close up today, I'd appreciate it."

Eldritch flattens himself against the open door to let his uncle slide by, but Calvin stops, pulling a pen from his coat pocket. "You know, on second thought, don't worry about calling Harry," he takes the list from Eldritch, crosses out the words "Call Harry about BRH," and hands it back. "I don't even know why I wrote that on there. Not something you need to deal with."

BRH. Birch-Rainey house.

"Is something wrong with the renovation?" Eldritch asks, curious and a bit concerned given his recent encounter with the house's contractor.

"Eh, I don't know. Harry has some questions. Don't worry about it," his uncle assures, "it's probably nothing." With that, he breezes past Eldritch and toward the front door, shouting a few instructions at Amir before the bell rings behind him.

The rest of the day is slow with only a handful of customers. The following day is the same. When Wednesday rolls around, Eldritch hops into his old Toyota Celica and drives over to his uncle's house on the lake. Calvin and Amy bought their house on Lake Murray eight years ago, the summer before the accident. Eldritch's parents always hosted Thanksgiving at their house—*his* house—a time-honored family tradition for as long as Eldritch could remember. After they died, Amy insisted she and Calvin host at their place so Eldritch didn't have to sit at home on Thanksgiving Day and think about the two people who should be there but aren't. What Aunt Amy didn't understand then, and doesn't seem to understand now, is a change in location doesn't matter. Gene and Louise are all Eldritch ever thinks about, whether it's a holiday or not.

When he pulls up, Amy is standing on the front porch, arms crossed, shaking her head. Eldritch reaches the bottom of the steps and looks up at her. "That bad, huh?"

"He's been cussing at that thing all morning!" she huffs. "If you don't get back there and set him straight, I might be cooking *him* for Thanksgiving dinner!"

Eldritch climbs the steps until he's two from the top and eye level with his petite aunt. They stare, stony-faced at one another, until Amy cracks a smile. They both laugh as she pulls him into a tight hug. "You never come around anymore!" she chastises, squeezing him as hard as she can. "I miss you."

"I know," he nods when she loosens her hold, "I'll do better. I promise."

Her smile fades as she sizes up her nephew, "you're too skinny. You're not eating enough, I can tell. Are you getting enough sleep?"

Eldritch appreciates her concern for his well-being and assures her he's eating and sleeping well enough. *She knows you're lying*, he tells himself but pushes the thought aside as he makes his way through the house and onto the back deck to help his uncle. He finds Calvin amidst a sea of scattered smoker parts, trying to bolt two sections together without much luck.

"Well, clearly you don't need my help," Eldritch jokes, laughing as Calvin jumps and drops his wrench.

"Daggumit!" his uncle shouts, and Eldritch falls silent.

The familiar expression, the cadence and tone, all serve as a reminder of his father. In times like these, Eldritch doesn't know whether he should laugh or cry—the resemblance, uncanny—but the moment passes, and he collects himself, slapping on a smile as he approaches his uncle and the surrounding mess of parts.

"I thought you were going to wait for me."

"Yeah, well, I woke up early and wanted to get a head start on this beast. So, here I am."

"You know, these things usually come with instructions..." Eldritch trails off as Calvin shoots him a look of contempt.

"I don't need instructions to tell me how to put a smoker together," Calvin grumbles in defense of his wounded masculinity. "It's not that hard—practically common sense."

"Uh-huh. And where exactly *are* those instructions?"

Calvin motions over to the smoker's empty, cardboard box. "In there, with the rest of the trash I don't need."

Two hours of fruitless effort later, Calving relents and agrees to let his nephew read the instructions to him, after which the two assemble the smoker with relative ease. When lunchtime rolls around, Amy comes out with sandwiches and sodas, and forces Eldritch to eat under her watchful eye. Once he finishes his ham and tomato on white, she slaps another one down on his plate and taps her foot to let him know she's not playing around. Eldritch eats half, and Amy appears satisfied. Before he leaves, she warns him that he is expected to get seconds and thirds at tomorrow's dinner, and she will not take "no" for an answer. Her tone is stern and unyielding, but when she hugs him goodbye, all he feels is love.

The following morning, Eldritch allows himself to sleep in, waking slowly from a dreamless sleep as bright sunlight filters in through the windows and falls across his eyes. He stirs, eyes blinking open, and lies there a few minutes before rising. He isn't expected at Uncle Cal's house until noon and is in no hurry to greet another Thanksgiving on his own. Grabbing his phone and padding barefoot across the wooden floor, he decides to forgo the robe since it's warmed up a bit in the last few days, and heads downstairs for some much-needed coffee.

The house is quiet—empty and still—the only sounds are his footfalls on the hardwood floor. If certain events had been avoided eight years ago, Thanksgiving morning at 129 North Main Street would paint a different picture entirely, and Eldritch allows himself a moment to pretend; allows himself a moment to act like nothing has changed. There was no accident. They are both still here, very much alive, and abuzz with an endless list of holiday preparations...

The smell of turkey hits him straight away as he bounds down the stairs. His mother has had one of the birds in the roaster for at least an hour already, and the aroma fills the house as it simmers. He can hear her on the phone in the kitchen as he rounds the corner at the foot of the stairs. From the sound of it, she's working on the dressing—Gran-Gran's recipe, a Thanksgiving tradition—and making sure Amy knows she and Calvin aren't expected to bring a thing.

"*Eldritch!*" she calls upon hearing his footsteps in the den, "*Put on a record, will you? Something Christmassy!*"

Eldritch laughs and obeys, grabbing the Carpenters' Christmas album—her favorite—and placing it on the Magnavox. Everyone in the Hayes family knows Thanksgiving isn't a holiday in its own right, merely the first phase of Christmas. "Christmas Waltz" crackles out through the worn speakers, and Louise begins to sing along as she ends her call with Amy and hangs up.

Eldritch hears a crash on the back porch and, looking through the screen door, sees his dad, fighting with the fryer. Turkey number two is always injected with hot sauce and deep fried. "*Daggum it!*" Gene shouts, trying his best not to burn himself with the bubbling oil. Eldritch shakes his head and smiles. *Some things never change…*

Reality always settles in when Eldritch reaches the kitchen and finds it empty. There is no turkey, no stuffing, no mouth-watering aroma filling the home, and no sweet chatter spoken over a phoneline long dead. There is nothing to be thankful for. Everything he ever cared about is gone.

He stands in the doorway of the kitchen and stares. The house is empty and still again. He listens for his mother's voice singing along with Karen Carpenter, but the sound has retreated to the confines of his memory once more. In a fit of anger, Eldritch stalks back into the den and rips the album off the center spindle of the record player. Fury and desperation course through him and, for a second, he wants to break the record in half. But he never could. This hokey Christmas album is a piece of his mother—one of the only pieces he has left. Instead, he brushes it off, places it back on the turntable, and drops the needle again.

Eldritch takes another look out the screen door and finds the back porch is just as empty as the kitchen.

Holidays are the worst.

Uncle Calvin's smoked turkey is a hit, and by the end of dinner, there's hardly enough food to pack up for leftovers. *That wouldn't be the case if Mama were in charge of the meal.* Louise always made enough to feed two armies, at least; the number of people she was expecting was an irrelevant detail. The temperature remains in the mid-seventies, and Eldritch relaxes on the back deck with his aunt and uncle, Amir, Larissa, and Lanny-Ray—who showed up out of the blue after declining Calvin's initial invitation.

Although social situations typically fill him with dread, Eldritch is at ease—at peace—in this moment with those he cares about. There was some apprehension over meeting Larissa for the first time, but Eldritch could tell right away she wasn't bringing anything to this gathering apart from her friendly disposition and obvious adoration for Amir.

He watches the two of them—sees their secret smiles, the brush of their hands, the stolen kisses when they think no one is paying attention. This level of casual intimacy is a mystery to Eldritch—foreign to him—as if it's the one thing everyone is capable of experiencing; everyone but him. He can't help the sting of jealousy he feels over what has been sacrificed at the altar of his ability.

He dated once. During his freshman year of college, there was a girl, Michelle, who said he had a nice smile. They went out for dinner a few times, caught a movie or two, and their blossoming romance seemed to have the potential to grow into something more. Eldritch worked up the nerve to kiss her on their third date. Michelle invited him up to her dorm with a wink, but he declined, certain neither Jesus nor his mother would approve. But the whole thing ended in disaster, thanks to his so called "gift," and Eldritch fights hard to suppress the bitterness he feels because of it in moments such as this.

"Did you get a chance to call Harry back?" Amir's question pulls Eldritch to the present, and he tunes back into the conversation happening around him. "I know you two were playing phone-tag Tuesday," Amir continues, addressing Calvin, "and he sounded *pissed* about something."

"Who's Harry?" Larissa asks, leaning forward in her seat, eyes alight with intrigue.

"Harry's the guy over the historical group, Restore SC," Amy explains.

"Nothing but a pain in the neck, if you ask me," gripes Lanny-Ray, "just like his daddy. *And* his daddy's daddy!"

"Lanny-Ray, Harry is like…70 years old," sighs Amir. "How would you remember his daddy and his grandad—you know what? Never mind. I don't know why I even bother."

Lanny-Ray says nothing, just sinks down into his chair, holding his cast-bound arm to his chest and closing his eyes.

Larissa turns her attention back to Calvin and works to get the conversation back on track, "And Harry's pissed about something? Calvin, did you call him back?!" Eldritch laughs at how invested she is in the story.

Calvin stretches in his Adirondack chair and shakes his head, "Yeah, I called him back. I don't know what he expects me to do about any of it."

"About any of what?" Eldritch and Larissa ask in unison, and she tosses a wink his way. He responds with a smile—genuine if a tad sheepish; they are co-conspirators now.

"It's Mark!" Calvin shouts, his voice bouncing off the planks of the deck and the siding of the house.

The levity of the moment evaporates, and Eldritch flinches—Mark's name not being something he expected to hear at his family gathering today. He glances over his shoulder in a knee-jerk reaction to make sure the man isn't standing behind him.

"And Mark is the contractor, the one working on the scary, old house, right?" Larissa confirms, settling down after her visible surprise at Calvin's abrupt response.

"Yes, Mark's the contractor." Calvin is getting huffy; whether at the direction of the conversation or his unhappiness at being caught in the middle of the drama between Harry and Mark, Eldritch is unsure. "Long story short: Harry can't seem to get a hold of the guy. Mark's not returning his calls, so naturally this is now *my* problem. Everyone's concerned about the renovation because it's like Mark just gave up. The house looks worse than it did when he started. At least, that's what all the folks at the historical society are saying. Harry's got his panties in a twist because he has this whole unveiling thing planned for the spring, but with the way things are going, the house won't be anywhere close to done."

Calvin takes a swig of his sweet tea and leans forward, voice dropping to a low whisper. "But just between us—" Everyone mirrors his motion, leaning in to hear what secret information he's about to spill; everyone except Eldritch who is sitting ramrod straight in his seat, clutching the arms of his chair in a white knuckled grip. *What's he doing? No, no, no, Uncle Cal. Not in front of Larissa, and Lanny-Ray!* Eldritch is relieved when Calvin glances up at him and sees the subtle shake of his head. A silent understanding passes between them, and his uncle stops mid-sentence. Eldritch hears the collective sigh of disappointment from the others as Calvin sits back in his chair.

"All I'm going to say is Mark has been MIA as far as Harry's concerned. He was supposed to come by the store Monday. I thought I'd be able to corner him and tell him to call Harry, but he didn't show."

"No, he did," Amir pipes up.

"What? When?"

"Monday. Like you said. He popped in for two seconds, asked where Eldritch was. I told him he wasn't around, and he split. Like, instantly. Just left. Dude's looking rough, by the way."

Calvin looks disturbed by this information and turns to Eldritch. "Did you know about this?"

Eldritch swallows and nods, "Yeah. Amir told me after it happened."

"Why didn't anyone tell me?"

"You were tied up on the phone in your office!" Amir rushes to his own defense. "And then it was time for my lunch break! And then...I just...kind of forgot."

"You should have told me immediately! I don't like this," Calvin rails on Amir before eyeing his nephew again. "I don't like him asking about you like that. Not after what—"

As Eldritch cuts his uncle off with another abortive shake of his head, the true reason behind his desperate need for discretion dawns on him: he isn't trying to protect the others from knowing the horrible truth about Mark's possession. He isn't even worried they'll laugh in his face or call him crazy. Eldritch realizes he is trying to protect Mark, the man. *It wouldn't be right for a bunch of people to know about the demon, when Mark doesn't even know.*

"I say we ban him," Amir states, voice firm.

"No." Eldritch is shocked by the strength of his own voice, shocked by his defense of Mark despite everything he's endured since that man walked into his life weeks ago. Yet, if anyone can understand the reason for Mark's behavior, it's Eldritch—Eldritch who has ignored the man's plight and played off Mark's spiritual predicament as if it were none of his business; Eldritch who now realizes he cannot abandon this man to the enemy like that.

"We can't just ban him," he speaks again, his words garnering strange looks from everyone. He tries to play it off. "Not while he's working on that house. It's not his fault he's—" Eldritch pauses, remembering Larissa and Lanny-Ray are present and know nothing of the *real* Mark situation. "It's not his fault."

"Eldritch, are you sure?" Calvin asks, his eyes communicating a deeper question the others are not privy to.

"I'm sure." And he is.

An uncomfortable silence falls over the group—Larissa looking to Amir, Amir to Calvin, Calvin to Amy, then to Eldrich who stares down at the deck.

After several minutes tick by, Lanny-Ray sits up straight and rubs his eyes with the hand of his uninjured arm. "Now who's Mark again?"

CHAPTER TEN

The Deliverance services continued until the year Eldritch turned thirteen. Reverend Holland kept him on a tight leash after the business with Nadine, making it clear that should Eldritch stray from his side, there would be consequences. Knowing the amount of damage the minister could do with just the wagging of his tongue, Eldritch and his parents plastered on their most convincing smiles and tried to keep in mind they were doing this to help people.

The Incident, as Eldritch and his parents would come to call it, occurred the week after his thirteenth birthday. Eldritch noticed the July and October services would have the congregation more keyed up than usual. In October, with Halloween on the way, they would be itching to combat the devil and his minions. Seeing the holiday as a threat to their ideology, they treated that month's Deliverance service as a call to arms with Reverend Holland leading the charge.

CALLING ELDRITCH HAYES

The July services, like the one in which *The Incident* occurred, were different—somehow *more* fervent. Eldritch blamed the intense summer heat and suffocating humidity, convinced something about it riled the parishioners up. The rising temperatures coupled with Reverend Holland's fearmongering about demons and devils among the people made for a powder keg of emotion and hysteria. Such were the conditions on the evening of July nineteenth.

The church was packed, and the AC unit had died just before service—an inevitable fate after struggling to keep up with the sweltering South Carolina summer for the last two months. The air was thick and heavy in the stifling heat, and every breath drawn felt sticky and damp.

Reverend Holland got the crowd going with a rousing rendition of "Stand Up, Stand Up for Jesus," and by the time Eldritch was escorted to the stage, the shouts and praises of the people were louder than the piano; the song becoming secondary to the moving of what they believed to be the Holy Spirit. Many began dancing and jumping in place, waving their arms in the air, crying and shouting with wild abandon. Their exertions did nothing to help the rising temperature in the crowded sanctuary, and Eldritch pulled at his collar, already soaked with sweat.

Reverend Holland continued to sing the last verse of the song, placing one hand on Eldritch's shoulder and lifting the other into the air.

> Stand up, stand up for Jesus,
> The strife will not be long;
> This day the noise of battle,
> The next the victor's song.
> To Those who vanquish evil
> A crown of life shall be;

125

> They with the King of Glory
> Shall reign eternally!

After singing it a third time, Holland motioned for the piano to cease and the congregation erupted in a "hand clap of praise"—as they called it—and cries of "hallelujah." The sound was deafening and served only to exacerbate the migraine Eldritch was battling. As the racket in the sanctuary died down, Reverend Holland leaned over and whispered in his ear, "Let's go get our crowns." The young man looked up at the minister, confused by his choice of words, but Holland soldiered on with a shout, "To those who vanquish evil, a crown of life shall be! Amen?!" Then, he raised his hand toward Eldritch and said, "You are the one God has chosen to help us vanquish the enemy, Eldritch Hayes. You are the banner of this church, held high on our mission from the Lord."

The words made Eldritch uncomfortable. From what he learned in all his years of attending church and reading the Bible, he was certain the only banner they were supposed to hold high was Jesus. Being a banner for anyone filled him with anxiety, and as of late, nothing about this "mission" made him feel lifted. Over the last few years, Eldritch had begun to feel a heaviness whenever a Deliverance service was on the horizon and found himself battling a severe headache more often than not. He used to think he was helping by identifying evil spirits and setting people free; but as of late, Holland hadn't used Eldritch's gift at all. There were fewer and fewer demons and spirits to identify, yet the Deliverance services had failed to lose any momentum, and Reverend Holland's influence had continued to grow. Eldritch felt his only job these days was to stand on stage before the crowd, a symbol of Holland's

crusade, while the minister did whatever he wanted in the pulpit—riling up the congregation and putting on a show.
Maybe that's what he means by me being a banner.

"Brothers and sisters," Holland continued in his address to the congregation, "are you ready to see a miracle from God this evening?"

The worshipers hollered out in affirmation, clapping and praising with unprecedented enthusiasm. Eldritch jumped at the sound and watched Holland revel in the excitement and applause, as if the praise were all for him and not the good Lord.

"We have beheld miracle after miracle, victory after victory, within the walls of this church, and tonight," Holland paused, Eldritch supposed, for dramatic effect, "we are going to do it again!" More cries of "hallelujah" followed the words. Eldritch looked up at his parents who seemed disgusted by the entire display, and the three of them shared a look of disapproval.

"This is ridiculous," Eldritch heard his father mutter under his breath, and he wondered if Holland heard it too. If he did, it never showed on his face.

"Church, we have a special guest with us here tonight," Holland went on, "I had the privilege of meeting her just before service, and I have to tell you, the Lord works in mysterious ways. Sister Jessie," he called to someone seated near the middle of the church, "why don't you come on down to the altar?"

As he spoke, a small-framed lady, who couldn't have been any older than twenty-five, rose from her seat and started down the aisle. Eldritch watched as the deacons, Dan and Lamonte—favorites of Holland's—marched behind her after receiving a nod from the minister.

Upon making it to the altar, she turned to face the congregation, gave an awkward wave, and started playing with a lock of her long, tangled hair. Dan and Lamonte were at her side now, and Jessie looked at them and grinned, swaying and twisting back and forth, making her long, floral skirt billow with the movement. Eldritch thought her actions were like that of a child—innocent and playful—happy to be included in the proceedings. Something about it made him uneasy. He looked over at his parents who were looking at each other, brows drawn together in confusion. Eldritch wondered if they were thinking the same thing he was: *What does Reverend Holland want with this girl?*

As if answering the silent question in Eldritch's mind, Holland introduced the woman at the foot of the stage. "This young lady here is Miss Jessie McLeod. Jessie just moved in with her aunt and uncle a few streets over. Now, sadly, her folks do not attend church. They don't have a church home of their own, but Miss Jessie here decided she needed to be closer to the Lord."

The congregation clapped and offered up a collective, "amen!" in approval.

Jessie nodded and grinned from ear to ear. "Yes, preacher!" she shouted, still twisting left to right and making her skirt swish. "I could feel the Lord calling me, so I walked out that house, and come down the road. I seen this church with the doors wide open, and I knew this was the right place! Hallelujah! Hallelujah!"

Her smile grew wider at the cheers from the congregation, and she waved her hands high above her head, repeating "hallelujah" over and over.

Reverend Holland gave a low chuckle, and Eldritch's stomach dropped at the sound.

"Indeed, sister," the preacher responded. "This is the right place, indeed."

With that, he looked from Dan to Lamonte and nodded a second time. The two men stepped forward and seized the young woman's upper arms, pulling them down to restrain her. A look of alarm flashed across her face, and she began to squirm in their grasp; but the deacons were much larger and stronger, and she was easily overpowered.

Holland raised his large hands into the air and cried out, "What this woman does not know is that the enemy dwells within her! The Lord has drawn her to our doors so that we may vanquish it and set this child free!"

Eldritch was confused. He hadn't felt any of the telltale signs that a demonic presence was near, and he was growing more and more anxious about the situation with every passing second.

"I knew it the second I laid eyes on her," Holland plowed ahead with increasing intensity. "I knew the Devil had her in his snare! When she opened her mouth to speak, the Lord confirmed it. When she moved about in a strange manner, I used the wisdom of God, and I *knew*—I *knew!!!*—she was sent here to be delivered from the demon dwelling within her!"

Jessie continued to grapple with her captors, bending her head in an attempt to bite their hands since Dan and Lamonte had limited the use of her arms.

"You get your hands off me!" she screamed and started cursing—saying words Eldritch had only ever heard the possessed utter—but this was different. He opened his mouth to say as much to his parents, but Holland's heavy hand was back on his shoulder and moving him across the stage until he stood above the captive girl at the altar.

"It's your turn, Eldritch," he said, voice just above a whisper before shouting, "Name this demon so we can cast it out!"

The unexpected change in volume was jarring, and Eldritch blenched, startled at the sound. He stared at Holland, more nervous and unsettled than he ever remembered being. The impatience in the minister's voice was unmistakable when he demanded Eldritch do as he was told and identify the possessing entity.

Eldritch turned toward the struggling lady, who was still cussing up a storm at being restrained, and he looked. He looked at her, around her, and looked beyond—looked through the veil, looked inside. He forced himself to concentrate, tuning out her fearful swearing, the cries of the congregation, and Holland's fervent shouts of "Name it!"

Eldritch looked and found nothing.

All that stood before him now was a scared young lady who was being held against her will at the church altar for reasons Eldritch failed to understand. Yes, her actions were odd, the way she spoke was a bit off, but she wasn't hurting anyone. *Is it because she's different?* he wondered and decided Reverend Holland was confused and misreading the situation.

Turning to the red-faced minister, he shook his head and said, "There's nothing there."

The shock of Eldritch's assessment was written across Holland's face. "What did you say?" he asked, his tone threatening, his hand squeezing the boy's shoulder like a vice.

Eldritch cleared his throat and spoke again, louder this time, "I said, there's nothing there."

The church grew silent, save for the sound of Jessie's fruitless struggle. There were no more "hallelujahs," no more "praise Gods." Holland to seemed notice the change and surveyed the quiet and bemused church members as they looked around—looked to each other, as if hoping their neighbor had an explanation for the sudden turn of events.

Reverend Holland's eyes were wide with panic, and his face grew a deeper shade of red. In a flurry of motion, he turned on Eldritch, grabbed him by the shoulders with both hands, and screamed at the top of his lungs, "DEVIL!!!!" his booming voice adding to the relentless pounding in Eldritch's head.

There was a collective intake of breath from the shocked congregation, but within seconds, it morphed into thunderous applause. Holland's flock had taken their shepherd's bait.

Eldritch heard his parents cry out, Gene shouting, "Len, get your hands off him!"

But Reverend Holland ignored the command, shaking Eldritch with a ferocity that sent the boy's head flying back, as he roared, "Get thee behind me!!!"

The hot damp of the preacher's breath still lingered on his face as Eldritch felt himself torn from Holland's grasp. He knew the hands that pulled him back, recognized the strength of his rescuer.

"I told you to get your hands off my son!" His father now stood between him and Holland and was pushing Eldritch back toward Louise.

Eldritch felt his mother's arms wrap around him and pull him away from the fight about to unfold. "It's okay, baby boy. It's okay," she whispered in his ear as she held him, back pressed tightly to her chest. "Never again. We're going home."

As he and his mother backed away and moved toward the steps of the stage, Eldritch saw the rage in his father's eyes—a rage he knew had been held in check for years; a rage begging to be unleashed. He heard his father shout, threatening the minister, railing on him for daring to touch Eldritch like that.

Reverend Holland stepped forward, pointed a finger in Gene's face, and delivered an impassioned passage from Isaiah, "'For the foolish person will speak foolishness, and his heart will work iniquity! To practice ungodliness, to utter error against the Lord!'"

His father wasn't backing down. "Man, you had that one in your back pocket, didn't you?!"

"You have been deceived by Satan, Gene Hayes!" Holland would not yield, crowding further into Gene's space, their noses an inch apart. "You have allowed him to lead you and your family astray! That boy of yours has become a mockery— a wolf in sheep's clothing!"

Gene pulled his arm back; Eldritch gasped, overwhelmed by the altercation unfolding before him. He had never seen his father ready to strike another person, and the sight rocked him to his core. *This is all my fault.* But before the punch could land, a group of deacons rushed to Holland's aid, grabbed Gene, and pulled him away from the preacher.

"Gene!" Louise called to her husband, the level of alarm in her voice a sharp contrast to the calm demeanor Eldritch was used to.

Gene managed to shrug one deacon off and turned to face his wife and son.

"Get him out of here!" he shouted, and Louise grabbed Eldritch by the arm and took off down the steps.

As they skirted past the pews on the far side of the church, Eldritch could see the faces of the members. Some looked confused, some looked angry—angry at *him*; he could tell. Some cried out for God to save him and rebuked the devil in the same breath. They had turned on him, and he couldn't understand why.

The swinging doors shut behind them as they entered the vestibule, safe from the angry congregation, but Eldritch ran back and peered through the windows, desperate to know what was happening to his father—and to Jessie. He saw his father arguing with the deacons around him, as he wrenched himself free. He shouted something at Holland and stormed off down the steps, taking the same path Eldritch and Louise had toward the back of the church. Before he reached the doors, Gene stopped and turned his attention back to the stage at the sound of Holland's voice sermonizing from the pulpit again.

The sounds from the sanctuary were muffled by the wooden vestibule doors, but Eldritch thought he heard Holland bellow something that had to do with Jessie, who was still being held by Dan and Lamont at the altar. His suspicions were confirmed when the deacons who had held his father descend upon her in a chorus of strange tongues. Whatever Holland said worked to rile the congregation into a frenzy again, and they all began moving closer to the altar. Eldritch lost sight of the poor girl in the ocean of bodies crowding around her.

Gene tried to make his way through the throng of frantic parishioners toward Jessie, but his efforts proved futile, and he turned away, making for the doors. Eldritch jumped back as his dad shoved them open. Gene looked at his wife and son and nodded toward the exit, "Let's go."

"But Dad, that lady. She doesn't have a demon in her. Why won't they just let her go?" Eldritch couldn't fathom why the Deliverance service was still moving forward, nor could he understand why everyone had turned on him for speaking the truth.

"I know, bud. Poor thing's just a little slow or off or something. It's not her fault, but Len the Almighty isn't listening. Not anymore."

"Gene, we can't just leave her," Louise insisted.

"We can't get to her. I tried," he said, shaking his head in defeat. "We're going home and calling the cops. That isn't the Lord's work in there. That's assault."

Gene pushed open the heavy wooden doors that led outside and ushered his family down the steps. The slamming of the doors behind them echoed down the street with a sense of finality; an audible indication that this part of their lives—of Eldritch's life—was finally over.

CHAPTER ELEVEN

The annual Sommerset Christmas tree lighting is the highlight of the holiday season. People from every part of town come together on the Friday night before the Christmas parade to watch the raising and lighting of the 20-foot Fraser fir. The mayor, several local level politicians, pastors, coaches, and business owners make appearances; some having prepared a festive speech or words of encouragement for the assembled community. Bands and choirs from the nearby schools provide the evening's music in the form of seasonal favorites and carols, and a few volunteers from the local churches are at the ready with hot cocoa and sweet treats for everyone present. It's the most anticipated event of the year—an event everyone makes a point to attend; everyone except Eldritch.

From his seat in the front porch swing, he can hear it all—the speeches, the songs, the prayers—courtesy of the cheap sound system set up in the town square, borrowed from the high school, no doubt. The event kicks off around 7:00 p.m.—once all the important people have arrived—and this year is no different. Eldritch sets a steady rhythm on the swing, a hot cup of coffee in his hands. It's Friday night, after all, and once the crowd clears out, there's a ritual he must see to; but for now, he sits. He sits and he listens, and he tries to grasp a bit of that holiday spirit, that sense of community he used to feel years ago.

The mayor, Eric Fulwood, kicks things off with an exuberant, "Good evening! Merry Christmas and thank you to all those who worked so hard putting this event together." After that, he welcomes a familiar name—a familiar face, as Eldritch pictures it in his mind—to the microphone to lead the community in a word of prayer. Pastor Michael Walsh of the First Baptist Church of Sommerset grabs the mic and begins to address the town. Eldritch smiles to himself as the soothing voice of Pastor Mike echoes off the buildings and storefronts of the town center and bounce his way. If there was ever a true "man of God" in this world, it was Pastor Mike. He was, and is, a kind man, an understanding man; a true example of what Christ wanted his followers to be. Eldritch wishes he could have been more like him, but that time has passed.

I bet Kelly's over there right now. Eldritch suspects she's standing nearby, supporting her father from the crowd, but he shakes all thoughts of her from his mind and refocuses his attention on the man speaking.

Pastor Mike is funny and endearing, telling a few seasonal jokes and leaning into that same self-deprecating humor that made Eldritch take a liking to him all those years ago. He was a younger man when Eldritch met him, barely forty. Now, though twenty-six years have passed, Pastor Mike seems as youthful and animated as ever. He leads the town in a beautiful prayer—a prayer of faith, love, and enduring hope during times of darkness. Eldritch hasn't seen the man in years, but he feels as though Pastor Mike is speaking to him—only him—and peering into the inner workings of his life somehow.

When the prayer ends, the assembly offers up a communal "amen" in response, and Mayor Fulwood introduces the middle school choir. They lead the crowd in a few familiar carols: "We Wish You a Merry Christmas," "Joy to The World," "Go Tell It on the Mountain." After a pitchy, yet vigorous rendition of "Jingle Bells, the middle school choir takes their leave, and the high school choir steps up to perform "In the Bleak Midwinter."

Eldritch remembers singing this number when he was in high school and calls the tenor part to memory as he joins in, his chorus days not entirely forgotten. To his relief, the high school choir is far better than their middle school counterpart, and the effortless blending of their young voices does justice to the song. It was always a favorite of his; the minor key, the haunting melody, and the lyrics—so simple, so poignant.

> "Angels and archangels may have gathered there,
> Cherubim and seraphim thronged the air."

Eldritch clutches his mug in his hands as a frosty gust of wind blows across the wide porch. The little boy in him thrills at the thought of a chilly Christmas tree lighting. It rarely happens in these parts. During a time of year when so much of the country is covered with snow, in South Carolina, you never know if you'll need to bundle up or grab your flip-flops to attend a local Christmas celebration. Eldritch is grateful for the drop in temperatures, especially after a Thanksgiving spent in shorts. He directs his attention back to the song, hoping he hasn't missed it while zoning out and thinking about the weather.

> What can I give Him, poor as I am?
> If I were a shepherd, I would bring a lamb.
> If I were a wise man, I would do my part.
> Yet what I can, I give Him: give Him my heart.

A brief silence hangs over the township as the choir steps aside and the microphone is passed off to someone else of note. Eldritch sits on his swing and listens as the program continues for another twenty minutes until the moment to light the tree arrives. He doesn't have to see the events to know exactly how they play out. The mayor connects one drop cord to another, the tree lights up, there is a collective gasp and applause, and the entire town joins together in a couple verses of "Silent Night"—the only two verses anyone knows by heart.

After the song and usual chatter die down, Mayor Fulwood takes possession of the microphone to wrap up the evening's proceedings. Once again, he thanks the volunteers, praises the council and committee members who were responsible for organizing the meager event, and moves on to introduce the final speaker—the person who will deliver the closing prayer. Eldritch shuts his eyes in preparation for the final invocation as Mayor Fulwood speaks.

"I am pleased and honored to introduce to you a man who has served this community for many years. I have known him since childhood, and let me tell you...this is a man of conviction, of integrity...and this is a man who knows the power of prayer! He was a pillar of faith in this community, and even though he and his beautiful wife, Debbie, retired to Beaufort several years ago—"

Eldritch's blood turns to ice water in his veins.

"—we are honored to have them here with us tonight, to close out this evening in prayer!"

No. Please don't say it.

"Citizens of Sommerset, please give a warm welcome to—"

Are you kidding me?

"—Reverend Len Holland!"

His jaw clenches at the mention of the name, teeth grinding together with enough force to crack a stone, and when the man begins to speak, Eldritch feels his skin crawl. He hasn't heard Holland's voice in over twenty-five years, and though weathered by age and less boisterous than it was in his prime, Eldritch would recognize it anywhere.

"Merry Christmas, Sommerset! What a glorious time of year it is to come together and celebrate the birth of the Savior!"

The beginning of what promises to be a rousing Christmas speech clamors through the town, assaulting Eldritch's ears as he rises from the swing and vacates the front porch, slamming the front door behind him. A muffled garble of words can still be heard through the walls, and Eldritch isn't at all happy about that man's voice attempting to infiltrate his home. He glances down at his watch and sees it's just after eight. The residents should start clearing out once Holland finishes; but knowing him, he plans to preach half a sermon before even getting to the closing prayer.

Eldritch flinches as a loud, piercing "hallelujah" rings out from the town square, and he marches to the back den. Sifting through the records, he grabs *The Hollies' Greatest Hits* and slams it on the record player, flipping the switch and dropping the needle to punctuate his resentment. The old Magnavox comes to life with "I Can't Let Go," and Eldritch turns the volume up as loud as it will go, hellbent on drowning out the distant sermonizing of Reverend Holland.

He stands in the center of the room, hands at his sides, clenching and unclenching, over and over. Despite years of telling himself that he's fine, that he is no longer affected by what Holland did to him as a child, Eldritch can't escape the feeling pervading his body. Years of being controlled, of being lied to and used, come flooding back. The shame and guilt that grew to anger and bitterness have returned, filling him up and making his body shake with a long-repressed rage itching to rear its head once more.

Before the scream registers in his mind, it's erupting from his chest and forcing its way past his lips with a ferocity that burns his lungs. His hands slide into his hair and pulls—the pain sudden and sharp, as the rage searches for a way out. Eldritch hits his knees in the middle of the den, hands still tangled in his brown locks. He feels the sting of tears pricking his eyes, but he won't let them fall. Holland doesn't get to have his tears, not now, not ever again. The scream dies, leaving his throat raw, and Eldritch falls back against the couch; hands dropping into his lap, legs stretching out in front of him.

He sits, staring at the wall across from him, for a solid twenty minutes, getting up only when he realizes side one of the album has come to an end, and the tone arm has risen and returned home. He makes his way over to the old Magnavox and flips the record over, but instead of playing side two, he listens. Holland's voice has stopped. Eldritch shuts the record player off and walks back down the hall to the front of the house. Peering out the large window in the living room, he sees the mass of citizens dispersing down the street. It's over. Holland will go back to Beaufort, and Eldritch never has to hear that voice again.

Eldritch plops down in front of the television in the living room and puts on a Christmas movie. *National Lampoon's Christmas Vacation* keeps him entertained for a couple of hours, and Eldritch cackles as if he hadn't had a complete meltdown moments before. As the credits roll, he stands up and checks his watch: 10:31 p.m. Contemplating whether he wants to take a shower now or wait until he gets back from his walk, he wanders into the living room and glances out the window to make sure there are no signs of idling townspeople. Pushing the lace curtain aside, sees the light of the newly lit Christmas tree reflecting off the storefront across the street, and in that light, on the sidewalk in front of Eldritch's house, stands the figure of a man.

It catches Eldritch by surprise, and he draws back, hand still gripping the curtain. Once the initial shock passes, he inches closer to the window, trying to get a better look at the man watching his home—watching *him*. Backlit by the reflection on the storefront window, nothing about the figure is discernible, apart from height and basic build, but that is enough for Eldritch; that and the demonic energy emanating from the man. Even through the single-pane glass and across the span of the front yard, he can feel it. It curls toward him, dark tendrils reaching out—ever-encroaching shadows in the dark of night.

Mark.

But Eldritch knows Mark's not the one in the driver's seat anymore. The minutes tick by, and neither moves. Eldritch is zeroed in on the figure, watching for any sign of a threat as the darkness looms across the street. He tries to look deeper, beyond the man, into the shadow. He knows the spirit is evil, knows it's demonic, but that's as far as he can get. Unlike the encounters from his past, there is no moment of recognition—

no name springing to mind. Just as it's done the handful of times they've crossed paths in the last month, the spirit conceals its identity. *The amount of power that must require...* The thought frightens Eldritch, but he doesn't turn away.

The standoff continues, and Eldritch can hear the pounding of his heart, the rush of blood in his ears. He feels the tension building; knows the fuse to the powder keg has been lit, and he braces for the inevitable blast. But something happens that Eldritch does not anticipate. After a silent, torturous stalemate, Mark turns and walks away. Eldritch tracks him through the window as he stalks down the sidewalk and disappears from view, obscured by the brick buildings that line Main Street to the right of Eldritch's front yard.

Going against his better judgment and ignoring every warning bell sounding in his brain, Eldritch grabs his coat and takes off out the front door, tailing Mark as discreetly as he can. When Mark reaches the stop light near the hardware store, he heads right, down McLeary Street—*toward the Birch-Rainey house*. Eldritch quickens his pace, his brisk walk becoming a light jog as he approaches the intersection. He cuts the corner just in time to watch Mark walk up the front steps of the Birch-Rainey house, jerk open the front door, and disappear inside.

Eldritch comes to a stop at the train tracks that cut across McLeary, weighing his options. He isn't sure why he tailed Mark to begin with, and he has no idea what the plan is should he follow him inside; but something pushes him onward, and moments later, he's climbing the front steps of the Birch-Rainey house.

He stands outside the front door, uncertain as to whether he's making the right decision. After five minutes of pacing back and forth on the porch, he raises his hand and knocks, unable to hide the quiver in his voice as he calls to the man inside, "Mark?"

There is no answer. Eldritch knew there wouldn't be and, taking several deep breaths to steel his nerves, he tries the doorknob. It turns—unlocked—and the door swings open.

"Mark?" he calls again, but still, Mark does not respond; so, Eldritch musters his courage and crosses the threshold, not bothering to close the door behind him.

He hasn't set foot inside the Birch-Rainey house in nearly twenty-five years. Even then, it had been long abandoned, decayed—the subject of urban legend and small-town lore. No one had touched it in an age, until Mark came to town with grand plans of renovation. But Eldritch is shocked at what he finds inside, expecting the project to be farther along than this. The man has worked day in and day out—Eldritch has seen it; has passed by to see Mark moving around, the sounds of hammers and saws cutting through the silence of midnight…*until recently*.

What Eldritch sees now is a construction site in disarray. Broken boards are strewn across a splintered, unfinished floor. Paint cans lie tipped over every fifteen feet or so; some have been there awhile, resting in dried puddles of yellow and white; the custom-made gingerbread trim is mangled—smashed to bits—the fragments scattered throughout the space. Even the rolls of insulation have been slashed open and shredded.

The house is shrouded in shadow; the only source of light a flickering bulb in the hallway just ahead. Eldritch moves with caution, eyes darting around every pillar and searching every dark corner for movement. When he finds none, he moves past living room and into the hall. The flickering light casts a myriad of shadows around him as he approaches a doorway on his right.

"Mark?" he calls into the room, searching for any sign of the man, "I know you're here. It's Eldritch, Eldritch Hayes. I saw you come inside a few minutes ago." The room is dark, illuminated only by a beam of moonlight streaming in through the lone window; but it's enough to notice that no one—no *thing*—is in there.

Eldritch steps back, eyes ever moving, straining to survey his poorly lit surroundings before pressing on. He makes it four or five paces down the hall when a thundering crash sounds behind him. He screams and spins around to find a broken workbench near the living room has given way, dropping a stack of paint cans onto the busted floor. Some of them are open, and the paint spills, streaking the wood in a splatter of pastels. Leaning back against the wall, Eldritch clutches his chest and closes his eyes, fighting to pull himself back from the precipice of full-fledged panic.

Breathe. Just breathe. It's okay. It was just some paint cans. You're okay.

There is one more room at the end of the hallway, and Eldritch pries himself from the wall, determined to check investigate, in spite of the fear coursing through his body. The door to the room is cracked about two inches, and he takes a tentative peek inside before pushing it open. With the aid of a small, overturned lamp in the corner, Eldritch takes in the scene before him, his jaw dropping in disbelief at the state of the ransacked room.

The bed is unmade, sheets and blankets twisted and ripped; even the frame looks bent or broken with the way the mattress dips in the middle. The contents of three suitcases have been thrown about—Mark's clothes and personal effects scattered everywhere. *This is where he sleeps.*

Eldritch ventures further into the room, heart pounding, fear lighting up each of his nerve endings. He takes short, careful steps, not wanting to tread on any of Mark's belongings, clearing his path with a gentle nudge of his foot. After reaching the center, he looks around, taking in the disaster that is Mark's bedroom; that's when Eldritch notices the walls. Mark just painted these walls not too long ago—a fact made evident by the faint smell of fresh paint that lingers in the air. But now…now they are completely marred, covered in scrapes and symbols from ceiling to floor. Eldritch moves over to the wall by the lamp for a closer look.

At first, they seem nonsensical, random scratches—deep scratches, not just in the surface of the paint, but into the wall itself—as if someone dragged their fingernails over the same spot for hours on end to carve them out. Eyes moving past the scratches, he notices a cluster of symbols—*no, not symbols, numbers: 66 12 7 8 9.*

Taking a step back, Eldritch scans the room and realizes every scratch, every symbol covering the walls is a variation of this series of numbers—each carved or drawn by hand, some painted in dark red; the same numbers, over and over. *66. 12. 7. 8. 9.*

What does that mean?

He moves to the adjacent wall and brings his hand up to touch it, to prove to himself that what he is seeing is real. When his hand makes contact with a painted group of numbers, he recoils at the sensation. *It's still wet? Did he just paint these on?* Pulling his fingers up to inspect them, he makes a startling discovery: *blood.* Eldritch jumps back from the wall and decides he's had enough heart-pounding terror for one night. Wiping his hand on his jeans, he flees the bedroom and heads for the front door. It's there, in front of him; just a few more steps, and he'll be free of this place.

Thump. Thump.

A noise overhead catches his attention. Eldritch stops, arrested by the sound, and listens.

Thump. Thump.

Footsteps.

Thump. Thump.

Footsteps on the second floor.

As his gaze shifts between the open door before him and the darkened staircase to his right, Eldritch comes to understand he is at a crossroads. The battle within him rages, but he cannot deny the severity of the situation—of Mark's situation—any longer. Another set of footsteps sounds from above and, in his mind, it becomes something else: *a plea for help*. He cannot abandon Mark to this entity any longer—despite what that may mean for himself. With a mumbled curse under his breath, Eldritch turns from the door and ascends the weathered staircase.

The stairs are old but most of the original wood remains intact. They creak and groan with every step he takes, and Eldritch swears he's never heard a louder sound in his life. With every stair he climbs, he takes a measured breath, trying to keep a level head and not hyperventilate. When he reaches the midway point—a small landing before the stairs begin again at the opposite angle—there is a change in the air. It becomes thick with animosity and a heaviness that can only be described as *despair*. Eldritch lifts his eyes to the top of the stairs, but the opening to the second floor is obscured by a sheet of plastic. Mark must have hung it there to keep the sawdust and debris from drifting down the stairwell to the floor below; or maybe to trap what little heat the generator produced on frigid December nights like this.

The plastic is loose on the right side where someone pulled it back to enter, the bottom corner wafting back and forth as if beckoning Eldritch to follow. He catches the plastic in his hand, waits, and listens. The footsteps have stopped, and Eldritch strains his ears to pick up any sounds from the other side of the sheet, but all is silent. Just as he contemplates turning around and going back the way he came, he hears it: a faint scratching sound. Eldritch thinks back to Mark's bedroom; the numbers scratched into the walls.

He's doing it again, Eldritch thinks to himself, and with a deep breath, he pulls back the plastic. The landing is large and open. There are no lights up here, but the moon shining in through the windows is bright enough for him to get an idea of his surroundings. There is no sign of Mark, but the scratching continues, and Eldritch focuses on it, trying to sense which direction it's coming from. *The right.*

The landing is shaped like a T with the two ends obscured by the adjacent bedrooms' exterior walls. Eldritch can't see what's around either corner, so he takes a few wary steps. The floorboards creak beneath his feet, announcing his presence on the second story. He halts his movements and waits again, but there is no response from Mark or the demon within. As he inches forward, the scratching grows louder—the rhythm of it offset from the pounding of his own heart—and Eldritch peers around the wall to the right.

Just beyond the beam of moonlight pouring through the French doors, cloaked in shadow, in the corner, stands Mark. His back is to Eldritch, and his right hand is raised, fingernails digging into the wall, wicked energy rolling off him in waves. The stench of death and rot hits Eldritch again, and he is overcome by a whirlwind of emotions—fear, anxiety, anguish, sorrow. He has to fight, with all his might, the urge to vomit and crumble into a sobbing mess on the splintered hardwood. The shadow extends from the corner of the landing and creeps through the moonbeam cast across the floor. It's reaching out for him, and Eldritch knows it. This is the strongest demonic force he has ever encountered, and it's taunting him, not even bothering to release its full power. But Eldritch stands his ground, swallows the bile that's climbed up into his throat, and waits to see if the demon will make a move.

Mark remains in his spot in the corner and continues to claw at the wall; but now, a new sound emerges: a murmur—a stream of harshly muttered words Eldritch can't decipher at first, but the longer he listens, the clearer they become.

"Sixty-six, twelve, seven, eight, nine. Sixty-six, twelve, seven, eight, nine. Sixty-six, twelve, seven, eight, nine," the voice coming from Mark repeats on constant loop, never pausing to take a breath.

"Mark?" Eldritch speaks at last, longing to put an end to the litany of numbers. "Mark?"

The muttering and scratching stops as Mark pulls his hand away from the wall and turns to look over his left shoulder. The movement is slow, glacial, and it feels as though seconds have become hours by the time his gaze falls upon Eldritch. What Eldritch sees in Mark's face makes his blood run cold, and his knees nearly buckle at the sight. Mark's eyes, which Eldritch remembers being a light, steel blue, are solid black—not just black—empty; an endless void of hopelessness contained within two hollow sockets. Even the structure of his face seems changed: the cheekbones are more prominent and sharper, cheeks sunken in, pallid skin pulled taut over muscle and bone, molded around distended, protruding veins.

Eldritch knows the truth, knows this isn't Mark, but he addresses the man and not the unidentified demon anyway, "Mark, what do the numbers mean?"

Neither answers the question.

Eldritch tries again, "Mark? Do you understand what I'm asking you?"

The demon cocks Mark's head to the side but does not speak.

Eldritch's anger begins to win out over his fear, and he raises his voice, "Mark! The numbers! Sixty-six, twelve, seven, eight, nine! What do they mean?"

Silence stretches between them, Eldritch and the demon eyeing each other from across the floor, until Mark's body rises from the ground. It takes a second for Eldritch's mind to comprehend what's happening, but once Mark is a solid two feet in the air, Eldritch jumps backward in alarm, tripping over his own feet. Mark's body levitates in front of him, stiff as a board, hands like rigid claws by his sides.

Eldritch can't believe what he's seeing. "Jesus," he utters on a breathy exhale, and the reaction is instant.

As soon as the name passes his lips, Mark's head is thrown back, and an otherworldly scream spews from his gaping mouth. The distorted roar is so loud Eldritch feels the entire house shake from the force of it, and he brings his hands up to cover his ears. The sound is cut short when Mark's body is thrown through the air and slammed up against the wall. Eldritch rushes forward to help the man, but as soon as he moves, Mark is thrown once more; this time through the giant, French doors that lead outside to the second-story porch.

He shouts Mark's name as the man's body, trapped in the demon's grasp, is sent crashing through glass and wood, shattering the door panels on impact. Eldritch dashes after, relieved to find Mark has landed on the small, upper-level porch instead of being launched over the railing and dropped to his death in the yard below. Eldritch steps through the mess of debris, calling out for him but receiving nothing in reply; Mark isn't moving at all.

"Come on, Mark, talk to me," Eldritch pleads as he kneels down beside him, wincing when a sliver of broken glass cuts into his knee. He slides his right hand under Mark's head, grips his shoulder with his left, and rolls him over. Mark's eyes are closed, and his face is covered in blood, littered with cuts and shards of glass. Eldritch places two fingers on his pulse point and lowers his ear to Mark's nose and mouth to make sure he's breathing. Satisfied Mark is still alive, Eldritch draws back and comes face to face with two black eyes, opened wide, and a split-lipped smile, dripping with blood. The demon grabs Eldritch by the front of his shirt and yanks him closer, their noses a hair's breadth apart.

With a low growl and a hellish voice that does not belong to Mark, the demon speaks: "Aren't you going to say hi, Eldritch Hayes?"

CHAPTER TWELVE

After *The Incident* unfolded at the final Deliverance service, Eldritch's father vowed he would never set foot inside a church again. Gene had called the cops once they were home, but nothing ever came of it. The town sheriff was good friends with Holland, and a big tithe payer, so the allegations of assault were dropped. It didn't help that poor Miss Jessie claimed she couldn't remember what happened that night and was later arrested for causing a scene in the town square. She was taken away in handcuffs, and Eldritch never saw her again—although word spread around town that she was diagnosed with some form of psychosis and sent to live someplace where she could be properly cared for. Members of Holland's flock called the diagnosis "nonsense" and claimed this world would say anything to disregard the existence of the devil and his minions.

Eldritch could tell his parents felt guilty about the situation he'd been placed in. After speaking with the cops, Gene and Louise had grabbed their son and held him tight, weeping into the embrace.

"I said I would protect you, and I failed," his father had said between sobs. "Please forgive me, Eldritch. I'm so sorry."

Louise was whispering things into his hair between kisses atop his head, "You did nothing wrong, love. You are good and strong. Jesus loves you. You are my brave, brave boy. We love you so much."

Eldritch never blamed his parents for what happened, knowing full well the blame rested with Holland and Holland alone. Even as a young teenager, he was wise enough to understand his parents believed God had gifted Eldritch with this ability for a reason and were trying to do right by Him. Although Eldritch was no longer convinced his gift served any great purpose, he didn't fault his parents for wanting to believe it did.

It can't be easy having a kid like me.

Reverend Holland's flock of militant believers did their share of talking after the showdown that Wednesday night. Rumors about Eldritch Hayes spread like wildfire across the township of Sommerset. Some said he was under attack and the enemy had blinded him; others believed he was possessed and had been sent to lead believers off the path of righteousness; there was even speculation that Eldritch was into witchcraft and practiced dark magic. It didn't matter if anyone actually believed these stories or not, Eldritch had been labeled a freak and an outcast in most circles.

At school, kids would jeer and joke. Even the teachers would exchange knowing looks as he trudged down the hallway from class to class. He had become a social pariah, the subject of scrutiny and speculation. The days of holding his head up and feeling special were long gone. Now, his head hung low, and his eyes stayed fixed on the ground; because if he never looked up, he'd never have to see any spirits, nor the smirks and sideways glances of others.

After an extensive family discussion following the outbreak of gossip around town, Gene and Louise decided it was in their son's best interest to pull him out of public school and homeschool him until the madness blew over. Eldritch was quick to agree, and for the next two years, he rarely left the house. To add insult to injury, his struggle with chronic headaches had increased, reaching a point where he could no longer remain silent about the pain, and he was prescribed a once daily medication to keep them at bay. The meds helped, and though the doctor assured him it was most likely hormonal or genetic, Eldritch wondered if his ability was to blame, or worse—if he'd done something to deserve this plight.

One day, around the time Eldritch turned fifteen, Louise came back from the grocery store with interesting news.

"Apparently, the Baptist church down the road has a new preacher. The older fella finally retired. I ran into Martha at the Piggly Wiggly, and she said they all really like him down there," she reported while Eldritch and Gene helped put the groceries away, "and she invited us to come hear him preach Sunday."

Both men stopped what they were doing—Gene pausing with the refrigerator door open and a jug of milk in his hand, Eldritch gaping at his mother with a mouthful of the cereal he'd just opened.

Louise continued on, as if she hadn't seen their shocked expressions, "I told her I'd have to check with y'all. If neither of you want to go, I may just go myself." Her voice grew quiet before adding, "I miss going to church."

Gene placed the milk in the fridge and shut the door. "Well, I suppose it couldn't hurt. I think we can give it a shot."

So much for that vow, Dad…

"Eldritch?"

He knew what his mother was hoping he'd say. He knew she longed for them to attend church as a family somewhere, but Eldritch wasn't ready, and he wasn't sure he ever would be. "Why don't y'all go and report back?" he countered and watched his mother deflate.

"That's fine!" she said, trying too hard to sound unbothered.

Eldritch responded by shoving another handful of cereal in his mouth, placing the box in the pantry, and retreating to his bedroom. Even with the door shut, he could hear his mother's sobs downstairs, and the guilt he felt for making her cry gutted him. Her cries were soon drowned out by the sound of Bread. "If" flowed from the Magnavox in the den, all the way up the stairs, and into his bedroom, and Eldritch knew his dad had turned it on to cheer her up. "If" was *their* song—their wedding song. Yes, it was cheesy, and yes, he let them know how much they needed to invest in new music every chance he got; but Eldritch sang along, word for word, happy his father could be there for his mother when he could not.

A few days later, Gene and Louise attended Sunday morning service at the First Baptist Church of Sommerset and came home raving about the new pastor.

"Nice. I'm happy for you," Eldritch said, voice clipped and apathetic, before walking out the backdoor to sit on the screened in porch. The screen door opened with a creak as Louise joined her son.

"He wants to meet you."

"What did you tell him?" Eldritch asked, worried the "freak" label had stuck over the years.

"Just that we have a fifteen-year-old son who has been hurt by the church in the past."

"So, he doesn't know I'm the town weirdo?"

Louise hesitated, and Eldritch nodded in understanding.

"He does know then. Well, I'm not sure what I expected. Small town. People talk," he sighed, taking a swig of his Coke.

"He's heard about you from a few people. He doesn't believe any of the gossip that came out of *that* church though," Louise assured her son, "but he knows you have a gift."

Eldritch snorted, "Still calling it that, are we?"

"Eldritch, it *is* a gift."

"I would say you could have it then, but apparently it's not something I can return or regift." He felt the venom in his words the second they left his mouth; knew he was being a brat. But the idea of stepping through the doors of another church, of having a new pastor to deal with, was too much for him.

"Sorry, Mama," he said, rising from his chair, "I just can't do it again." He headed for the door, but Louise stood and intercepted him before he could reach it.

"What if you just give him a chance? You don't have to go to the church. I'm not forcing you to do that. But I would like you to meet him. We can invite him over for dinner, and you can see for yourself."

The suggestion grated on his nerves and drew a petulant eyeroll from the teen.

"Don't you roll your eyes at me, young man. I know you've been through a lot—more than I will ever know or understand—but I am still your mother." Her voice was raised, a sound Eldritch seldom heard, and the admonition made him regret his insolence.

"Sorry, Mama," he apologized, eyes focused on the tops of his shoes.

Louise reached up to touch her son's face—he had grown so much in the last two years and was now taller than her—and placing her hand under his chin, she lifted his face upward.

"Look at me," she said. "I wish you would hold your head up, baby boy. You're too handsome to be staring at the floor all the time." She kissed his cheek and turned to go inside.

"Mama—"

She paused and faced him again. "Yeah?"

"I'll give him a chance. For you, I'll give him a chance."

To say Michael Walsh was nothing like Len Holland would have been an egregious understatement. In Eldritch's mind, no two men who claimed to be on the same side of something could be more different in personality and approach. From the moment the man entered their home, Eldritch felt at ease. He was courteous and friendly; approachable and funny. There was no air of piety or arrogance about him, and his warm smile seemed to come from a place of genuine joy and love. Despite his resistance, Eldritch liked him.

At first, he'd begged them to just call him "Mike," but the properly southern-bred Hayeses wouldn't have it, so "Pastor Mike" it was. Pastor Mike wasn't one to stand on ceremony and said as much to the family that hosted him over Louise's classic pot roast dinner—Eldritch's favorite. The roast had been in the crock pot all day, simmering with carrots and potatoes in a thick brown gravy that made his mouth water just thinking about it. Eldritch knew her choice of supper was gesture of gratitude for agreeing to meet Pastor Mike, and he was happy to accept the offering.

"So, Eldritch, you are starting high school this year?" Pastor Mike asked after chasing a forkful of roast with a swig of Gene's family-famous sweet tea.

"Yes, sir. I'm going back to public school this year."

"Oh, wow! That's exciting!"

To Eldritch's surprise, the man's interest seemed sincere. Pastor Mike didn't appear to be putting on a front as a means to an end, which was what Eldritch was used to.

"I haven't been to public school in a couple of years," Eldritch admitted. "I'm a little nervous."

Pastor Mike gave him an understanding smile, "I'm sure it'll be a big change for you, but I bet it will be a lot of fun! Some of my fondest memories are from high school."

He smiled as the man began to regale the family with tales of his wayward youth, and Eldritch couldn't remember the last time he'd laughed so hard.

As the evening drew to a close, Pastor Mike rose from his seat and thanked Gene and Louise for the invitation. "Best meal I've had in a long time!" he beamed, before adding a sheepish, "but don't tell my wife I said that."

"Eldritch," Louise said after their laughter had settled down, "why don't you see Pastor Mike out? I'm going to get started on these dishes."

Eldritch walked Pastor Mike to the front door and followed him out onto the porch. They stood in the sweltering heat of a southern, summer night—Pastor Mike rocking back and forth on his heels, Eldritch staring down at his feet out of habit.

"You do that a lot, don't you?" asked Pastor Mike.

Eldritch lifted his eyes, his brow furrowed—a silent question.

"Your eyes, they're always downcast," Pastor Mike clarified. "I noticed it earlier when we first met. You look down a lot."

"Yeah," Eldritch agreed, rubbing at the concrete of the porch with the rubber toe of his sneaker, "defense mechanism. I think that's what it's called."

Pastor Mike hummed but didn't press the subject further. "Would your parents mind if you took a walk with me?"

The question caught Eldritch off guard, but he shook his head, "No, I don't think so."

"I don't want to come across as some creepy, old dude. I promise, I'm not crazy or anything, but there's something I'd like to show you—something I think could help us understand one another a little better."

Eldritch heard the earnestness in the man's voice, the genuine desire to get to know and understand him. Eldritch wasn't exactly an open book, but Pastor Mike seemed content with reading the back cover and what little excerpts Eldritch was willing to share. He opened the front door and called out to his parents, "Hey! Pastor Mike wants me to take a walk with him. That okay?" They shouted back their permission, and Eldritch set out into the night with the curious new preacher.

They talked as they walked—down the sidewalk, through the town square—their path never taking them near Holland's church. The move was intentional; Eldritch was certain of it and appreciated it. They crossed over the highway that paralleled Main Street on the other side of the square and turned left. Eldritch and his parents never took this route on their Sunday strolls—strolls which, as of late, were taken later and later at night to avoid running into any unwanted acquaintances.

Pastor Mike told him all about his family, which was quite large. He had three daughters and one son—all a great deal younger than Eldritch—with the exception of his eldest daughter, Kelly. Kelly was only one year his junior, and Pastor Mike said he would be happy to introduce them if Eldritch wanted to meet her. Eldritch made a noncommittal noise, and Pastor Mike moved on.

"I know you're not an idiot, Eldritch," he said when the well of neutral topics ran dry. "I know you know that I know."

"Yeah, I figured you did."

"People love to talk, but I don't care for gossip. I want you to know that." The man stopped walking and turned to face Eldritch head on. "I have heard some wild stories about you, Eldritch Hayes, but all I know for sure is that you must be a strong and remarkable young man to play the hand you've been dealt."

Eldritch fought to maintain a guise of stoicism, determined to keep the storm of emotions he felt inside from showing on his face. It had been so long since anyone besides his family had made him feel valued or understood. Now, this man stood before him—a stranger by all accounts—telling him he was strong and remarkable. It baffled him.

"Why are you being so nice to me? You don't even know me, not really."

"Eldritch, I can't imagine the heartache you've had to endure because of what you can do, but all that is secondary to *who* you are. You are my brother in Christ, and I am supposed to love you as such. I know that sounds like some kind of lame, Christian cliché," he admitted with a sigh, walking along the path again. "Look, Eldritch, I don't know much. I'm not some theological genius or anything. I struggle like everyone else. I'm just trying to love like Jesus."

Eldritch appreciated his candor. How strange that in all his years as a member of Reverend Holland's congregation, never before had he heard such sentiment expressed. Holland wasn't concerned about loving like Jesus, imitating Jesus. The only person Len Holland was ever concerned about imitating was a more exalted version of himself.

Pastor Mike stopped again, but this time in front of a set of concrete steps that lead from the sidewalk to a modest brick house. It was an older home, but not terribly so—nothing like the scary Birch-Rainey house on McLeary Street.

"Whose house is this?"

"Mine," said Pastor Mike. "My wife and kids are moving up from Vidalia next week, but I brought the dogs and went ahead and moved in once I got the position at the church."

"Dogs?"

"Yeah. We have two greyhounds."

Eldritch had never seen a greyhound in person. He knew they raced down in Florida but wasn't aware people owned them as pets.

"Eldritch, if you're comfortable, I would like you to take a look at something in this house. I promise it's not anything scary—at least, I don't think it is. I just need confirmation about something."

Eldritch nodded and followed him up the steps. The door opened to the tip-tapping of clawed feet on vinyl, as he and Pastor Mike were greeted by two large, muscular greyhounds. They were well-mannered and didn't jump, but one seemed more eager than the other to meet their owner's strange, new guest.

"The brindle one, that's Fuzz," explained Pastor Mike as Fuzz approached Eldritch in search of attention and head rubs.

Fuzz's fur was a rusty brown with black stripes—almost like a tiger—but his broad chest was bright white, as were all but one of his paws. Eldritch patted Fuzz's head and scratched behind his ears. The dog panted and looked up at Eldritch with his big, brown eyes, beaming at the stranger who had rubbed his head so nicely.

"The white one over here is Topper."

Eldritch looked to where the pastor stood and took note of the large white dog beside him. Topper was beautiful—completely white with the exception of his ears, which were a dark grey. Where Fuzz was stocky, broad, and thick, Topper was tall, toned, and lean, but there was something else—something beyond their physiques in which Eldritch noticed a marked difference. This dog was far more skittish and reserved than his counterpart, Fuzz. When Topper lifted his head to assess the visitor, their eyes met and Eldritch knew: this dog had seen things. Eldritch could empathize.

"How long have you had them?"

"About three years. We got Fuzz first, then Topper about six months later. We adopted them after they retired," Pastor Mike explained.

"From racing?"

"Yep. They both raced until they were five years old, and then they had to retire. Topper was an A-list racer—top notch, at least that's what we were told. I have his track records around here somewhere."

"He seems sad," Eldritch mused aloud as Topper averted his eyes and stared off into the corner of the room.

"Topper has been through a lot." Pastor Mike let out a heavy sigh with the words and knelt down to Topper's level.

"He was abused by his trainer and left in his kennel during a hurricane. I had to get down on my hands and knees to approach him at first. He's made amazing progress though, haven't you, boy?" He kissed the dog on the crown of his head and stood back up, "I figured everything was smooth sailing, but now I've got this going on."

"Got what going on?" Eldritch asked, afraid he'd missed something.

Pastor Mike walked across the living room and stood by the fireplace. "You see this?" He motioned toward a large painting displayed atop the mantle, "I bought this shortly after the boys and I moved in. I got it from that big antique store on Main Street. You can see why."

Eldritch walked closer to where Pastor Mike stood and took in the painting, every detail. The subject was a tall, elegant woman in what he assumed was Victorian clothing. Her ivory dress was long and had a sheen to it—silk, perhaps—with a muted purple overcoat. The feathers in her dark purple hat were a vibrant gold, and a pearl necklace lay against the pale, white skin of her neck; but the most intriguing detail was the dog standing to her left. It was a greyhound with fur white as snow, save for the grey of his ears.

"He looks just like—"

"Topper, I know," finished Pastor Mike. "Now you see why I had to buy it."

"It's crazy," whispered Eldritch, eyes darting between Topper and the dog in the painting, "like…uncanny."

"Cool, right?"

"Totally," Eldritch couldn't help but smile at the peculiarity of the situation. *What are the odds?*

"To be perfectly honest with you, Eldritch…it could be cooler," said the pastor, smile fading as he took a seat in the recliner; Fuzz following after and lying down at the foot of the chair.

Eldritch sensed a shift in the tone of their conversation—the sudden seriousness in Pastor Mike's voice and face making him nervous. "What do you mean?" he asked, unsure whether he should be sitting down as well.

Pastor Mike seemed to notice his indecision and motioned for him to sit on the couch., "Have a seat. If you don't mind waiting a little while, I was hoping you'd be able to tell me a thing or two."

"A thing or two about what?"

"About what's been going on in my house…with my dog."

The room grew quiet, the only sound the ticking of the clock on the living room wall. Eldritch wasn't sure what to say. He watched Pastor Mike's face for any sign that he was poking fun at him or setting up some elaborate joke, but Eldritch found none. He could tell the man was leaving something out on purpose—probably as a test to see if the rumors around town were true.

He was about to tell Pastor Mike that he didn't sense anything in his house—that it was getting late, and he needed to head home—when out the corner of his eye, something moved. On the floor, across from him, Fuzz lifted his head and stared off in the same direction, and Eldritch knew the dog had seen it too.

Eldritch turned his head to the left and saw Topper standing on the other side of the room. The dog's head was bowed, the hair of his back bristled, and he wasn't alone. Crouched down beside him, stroking the fur that stood on end, was a woman; but not just any woman—a woman dressed in ivory silk and purple. Eldritch's jaw dropped at the sight of her. As if she had climbed down from her place over the mantle, there she was: the woman from the painting. She cooed and murmured to Topper, telling him what a good and beautiful boy he was, but she called him something else—another name. *Achilles*

"Eldritch?" Pastor Mike followed the boy's gaze across the room to an agitated Topper. "Do you see something?"

"She calls him Achilles," Eldritch responded, his voice quiet and filled with something akin to wonder as he watched the woman with Topper. He could tell the dog was letting his guard down as she carried on petting him and singing his praises, and eventually, he turned to face her head on. She chuckled as he did, placed a kiss on the tip of his nose, and vanished. Topper looked around in search of the lady but, finding no trace of her, retired to his dog bed in the corner.

Eldritch turned to Pastor Mike. "I don't think you need to worry about her."

"Her," Pastor Mike confirmed.

Eldritch said nothing but glanced at the painting above the fireplace.

"So, it is *her*, then?"

"She thinks Topper is her dog. She was petting him."

"Sometimes she lets him outside too. The backyard's fenced in, so I'm not too concerned about it. I knew something was going on, I just needed to know what. If you say she's not a threat, then I'm fine just letting her be…especially if Topper can bring her some joy in the afterlife." Pastor Mike's smile had returned as he looked over to where Topper lay, curled up in his bed.

"She's a ghost," Eldritch said, bewildered by the man's reaction to this news.

"I figured as much," Pastor Mike laughed, "I didn't feel anything evil or threatening in the house. Just curious if you could give me an idea of who it was. And you did."

"So, you aren't going to give me some lecture about ghosts not being real?"

"And why would I do that?"

Eldritch didn't respond, unsure how to explain that with Reverend Holland, the subject of ghosts was not up for discussion.

When he didn't say anything, Pastor Mike continued, "Eldritch, I'm not going to give you any kind of lecture on the subject of spirits. I'm not one of those self-proclaimed 'theological giants' who thinks they know everything about this life and the next. There are so many mysteries that we can't understand—that we're not *supposed* to understand—not yet at least. You've seen more than I could even begin to comprehend, and it's not my place to tell you what you're seeing or how to describe it."

Being spoken to this way by a pastor was making his head spin. The only spiritual leader Eldritch ever knew used and abused him; treated him like an instrument to be played for that man's own personal glory. Eldritch wanted to trust Pastor Mike, wanted to believe him, but Eldritch also knew people lied, and he'd experienced more than enough lies and manipulation in his lifetime.

"It's getting late," he said instead, rising from his seat on the couch, "my parents are probably wondering where I am."

Pastor Mike stood as well and accompanied him out the door and onto the front porch. "Want me to walk home with you? It's pretty dark."

"No, sir," Eldritch shook his head, "I like walking at night. Thank you though."

"Thank *you*, Eldritch. Thank you for sharing your gift with me. I know that couldn't have been easy."

Something about this new preacher made him feel comfortable; like it was okay that he wasn't perfect, it was okay that he was damaged. Pastor Mike made him feel like an actual person—a person to be seen and heard—not some pawn to perform on command; yet Eldritch still refused to lower the walls he had carefully constructed around his heart these last few years.

Before starting off down the sidewalk, he turned and called back to Pastor Mike, "Goodnight. Maybe I'll see you around."

"That'd be great," Pastor Mike smiled at him, "and if you ever need my help with anything, Eldritch. I'm just phone call away."

CHAPTER THIRTEEN

Eldritch makes it down the stairs, out the front door, and onto the lawn before he drops to his knees and retches, spilling the contents of his supper into the dirt. Above him, on the second-story porch, the laugh persists—the laugh that chased him away from Mark's bleeding body and out of the house. He scrambles to his feet and sprints down McLeary Street to Main, running, running as fast as he can back home. Once safely inside, he locks the doors, draws the curtains, and dashes up the stairs to his parents'—*his*—bedroom.

He strides with purpose over to the bedside table and, yanking the drawer open, grabs the weathered Bible from within. His hands run over the cover—high-quality, imitation leather—and his fingers trace the name embossed on the lower right corner. *Robert Eugene Hayes, III.* Eldritch goes to open it, not caring which passage unfolds before him, but finds he is unable to do so. Despite his encounter moments ago, Eldritch hesitates with the Good Book in his hands. He wants to open it. He wants to find sanctuary in its scriptures, comfort in its promises, but something stays his hand—something angry and complicated that made its home in his aching heart eight years ago.

Instead, he squeezes the book and holds it to his chest, and although he can't bring himself to recite the words out loud, they cycle through his mind for the first time in a long time.

> *Our Father, which art in Heaven,*
> *Hallowed by Thy name.*
> *Thy kingdom come,*
> *Thy will be done,*
> *On Earth as it is in Heaven.*
> *Give us this day our daily bread,*
> *And forgive us our trespasses*
> *As we forgive those who trespass against us,*
> *And lead us not into temptation,*
> *But deliver us from evil…*
> *Deliver us from evil.*

Deliver me from evil.

The entire prayer boils down to that one thought—*deliver me from evil*—and Eldritch mouths it over and over until he passes out.

When Eldritch wakes the next morning, he finds he's lying atop his still-made bed, dressed in his clothes from the night before, with his father's old Bible resting on his chest. He sits up and looks over at the window to gauge the time of day when a sharp pain shoots through his neck. He tries again, turning his head to the right, but the stiffness is unrelenting. *That's what I get for falling asleep like that.* Scooting to the edge of the bed, he places the Bible back in the bedside table—dragging his fingers across the gold letters of his father's name before shutting the drawer.

When he stands and tries to pop his back—also stiff and angry from the night before—his phone tumbles out of his pocket. Eldritch picks it up and checks the time: 6:02 a.m. *The sun won't be up for at least another hour*, he thinks, walking over to the window to look out at the street below. A few cars pass; their headlights cutting through the shroud of an early December morning that still covers the sleepy town.

Though dawn has come, the darkness of night still lingers, not wanting to relinquish its grip; but Eldritch knows in an hour's time, when the sun rises, the darkness will have no choice but to retreat. It will slowly seep into the alleyways and behind the large storefronts and houses. It will linger beneath the canopies of trees and under bushes and parked cars. When the sun rises, the darkness will shrink into shadows cast about town and await the evening when it can swell and spread once more.

Darkness is inevitable. How do we face it alone?

The thought spurs him to action, and he's down the stairs and out the door in a flash, taking the same path he did last night. His breaths are even and steady as he braces himself for what he's about to do, watching the condensation of every exhale in the early morning cold. *Breathe. Breathe. Breathe. Just breathe,* he reminds himself, as he stalks along the sidewalk in the dark.

In less than five minutes' time, he stands before the Birch-Rainey house once more. The front door is wide open from when he fled the scene last night, and Eldritch admonishes himself for not having the presence of mind to close it on his way out. As he travels up the concrete walkway leading to the front porch, he glances up at the second-story porch where he abandoned Mark hours ago. *It's empty*. He climbs the steps and crosses the threshold, knocking on the open door to announce his presence before pulling it shut behind him.

"Hello? Mark?" he calls into the black around him; the one flickering light in the hallway having exploded above his head during his rapid getaway. He pulls his cell phone from his pocket and flicks on the flashlight app, pointing it here and there, into every corner, as far as the beam can reach. There is no sign of Mark downstairs.

"Mark?" he calls again, and again, and still—nothing. "For once, just *once*, it'd be nice if this guy answered when I called," Eldritch mumbles to himself, creeping past the living room. *You know where he is*. Eldritch stops and turns toward the weathered staircase just as raspy voice answers from above.

"Here."

"Mark?!" Eldritch shouts, moving to the base of the stairs.

"I'm up here," Mark replies, voice rough with exhaustion and strained from misuse.

It's just Mark. The concern Eldritch feels about having to face the full manifestation of the demon again diminishes, and he ascends the staircase in a hurry, taking the stairs two at a time. When he reaches the top, he pushes the curtain of plastic aside and steps onto the second-floor landing, eyes darting everywhere in search of Mark. Shining his light across the open space, he spots him sitting against the wall to the right, legs stretched out in front of him. Eldritch rounds the corner and shines the phone right at Mark, who raises a hand to shield his eyes against the light.

"Put that thing away," Mark mutters. "You've found me, yeah?"

"Sorry," Eldritch apologizes and fumbles with his phone until the app is closed, "it's just…dark in here."

Mark grunts and knocks his head back against the wall, "It's always dark in here, even with—" he stops, looking away from Eldritch and out the jagged opening of splintered wood and shattered glass where the French doors once stood.

"Even with what, Mark?" he presses.

Mark doesn't turn to face him but answers, his voice a hollow whisper, "Even with the lights on."

Ignoring the knot he feels in the pit in his stomach at their proximity, Eldritch shuffles closer and takes a seat on the floor beside him, back resting against the wall in a similar position. The sun is rising, and the early morning light filters in through the broken doors to their left. They sit in silence for some time, the demonic presence within Mark still buzzing beneath the surface, the shadow still swirling about him, but muted as if it too is exhausted from the events of last night. Mark continues to stare out at the sky; Eldritch keeps his eyes forward and watches the sheet of plastic sway back and forth at the top of the stairs. Mark is the first to speak, looking over at the man beside him.

"Why are you here?"

Eldritch sighs, "Honestly, I've been trying to figure that out myself."

"Aren't you going to ask what happened?" Mark motions toward the broken doors and at his bleeding face.

Eldritch takes a hard look at Mark's face for the first time since he found him and cringes at the multitude of cuts decorating the man's flesh. There's a deep laceration across his left cheekbone, and Eldritch can see bits of glass stuck into the skin of his cheeks and forehead, gleaming in the newly risen sun. Mark brings a hand up to pick at a large shard stuck in the gash above his cheek, wincing with a sharp inhale as he pulls it free. He tosses it into the opposite corner and turns to Eldritch, who realizes Mark is waiting for an answer to his question.

"Oh. Um...no. I-I don't have to," he stammers, wondering if Mark has any recollection of what transpired in this very spot last night. But Mark's face is a picture of confusion, so Eldritch continues, "I was here last night. For a little while. When...all this happened."

Mark doesn't respond, and Eldritch can't imagine what must be going through the man's head.

"Mark, you know something's...off, right? You know something is happening to you?"

Mark's eyes glisten with tears, but the contractor does a good job of holding them back as he speaks, "I've been losing time. I don't really know how to explain it, but sometimes I wake up, and the place is a wreck." He clears his throat before continuing, "Stuff's broken, lights are busted—doesn't matter how many times I replace them—and you should see the bedroom—"

"I have," Eldritch interjects, "I did. Last night." Mark closes his eyes and hangs his head, and Eldritch wonders if he's embarrassed—embarrassed by the state of the house, embarrassed by the trashed bedroom and the condition in which he was discovered; but Eldritch needs answers, so he presses on.

"The numbers on the walls. What do they mean?"

"Hell if I know," Mark snaps, causing Eldritch to flinch and avert his eyes. "Sorry," Mark amends with a heavy sigh, "It's been a rough few weeks."

"You were reciting them last night, over and over—well, it wasn't you, but it was using your mouth, your vocal cords." He knows how this must sound. *He's gonna tell me I'm crazy and kick me out.*

But he doesn't. Instead, Mark brings a hand to his throat and swallows. Eldritch resists the urge to ask if it's sore. The the growls and shrieks torn from it last night must have hurt, and he imagines Mark is feeling the aftermath of that this morning.

"Do you want some water?" he asks, growing more and more concerned about the state of Mark's throat as he thinks back to the demonic voice. Eldritch moves to stand up, but Mark grabs his arm.

"Eldritch," Mark says, the sound tired and broken, "You know what's wrong with me, don't you? It's all over your face. When you can bring yourself to look at me, that is."

Eldritch knows it's time, knows he's allowed this to go on too long. Mark has sunk most of his money into this renovation, and in the span of a few weeks, the entity within him has wrecked it—has wrecked the renovation, has wrecked the man himself; his body, his mind, his spirit—and Eldritch stood by and said nothing, all because he was afraid. He is still afraid, as he sits shoulder to shoulder with the most diabolical spirit he has ever encountered; but he can't run from it anymore.

"Mark," he begins, slumping back against the wall in resignation, "there's a reason I can't look at you. There's a reason I have a panic attack the second you enter a room…and it's not your fault." Mark remains silent, allowing Eldritch to explain. "I know you asked around town about me, and people told you some crazy things. The problem is…it's all true. I can see spirits. I see ghosts, I see demons. I've been seeing them for as long as I can remember. It's my curse."

Eldritch chances a look at Mark's face, unsure of what he'll find there, but the man's expression is neutral—stoic, even—

as he asks in a quiet voice, "But what does that have to do with me?"

And there it is: the point of no return.

Here goes nothing. "Mark, I believe—no, I *know*—you are the subject of demonic possession."

Mark stares at him, unblinking, bleeding face devoid of emotion, and Eldritch takes that as a sign to continue. "Every time I'm around you, I see it, I feel it. I feel it right now, even though it isn't manifesting. It's a shadow, a darkness. It's all around you, it's inside you. Whenever I get near you, it's like…it reaches out for me." He pauses, watching as Mark looks down at his own body and runs his hands up his arms, like he's trying to feel the demonic presence Eldritch described.

"Is it my fault?"

Eldritch's heart breaks a little at the shame behind the question. "No, Mark," he insists. "Look, I don't know why it picked you. I don't have all the answers here. I just know what I see."

"And what did you see last night?"

Eldritch hesitates, trying to decide if he should sugarcoat the details of last night's episode, but in the end, he believes Mark deserves the truth.

"Did you go to the tree lighting last night?"

"What? Yeah—maybe? I don't really remem—what's that got to do with anything?" Mark stammers, his air of stoicism giving way to testy agitation. Eldritch knows Mark's frustration has less to do with the question itself and more to do with Mark's inability to recall what happened. He doesn't take it personally.

"Do you remember standing outside my house?"

Mark doesn't respond immediately, and Eldritch gathers he's searching as best he can for any memory of the night before.

"No," Mark says with a shake of his head, "I don't even know where you live."

Eldritch doesn't like the sound of that. Mark doesn't know where he lives, but *it* does. He looks at Mark again—really looks, looks around him, looks inside—and it's still there, lurking. Eldritch feels the chill, feels his little hairs stand on end like they always do when demonic spirits are near; but there's something about this one, something that sets it apart. *It's different—stronger, smarter, and…crafty?*

"I followed you," he says, refocusing on the story at hand. "When you left, I followed you all the way back here. I knocked, but you didn't answer, so I let myself in. The whole downstairs was trashed, man, like you haven't done any work in weeks, or wrecked all the work you had done."

"Like I said," Mark rasps, "I've been losing time. Sometimes, I wake up…and I'm in some random part of the house, broken boards all around me, or a massive hole in the wall…and I have no idea what happened. All that custom trim I ordered through y'all's guy? Smashed. Like I took a sledgehammer to it. And you saw what I did to my room—all those numbers on the wall—I don't remember any of it."

"Yeah, the numbers…they were everywhere," Eldritch recalls the scene in the bedroom, "and there was blood on the wall."

Mark lifts his hand to show Eldritch his fingertips. They're bloody, scraped. The skin is torn, the nails chipped and broken. The nail on his right index finger is split down the middle and caked with blood. "I think I clawed them into the wall."

Eldritch winces at the sight, "We need to get those cleaned up."

"And my face? What about that?" Mark asks.

"We'll get that cleaned up too. You've still got some glass—"

"That's not what I meant, and you know it," Mark interrupts.

"It threw you through the doors!" Eldritch blurts out, tired of struggling to find the right way to phrase this, tired of trying so hard to be delicate. "I came up here and you were standing in the corner digging into the wall with your nails. It had fully manifested inside you…and then you were in the air and—BOOM—out the doors. Through the glass, through the wood, everything. I ran to check on you, but when you turned over…it was looking at me—*it*—not you. And it spoke to me…" The words are flowing now and Eldritch is powerless to stop them "…it spoke to me, it knew my name, and I ran, Mark. I ran, and I left you here."

"Eldritch, Eldritch, hey," Mark's tired voice cuts through Eldritch's guilt-ridden confession, "cut yourself some slack, man. I would have left me too. I can't imagine what you're going through right now, just sitting next to me when I'm *not* going all Linda Blair on you."

The comment strikes Eldritch as funny, and despite the seriousness of their situation, he erupts into a fit of laughter. Mark watches, wide-eyed, for a moment, before losing it himself. They laugh until the tears they'd both been holding back begin to fall, shoulders shaking, heads leaned back against the scratched, wooden wall.

Mark gains his composure first, and looks over at the man beside him, still trying to catch his breath between giggles. "I wasn't sure you ever laughed. Or smiled, for that matter."

"I laugh," Eldritch chokes out, managing to get himself under control, "but only in incredibly inappropriate situations."

"So, speaking of Linda Blair..."

"You're going to need an exorcism," Eldritch finishes.

"Do you do those?" The question is sobering as Mark adopts a serious tone once more.

Eldritch shakes his head, "No. I don't." Mark sighs, a broken, defeated sound—a sound Eldritch decides he hates, so he's quick to add, "But I know someone who does," and sees a glimmer of hope return to Mark's eyes. "I'll give him a call. We're not Catholic, so it's not like the movies. No fancy Latin phrases or holy water. Nothing like that."

"But you'll be there?"

Eldritch isn't sure how to answer that question. Being present for an exorcism is not something he's ever enjoyed, even as a kid; and with a demonic force *this* powerful, he doesn't know if he'd be able to stomach being in the room with it once it's cast out. "I don't know, Mark. That's not really my scene anymore."

"You don't have to be in the room. Just...around. Somewhere nearby. I'll feel a lot better about the whole thing if you're there." He is so earnest and open in his plea, that Eldritch has no choice but to nod in acquiescence.

"Thanks, Eldritch," he says, slapping the man's knee in appreciation. "By the way, did your parents hate you?"

"What?"

"They named you Eldritch. What's that about?" Mark quips, and the corner of his mouth pulls up into a half smile.

"Oh. Yeah, it's a family name," Eldritch explains, "I was named after my great-grandfather..."

"That makes sense. I was going to ask if they picked it out of a D&D manual or something."

It's Eldritch's turn to joke this time. "Come on, Mark. You know D&D is of the devil."

The two men fall into another fit of giggles, and Eldritch feels a slight surge of pride at being able to make someone laugh again—something he hasn't done in a long time. As their laughter dies down, Eldritch pushes himself to his feet and holds out his hand to Mark, who grabs it and curses in pain.

"We also need to see to those hands."

"Yeah, I'm going to go wash them and look for some bandages," Mark grits through the pain, allowing Eldritch to help him up.

Eldritch scrolls through the short list of contacts on his phone, as they head toward the plastic sheet, now illuminated by the rising sun shining through the stairwell window. He selects a number and presses the "call" button. The other line begins to ring, and Eldritch holds the phone to his ear with one hand while reaching out to help Mark down the stairs with the other.

"Oh, and for the record," he says before his call is answered, "my parents loved me very much."

CHAPTER FOURTEEN

The Birch-Rainey house had long been the subject of local lore and legend. No one had lived in it for over half a century, and before it was abandoned, the owners had done a poor job of keeping it up. With the exception of a few modern upgrades, like electricity and running water, the house had largely gone untouched since its construction in 1890.

Formerly the residence of a prominent family in town, the structure now housed nothing more than the occasional group of teenagers bored with the monotony of small-town life, and the few cases of beer they managed to filch from someone's father. Once, the pitter patter of small feet echoed on the stairs after dinner, refusing to be put to bed, and important business was being discussed over cigars and brandy in the sitting room. One hundred years later, the only sounds the abandoned house boasted were that of hushed laughter on a Friday night, whispers in the dark as someone watched out for cops, the smacking of awkward first kisses, and bets on whether or not the place was haunted.

It was on a Friday night, much like this, that a seventeen-year-old Eldritch Hayes found himself sneaking around the back of the Birch-Rainey house and climbing in through a broken window. There were seven of them all together. Ryan, Denise, Tiffany, Scott, and Devin were a tight-knit group of friends who traveled in a pack up and down the halls of Sommerset High. They weren't popular in the football-cheerleader sense of the word, and they had zero interest in academic achievement, but people thought they were cool, nonetheless. There was a devil-may-care attitude they all possessed, and Eldritch wished, on many occasions, that he possessed it too.

Ryan, who sat in front of Eldritch in homeroom, had turned around one Thursday morning and asked Eldritch what he knew about the old Birch-Rainey house. Eldritch had shrugged and confessed he didn't know much.

Undeterred, Ryan had continued with his line of questioning, "So, is it haunted?"

Eldritch looked up from his physics homework a second time, growing irritated with the line of questioning. "How would I know?"

"Really, dude? Don't play dumb, Hayes. Everybody knows about you."

Eldritch had returned to public school at the start of tenth grade, and by this time—well into his senior year—he'd had minimal occurrences as far as seeing spirits and addressing local gossip went. Eldritch had planned to keep it that way, which is why he gave no response to Ryan's insinuation and diverted his attention back to his homework.

"You've never been inside?"

Boy, he just won't give up, will he?

"No, Ryan, I have never been inside the giant, scary, allegedly haunted house," Eldritch snapped. He'd known his defensive behavior was unwarranted, but he didn't know Ryan's intentions, and that had bothered him. "I'm sorry," he'd amended, "I just didn't get this physics assignment done, and I'm kind of freaking out about it."

Ryan seemed to buy it and craned his neck to see the assignment in question. "Ugh, physics. No thanks."

"Tell me about it," Eldritch gave an overdramatic sigh and planted his face in the middle of the book, which had garnered a laugh from Ryan. Eldritch lifted his head at the sound, smiling for once. He liked that: making someone laugh. He'd made such a point to distance himself from his peers—from anyone, really—that he'd never truly paid attention to how it felt to make an actual connection, no matter how brief, with someone else. He decided a little conversation with a classmate wouldn't hurt.

"So why the sudden interest in the Birch-Rainey house?" he'd prodded, eager to make small talk for once.

"A few of us were thinking about checking it out tomorrow night. It might be a cool hangout spot…but…"

"But what?" Eldritch had an idea of where this was going.

"Tiffany and Denise, they're afraid it's haunted. I'm not. I could totally handle some ghosts."

Eldritch had known that was a lie. One look at a legitimate spirit and Ryan would bolt, making a brand-new doorway in whatever room he was in at the time.

"Well, I hate I can't be of more assistance. I've never been, so I don't know."

Ryan had hummed in understanding and turned back around in his seat. Eldritch hated to admit he was a little disappointed the conversation had ended so quickly, and the knowledge that no one would ever find any use for him beyond his ability had settled in his mind. He stared down at his physics homework again and decided to give up; none of it made sense anyways. He'd put his textbook and notebook away and was zipping up his bookbag when Ryan turned around again.

"You know, you could always come with us."

Thirty-eight hours later, Eldritch was being hoisted up by Ryan Meares and Scott Connelly, and trying to grab the ledge of a busted window at the back of the Birch-Rainey house. He had clear instructions, once inside, to take a look around the place and make sure there were no ghosts. If he deemed it free of spirits, the rest of the group would climb in after him.

Eldritch was able to reach the window with the help of his new friends and pushed down on the busted, wooden frame for leverage as he lifted himself inside. The palm of his left hand caught on a jagged shard of glass, and he cried out in pain, tipping forward into the room. His reflexes kicked in, and he threw his right hand out in front of him, catching himself at the last second to keep from landing on his face.

"Eldritch! Are you okay?" a concerned female voice cried from outside, followed by a chorus of shushes and an annoyed, "*Kelly,* be quiet!"

He picked himself up from where he'd fallen and looked at his injured hand, which was dripping blood onto the dusty, moldering floor. The cut was deep, and he flexed and extended the muscle below his thumb, wincing at the stinging pain that radiated from the gash, but he had to play it cool. Eldritch never got invited out—often had no desire to *go* out—but this time, he wanted to fit in, and crying about a cut on his hand wouldn't do. He stepped over to the window and stuck his head out, looking down at the others below.

"I'm good. Just cut myself is all. Ryan, can you throw me a flashlight?" he asked in a harsh whisper.

"Here you go!" Ryan called back, tossing a flashlight up to Eldritch in the window.

"See any ghosts yet?" asked Scott, trying—and failing—to hide his nervous laughter.

"Not yet," Eldritch responded, clicking the flashlight on and shining it down at the group. "Give me a few minutes to look around. I'll be back."

He turned his attention and his light to the room in which he stood. It was empty, with the exception of a broken-down water heater to his right, which he guessed hadn't worked in decades. There were loose fittings and wires strewn here and there about the floor, and several of the hardwood planks were rotted or missing altogether. He shone his light down at the floor and, in certain spots, he could see all the way down to the dirt beneath the house. *Definitely need to watch where I step.*

Eldritch walked forward, eyes alternating between the treacherous flooring and the room ahead of him. When he passed through the doorway, he found himself in what he believed to be the kitchen. Moving the beam of light around, he saw bare, wooden counters in poor condition, cabinets hanging off the hinges, and an antique stove toppled over in the corner. Eldritch remembered seeing one like that in the antique store, polished and in excellent condition, and felt it a shame this one was left to such a fate.

Upon leaving the kitchen, he entered a short hallway; on one end of which was a door that led outside to the wraparound porch. The door was boarded up and nailed shut, probably with the intention of keeping vandals and squatters from trespassing. *Might want to do something about the windows, y'all.*

Across from him, under the grand staircase, was a little closet. Eldritch crossed the hall and brought his flashlight up to peer inside the open door. It was clear this small space had been used for storage in the past. There were a few cans of paint, an old sink, a wooden ladder, broken picture frames, and piles of loose papers scattered throughout the tiny room.

He stepped back and shone his light upward, illuminating part of the massive staircase that rose high above his head. The stairs stopped and turned onto a small landing, then bent in the opposite direction up, up, up again to the expanse of the second floor. His lone beam of light barely reached the place where the stairs ended and the mysterious second story began.

Eldritch lowered his light and listened—listened to the house around him, the way it settled in its old bones and caught the early, spring breeze that filtered in through the cracks in its shell, as if it were taking breath after breath. The house was tired, broken, used, and tossed aside. Eldritch could relate. He wandered around the first floor a few minutes more, taking in the size of the place; his light hitting sections of elaborate trim and woodworking—architectural and artistic genius crumbling into ash and dust. In one room and out again, he went; then on to the next, and the next, until his search led him back to the foot of the stairs.

Nowhere to go but up.

He made it halfway up the first flight when the stairs groaned beneath the weight of him. Eldritch shut his eyes and froze, waiting for the tell-tale cracking of wood; waiting for the entire staircase to collapse, taking him down with it, burying him in a mountain of debris. There he would remain, lost to the splintered wood and earth, laid to rest on a foundation generations had forgotten.

Bury me there. Let me sleep in the dirt below this wreck.

Eldritch opened his eyes and glanced around. The stairs still stood; the house was silent again, and he resumed his ascent. The second floor was more vacant than the first, large and open. He scanned the space with his flashlight, but his beam caught nothing but empty walls of peeling, ivory paint and faded, brown trim. The floorboards were in much better condition up here, although in desperate need of refurbishing. He walked around upstairs for a bit, examining the four bedrooms, one after the other, but each proved just as desolate and deserted as the last. Two of the rooms had fireplaces; fireplaces left in shambles with bricks and stonework crumbling away and spilling out onto dust-covered floors.

Eldritch wondered how many fires burned within them long ago, how many nights had they kept the tenants of their rooms cozy and warm. It didn't matter now. Now they were useless, left to rot and disintegrate, no longer serving a purpose. Eldritch did another scan of the large landing after checking the last room. There was nothing—no one—in this house. Sure, it was old, dilapidated, frightening to the casual observer, but this house wasn't *haunted*. It was worse than that. This house was forsaken.

"What took you so long?" Ryan whisper-shouted when Eldritch appeared at the back window again. "We saw a patrol car circle twice. Devin got stabbed by a stick diving into the bushes!"

"Shut up, Ryan. He's just doing what you asked him to do," Kelly hissed from the back of the group. "Did you see anything, Eldritch?"

"No. It's not haunted. You guys are good to come on in," he reported, lowering the ladder he'd found in the closet beneath the stairs. "I found this. Careful—I don't know how sturdy it is," he cautioned as one by one, they began to climb. "And watch out for glass. There's still some sticking up in the window frame."

Ryan and the others started whooping and hollering the second they made it inside, running out of the room and chasing one another through the abandoned house. The sound of someone falling reached his ears, followed by hysterical laughter and Scott shouting, "Careful with the beer, Devin!" Eldritch shook his head, aggravated by their lack of respect for the home.

Kelly was the last one up the ladder, the group of five making a point to jump ahead of her—just another way to make her feel left out. Kelly Walsh hadn't been invited to this gathering, but she had overheard Devin and Denise talking about it in economics class. As soon as they'd mentioned Eldritch's name, she had invited herself, unsure of their motives. Kelly was Pastor Mike's eldest daughter and self-appointed watchdog over Eldritch Hayes. They didn't speak that much, nor did they run in the same circles—Eldritch not running in *any* circles, and Kelly spending most of her time with the art kids—but although it went unspoken, they shared a deep respect and appreciation for one another. Kelly made it known she did not approve of anyone making a mockery of Eldritch or planning some elaborate prank at his expense.

Eldritch held his right hand out when Kelly reached the top rung, and she took it with a smile as he helped her clear the glass at the bottom of the window. She stood upright when her feet hit the old, wooden floor and began brushing off the front of her jeans where they'd made contact with the dusty ladder.

"Watch where you step," Eldritch said to her when she finished cleaning off her pants, "the floor's in bad shape." He shone his flashlight on the large holes peppered throughout the room, and her eyes followed the beam across the room and back again.

"Eldritch, what happened to your hand?" she gasped, gaping at the blood dripping down his arm and onto the floor, visible just outside the beam of light. Kelly snatched the flashlight from him and turned it on the deep gash in his left palm.

"Oh, yeah," he shrugged, trying to play if off as nothing, "I cut myself climbing in."

"Yeah, I heard you, but this isn't just some cut, Eldritch." She tucked the flashlight under her arm, reached into her black, crossbody bag and pulled out a pack of tissues. Grabbing a handful of them, she placed them on the gash and pressed down. "Keep some pressure on that," she instructed, using the rest of the tissues to clean the tracks of blood from his forearm.

"Kelly, it's fine. You don't have to do th—" but the look she shot him made the words die on his tongue, and he decided to rephrase: "Thank you."

The corner of her mouth lifted in a half smile, "You're welcome, Eldritch Hayes," and tossing the bloody tissues on the ground, she used the flashlight to guide them safely out of the room, all the while reminding him to keep pressure on the tissues over his wound. They exited the abandoned kitchen to the sound of Tiffany and Scott running up the rickety stairs— the same stairs that had groaned in discomfort when Eldritch had tested their stability. He couldn't imagine how they felt with these idiots bounding up and down them.

"I'd stay off the stairs! They aren't very sturdy," he lied. "They could go at any second."

Tiffany and Scott exchanged a worried look and descended in haste, Scott proceeding to chase a squealing Tiffany into the living room at the front of the house where the rest of the group had gathered.

"Awww, look at the happy couple," Devin snarked as Kelly and Eldritch entered the room. Kelly rolled her eyes and took a seat on the floor by Denise, Eldritch following after.

"Hey, Hayes!" Ryan called, "Heads up!" Eldritch turned in time to catch the item being lobbed in his direction and eyed it curiously. It was a can of beer, some German name he couldn't pronounce.

"What's this?" he asked, more out of shock than anything else.

"What's it look like? It's a beer, Hayes!" Ryan shouted.

"I know what it is, I just don't know why you're throwing it at me."

The five friends glanced at each other before erupting into fits of raucous laughter. Eldritch knew they were being overdramatic on purpose, trying to get under his skin, ganging up on the weird kid. He looked over at Kelly who was shaking her head, mouth fixed in a downward curve.

"We want you to drink it, Eldritch!" barked Tiffany, red faced and teary-eyed from laughing.

"Don't tell me Eldritch Hayes, the son of Satan himself, is too good to drink a beer with us lowly mortals!" Scott added in a poor attempt at a British accent.

"Son of Satan? What—?" Eldritch, blindsided by the comment, struggled to form the question.

"Shut. Up. Scott."

Scott sneered at Kelly's scolding, laughed again, and cracked open a beer of his own.

"That's what they say about you, you know," Ryan added after chugging an entire can. "Man, if my mom knew I was in this dump, less than five feet away from Eldritch Hayes, she'd lose her mind."

"Is that so?" Eldritch asked, going for disinterested, while on the inside he was screaming.

"Yeah, man! You're practically famous!" Ryan belted, with an enthusiasm that hit Eldritch like a slap in the face.

"Infamous," Denise, the know-it-all, corrected his choice of words.

"What's the difference?"

"Infamous is when you're famous…for *bad* stuff," she leveled her gaze at Eldritch as she emphasized the word.

Kelly scoffed, eyes narrowed at Denise, "Eldritch hasn't done anything bad."

"Kelly, it's fine," Eldritch whispered under his breath, finding himself on the receiving end of one of her death stares as a result.

"Not according to Len Holland," Ryan muttered before taking a sip from his second beer of the night.

"Len Holland talks too much," Kelly snapped.

"Yeah, he does," Ryan laughed, "and boy, does he talk a lot about you, Eldritch Hayes. Says you're evil, corrupted by the devil himself."

Eldritch looked down at the beer in his right hand, absorbing every word and barb being shot at him, before lifting his eyes to meet Ryan's malicious gaze.

"Well, if Holland says it, it must be true. So…I might as well enjoy the corruption." He popped the tab on the beer, and chugged. He could hear the cheers and howls of excitement from Ryan and company as he downed the drink, trying to ignore the bitterness that fizzed on his tongue. The taste wasn't anything to write home about, and Eldritch wondered why anyone bothered with this stuff at all. *Give me a Coke any day*, he thought and tried to imagine the sweetness and burn of the soda as he downed the beer. When he choked down the last drop, Eldritch crushed the can in his right hand and chucked it across the room. It landed somewhere behind Ryan who screamed out, "My man!" and tossed Eldritch another beer.

Kelly caught his eye and mouthed a "don't" in his direction, but he held her gaze and chugged the second one anyway.

"Hey, Eldritch," Tiffany called from her spot in Scott's lap, "truth or dare?"

"Oh, for God's sake," he heard Kelly mutter under her breath.

"Uh…truth, I guess."

"Do you think you're cursed?"

All the air seemed to be sucked out of the room at once, and Eldritch found himself face to face with the question he dared not ask aloud. *Am I cursed?* For thirteen years, he'd heard his parents refer to his ability as a "gift," but Eldritch wasn't so sure anymore. As far as he was concerned, this "gift" had brought him nothing but nightmares and pain. Sure, there had been a brief moment in time where he was loved, admired, and under the delusion that he was helping people, but those years were over. Now, he was an outcast, the butt of a poorly timed joke. He never left his house, never looked people in the eye. He had no friends, he didn't hang out, he didn't date. He lived in fear.

How is that a gift?

"You know what, Tiffany?" he asked with a forced smile. "I believe I am."

Eldritch was surprised they didn't erupt into another fit of laughter or a chorus of cheers. Instead, the five friends stared at him as if his response had caught them by surprise. It was Ryan who broke the spell of silence, piping up with another, "Truth or dare, Eldritch Hayes?"

"I don't think that's how it works," Denise began. "Now he has to ask—"

"Shut *up*, Denise!" hissed Tiffany.

Denise's mouth snapped shut and the five of them waited for Eldritch's response.

"Don't be boring, Hayes," Ryan chided, and Eldritch knew what was expected of him.

"Dare," he said, lifting his chin in an act of defiance. He knew they were trying to get the better of him, but he didn't care at this point. The two beers he'd chugged were flowing through his system, and he felt loose, uninhibited. If they wanted him to play ball, he was game, and he cracked open a third beer and drank it down to drive his point home.

"Ooooo," purred Tiffany, "the possibilities are endless. What do you think, Denise?"

Denise smiled back at her friend, "Oh, I don't know!" Then, she turned to Eldritch and adopted a sultry tone, "You know, Eldritch, you're actually kind of cute. I bet girls flirt with you all the time, don't they?"

Eldritch swallowed another mouthful of beer and shrugged, "Sometimes."

Scott snorted from over Tiffany's shoulder, "Yeah, until they find out who you are right?"

Eldritch could see the muscle in Kelly's jaw twitch as they teased him.

"I don't know," Denise spoke up from beside Eldritch, much closer than she'd been a minute ago, "I could go for a little seven minutes in heaven with Eldritch Hayes."

"Oh, can it, Denise!" Kelly cried out. The five friends didn't respond to her outburst but looked amongst each other and snickered.

Turning back to Eldritch, Denise brought her mouth close to his ear and whispered, "What do you say, Eldritch? You ever been kissed before?"

Eldritch knew he was blushing, and he cleared his throat to answer, mouth suddenly very dry, "I—"

"Leave him *alone*!" Kelly interjected, and Eldritch appreciated the save. He wasn't ready to reveal to this crowd that he'd never even held hands with a girl, much less kissed one.

The friends were laughing again, and Ryan spoke up to get their game of truth or dare back on track. "Okay, okay. Eldritch, I dare you to go into that little room under the stairs," Ryan paused, looking between Kelly and Denise, "and make out with..." Eldritch swore he could hear the alcohol rushing through his veins, "...Kelly for seven minutes!"

There was a collective intake of breath from the group. Scott made a suggestive growling noise in the back of his throat, while Tiffany tried to hide her giggle fit behind her hands. Denise looked far less amused and shot Ryan a dirty look. Eldritch couldn't help but look over at Kelly who was staring right back at him in shock. Kelly *did* have beautiful eyes—soulful and brown—which complemented her pale skin and blonde hair. *She has a nice mouth too...*

Eldritch knew his mind was wandering, trailing off in a direction foreign to him, but the alcohol made things fuzzier— or maybe it clarified them. Kelly *was* attractive, there was no denying that, and she was always so kind to him. If Eldritch was to have his first kiss amidst a childish and clichéd game of truth or dare, at least Kelly was here to make it good.

Rising from his seat, legs a bit wobbly from the three beers he'd chugged in rapid succession, Eldritch extended his uninjured hand to Kelly and smirked, "Why not?"

Kelly said nothing but shot daggers in his direction as she placed her hand in his. She rose from her seat on the floor to the sound of cat calls and whistles, and walked, dutifully, to the closet beneath the staircase. Eldritch reached for the door to hold it open for her, but Kelly batted his hand away and pulled it open herself, shining her flashlight on the small space within.

"Well, what do you know?" She said, voice dripping with false disappointment, "There's a sink in the way. Guess we'll have to take a rain check."

The group rushed to the doorway to take a look, but Eldritch walked into the closet, hauled the sink out with his cut hand, and slung it, against the wall in the short entryway.

"Eldritch, your hand!" shouted Kelly.

"It's fine." He shrugged and nodded in the direction of the closet, "After you."

Kelly pinned him with a glare but walked in anyway. Eldritch followed, after being handed another beer by Devin, and shut the door behind them. The five on the other side shouted their approval at the sound of the latch clicking.

"Morons," Kelly growled, taking a seat on the floor between musty piles of junk. "If a spider crawls in my hair and lays eggs in my scalp, I'm holding you personally responsible for any and all damages, Eldritch Hayes." The threat was thin, and the fact that she was failing to conceal a smile did nothing to convince him of her sincerity.

"Yeah, yeah," he drawled, pushing the paint cans aside and sitting across from her, "bill me."

The space was narrow and cramped, and Kelly set the flashlight on the floor so the beam was shining upward, illuminating as much of the tiny room as possible.

"So, how do you want do this?" she asked, and Eldritch couldn't tell if she was joking or not.

"Uh…ummm…well, maybe…"

"Should I straddle you? Sit in your lap? Are we talking full tongue? No tongue?"

"Kelly!" he shouted into the small space between them, shocked by her candor, despite how his body warmed at the picture she painted.

She shrugged. "Well, you're calling the shots here, Eldritch. I'm just along for the ride, apparently."

"You're mad at me," he observed, ginning as he leaned back against the wall of the closet. The alcohol was settling in his system, and Eldritch felt relaxed; felt the urge to flirt. He had never flirted before. This was new and uncharted territory, but his brain was yielding to the effects of the drink in his hand, and he succumbed to the comfort it offered.

"Mad at you? Please!" she snapped. "Eldritch, do you even know why I'm here?"

"Because you want to make out with me?" he joked.

Kelly rolled her eyes for the thirtieth time that night, "Not in this closet, idiot. In this house! Eldritch, I tagged along because I was worried about you!"

Eldritch held a finger to his lips and shushed her as her voice rose in exasperation. "We're supposed to be making out. If they hear you yelling at me, they'll know your tongue isn't down my throat."

"I'm not putting my tongue down your throat, Eldritch."

"Ah, well, a fellow can dream, can't he?" He flashed her a lopsided smile and did his best to come across as charming.

"Why are you here, Eldritch?"

"Because I was invited."

"But you didn't have to come," she countered.

"Maybe I just wanted to spend some time with my new friends."

"They're not your friends, Eldritch! You can't trust them!"

Eldritch had no rebuttal for that, knowing full well the notion of anyone inviting him somewhere as a friend was ludicrous. In lieu of a response, he opened the beer Devin had given him and took a swig. Kelly's irritation at the situation rolled off her in waves.

"So, are you going to college in the fall?" Eldritch asked after some time, attempting to diffuse the uncomfortable tension between them.

"Yeah, USC," she answered, the fight draining out of her as she relaxed against the wall.

"Well, Go Cocks or whatever," he smiled at her. "You majoring in art?"

"That's the plan. I'm sure I'll be perfectly un-hirable and poor, but yeah, art it is," she laughed.

"You'll do great. I like your paintings," and it was true. Eldritch had always admired Kelly's artwork, which was displayed in the arts hall of the high school on a regular basis.

"Thanks," she smiled and turned away, but Eldritch was certain he saw a blush creep into her cheeks at the compliment. "What about you?" she asked.

"College of Charleston," he grumbled, chasing the words with another swallow of beer.

"You don't seem too excited."

Eldritch looked down at the upturned flashlight, his eyes following the edge of beam from the floor to the ceiling. "I'm not sure there's anything to be excited about," he murmured, zoning out as he stared at the point where the light could no longer keep the darkness at bay.

"Eldritch?"

He snapped out of it and turned his attention back to Kelly.

"You can talk to me," she said, reaching out to brush back a lock of hair that had fallen across his eyes.

No one had ever been like this with him. Outside of his parents, no one ever asked him to share his thoughts, his feelings. No one cared what was going on in his head. The openness and compassion on her face, in combination with the alcohol in his bloodstream, compelled Eldritch to speak.

"My mom went to the College of Charleston, and she loved it. It's close to Gran-Gran. She's in her 80s now, so I like the idea of being able to see her…"

"But?"

"But it's so far away from everything I know. It sounds stupid, but I've never been that far away from my parents. That's really lame, I know, but they're all I have. They're the only ones who know what it's like to…be me."

His speech was slow and starting to slur, but Eldritch couldn't stop the words pouring from him if he tried. Kelly didn't interrupt, didn't interject, simply listened to every word he said.

"The whole campus is supposed to be super haunted, and honestly, I don't know if I'll be able to stand it. I'm terrified of what I'm going to see. I'm so sick of it—never knowing what I'm going to see when I open my eyes or meet someone new. That's why I'm always staring at the ground. I never know what's going to be around me when I lift my head. It's exhausting, Kelly. I didn't ask for this. I don't want it." He paused and took a deep breath, his body trembling on the exhale as he fought the urge to cry.

A sad smile graced his lips as he closed his eyes. "But I have to say…this—" Eldritch held up his beer, shaking the remainder of it to emphasize his point, "this seems to be helping." He drained the rest in one gulp and let the empty can drop to the floor beside him.

Kelly reached out to cover his injured hand with hers. Eldritch choked out a sob at the tenderness of the act, and he clutched her fingers, relishing the pain radiating from the gash. Kelly didn't seem to mind that he was bleeding against her skin. He knew she could feel it, the wet warmth of his blood spreading between their palms.

"It's all I am. It's all I'll ever be," he continued. "I'm not just Eldritch Hayes. I'm Eldritch Hayes, the boy who sees ghosts. I'm Eldritch Hayes, the guy who sees demons. And, apparently, I'm now Eldritch Hayes, the son of Satan."

"Thirty seconds!" a voice called out from somewhere on the other side of the door, disrupting the safe space they'd created with one another.

Kelly grasped his hand even tighter, the pain of his cut intensifying as more blood spread from his palm to hers. "I don't know what it's like to be you, Eldritch," she whispered, so close he could feel her breath on his cheek, "but I believe you can do whatever you want to in life. What you can see, what you can do…it's a big part of who you are…but it's not *all* you are," and with that, Kelly closed the gap between them, placing a chaste kiss on his lips.

Eldritch closed his eyes at the sensation, losing himself in the moment—his first time feeling another's lips on his. It lasted only a second, and Eldritch leaned forward, chasing

Kelly's mouth as she pulled away. He opened his eyes and saw she was already standing, turning the handle of the door that stood between them and the rest of the world. Eldritch schooled his face, masking his disappointment, and stood on unsteady legs to follow her out of the closet. The shouts and jeers from the other five teens pierced his ears, and Eldritch wanted nothing more than to crawl back and hide himself away in the little room. *Would she hide with me if I asked?*

The next few hours passed in a blur, the alcohol taking its toll on Eldritch as he took whatever drink was sent his way: beer, then something much stronger from a bottle. The antics of the group faded into the background for the most part, and Eldritch spent the remainder of the time touching his fingertips to his lips and staring down at the blood drying on his palm. Sometimes, he would look up to catch Kelly staring back at him. He glanced down at her hand and noticed his blood smeared across her skin; she hadn't wiped it off.

It was half past one when the group called it a night and began stumbling out of the old house the way they had entered. Devin, refusing to let go of whatever bottle he had in his hand, ended up falling out of the window headfirst but was spared any serious injury. Eldritch stood inside and held his bloody hand out to Kelly as she stepped over the windowsill and onto the top rung of the ladder. She took it without hesitation.

Once they had all reached the safety of the ground below, Kelly yawned and remarked that she needed to get home before her parents realized she was gone. Eldritch caught her eye once more, and she gave him a shy smile before turning to go. He watched her walk away, only turning his head when she had disappeared from view. Eldritch knew whatever happened between them that night would stay in that closet under the stairs, but he didn't care. It had been enough.

"Nice going, lover boy," Ryan jeered. "You can thank me later. Did you get her number?"

Eldritch smiled as he answered, "No. We're both going off to college in the fall. Besides, it wasn't like that."

"Oh yeah? Well, what was it like then?"

"It was perfect," he whispered. "For one second, it was perfect."

He heard them snicker behind him but tried not to care. Despite their snide comments and jokes at his expense, Eldritch still wanted them to like him and hoped they could come to accept him as one of their own.

"So," he began, "we doing this again sometime? Next Friday?" He waited with bated breath, hoping he'd be included again.

"Oh, well, about that," Ryan put his arm around Eldritch's shoulder. "You don't have to come back. Now that we know the house isn't haunted, it's all good. You won't have to bother with us anymore."

Eldritch felt something wither inside him; something fresh and new that he'd had high hopes for, but it died on the vine, cut down it before it had the chance to grow. The false consideration in Ryan's voice was at odds with the look in his eyes—a look that conveyed his true response to Eldritch's question: "Not on your life, Hayes." The five friends burst into laughter and moseyed along, leaving Eldritch alone in the shadow of the old house.

CHAPTER FIFTEEN

Saturday and Sunday were grueling for Mark as the demon strengthened its hold. Eldritch refused to leave his side, despite the effort it took to remain in the entity's presence. By Sunday morning, Mark was unable to walk under his own steam and required Eldritch's help moving to and from the bed. There were moments where Mark seemed catatonic, staring off into some nameless void—a living corpse wrapped in tattered, sweat-soaked sheets. But then, Eldritch would sense a change in the room: the air would grow thick and heavy, and the vibrations of evil that always hummed just below the surface would swell, pervading his senses. The nausea would hit, and he'd have to fight the urge to sprint from the room and vomit. In these moments, if he could manage it, Eldritch would look over and find the demon smiling at him using Mark's face; eyes black, veins protruding, with that ungodly growl clawing its way out of Mark's throat.

Eldritch would excuse himself and step into the hallway, always to the sound of the demon heckling him and calling his name in an eerie, sing-song voice. It was late morning when Mark, coming back to himself, insisted Eldritch sit outside on the porch and wait for Pastor Mike to arrive. Eldritch acquiesced, but only because of the fear evident in the man's voice—as if he knew something Eldritch did not.

It's just after noon when Pastor Mike's truck pulls up beside of the Birch-Rainey house. Eldritch rises from his seat at the front of the wraparound porch and walks the length of it to greet him. When Eldritch called him yesterday morning, Pastor Mike had been visiting family in Georgia but insisted he would be there following church Sunday. He was true to his word, not even stopping for lunch before coming to Mark's—and Eldritch's—aid.

Pastor Mike shuts the driver's side door and comes around the front of the truck, grinning at Eldritch. "Eldritch, my friend! How's it going?"

Eldritch holds out his hand, and Pastor Mike catches it in his strong grip as he reaches the top step. "Thank you so much for coming, Pastor. I didn't know who else to call."

"Anytime, Eldritch, anytime. It's so good to see you!"

The hug is unexpected, but Eldritch melts into the embrace as the preacher wraps his arms around him. When Pastor Mike lets him go, Eldritch feels stronger, supported, and he holds his head a little higher.

"Alright, Daddy, don't smother him," a familiar voice rings out from beside the truck. Eldritch looks over Pastor Mike's shoulder, smiling when his eyes land on Kelly, who smiles back, head cocked to the side and a hand on her hip.

"I'm not smothering him! I'm just happy to see the boy!" He slaps Eldritch on the back before switching gears and addressing the matter at hand. "I take it he's inside?"

"Yeah, if you walk in through this door," Eldritch motions behind him at the side entrance, "go straight ahead, and the room is across the way on the left. It's been a bad few days. Last I checked, he was asleep, but that can change at the drop of a hat with this thing."

"You mentioned it was strong. Can you tell me anything else?"

Eldritch shakes his head, "I don't know its name. It's like it's keeping it from me somehow. I've never seen anything like this, Pastor Mike."

"That's fine, that's fine. You've done an excellent job helping this man out, Eldritch. And his name is Mark, correct?"

"Yessir, Mark Satterfield."

Three more cars pull up and park along the side street, and Eldritch watches as six people make their way toward the house, each greeting Kelly upon their approach. Kelly smiles and waves, making small talk with a few of them. Eldritch doesn't know these people, but it's obvious Kelly does, and that knowledge puts him at ease.

"I hope you don't mind," says Pastor Mike, "I've invited a few people to help me today. If this thing is as strong as you say it is, we're going to need some prayer warriors in there. Don't worry, they're good people."

The newcomers ascend the steps, one by one, and shake Eldritch's hand, introducing themselves. There are three women and three men, each a member of Pastor Mike's church and glad to be of service this afternoon. Once the introductions are out of the way, Pastor Mike gives them the rundown of the situation. None of them seem fazed by the circumstances described, and Eldritch trusts Mark is in good hands.

Before going inside, Pastor Mike has everyone gather around and join hands with the person next to them. As Eldritch closes his eyes, offering his right hand to the pastor in the circle, someone grabs his left and runs their thumb over the scar on his palm. *Kelly.* Her hand is small and warm in his grasp, and he pretends the gash is fresh and bleeding—as if it never healed and her hand never left his. She squeezes once, and Eldritch responds in kind. *She remembers it too.*

Pastor Mike says a short prayer of protection for everyone present and a special blessing over Eldritch. Eldritch is touched by his kind words and almost sends up his own prayer of thanks for the Walshes and those here to help them—almost. At the final "Amen," Pastor Mike pulls open the door, and he and his six helpers file inside, ready to do battle on Mark's behalf.

Eldritch grabs the door from Pastor Mike and holds it open for everyone as they enter, winking at Kelly as she falls in behind them. The group of seven make their way to Mark's room, but Kelly hangs back beside Eldritch in the short hallway beside the grand staircase.

"Aren't you joining them?" he asks.

Kelly shakes her head, "I'm not here to help them. I'm here for you."

The answer is unexpected, and his face asks the question before his lips can form the words.

"Daddy told me you weren't taking part in it, but that you'd be outside the room, at Mark's request. I didn't want you to be alone out here with all that on the other side of the door."

Her words wash over him like a warm breeze, and for a second, Eldritch can't even feel the chill of the mid-December air. The fact that Kelly Walsh, the girl he shared a kiss with in this very house, the girl who held his bloody palm and told him he was more than his gift—now the woman he sees maybe twice a month when he needs coffee—is standing in front of him because she didn't want him to be alone.

Eldritch doesn't know what to say in response, so he settles on the first thing that comes to mind, "I'm sorry about the other week, in the café. I was all over the place. I felt like such an idiot afterwards."

"Eldritch, what—? Oh my God. Eldritch, you don't have to apologize for that." She smacks him on the arm, and Eldritch wishes the floor would open up and swallow him. "It makes total sense now. Don't you ever apologize to me for something like that, okay?"

"Okay. I'll try to remember."

Kelly's eyes drift to the closet under the stairs. "Now, *this* brings back memories," she laughs, sauntering over and pulling open the door. Mark must be using the space for storage now because it's packed full of building and cleaning supplies. "We couldn't fit in there if we tried," she laughs, shutting the door. "And you probably have no idea what I'm talking about, do you?"

It's Eldritch's turn to laugh as he leans against the wall. "Pretty sure your first kiss is something you're supposed to remember."

"Was I really your first kiss?!"

"Oh, come on, Kelly. Don't act surprised. You remember what I was like in high school—what I'm like *now*."

She cuts her eyes at him and smirks. "I don't know. I'd never put anything past you, Eldritch Hayes. You're a dark horse."

"Oh yeah, you know me. Secretly living it up with all the ladies."

Kelly shakes her head, staring up at Eldritch with a look that has him tugging at his collar. "I still can't believe I got to be your first kiss. You weren't mine, sadly."

"Well, that doesn't surprise me," he says before he has time to think about how the comment sounds. Kelly's look of mock horror clues him in, however, and he's quick to amend his statement, "No, no, no. Not like that. I don't mean I thought you were running around kissing everybody! Just that…you know…boys like kissing pretty girls."

"Is that so?" she asks, eyebrow cocked, and arms crossed.

"Oh, absolutely."

"So, you thought I was pretty?"

Eldritch feels like he's seventeen again, about to crawl into a cramped, dark closet with the prettiest girl in school. "Of course," he admits, looking down at the floor, embarrassed. "Still are."

Kelly's face changes. The coy smile and mischief in her eyes are replaced by something more serious. Eldritch fears he's taken their playful banter too far, but there's a softness to her expression that wasn't there before. Kelly takes a step toward him and grabs his left hand, turning it so his palm is facing upward. Her fingers dance along the scar below his thumb and Eldritch shivers at the touch. She opens her mouth to speak, but Pastor Mike appears in the hallway, breaking the spell.

"I'm sorry to interrupt," he says, eyeing the two of them—inches apart, Eldritch's hand in Kelly's, "but Eldritch, he's asking for you. Wants to talk to you before we begin."

Kelly drops his hand, and Eldritch follows Pastor Mike into Mark's bedroom. The sinister presence is a punch to the gut after being away from it for so long. He steadies himself against the doorjamb and adjusts to the feeling.

"Hey, Mark," he says, approaching the bed.

"They told me you were here, but I wanted to make sure." Mark lifts his head as much as he can and extends a hand in Eldritch's direction. Eldritch takes it, fighting his instinct to pull away.

"I'm here. I wouldn't just leave like that."

Mark grasps his hand tighter and chokes on a sob, "What if I'm not strong enough? What if it takes me? Eldritch, I'm scared."

"It's not going to take you. These people are here to make sure that doesn't happen. You're in good hands, Mark." Eldritch observes the demon's handiwork, considers what it's done the man clinging to him for dear life, and a righteous anger builds within him. "This ends today. You hear me? This ends today."

The grip on Eldritch's hand grows even tighter, bordering on painful; but before he can free himself, he's yanked forward by an impossible strength and finds himself nose to nose with Mark. *No, not Mark. Not anymore.*

The demon bares its teeth, contorting the features of Mark's face as it snarls, "Careful what you wish for, Eldritch Hayes!" The mouth opens wide, as if it were trying to swallow Eldritch whole, but Pastor Mike and the other men pull him back, wrenching him free of the demon's iron grip.

"Eldritch, get out of here! It's too fixated on you!" Pastor Mike shouts, and Eldritch is shuffled from the room by two of the prayer warriors. The door slams behind him, and he stands in the main hallway, staring at Kelly in shock.

"Are you alright?" she asks, hurrying to his side.

Eldritch nods in a daze; then, he's gagging, the contents of his stomach rushing up through his throat and into his mouth. He covers his mouth with his hand, but the attempt to stop it escaping is futile, and Eldritch throws up all over the floor between him and Kelly.

Kelly springs into action as Eldritch stands, motionless, attempting to process what just happened. She runs to the kitchen and returns with a roll of paper towels and a black trash bag. It isn't until she drops to her knees at his feet that Eldritch comes back to himself and notices Kelly cleaning his vomit off the floor.

"Kelly, no. Don't do that."

"It's fine, Eldritch. I got it," she insists, refusing to pause her efforts.

Eldritch joins her on the floor and tries to take the paper towels from her hands, "Let me at least help."

"Stop! Let go!" she shouts at him.

Stubborn as ever.

Eldritch knows when he's been beaten, knows there's no arguing with Kelly when she has her mind set on something, so he sits back and unfolds his legs from under him, giving his knees a break from the hard floor.

Kelly mops up the vomit and deposits the soiled paper towels in the black trash bag. "There, all done. See? No big thing." She walks over to the purse she set on tool bench by the stairs and fishes out a bottle of hand sanitizer, squeezing some into her hands and rubbing them together.

"I'm sorry." They're the only words that come to mind.

"I swear, if you apologize to me one more time—"

Her scolding is cut short by a monstrous scream from within Mark's room. Eldritch, whose back is inches from the bedroom door, spins around as it shakes and rattles in the frame.

"Eldritch, get away from there!" Kelly cries, and Eldritch does as he's told, backing away and meeting her in the middle of the hall.

The inhuman sounds coming from the room assault Eldritch's ears, and he brings his hands up to cover them. In an instant, he's a child again, standing on the stage of Sommerset Pentecostal Holiness Church as Reverend Holland and his deacons grapple with the forces of darkness in front of him. He can hear the shrieks, the curses, the howls, the demonic laughter. He can feel the darkness surging from the poor, possessed human vessel. It reaches for him—it's always reaching for him. Chills run up and down his arms and spine as he backs away, backs away, backs away again. He's scared. He's vulnerable and out in the open, and no one is here to protect him, to hoist him in their arms and pull him away from the threat.

His father isn't here this time.

But then, there's a hand on his shoulder, and he turns to see Kelly at his side. "It's okay," she says, "it can't hurt you."

Another sound joins the tumult, rising above the howls and sinister screams. It's the prayers of the saints in the room, locked away inside, opposing the spirit with fervent prayer. Eldritch hears them call upon the name of the Lord, spouting scripture and the promises of God, commanding the evil presence to depart and free this man.

The sounds intermingle—prayers and shrieks, the name of God mixed with curses against Him. A spiritual war is raging on the other side of the clattering door, which rocks on its hinges and threatens to give way. The demon is strong, Eldritch can feel its power radiating outward. He turns his back and sees the door to the outside world is only a few paces away. He takes a step in its direction, but his promise to Mark hangs over his head and halts his steps.

"*I'm here. I wouldn't just leave like that.*"
I wouldn't just leave like that.

Eldritch has no choice but to stick it out. He can be strong this time, he can be strong for Mark. With his eyes slammed shut, he fights the urge to flee, fights the urge to double over and fall to the ground as the cacophony of sound overwhelms him and rocks the very foundation of the house. Then, Kelly is in front of him, her hands over his ears, bringing his face down so their foreheads touch. She says nothing aloud, but Eldritch opens his eyes a fraction and sees her lips moving in a silent prayer, her eyes closed in supplication. He follows suit and lifts his hands to rest a top hers.

They stand together in the midst of the maelstrom, eyes closed, hands touching on the sides of his head, Kelly praying, Eldritch reminding himself to breathe, on loop. He feels the floor shake, the old house trembling from the force of the demon's rage—this house where he once bared his soul to the woman cradling his head, this house that once cut his hand in a plea to be seen and understood. Amidst the chaos around him, Eldritch thinks back to the blood he shed here in his youth and wonders if it still stains the floor in the back room and in the closet under the stairs. He stands here now, a grown man, pouring more of himself into this place. His vomit, his fear, his tears—all of them, a part of this house now.

And then, it stops. The demonic howls, the prayers, the quaking all cease, and silence settles throughout. Eldritch and Kelly open their eyes, and he curls his hands around hers, pulling them away from his ears. Their hands drop to the space between their bodies and remain connected.

Eldritch wants to speak, wants to open himself up to Kelly like he did all those years ago, feet away from where they stand, but he doesn't get the chance. The air feels electric. Something has shifted. Eldritch knows the door is about to open, but seconds before he can act on the intuitional warning, it flies off the hinges, crashing into the wall at the end of the main hallway. Pastor Mike and his helpers run from the room, still praying, still admonishing the beast using Mark's form as a puppet as it emerges behind them.

Eldritch let's go of Kelly's hands and pushes her back. She stumbles and falls, landing on the floor with a thud. He glances over his shoulder to make sure she's okay and, upon seeing she's fine, turns back to face the demon; but he isn't fast enough. The demon is already on him, in his face, grabbing him by the shirt and pulling him close.

"Eldritch Hayes. The boy who sees all. I know your name. I have whispered to you. Just one look. Just one look." The demon repeats the familiar phrase over and over, clutching Eldritch to its chest.

Pastor Mike and the men of the group appear at his side, pulling the demon away, prying Eldritch's shirt from its rigid fingers. The laugh it releases as it is hauled away from him is maniacal, and Eldritch feels the need to vomit again. He looks down and notices his shirt is ripped where its fingers had dug into the fabric.

Such a simple thing, the ripped shirt, but it sends Eldritch into a fury all the same. He looks up at Mark's body as it thrashes and twists against the arms holding it in place, and he shouts with a rage unlike any he's ever felt, "Tell me your name!"

The laughing ceases for a fraction of a second, but then the demon, manipulating and abusing Mark's vocal cords, begins

CALLING ELDRITCH HAYES

to chant "Sixty-six, twelve, seven, eight, nine. Sixty-six, twelve, seven, eight, nine."

It continues over and over again, until Eldritch feels it's nearly driven him mad with the repetition of it, and cries out, "Enough! Let him go! You want me? Is that it? I'm right here! Let Mark go!"

In his fit of rage, Eldritch fails to notice Pastor Mike running between him and the demon, holding the Bible up in his right hand and shouting at the top of his lungs, "'In my name they will drive out demons; they will speak in new tongues!' In the name of Jesus, I command you, servant of evil, come out!" The demon lunges from the hold of the men around him and falls to its knees. Eldritch watches as it heaves three times. On the third, a dark substance, similar to the one which slithered out of Charlie Haskell thirty-five years ago, spills out of Mark's mouth.

Mark falls prostrate on the hardwood floor, and the black matter lands beside him, moving around of its own accord. The exorcised spirit languishes on the ground before rising high above their heads, yet no one but Eldritch seems to notice. The others are running to Mark's side, checking his head, making sure he's breathing.

Eldritch stands still, eyes fixed on the demon's incorporeal form. It swirls about between their heads and the ceiling before darting in his direction. The shadow encircles and surrounds him. He can feel it trying to penetrate his flesh, trying to find a way inside, but its attempts to possess prove fruitless. Eldritch feels the malice, the hatred, the evil pressing in on him, and the weight of it is more than he can bear. He falls to his knees and screams. There is a sound—similar to that of a sonic boom—the walls shudder and quake. In the distance, Eldritch hears the shattering of glass, and then all is silent as he hits the floor, unconscious.

When he wakes, it's to the feeling of a cold rag on his head and the sound of someone's voice humming an unfamiliar tune in his ear. He opens his eyes, and the first thing he sees is Kelly's face, upside down, where she holds his head in her lap, hands pressing the wet cloth against his temple.

"Easy, easy," she says as he sits up, "you hit the floor pretty hard."

"Am I bleeding?" he asks, hand moving to the back of his head to check for damage.

"No, but I wouldn't go operating any heavy machinery if I were you. At least not for a while."

Eldritch tries to get a sense of his surroundings—he's not at home, he's not at work. "Where am I?"

"I haven't moved you," she says, voice quiet, breath tickling his face. "Birch-Rainey house, remember?"

Birch-Rainey house? But the last time I was here...

"You kissed me," he sighs, lost in the memory of their time under the stairs.

"Not today."

It comes back to him in a rush as he sits up—the house, the exorcism, Pastor Mike, Kelly...Mark.

"Mark! Oh, God, Mark!" Eldritch looks around, searching for the man.

"It's okay! Eldritch, he's okay," Kelly assures him, pointing across the hall.

He spots Mark, leaning against the wall next to the splintered doorframe. Pastor Mike is crouched beside him, and they're engaged in quiet conversation with one another.

"Mark," Eldritch calls, and Mark turns to face him.

"Hey, man," Mark responds. His voice is hoarse, and Eldritch wonders how his throat isn't bleeding.

Kelly helps Eldritch to his feet and over to where Mark sits. Mark looks up at him and leans back, the wall the only thing keeping him from falling over and collapsing on the dirty floor. He must be tired, exhausted from the gauntlet the demon put him through. His body has been used and exploited, pushed to its physical limits by supernatural means, yet Mark smiles. He smiles because now, he is free. It is a sentiment he doesn't have to voice. Eldritch can *see* the truth of it, can feel it in the air.

"It's gone, isn't it?" he asks.

Eldritch kneels down and looks at the man—at his friend—and for the first time, all he sees is Mark. No longer is there a shadow hovering about him. No longer is there an undercurrent of evil pulsating from within. This is Mark and only Mark, and Eldritch laughs, a sound of pure joy bubbling up from inside him.

And for the third time today, there are hands on him, pulling him in and holding him tight. Mark hugs him, thanks and gratitude rolling off his tongue, uninhibited.

Eldritch smiles and pats his back, "It's okay, Mark. It's gone."

It's all over now…

PART II

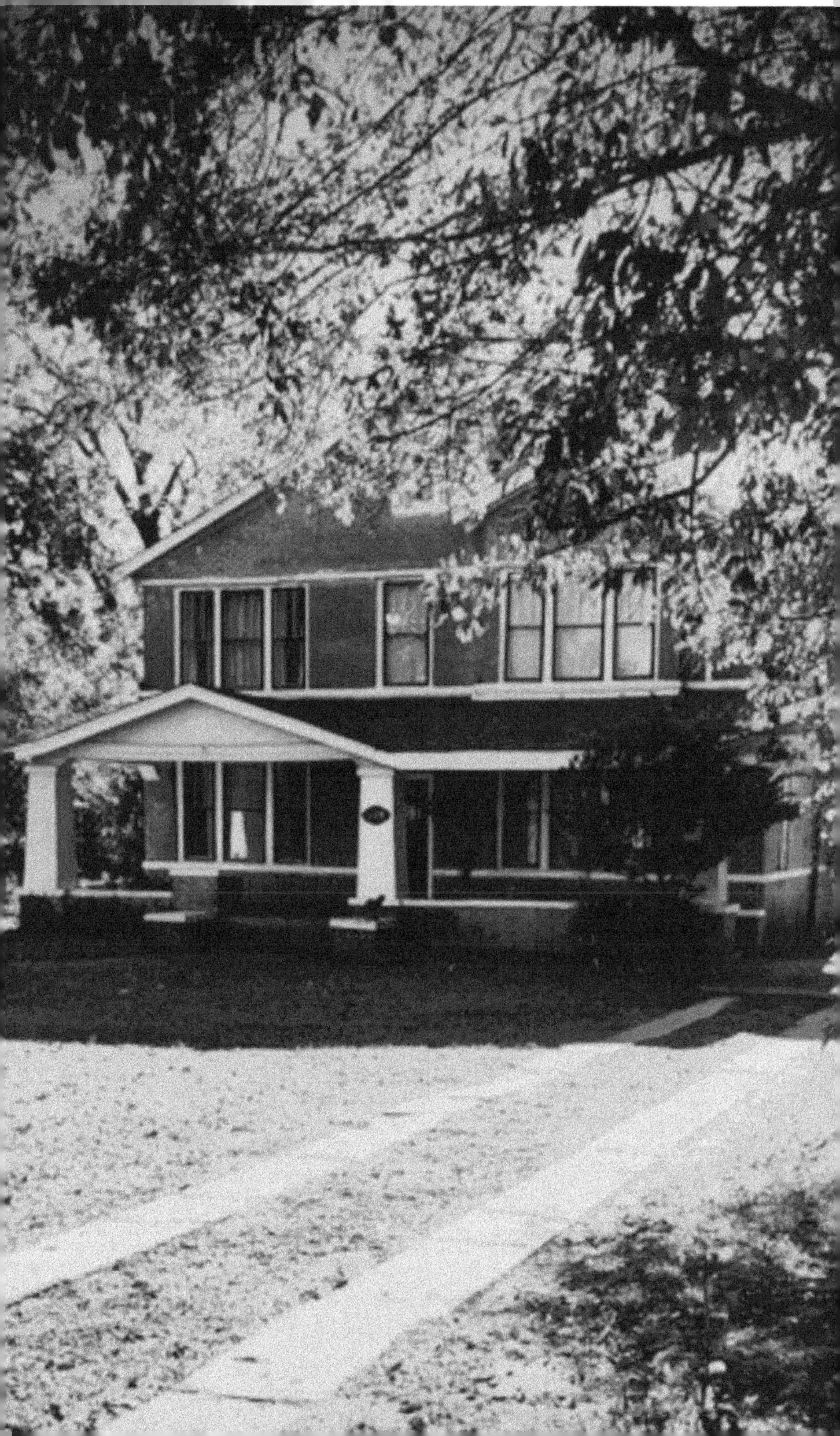

CHAPTER SIXTEEN

"Alright, I got you some ginger ale right here," Calvin says, setting the glass down on the end table beside the couch in the den, "and Amy sent you some potato soup. It's in the fridge when you get hungry. I stocked your pantry with snacks in case you don't want that. You still like Gushers, right?"

"Uncle Cal, I'm fine. It's not the flu. I just passed out," Eldritch insists. He appreciates it, but the extra care is unnecessary.

"You've been through a lot, Eldritch. Let the man take care of you," Kelly scolds from her seat on the arm of the sofa, down by his feet.

Following the exorcism, Kelly escorted Eldritch home, insisting he call his uncle on the way. Calvin dropped everything and came rushing to his nephew's side, arriving with grocery bags full of snacks and Amy's cure-all for everything: potato soup.

"I'm not the one who needs all this coddling," Eldritch protests, attempting to fluff the stiff and scratchy accent pillows under his head before giving up and tossing them on the floor, content to rest his head against the arm of the couch. "How's Mark?" he asks, sinking into the couch again.

His concern isn't unwarranted. Although his mind and spirit were much improved, the possession had taken its toll on Mark; and the exorcism, which didn't take as long as Eldritch expected, pushed his body beyond its limits.

Why didn't it take that long? The question won't leave him alone, and Eldritch hates how much he's stewed on it.

"Daddy took him to the hospital. He's dehydrated and has some minor injuries, but he's going to be okay," Kelly promises, squeezing his foot, and Eldritch assumes she mistook the disturbed look on his face as concern for Mark's well-being.

"Geez. I can't imagine how they're going to explain that to the doctor," Calvin sighs, searching for a coaster to put under Eldritch's drink.

"Construction accident caused by sleep deprivation or something. Daddy played it off."

Calvin locates a coaster on the mantle and slides it under the glass of ginger ale on the end table, "There we go." Eldritch catches his uncle watching his and Kelly's interaction. "Well, I'm going to get out of your hair. Kelly seems to have this under control," Calvin adds with a wink at his nephew. Eldritch tries to prevent the heat from rising to his face at his uncle's insinuation but fails, diverting his eyes to the back of the couch.

Seeing his way out of the den, Calvin gives Kelly a quick hug, and Eldritch doesn't miss the "Thank you," his uncle whispers to her before leaving.

"Bye, Uncle Cal," Eldritch hollers after him when he hears the man open the front door to leave.

"Bye, bud," Calvin calls back, shutting the door behind him. The uncanny similarity strikes again, and Eldritch must take a second to compose himself.

"Everything okay?" asks Kelly.

Eldritch hums in affirmation, a soft smile tugging at his lips. Kelly smiles back, and it's the most beautiful thing he's ever seen. He allows himself a moment to bask in it until a stabbing pain shoots through his head, causing him to wince and bring a hand to his temple. He rises and swings his legs over the side of the couch, but Kelly is up and pushing him back down, her hand firm on his chest.

"Whoa, where you going?"

"Just to get something for my head."

"No. Sit. I'll get it," she insists. "Where do you keep the aspirin?"

"I don't." Over-the-counter or not, he knows in the wrong frame of mind, he can make do with whatever is available.

Kelly doesn't ask why. He knows she knows—not the specifics, not the gritty details, but she knows it happened. *Everyone does.*

"I was just going to make some coffee," he explains, sitting up again.

Without a word, Kelly disappears into the kitchen; and soon, the sound and aroma of brewing coffee fills the house.

"I don't know how you do it, Eldritch," she says, returning to the den. "I don't know how you handle seeing that kind of thing constantly. That was my first time seeing anything like that. I was terrified."

Eldritch shrugs and lowers his eyes.

"People don't get it. They don't understand because...how could they?" she continues. "Until you've seen it...Eldritch, it was pure evil, and it was staring you down, speaking to you. I've always known you've had it rough, but I didn't realize just how bad it could be." Kelly drops to her knees in front of him and reaches up to touch his cheek. "I'm so sorry for not understanding."

Eldritch covers her hand with his own and leans into the touch. God, he loves it when she touches him, no matter how brief—how fleeting—that touch may be. He's gone without the touch of another person for so long, and all he wants to do is melt into her. "No apologies about this, remember?" he says, harkening back to her words in the Birch-Rainey house.

Kelly nods, moving to sit beside him on the couch. "So, was that as bad as it gets? Exorcism-wise? Is it technically called an exorcism since we're not Catholic?"

"I have no idea. Probably not," he shrugs, "and yeah, that was bad, but—" he hesitates, not wanting cause her any undue worry.

"But what?"

Eldritch relents, knowing full well she isn't going to let this go, "Do you think it was too easy? I mean, it was over in minutes. And that thing was so strong...stronger than anything I've ever felt, and then boom! It was over."

Kelly leans in and runs her fingers through his hair. "I know demons and spirits aren't my area of expertise, but I think maybe you're worrying too much. You're so used to everything being terrible all the time, maybe you're just not used to having something go right. You're allowed to breathe, Eldritch. Take the win and breathe."

Eldritch closes his eyes and leans against her, desperately wanting her words to be true.

Maybe it is over. Maybe I can breathe now.

Eldritch and Kelly are nearly inseparable in the days that follow. Uncle Cal calls Eldritch later Sunday evening to tell him he's getting an early Christmas present: the rest of the year off. Eldritch tries to argue, but Calvin says he's the boss and his word is final. Eldritch has weeks of unused vacation time that keep going to waste, and Calvin wants him to rest and recover from the month-long, demon ordeal. He assures his nephew that he, Amir, Lanny-Ray—who was just cleared for light work—are more than capable of holding down the fort while Eldritch takes some much-needed time off.

Every day after two o'clock, when Kelly closes the doors of The Grind, Eldritch opens *his* door to her smiling face. They cook dinner, watch movies, and talk for hours. Tuesday, she convinces Eldritch to decorate for Christmas, and before he knows what's happened, they're both hauling boxes upstairs from the basement. Eldritch hasn't decorated for Christmas in years. Something about it never seemed right; but now, as he watches Kelly rearrange the ornaments on the Christmas tree for the fourth time, he thinks maybe that has changed. She's talking to herself, trying to figure out what looks best on each branch, and it hits Eldritch that he would be content to watch her do this all day.

After dinner, they sit on the couch, side by side in the den. Karen Carpenter serenades them in the background, "Merry Christmas, Darling" spinning on the old Magnavox. Eldritch fidgets, longing to put his arm around Kelly, but not wanting to look like a fool in the event he's reading more into the situation than he should. For all he knows, Kelly is just trying to be a good friend—trying to keep him from feeling alone during the roughest time of the year.

She's kind of leaning on me. She could just be tired though. She helped decorate my house and she cooked dinner. That's got to mean something...or she's just being nice. One kiss in an abandoned closet over twenty years ago does not a relationship make.

His thoughts continue to spiral until Kelly, in her infinite mercy, grabs his arm and places it around her shoulders.

"There," she says, "that wasn't so hard, was it?"

Eldritch feels his face turn red and chuckles at his own insecurity. *This. I could get used to this.* They sit in companionable silence for the better part of an hour, wrapped in the music from the record player—Eldritch rubbing circles on her arm, Kelly resting against his side.

"So, did you ever see the ghost lady in our house?"

Eldritch barks out a laugh, "Random!"

"I can't help it! I've been wanting to ask for so long!"

He shakes his head, smiling at her curiosity, "Yeah. I saw her. The first night I met your dad, he took me to the house. I saw her petting the dog, the big white one—what was his name again?"

"Topper."

"Topper! That's right. She still in the house?" he asks, not having thought about the ghost lady since he was a teenager.

"No. We had to put Topper down back when I was in college. He got bone cancer real bad. After he died, she just sort of...disappeared."

From there, the conversation flows with ease between them. Eldritch tells her stories of the different ghosts he's seen through the years, along with memories of his parents. Kelly talks about growing up with three siblings, her artwork—which she still dabbles in and sells at The Grind—and her college years in Columbia.

"We were young—well, *I* was young," she says when the topic of her first marriage comes up.

Eldritch doesn't like the way she says that, but he remains silent and lets her continue.

"He was…controlling, and after a while, he got mean. He hit me once, and once was enough."

Eldritch tenses, left hand clutching the arm of the couch in a white knuckled grip, while his right hand halts its movement on her arm. He's angry, angry at this man he's never met who dared to lay hands on Kelly.

"What did you do?"

"Hit him right back and called my dad," she grins, all strength and grit, and Eldritch is certain Kelly is the rarest breed of human—one he's proud to have in his life now. "That was probably the only time anyone could ever question my daddy's Christianity. I thought he was going to kill Aaron."

After sharing about her abusive husband and divorce, Kelly feels emboldened to ask about what happened seven years ago. Eldritch is not surprised when the subject arises. He knew it was only a matter of time before Kelly asked about it, and part of him is relieved when she does—not only because he longs to unburden himself to someone without judgement, but also because it lets him know Kelly cares about the details, cares about his deepest, darkest secrets, cares about getting past the surface and into the substance of Eldritch Hayes. He shares what unfolded that morning and the weeks that followed.

"I'm not proud of it, but after it happened, I quit drinking. Been sober ever since."

Kelly's hand finds his resting on her arm, and she turns her head to kiss it. "I'm glad your uncle found that spare key and got to you in time."

The suicide attempt was no secret around town after it happened, but for the most part, everyone had the decency to not say anything to his face. Behind his back was a different story. Eldritch knows for a fact many a busybody received a tongue lashing from Kelly for saying something off color about it in front of her. He has always appreciated her loyalty, even before they were whatever they are now.

"I feel like you've always known about me, like you've always been in on the loop. You've always tried to understand. I don't get why it's taken us so long to just…talk. After that night in the Birch-Rainey house, I don't think we'd spoken two words to each other that didn't involve a coffee order…until now. And I hate myself for losing all that time with you," he whispers his confession in her ear.

"I think I was always afraid of crowding you. Of being there when you didn't want anyone to be. You kept to yourself, and I thought that was what you wanted," she squeezes his hand and places another kiss to his knuckles, "but I've always been your friend, whether it was obvious or not."

They talk for hours, until Kelly realizes it's after eleven and she has to be at work at five tomorrow morning to prep the café. She leaves for the night, and Eldritch goes to bed with a smile on his face for the first time in years.

Amir calls him Thursday to check in, and Eldritch is happy to hear his voice. He is less happy about his and Kelly's blossoming relationship being the main topic of discussion at the hardware store. By the end of the phone call, he and Kelly have been roped into a double date with Amir and Larissa. Kelly is—much to his surprise—excited and asks if Eldritch would be more comfortable hosting at his house.

"Yeah," he admits, touched by her consideration, "I think that would be easier."

Larissa, who works as a nurse in Lexington, has a complicated schedule, so the dinner is planned for the following Tuesday, Eldritch and Kelly work together in the kitchen, preparing dinner side by side, and he is drunk on the domesticity of it all; yet a shadow looms in the distance. Tomorrow will mark the eighth anniversary of the night he lost his parents. Eight years, and the pain has yet to lessen like everyone promised it would.

"Time heals all wounds." What a trash philosophy.

He knows Kelly sees the sadness in his eyes. She's extra affectionate with him this evening, her touches lingering longer than usual.

Amir and Larissa are right on time, and they both take a liking to Kelly. Of course, Amir has met her in passing at The Grind, but he has never had the chance to speak with her until now. Kelly asks about Larissa's work as a nurse while Amir and Eldritch talk shop. Eldritch won't admit it, but he's eager to hear how things have been panning out with Lanny-Ray back at the store and down an arm. As he suspected, it's been a disaster.

"I miss you, man," Amir groans. "Do you know what it's like being stuck up there with Lanny-Ray and Cal? No offense, I know he's family, but…dude."

Eldritch laughs, "I get it. Believe me, I do. But order are orders. I can't come back until after the new year."

"You're good, man. I'm glad you're taking some time off. You need it." Amir shoots him a pointed look which tells Eldritch Amir knows all the details about the Mark situation. *Thanks, Uncle Cal.*

Once they finish off Kelly's Caribbean barbeque chicken, Eldritch brings out his crème brûlée, and the couples begin discussing holiday plans. Amir has no plans of his own, with his parents visiting relatives in Saudi, but he'll be joining Larissa for Mass in Lexington.

"Do you go to Corpus Christi?" asks Kelly.

"I do. Not as regularly as I should, but yeah." Larissa answers. "What are y'all's plans? Your dad preaching a special service or anything?"

"No, no special service. We're actually leaving for Georgia Thursday evening and won't be back until the twenty-sixth. The associate pastor will preach Christmas Eve. We have family in Vidalia, so we go there every year," she explains.

The information delivers a stinging blow, but Eldritch is determined to hide the pain behind a mask of casual indifference. The thought of Kelly being so far away on Christmas makes him ache, and he comes face to face with how effortlessly she has woven herself into his life and how much he needs her there. He wishes he could keep her here with him. Images of the two of them waking up together, easing into the day without rushing, and opening presents by the fire cycle through his mind, but he forces himself to push them away. *We aren't to that point yet. It's only been a week. Stop being a creep.*

"What about you, Eldritch?" Larissa asks. "You going to the Christmas Eve service?"

He shakes his head, "No. No I don't do services."

"Eldritch doesn't do church anymore," Amir chimes in.

"Oh, I'm sorry!" She's worried he's offended, Eldritch can tell by the blush spreading across her cheeks. "There's a lot of religious décor; I just assumed that was your faith. I didn't mean to overstep."

"No, it is my faith. I believe in God. I believe in Jesus. I have a harder time believing in His people," he clarifies. Everyone looks down at their ramekins, focusing on the crème brûlée in lieu of responding. Eldritch fears he's ruined the tone of this casual double date and tries to explain his comment further, "I've been hurt by the church, so it's easier for me to distance myself and worship in my own way."

"Except he doesn't," Amir's commentary earns him a displeased look from Eldritch. "What? We've had this discussion, dude. You have issues with church people, and you know what I have to say to that. You can't judge a perfect God by the actions of imperfect people. You just can't, so—"

"I know that. I don't judge Him based on the actions of others."

"So why are you so angry at Him all the time? That's the real reason you don't go to church or anything like that. Not because you were hurt, but because you're angry."

The atmosphere has changed—the idle chitchat and lighthearted banter veering into uncomfortable, personal territory.

"Look, Amir. I know you don't fully understand where I'm coming from, but God and I...we have a complicated relationship at the moment. Let's just leave it at that, okay?"

Amir stares at him and says nothing. Dessert is finished in silence.

When Larissa and Amir go to leave, Amir pulls Eldritch into a tight embrace.

"You call me if you need anything, yeah? I love you, man."

Eldritch returns the hug and the sentiment, grateful he has a friend who refuses to turn tail and run when his issues and hangups take center stage.

They are alone in the kitchen when Kelly asks the question he was hoping to avoid. "Why is your relationship with God complicated?"

I should have known she wouldn't let that slide.

He decides honesty is the best policy with Kelly, convinced she'll be able to tell if he's lying anyway. "Because I feel like He cursed me with this so-called 'gift,' and then ripped the only two people who made me feel safe out of my life forever. I'm angry. I'm dealing with it, but I'm angry."

She doesn't feed him a sermon about God's ways being higher than his own; she just hugs him and thanks him for being honest with her.

It's after midnight when Kelly decides she needs to get going. "Unlike some people here, I actually have to work in the morning," she teases as Eldritch walks her to the door, where they linger, hesitant to bring the night to a close and go their separate ways.

Eldritch's hand is on the doorknob, but he can't bring himself to open it.

"Maybe…you could stay." He can't believe he's said it even after the words have left his mouth and are hanging in the air between them.

Kelly takes a step forward, sliding into his space as her eyes drift closed, and just like that moment years ago in a dark and dusty closet, her lips are on his—but this time, it isn't fleeting; this time, she doesn't pull away. Eldritch leans into it, presses his mouth against hers and mirrors the movement of her lips. His hand is off the door handle and snaking around her back, clutching the soft fabric of her t-shirt. Kelly presses into him, and as he gasps at the sensation, he feels the slide of her tongue against his, soft but insistent. He can taste the vanilla from the crème brûlée and the herbal tea she drank after dinner. They remain that way for some time: kissing, basking in the feel of being in each other's arms, savoring a moment that is long overdue.

They break apart, breaths coming in heavy pants, and he brings his forehead to hers. When Kelly speaks, her voice is hoarse and dripping with want, "Maybe I could stay."

His mouth is on hers again as he hums his approval, one hand at her back, pulling her flush against him, the other in her hair. How he's longed for this, longed for this connection. In all forty-one of his years, he's never experienced anything like it, and it's all because of her—because of the woman she is and the man he knows she can help him become.

Kelly breaks the kiss and moans his name, equal parts desire and reluctance, and Eldritch braces himself for what he knows is coming.

"But I can't," she whispers against his lips.

Eldritch agrees; he hates himself for it, but he agrees. He knows she's right. He's been through a lot recently and throwing sex into the equation would only complicate things. This new relationship is important, precious to him, and neither he nor Kelly want to screw it up by doing something impulsive.

He forces himself to step away and opens the door. The temperature is dropping outside, and they huddle close to one another as he walks her to her car. The horrible truth that she's leaving him here alone tonight is an impossible weight which threatens to crush the very heart of him, but he pushes past the pain and tries to be happy. He *is* happy; happy in *this* moment with *this* woman, and part of him is terrified of enjoying it because he doesn't want it ripped away.

"What's wrong?" she asks.

"Just waiting for the other shoe to drop, I guess."

Kelly grabs his left hand and kisses the scar on his palm, "You can't live like that, Eldritch. Try to be happy, love." She kisses him again, and Eldritch has to tear himself away, recognizing he's on the verge of sweeping her off her feet and carrying her back inside. Kelly wraps her arms around him and kisses his cheek before shutting the door and driving off. Eldritch watches her taillights disappear around the corner and decides it's much colder with her gone.

It takes him a while to fall asleep, mind mixing with thoughts of this exciting, new territory he's ventured into with Kelly and the dread of tomorrow. Eldritch knows he will wake in the morning to the stark reminder that things will never be what they should, and no matter what good finds its way into his life, Eldritch will never be—*can* never be—whole.

When sleep comes to claim him, he finds himself in a familiar place: The Birch-Rainey house. It looks much like it did over a week ago. Eldritch can hear the wails and growls of the demon on the other side of Mark's door, but this time, it's different. This time, he's alone. He cannot hear the prayers of Pastor Mike or the other saints. He looks around, and Kelly is nowhere to be found. To his left, where there should be a doorway leading into the kitchen, there is a wall with a broken window. In the lower corner, a trail of blood drips on the edge of the jagged glass. *That's my blood*, he thinks and looks down at the scar on his hand. But something is wrong. There is no scar, and his hands are small, much smaller than they should be— the hands of a child. Eldritch stares into the glass of the window and catches his reflection. He is not himself—not as he is now—he is young, around the age of six, if he had to guess.

A loud shriek shakes the house, and Eldritch hears the splintering of wood. He turns to face the bedroom as the door flies off its hinges. The demon emerges, stalking toward him—not Mark, but a large, shadowy figure. It has no face yet moves like a man. Eldritch trembles and longs to cry out, but his voice is stolen away—silenced by the inescapable truth that this is where he will always find himself; this is where he belongs. He is all alone in this great, big house with no one to pull him away from this monster—but then, there's a hand in his. Beside him, someone has grasped his left hand and is holding it in a firm grasp. The demon roars in front of him, reaching out, but Eldritch feels stronger now. There's a hand in his, and it's rubbing over the scar that has reappeared on his palm. *Kelly.* He feels the familiar, wet warmth pool between their skin and looks down at their entwined fingers. But what he sees is unexpected.

Eldritch isn't bleeding. The blood is flowing from the other person's hand and running all over his, covering it in a river of red. *Why is Kelly bleeding?* He looks over at the face of the woman next to him, but to his horror, Kelly is not who he finds. Instead, the bloodied and bruised face of his mother stares back at him. There are pieces of glass stuck in her skin and hair, and she's dressed in the same outfit she was wearing when she left for Charleston the morning of December nineteenth, though now it is soiled in blood, asphalt, and bits of metal. The demon screams in his ear, so close Eldritch can feel its breath on the side of his face, but he doesn't turn. Try as he might, he cannot tear his eyes away from the image of his dead mother. Her mouth opens, and in a voice he hardly recognizes, she rasps, "Be on your guard!"

TORI LEWIS

Eldritch wakes to the sound of his own screams echoing through the empty house.

CHAPTER SEVENTEEN

Eldritch tried his best to be quiet upon returning home, but the amount of alcohol he'd had back at the Birch-Rainey house was working against him, and he stumbled through the front door, sending it swinging backward and slamming into the wall with a bang. He hissed a shush through gritted teeth, begging the door to keep it down so his parents wouldn't hear him sneaking in, but it was too late. The sound of footsteps could already be heard on the stairs, and Eldritch braced himself for whatever lashing he was about to receive.

"Eldritch?!" came his mother's cry from the stairwell, equal parts fury and relief.

The light in the den switched on, and his father came bounding from the back of the house toward the living room. "Where have you been?! Do you have any idea what time it is?!"

His parents converged on his position by the front door, eyes blazing and faces red.

"I was out, and no, I have no idea what time it is," he answered with an eyeroll, words slurring just enough to betray him. "Also, I don't care, sooo—"

"Are you—Eldritch, are you drunk?" Gene crowded into Eldritch's space with an investigative sniff and looked into his son's eyes. "You're not drunk. You're hammered!"

Eldritch scoffed at his dad's assessment, swaying on unsteady feet, "No, I'm not."

"You smell like a keg and your eyes are all glassy! What have you been doing?" his father demanded.

"Well, drinking, obviously," Eldritch snorted, "as you just pointed out. Well done, Mr. Holmes."

Even in his drunken state, he could see the looks passing between his parents and knew he was in for it.

"You've got five seconds to drop that attitude and give me a straight answer. I'm not playing here, son."

Eldritch had never heard his father take that tone with him before; largely because Eldritch had never done anything to warrant being reprimanded in such a way. Somewhere in the sober recesses of his mind, he knew he was in *actual* trouble—knew he was being disrespectful, but he didn't care; at least, he didn't *want* to care.

"I got invited to go out with some people from school."

"Yeah, you told us y'all were going to catch a movie at 7:30, and we told you curfew was at eleven. It's almost two in the morning, Eldritch! Where have you been?!"

"The old Birch-Rainey house, alright?!" he shouted, and his parents' jaws dropped at his outburst. "A guy in homeroom wanted me to go with them to check it out. It was just a few of us. We were fine. A couple of the guys brought some beers, and I had a few, okay? So, forgive me for trying to be a normal teenager for once! I'm *so* sorry!" He held up his hands in mock surrender, revealing the bloody gash on his left palm.

"What happened to your hand?!" his mother gasped, grabbing his forearm, and bringing his palm up for closer inspection.

"I cut it on a window," he shrugged, "It's fine. Kelly took care of it."

"Kelly? Kelly who?" she asked, not waiting for an answer as she dragged Eldritch toward the kitchen. "This needs to be cleaned and bandaged. You're lucky you don't need stitches."

He tripped over his feet as she tugged him along, trying to find his footing with the alcohol dulling his motor skills.

"Kelly Walsh. She tagged along, to make sure I was okay. They dared us to make out in a closet," he admitted with a smile on his face, thinking back on the moment. *It was a good kiss.*

"WHAT?!" both parents shouted, his father entering the kitchen behind them as Louise turned on the faucet.

"It's fine! Nothing happened. We didn't make out. No one's pregnant. Calm down!"

"You watch that mouth right now, young man!" his father bellowed. The sound startled Eldritch, and he wanted nothing more than to make himself small and hide away. "You don't get to disappear on us like that, stay out all hours of the night—when we have no idea where you are or if something has happened to you—and then traipse back in here, drunk as a skunk, with that cocky grin on your face and talk to us like that!"

His father was angry, Eldritch was well aware of that, but there was something else under that anger—something else colored the words he shouted at his son.

Fear.

The realization crashed against Eldritch like a wave, leaving him foundering in a sea of shame. Of course, they were upset with him. He'd lied and ran off with people he barely knew with no way for his parents to contact him. The warm water from the faucet poured over the cut in his hand, and he watched the blood flow down the drain. He wished he could follow it down there—down the drain, through the pipes, and into the sewer where he belonged. He lowered his head as his mother grabbed the soap and began to clean the wound. It stung, but Eldritch felt he deserved the pain.

"I'm sorry," he said, voice small. "I just wanted someone to like me, to want to be my friend."

Louise rinsed his hand one last time, shut the water off, and grabbed a handful of paper towels to dry it with. "Sweetie, those aren't the kind of friends you want or need. With the exception of Kelly. She seems like a nice girl." She tossed the paper towels in the trash and rummaged around the medicine cabinet for some ointment and bandages.

"Well, it doesn't matter. Apparently, I'm evil, so in the grand scheme of things, drinking doesn't seem all that bad."

"What did you say?" Gene asked, coming to stand in front of Eldritch.

Louise stopped wrapping Eldritch's hand and looked up at her son. "What do you mean you're evil?" she asked, shooting her husband a concerned look.

Eldritch could feel the tears threatening to flood his eyes, the effects of the alcohol making him more emotional than he wanted to be over this. "That's what everyone is saying," he sniffed, wiping his nose and eyes with his uninjured hand. "Reverend Holland's been spreading it all over town. 'Eldritch is evil. Eldritch is a wolf in sheep's clothing,' and people are just running with it, I guess. Someone's out there calling me the son of Satan. So, I figured if I'm evil, might as well enjoy the sinning. That's the fun part, right?" The tears began to flow against his will, and Eldritch buried his face in his mother's shoulder.

With the dressing on his hand wrapped and secured, she brought her arms up and pulled him into a tight embrace, whispering into his hair, "It's okay. It's all going to be okay."

Eldritch pulled back to look at her face, vision still blurred, and she wiped the tears from his cheeks. There was so much he wanted to say, but before he could open his mouth to speak, a convulsion wracked his chest and throat, and his eyes grew wide at the sudden onset of nausea.

"I think I'm gonna be sick," he croaked, and his father's hands were on him in an instant, helping from the kitchen to the bathroom. They reached the toilet just in time, and Eldritch hit his knees, spilling the contents of his stomach into the bowl. Gene stood behind him the entire time, one hand patting his back and shoulders, the other resting on the crown of his head. When Eldritch was finished, he pushed down on the handle to flush, and slumped backward against his father. Gene let him rest for a moment before helping him to his feet so he could rinse his mouth out at the sink.

Climbing the stairs to his bedroom was a struggle, but they managed it together; Gene cradling him while Eldritch clutched the railing for extra stability. When they made it to his room, his father turned the sheets and comforter back and set him down on the bed. Eldritch tried to reach down to untie his sneakers, but the room started spinning, and he pitched forward.

"Hey, hey, I got it," Gene said, catching him by the shoulders and sitting him upright again. He removed the sneakers and set them inside Eldritch's closet. Moving back over to the bed, he helped his son lie down and pulled the covers up over him.

"You know, when I was your age," Gene began, taking a seat on the floor by the bed, stretching his legs out with a groan, "I used to get in way worse trouble."

"Nuh-uh," slurred Eldritch, closing his eyes and relaxing into the mattress.

"Yeah, I did," his father laughed, "I was the bad kid. Calvin was the good one, but I guess he figured he had to be after all the hell I put our parents through."

"Did they ever catch you coming home drunk?"

"More times than I can count."

"I'm sorry I did it. I'm sorry I was disrespectful." Eldritch rolled over onto his side and looked down at his father on the floor. "I drank the first one, and it made me…I don't know, chill or something. I felt good, so I had another; and then they just kept giving them to me. I just wanted to forget for a little while, you know?"

"Forget what, exactly?"

"What it's like to be me. What it's like to be messed up—an outcast. I must be such a disappointment."

"You know, bud… your mom and I will never know what it's like to be you, but I don't want you to think for one second that we ever wished you were anyone else. Do we wish you had it easier? Do we wish you'd been dealt a better hand? Absolutely. But we wouldn't trade you—who you are—for anything in this world." There were tears in his father's eyes, and Eldritch's heart broke a little. "You're a good kid, Eldritch—the best. Yeah, you did something stupid tonight, and I won't lie, I wanted to ring your neck when you came through that door, but I want you to know…we forgive you.

Your mother and I are not happy with your actions, and there will be consequences. We are disappointed in your *choices* and your *behavior* tonight—" Eldritch could hear the emotion in his father's voice as he paused, "but *you* are not a disappointment. You could *never* be a disappointment to us."

Gene rose from his spot on the floor and patted him on the shoulder. "I guess this means you're grounded. No hanging out with friends or going anywhere that isn't school for two weeks."

"Man, what a change that'll be to my everyday life," Eldritch snorted.

"Hey, you're the one with all the friends now, tough guy."

Eldritch wished that were true. He longed to have a group of friends to call his own, but he remembered how Ryan had blown him off, how he'd told him he wasn't part of their group without saying the words.

"Not really," he admitted to his father. "They didn't want to be my friends. Just needed to make sure they weren't walking into a haunted house. They didn't want Kelly there either; she was just looking after me. They didn't want either of us around."

"Well, that makes them idiots, and you shouldn't be hanging out with idiots no way." Gene cocked an eyebrow at him before turning toward the door. "Oh, and just out of curiosity," he added before leaving, "did you at least get to kiss Kelly Walsh?"

"*She* kissed *me*."

"Attaboy," he grinned, winking at his son as he walked out, passing Louise as she entered the room.

"What was that about?" she asked.

"Oh, nothing," Eldritch smiled. He felt the dizziness begin to wane, the spinning room begin to still, but he couldn't help the loopy smile he flashed his mother as he snuggled down into the comforter.

"You need to try and drink this before you fall asleep," she said, placing the glass of water on his nightstand. "Do you think you'll throw up again?"

"Nah. I'll be fine."

"Good. You need to take your migraine meds before you fall asleep. But I doubt that'll help with the headache you're gonna have in the morning, so I'm putting some aspirin right here for you." She set the pills down by the glass and brought her hand up to stroke his hair—something she'd always done when he was little; something Eldritch figured she'd never stop doing, no matter how old he was.

He sat up and took his medication, drinking half the glass before setting it back down. "Thanks, Mama."

"I don't want you to give another thought to all that trash Len Holland has been spreading, you hear me?"

Eldritch's eyes were closed as he laid back down, but he hummed a sleepy "mmhmm," letting her know he understood.

"I'm probably going to have to talk your father down from marching over to his house and punching his lights out. You know how he gets."

Eldritch cracked his eyes open, smirking at the scenario she painted. "But you can't do that. Holland has friends in the police department. Daddy'd probably get life without parole for crossing the almighty Len Holland."

Louise grinned from ear to ear, and Eldritch watched her bask in the assurance her teenage son still needed her after all. He could see himself reflected in her eyes, could see the little boy tucked away in bed.

"Want me to sing you to sleep? Like I used to do?" she asked.

"I'm not a baby anymore." The light in her eyes was overtaken by the shadow of disappointment, and Eldritch was quick to add, "But sure, go ahead."

Her face lit up again, and she replied, "Only if you sing with me."

Eldritch let her begin, but after the first couple of lines, he joined in.

> Little ones to Him belong.
> They are weak, but He is strong.
> Yes, Jesus loves me.
> Yes, Jesus loves me.
> Yes, Jesus loves me.
> For the Bible tells me so.

Both fell silent; Louise stroking his hair as he lay there, Eldritch teetering on the edge of sleep. After a few minutes, his breathing evened out and Louise called his name. When he didn't respond, she picked up his left hand and ran her fingers over the bandage she'd applied earlier; then intertwining her fingers with his, rested her free hand atop his head, and began to pray.

"Father, please keep your hand upon Eldritch. He's been through so much, Jesus, and everyday must feel like a battle for him. Please wrap your arms around him and let him know that even when it feels like no one cares and no one could possibly understand…you do. You do, and you're right there with him. Help him to realize he is not alone, no matter how lonely he may feel."

After a shaky, tear-filled, "amen," Louise released his hand, kissed his head, and whispered in his ear, "'Be on your guard, stand firm in the faith. Be courageous. Be strong.' Be strong, baby boy."

She turned off the lamp and left the room.
And Eldritch drifted off to sleep.

CHAPTER EIGHTEEN

Nothing remarkable accompanies the rising sun to herald the importance of the day. The morning of December nineteenth arrives as all mornings do. Everyone in Sommerset wakes up, sees to their morning routines, and goes about their lives—filling the streets and shops in a mad dash to conquer their to-do lists with Christmas less than a week away.

When Eldritch wakes, the significance of the day is inescapable. The usual weight he carries around—on his shoulders, in his heart, in his spirit—is crushing, and despite the years that continue to pass, every December nineteenth is just as difficult as the last. After he'd awoken, screaming in a tangle of sweat-soaked sheets, the image of his dead and bleeding mother refused to leave his mind. The rest of the night's sleep was fitful and disturbed; the entire ordeal serving only to exacerbate the pain.

He grabs his phone from the bedside table and walks downstairs, checking his notifications as he goes. There are two text messages from Kelly.

> *6:36 a.m. – Hey, handsome. Thinking about you this morning. I'm here if you need me.*
>
> *8:13 a.m. – Is it ok if I stop by later? I understand if you want to be alone today. I just don't like the thought of you over there all by yourself.*

Eldritch smiles as he reads them. For the longest time, no one—apart from Uncle Cal and Aunt Amy—seemed to care about him this much, and he wonders how he's gone so long without Kelly in his life. He types out a response as he sets his coffee to brew.

> *9:07 a.m. – Sorry. I kinda slept in. I'd love to see you today. I gotta meet Uncle Cal when he closes up at 6, but I'm free before then.*

Eldritch and Calvin have a standing appointment every December nineteenth. After the store is closed for the evening, they walk to the cemetery together and spend time at Gene's and Louise's graves, reminiscing and telling old stories from years ago. Eldritch doesn't mind rehashing the same memories over and over again. It's the one part of this day he looks forward to.

His phone buzzes with another incoming text.

> *9:09 a.m.– I'll come by after work. It hasn't even been 12 hours and I want to see your face again. I'm such a sap.*

His heart swells as he reads her message. He wants to see more of Kelly too and wishes she hadn't left last night. Waking up this morning might have been easier if he'd woken up in her arms. Eldritch is tempted to convey this via text but decides that would come across as a little *too* eager. *Geez, now I'm the sap.* He deletes the words he typed and goes with the only other thing he can think to say.

9:10 a.m. – I want to kiss you again.

He blushes as he sends it, amazed at how just over a week with Kelly has turned him back into a seventeen-year-old boy. Eldritch know he's falling, and he's falling hard. He pours a cup of coffee, setting his phone aside to keep himself from staring at the screen while waiting for her response. He hears the tell-tale buzz but makes a point to stir two spoonful's of sugar and a splash of milk into his coffee before grabbing it. *Try to play it cool, for God's sake. You're a grown man.* He takes two sips from his mug and decides just over a minute is more than enough time to wait. Eldritch doesn't want to admit it, but part of him is a little afraid of what Kelly's response to his last text will be. He can't remember the last time he flirted with someone, and he's well aware his skills are rusty.

His hands tremble in anticipation as he opens the text thread.

9:13 a.m. – A repeat of last night's performance can easily be arranged. ;-)

Eldritch feels flush, heat burning a path from his cheeks to his chest as he reads her words, but before he can shoot off a witty retort, another text is coming in.

9:15 a.m. – Hey babe, the café is super slammed right now, so if you don't hear from me for a bit, don't worry. I'm not ignoring you. Just crazy busy. But I'm kissing you the second I see you later.

Eldritch stares down at his phone in disbelief and reads the text again and again. Kelly had called him "babe." No one has ever called him that, ever given him a romantic, pet name before. Then he remembers last night, when she was climbing into her car, she called him "love." *So, this is actually something then. I mean something to her.* Rubbing the back of his neck, he fires off one last text.

9:18 a.m. – no worries. I'll let you get to it. I'll see you later.

He slides his phone into the pocket of his pajama pants, grabs his coffee, and heads into the den. Reality tears through his cocoon of giddy, schoolboy euphoria when the record player comes into view, and Eldritch is reminded of what today is, what today means. It took ten minutes—ten minutes of a text conversation with Kelly—and he allowed himself to forget. He wonders if that's a good thing or a failure on his part as a grieving son. It's the eighth anniversary of his parents' accident, and for ten minutes he'd forgotten to be sad. Eldritch decides that isn't something he wants to unpack at present, so he files it away to be addressed later.

He stoops down to look through the library of records stashed in the Magnavox, searching for a song befitting the day. Bread's "Everything I Own" is the obvious choice, but that song carries with it another memory—a memory Eldritch would rather not replay today—so he settles on "The Best of My Love" by The Eagles.

CALLING ELDRITCH HAYES

The record spins. The needle is dropped. The song begins. Eldritch turns up the volume and, grabbing his mug, walks out of the den and into the living room. Sunlight from the early December morning pours through the windows, painting the room in streaks of gold and white. There isn't a cloud in the sky, and if Eldritch is honest, it bothers him. The sun shouldn't be shining, not today of all days. He wishes it would rain.

There have been eight December nineteenths, and Eldritch can only remember one instance in which the weather reflected his mood. It doesn't seem fair; it doesn't seem right. His parents are gone, and this date is a constant reminder of that. The least the sky can do is cloud over for him—*for them*.

He spends the majority of the day listening to records and watching his parents' favorite movies: *JAWS* for his father and *Dirty Dancing* for his mom. Around 1:30, he grows restless and decides he needs some air. The Grind will be closing in half an hour, and Eldritch figures Kelly may appreciate some help closing up. He dresses, throws on his coat and walks the short block to the coffee shop his girlfriend owns. The term enters his mind unbidden—*girlfriend. Is that what she is? Can I call her that?* Eldritch starts thinking of a casual way to slide that question into conversation at some point in the near future.

Two patrons pass him on their way out, and Eldritch lowers his head, focusing on the floor, only looking up when he hears Kelly's voice.

"Hey, you," she beams, and he is struck again by how happy she is to see him.

"Hey," he says, returning her smile with his own. "I was going a little stir crazy over there. I hope you don't mind me showing up like this."

"Are you kidding? Things always die down after one." She moves from behind the counter and wraps her arms around his neck. "How you doing, all things considered?"

Eldritch slides his arms around her back, "Well, actually—"

"Ms. Kelly?" They're interrupted by a young, female voice, calling from the entrance to the kitchen. Eldritch and Kelly look over to see two of her teenage employees standing in the doorway. "Would it be okay if we took off early? I've already got the kitchen cleaned up, and Chloe took care of the dining area."

Kelly nods, "Yeah, that's fine. I'll take care of the last couple of tables and the deposit. Y'all get out of here."

The two girls sprint through the kitchen and out the back door, giggling as they leave.

"You know they're laughing about us, don't you?" he asks, eyebrow raised as he looks down at the woman in his arms.

"Oh, one hundred percent," she answers, and stands on her tiptoes, bringing her face closer to his, "but I can't find it in me to care."

Eldritch follows her lead, and soon, the space between them disappears.

He's waiting in the parking lot when his uncle flips off the store lights and locks the front door for the evening.

Calvin jumps when he first spots his nephew and lets out a yelp of surprise. "You know, you could have walked inside."

"And risk you putting me to work? Nuh-uh. It's my day off."

Calvin shakes his head, pulling his nephew into a tight embrace.

"You alright?" Calvin asks. "I know today sucks."

Eldritch pats his uncle on the back. "I'm okay. Got a little extra help to get me through it now."

Calvin gives him the side-eye, "You mean—?"

"Yep."

"Attaboy." And there it is again, that eerie likeness Calvin has to Gene, creeping into the smallest of moments when Eldritch least expects it.

Sometimes Eldritch forgets he wasn't the only one affected by the accident that night. He lost his mother and father, but Calvin lost a brother. As an only child, Eldritch has no idea what that brand of heartache feels like. Even though they were several years apart in age, Calvin and Gene were very close. Eight years ago today, Calvin's world changed just as much as Eldritch's did—maybe not in the same way, but he knows Calvin also carries a gaping hole within him that nothing can ever fill.

"You ready?" Calvin asks, tone light and conversational, as though they're about to stroll up the street for a cup of coffee.

"Yessir."

They set off on a path Eldritch knows well. He made this journey just a few nights before, after Kelly went home last Friday. The subject of his Friday night ritual has never come up, and although he isn't necessarily keeping it a secret, Eldritch isn't prepared to discuss it with anyone. The last thing he wants is for Uncle Cal to find out and tell him his grief has turned to obsession; or worse, for Kelly to find out, realize he's crazy, and stop coming around. Part of him knows neither would react that way, but he can't be too careful. He has few relationships left, and he doesn't want to lose the handful of people he loves.

Loves?

"So, what you been doing with your time off?" His uncle's question cuts the thought short.

"Nothing much, really," Eldritch shrugs, "mostly just hanging around the house with Kelly."

"Are y'all officially a thing now?"

"I'm not sure," he admits, "I think so, but I don't want to assume anything."

"What all have y'all been doing exactly?" There's no mistaking the suggestive edge to Calvin's voice.

"Oh, come on, Uncle Cal! Really?" Eldritch feels his cheeks flush at his uncle's insinuation.

"You said you hadn't left the house!" Calvin shouts in defense of himself.

"You dirty, old man."

"Hey now!"

"We just hang out. We cook dinner, we watch TV, we talk. That's it. I swear. I mean, we've kissed…a few times. Earlier today, actually." Eldritch grins the insuppressible grin of a man well and truly smitten, and Calvin slaps him on the back in approval.

They reach the cemetery, and all is silent save for the crunch of gravel and dead grass beneath their feet. The flashlight Calvin snagged from the store lights the way, cutting through the darkness left in the wake of an early-setting, winter sun.

"Did I ever tell you about the time your daddy and I hopped the fence in Marshall Garvin's pasture, and that bull ran us out of there?" Calvin's voice sounds above the rhythm of their steady footfalls, and Eldritch smiles.

He *has* heard this story—many times—but he doesn't mind hearing it again. He never minds hearing it again. He says nothing, and Calvin launches into the tale, like he does every

December nineteenth. He tells of how he stalked further into the pasture even after Gene had spotted the bull and yelled at him to run back to the fence.

"I wouldn't listen, of course, and your daddy was so mad. He couldn't have been more than eighteen. I was a stubborn little seven-year-old, showing him I was just as big as he was." Calvin is laughing, but all Eldritch hears is a sadness that refuses to be concealed. "Then that old bull—Coach, that was his name—ol' Coach came charging after us. Your dad ran and scooped me up and threw me over that fence. He hopped over just in time. Ol' Coach was inches away from goring him. His hand got all ripped up on the barbed wire though. Mama and Daddy were so mad…" his voice falters, and Eldritch sees the pain in his eyes.

"He was always watching out for me. Always. Sometimes I felt kind of bad for him. Older brother, built in babysitter, you know? But he never complained. Said he liked having me around. I'm just glad Mama and Daddy went on before he did. They couldn't have handled it. Louise's grandma either."

They go on like that for a while, exchanging stories, reliving memories of Gene and Louise. Eldritch tells his uncle about the time he came home drunk in high school, which he's recounted many times before. Calvin gets to talking about when Gene and Louise first met, and how vividly he remembers their wedding day.

"Your daddy was so nervous. He wasn't even twenty years old yet, but he loved your mama so much. Said he knew it the day he saw her. They only dated six months. This May would have been forty-five years…but at least they had thirty-seven. Thirty-seven years together. I can't even imagine what that's like. Amy and I only got twelve under our belts."

"Lightning in a bottle," Eldritch muses. "That's what it was. Not everyone gets it, but they had it."

Another hour passes before Calvin rubs his hands together and clears his throat, "I ain't going to lie, I'm freezing out here. You hungry? Amy's cooking spaghetti tonight if you want to come over."

"No, I'm good. Thank you, though. I think I'll stay a little longer."

Eldritch knows his uncle understands—understands that Eldritch wants some time alone with them.

Calvin pulls him into a fierce hug. "They loved you so much, you know that, right?"

"Yessir. I do," Eldritch breathes into his uncle's shoulder.

"And I love you too."

"I know, Uncle Cal," he says, pulling back from the hug. "I love you."

Calvin claps a hand on Eldritch's shoulder—like he always does—gives it a squeeze for good measure, and disappears into the darkness. Only when he knows his uncle is no longer within earshot, does Eldritch begin to speak.

"Hey. I know I was just here a few nights ago, but you know…with today being what it is and all…"

He won't say it. There's something about saying the word out loud that harbors a finality he cannot escape. He can visit their graves, hunt for signs of their spirits, but he cannot—he *will* not—bring himself to say, "Today is the day you died."

"Oh, so you know how I told you Kelly and I had started hanging out? Well, I think we're an item now. Thought that bit of news would make you happy. And yes, Dad, we have kissed."

He pauses, hoping against hope for any sign that they can hear him—the rustle of leaves, a phantom draft of wind—but nothing happens. The air is as still and silent as the graves at his feet.

"It's been eight years, and I just miss you both so much. I keep looking. I know I always say that, but it's true." Eldritch knows he'll never receive a response from the headstones, but having something physical in front him always makes it easier to speak—easier than casting his words up to the wind and hoping they're carried off to wherever they need to go.

The crash site is just as quiet; but still he waits, humming the melody of Bread's "It Don't Matter to Me"—a favorite of his dad's—as it pops into his mind. After another hour ticks by with nothing on his radar but the passing traffic, and Eldritch decides to call it a night.

It's just shy of ten o'clock when he passes by the Birch-Rainey house. A single light shines inside the living room window, and all is quiet—the sound of power tools has yet to return.

Mark must be taking time off to rest. Good.

He jumps when a voice calls his name from the front porch, and he looks over to find Mark sitting on the front steps, smoking a cigarette. Eager to see how the man's doing after such an ordeal, Eldritch crosses the road and treks up the pathway leading to the front porch.

"Sorry. I didn't mean to scare you. Still jumpy, I see," Mark snorts.

"Oh, you know me. Always on high alert." Eldritch reaches out to shake the man's hand, amazed at how different things are between them now. With the steady undercurrent of evil gone, Mark's just a regular guy.

"You look good," Eldritch says. "How you feeling?"

"Tired, mostly," Mark admits, "but better. Much better."

"I'm glad to hear it."

"Well, you look like you aren't about to throw up or run away, so I guess it's safe to say I'm in the clear here?" he asks with a smile.

"You're in the clear."

"I didn't mean to interrupt your walk or anything. Just wanted to say hey and, you know…thanks, obviously." Mark puts the cigarette out on the step beside him and tosses the butt in a trash bag to his right.

"No, it's fine. I was just…I was at the cemetery."

"Not exactly the first place I'd expect you to be, but okay."

"My parents," Eldritch begins, "It's been eight years since… Today's the anniversary, so I was just…visiting them. They're in there—in the cemetery."

Eldritch hopes his bumbling explanation is enough for Mark, and much to his relief, the other man doesn't pry or ask for details. The two of them haven't had many conversations as it is, and Eldritch only remembers mentioning his parents once before.

"They loved you very much," says Mark.

"Yes. Yes, they did." Eldritch smiles at the allusion to his comment on the stairs that morning.

"I lost my dad too. I was sixteen."

"I'm so sorry." Eldritch doesn't know what else to say. He's curious, but he knows from experience how unwelcome certain queries can be.

"He was a pilot. Died in a plane crash," Mark says, answering the unspoken question hanging between them.

"That's terrible!"

"He was the only casualty. It was a little puddle jumper. He got reckless. No one else was killed."

"I meant for you," Eldritch clarifies.

Mark shrugs, "It is what it is. He wasn't all that great. Didn't really have the same relationship with him I suspect you had with your dad."

"What about your mom?"

"She's around, over at an assisted living facility in Lexington. I check on her every week."

"You an only child?" asks Eldritch, intrigued about the life of the man with whom he feels so intertwined.

"Nope." It's short, clipped, and Mark offers no further information on the subject. Eldritch takes it as a sign to move on.

They chat a little while longer and exchange phone numbers so they can catch up sometime. Eldritch is rather pleased with himself on the way home—he's never had this many contacts in his phone before. *Watch out, Eldritch, you might be well on your way to having some semblance of a normal life*, he thinks as he pushes open the front door and steps inside.

He's shedding his jacket and kicking the door shut when he feels it: *something is wrong*. Eldritch freezes, one arm still trapped in the sleeve of his jacket. His heart begins to pound, his breaths become quick and shallow, and his stomach churns as he's hit with a wall of sinister energy. Understanding dawns on him, sending a spike of fear up his spine to settle in the forefront of his mind.

The few lamps he turned on earlier cast shadows across the house. Eldritch tosses his jacket on the couch and crosses the living room as quietly as he can. His eyes dart back and forth, combing every square inch of the house he can see: the living room, the sitting room, the dining room. When he enters the hall and approaches the doorway to the back den, he sees it. One of the shadows moves. It walks, like a man, upright on two legs, from one side of the den to the other. The scent of rotting flesh—the stench of sulfur and death—trail in its wake, and Eldritch doubles over. The urge to vomit is strong, but he fights against it, swallowing the excess saliva as it fills his mouth.

It's back, and it's in my house.

Eldritch stands to his full height in the hallway, waits, and listens. The frantic beating of his own heart is all he hears until the sound of something being shuffled around pricks his ears, followed by a series of clicks; then, silence. Eldritch closes his eyes—*it's now or never*—opens them, and with a deep breath, charges into the back den, ready to face the spirit...but the room is empty. There is no shadowy figure, no distorted shape of a man walking around. Eldritch blinks and scans his surroundings but finds he is very much alone. He turns to investigate the kitchen, but before he can leave the den, the unmistakable sound of The Hollies comes blaring out of the old Magnavox at full volume.

He spins around with a scream, clutching his chest as his heartrate spikes again. His body locks up at the sudden shock of sound, and Eldritch must fight against instinct and his own nervous system to gain control of his legs and inch toward the record player. *The Hollies Greatest Hits* is spinning on the turntable, where The Eagles sat earlier that evening. Eldritch is bewildered and disturbed by this turn of events, but as he reaches to shut the record player off, it dawns on him exactly *what* song is playing.

"Just One Look."

The lyrics wrap around him like a snake, stealing the air from his lungs, holding him captive in the coils of unadulterated terror. In his mind, they tighten, and he is transported to the back of the old church. His six-year-old self is watching as Amaymon spins Charlie Haskell's head around, and the words spill from his mouth—the words Eldritch has dreamt about for years—the threat, the promise of some unknown malice that was to come.

"Just. One. Look. He will find you. Just one look, and he will know. He is coming for you, Eldritch Hayes!"

He's here.

Eldritch slams the lid of the Magnavox, killing the music, but it plays on in his mind despite his efforts. The fear coursing through him is unlike any he's ever felt before. Facing demons, calling them by name, watching as they use someone else as their vessel, that was all doable. Eldritch has faced such things many times; but having one enter his home, having one actively stalk him, is unprecedented.

He can feel it, but he can't see it, not from where he stands now. But the chills running up and down his spine, the gooseflesh breaking out on his arms and neck, the nausea twisting deep in his core, all tell him it's here, and it's close.

Eldritch knows this isn't something he can face on his own. This entity has it out for him. It told him so before being expelled from Mark.

"Eldritch Hayes. The boy who sees all. I know your name. I have whispered to you."

It knows him, it has called to him.

"Do you remember standing outside my house?"

"No. I don't even know where you live."

But *it* did.

Eldritch remembers holding Mark's hand and telling him it was almost over, that it would end then and there, in that room.

"Careful what you wish for, Eldritch Hayes!"

Eldritch reaches into his pocket and grabs his cell phone. He knows he needs to call someone—Kelly or Pastor Mike—

and get them over here to help with this. He presses the side button to unlock it, but nothing happens. The screen does not light up, the fingerprint recognition does not appear. He pushes every button he can think of, but the screen remains black. The phone is dead.

Impossible.

He made a point to charge it before meeting up with Uncle Cal, and it was working just moments ago with Mark, yet the battery is drained.

He flees the den, knowing he has to make it to the front door. His cell phone is his only means of communication with the outside world, the only working phone in the house. With it out of commission, he'll have to get help the old-fashioned way. He makes it to the hall when he hears a noise behind him. He stops and turns around; stops and waits. He can't see much, just the stretch of room visible through the doorway, where the sofa rests against the wall. Another sound follows, a sound he recognizes: the opening of the Magnavox lid; then, nothing—no noise, no movement. Just as Eldritch begins to wonder if he imagined it, The Hollies vinyl goes flying across the den and slams into the wall opposite the record player; thrown with such force that it becomes lodged into the drywall and stays there.

Eldritch backs away down the length of the hallway, afraid to turn his back on the entity. It's already shown him it can manipulate and move things on its own, no physical host body required. This thing is even stronger than he realized, and despite his best efforts, he still can't identify it. His mind is racing, his heart is pounding; he's in over his head.

I gotta get out of here.

When he reaches the living room, he still doesn't have a visual on the spirit but decides now is his chance to make a break for the front door. He snatches his coat off the back of the couch and turns, racing toward the front of the house. His hand grasps the handle, he pulls the front door open…but stops as an unexpected sound reaches his ears—a sound he hasn't heard in over a decade.

The phone is ringing.

Not his cellphone.

The landline.

This should not be happening. How…?

Against his better judgement, Eldritch turns from the door, drawn to the sound of the disconnected phone. As he approaches its spot on the kitchen wall, he catches the shadow in his periphery. It leaves the den and moves toward the stairwell, as if trying to skirt by, just out of Eldritch's field of vision. Part of him wants to keep his eye on it, to track its movements, but the phone is still ringing, and Eldritch is compelled to answer.

Eldritch lifts the receiver from the wall mount and brings it to his ear. "Hello?"

There is no answer, only the crackling of static.

"Hello?" he repeats, louder this time.

There is still no answer.

"Who is this?" he demands.

But silence is the only answer he receives, and he slams the phone down on the hook.

As he turns to walk away, it rings again. Eldritch hesitates, but after the third ring, he gives in and picks it up. He waits, listening to the static on the other end before speaking.

"…hello?" His voice a whisper, part of him afraid of who—or *what*—will answer back.

The static gets louder, the popping and crackling reaching a crescendo in his ear; then it dies, and another sound breaks through: the sound of two voices speaking. He can't make out the words at first, but they grow louder; and before long, the voices are crystal clear, cutting through the static of the dead landline.

"Daggumit! I swear, no one around here knows how to drive!"

Eldritch can't believe what he's hearing. The words, so familiar; the voice, unmistakable. "…Dad?"

His father does not respond, but another voice filters through the receiver.

"Gene, watch that guy, he's going to try to jump over in front of you. Look at him! Didn't even use a signal."

He knows it's them. He would recognize their voices anywhere. "Mama?! Dad?!" He shouts into the phone; he *has* to get their attention.

"Oh, yeah—hey son," his father speaks. "Sorry, just a bunch of idiots on the road today."

"Everything okay, Eldritch?" Louise chimes in and, oh, how Eldritch has missed that sound. He breath catches in his throat, and he chokes back a sob. They've been gone eight years, eight years to the day. He has been patient and diligent in his search for them, and here they are, calling him on the phone, voices piercing the veil between this world and the next. He has never been happier in his life.

"I'm fine. I'm fine," he tells them, laughing through tears of joy. He waits for a response, but the static has overtaken the voices. "Mama! Mama, can you hear me? Dad?!" He begins to panic, shouting into the receiver, begging them to answer, but the static stops and the line goes dead. Eldritch clicks the switch hook several times, trying to make something happen, but all is silent on the other end.

Eldritch slams the receiver down, emboldened by his anger and the brief contact with his parents.

"You can't be here," he snarls, addressing the spirit he knows is lurking nearby. "I know you can hear me. I want you out of here!" The rage boiling beneath his skin spurs him on, and he shouts a final, "Get out of my house!"

The back door slams, and Eldritch feels the fear and anxiety drain from his body. Out of curiosity, he reaches for his cellphone and hits the button on the side. The screen lights up. Battery: 73%.

It's gone.

Eldritch breathes a sigh of relief and walks around the house, turning on every light and locking every door. He can't get the sound of his parents' voices out of his head. *How is it possible? Did they know I was in trouble and call to help?* Convinced that must have been it, he does a quick sweep of the house to make sure the spirit has indeed departed. *They're watching out for me. I'm not alone after all.* He smiles at the thought and, satisfied that the house is clear, turns the lights back off. He hangs his coat up in the closet and starts up the stairs, pulling his cellphone out to call Kelly.

Before he can make it to the top, the landline rings again. Eldritch drops his cell and spins around, and by the second ring, he's made it to the bottom of the stairs. He crosses the house in a flash, snatching the phone off the hook and holding it to his ear.

"Mama? Daddy? Is that you?" He waits for his parents to respond.

When the voice on the other speaks, Eldritch recognizes it immediately, though it belongs to neither of his parents. With unmistakable clarity, *his* voice answers back with a question of its own.

"Do you think it was too easy?"

Eldritch drops the phone and lets it fall to the floor. Those were his words, words he'd spoken to Kelly over a week ago. He sprints up the stairs, locks his bedroom door, and hastens to the bedside table to grab his father's Bible. But yanking open the drawer, he is astonished to find the Bible is gone.

CHAPTER NINETEEN

His freshman year of college, Eldritch developed a strategy to help make living away from home easier. He left his dorm for only two reasons: to attend class and to grocery shop when his mini fridge was bare. During lectures, he kept his head down and concentrated on his notes, making a point to keep his eyes from observing anyone too closely and his supernatural sense in check. His strategy proved successful for the majority of his first semester. There had been no demonic activity, and the occasional ghosts he'd spotted hadn't bothered him. Charleston was notoriously haunted; but so far, Eldritch's fear of enduring a barrage of disturbing encounters had proved unwarranted.

On a whim, he signed up for Psych 101, and found himself captivated. Neuroscience, nature versus nurture, perception, personality, and studies in abnormal behavior had him poring over his textbook and checking out additional materials from the library. Eldritch excelled in the class—so much so that the teaching assistant chose him to lead a study group before the midterm. Ten other students were assigned to his group, and they all agreed to meet at the library around 6:30 Friday evening.

Desperate to prove himself—to be seen as normal and capable of handling this assignment—Eldritch slaved over his notes and developed an outline, arriving early to make copies for everyone. His classmates began to trickle in around 6:15, and Eldritch gave them each a quick once-over as they entered, relieved to find there were no unwelcome guests.

About an hour into the session, their initial vigor for studying began to wane. One classmate, Jonathan, tossed his notebook on the table with a sigh.

"This is all well and good," he said, fist coming to rest under his chin, "but I'm ready for some actual in-depth psychology. Where are the personality disorders? The mental illnesses? The psychos who murder their families? Give me something interesting to study. Not just theory and boring foundational stuff."

"Well, it's Psych 101…emphasis on the '101,'" replied Eldritch, fighting to keep his irritation at his classmate's hubris from showing on his face. "I think that's kind of the point of the course."

Someone else chimed in—inspired by Jonathan's rant—a female student. *Lauren? Is that how she introduced herself?*

"No, I totally agree. No one signs up for psychology for the boring stuff. We all want to study the Hannibal Lectors, right?"

Eldritch felt a stab of disappointment as his study group devolved into a series of unrealistic complaints, but he tried his best to salvage it. "Well, you have to walk before you can run—"

Another student joined in, bowling over Eldritch's interjection and taking the conversation in a different direction. "So, I grew up Catholic, right? You guys wouldn't believe the number of mentally ill people the Catholic Church insisted were demon possessed."

That got Eldritch's attention. All thoughts of refocusing the session left his mind and his mouth snapped shut.

"No joke!" someone shouted from the opposite end of the table—*Todd*—and was reminded by half the group to keep it down—this was a library after all.

"Sorry," he said, lowering his voice, "Leave it to the church to keep up this medieval mindset of demons and evil spirits. What's sad is the absolute disregard they all have for science and modern medicine."

Eldritch did not appreciate that comment. He, for one, was perfectly capable of separating mental illness from demonic possession. Granted, he had a leg up on everyone else; but his parents weren't blind to the existence of mental disorders and the notion that not everyone who acted out was under the influence of an evil spirit. He did know, however, there was some truth to Todd's statement. Reverend Holland was a prime example; but making a blanket statement about all Christians and the church as a whole was unfair. As much as he wanted to address this fallacy, Eldritch knew that wasn't an option. His inability to chime in with his own knowledge on the subject was just another reminder that he would always have to keep a part of himself hidden away.

Eldritch chose to tune the conversation out, staring at the clock on the opposite wall as his study session spiraled down the drain. As 7:30 drew near, books and notebooks were slammed shut and stowed away for the night. Several members of the group were planning to attend a party at McConnell Hall and, much to his surprise, an invitation was extended his way.

"Join us, Hayes," Todd insisted, as they brushed shoulders exiting the library.

At first, Eldritch wasn't sure whether the invitation was legitimate or if he was about to be the butt of another cruel joke. Scenes from that night in the Birch-Rainey house sprang to mind; flashes of Ryan, his crew, and their casual cruelty. He remembered waking up the morning after, hungover and ashamed—embarrassed he'd had the audacity to believe they wanted him to join their circle. In his mind, he'd come out of that night with only two things: a perfect kiss from a girl he may never see again and further proof he was indeed a social pariah.

He stood there, unblinking, staring at the group and waiting for someone to cue the laughs, but none came. "You want me to go with you? To the party?"

"Yeah, man. We've been in the same class for half a semester, it's time you actually got to know some of us."

Eldritch looked from one member of the group to the next, and once convinced he wasn't being mocked or set up, he agreed to join them—his new friends.

The party at McConnell Hall was in full swing by the time Eldritch and the group arrived. The hallways were packed with people—all blowing off steam after hours of studying for midterms—and music was blaring from a makeshift sound system. The rumble of the bass was deafening, and the environment was unlike anything he'd ever experienced. Strangers were pushing in on him with every step he took, and Eldritch soon became lost in a sea of unfamiliar faces.

Reminding himself to breathe, he fought to stave off the panic threatening to take hold of him. He searched the crowd for Todd and Jonathan, but it was no use. As his eyes darted back and forth across the room, they landed on a small group of friends talking and drinking near the doorway of a dorm room. A young woman in the group met his gaze, and Eldritch jumped back a step, startled at his discovery. She was filled with a swirl of black—surrounded by it—the darkness swelling within her and seeping beyond the confines of flesh and bone.

Halphas.

The name came to him seconds later. She continued to stare at him, and Eldritch wondered if she was curious as to why he was staring back, or if Halphas was the one in control. With some of the lesser demons, it was hard to tell when they were fully manifested. Whatever Halphas was, it wasn't as strong as some of the other demons Eldritch had encountered and identified, demons like… Amaymon.

Eldritch suppressed a shudder at the memory and resolved he would have none of that tonight. No demons, no spirits, no special ability was going to ruin this party for him.

Eldritch Hayes is going to be a normal college student and have fun for once. He turned his back to the woman—and the demon lurking within—and crashed into Jonathan who sloshed the contents of two plastic cups onto Eldritch's shoes.

"There you are! We thought you ditched us, Hayes! Here," he shouted, shoving one of the cups into Eldritch's hand, "drink up."

"What's in this?" Eldritch asked, straining to be heard over the blaring music as he sniffed the fruity liquid in the cup.

"I don't know, man. Vodka and some kind of juice. Who cares? It'll get the job done, trust me."

Eldritch looked over his shoulder at the possessed student in the hallway. She was no longer watching him, but he could sense the entity within her all the same—lurking and ever-present, like the shadow of Eldritch's ability over his entire life.

"I'm through living like this," he said aloud, earning a confused look from Jonathan, and with a heavy exhale, lifted the cup to his mouth and began to chug.

"Whoa, whoa, easy, Hayes. Derrick makes 'em strong," Jonathan cautioned, but his words fell on deaf ears.

Eldritch drained the cup in seconds and asked for another.

"Why don't we find you a nice place to sit down, dude? I'll grab you another when I'm sure you won't fall over," said Jonathan, guiding Eldritch to a spot the rest of the psychology group had secured in the common area. "Have you ever even drank before?"

"Absolutely!" Eldritch shouted, "I had a bunch of beers one night in April. Like…a bunch of them. *And* something from a bottle." Eldritch could already feel his lips loosening, his guard dropping. He felt free again—free and relaxed—like he had that night in the closet with Kelly. He'd had several drinks that night, but just *one* of these concoctions, created by some unknown Derrick in the room, was already doing the trick. *Morning after, be damned*, he thought, and admonished himself for the language in a knee jerk reaction.

Jonathan laughed at his admission, "Wow. One whole night of beer *and* something from a bottle. That's pretty impressive," and motioned for Eldritch to take a seat on the couch their group had claimed. It was a tight squeeze, with multiple students crowding onto the sofa, and Eldritch looked to his left to see whose personal space he'd just invaded. It was another classmate, a brunette named Michelle. She hadn't been part of their study session earlier that evening, but Eldritch remembered her from class. She participated a lot, asked questions, got involved in discussions.

"So, *you're* Eldritch Hayes," she said with a sly smile.

Eldritch nodded, "Yep. And you're Michelle."

She arched an eyebrow. "How—?"

"Professor Ritchie calls on you a lot in class," he explained.

"Gotcha."

"You weren't in our study group."

Michelle giggled and took a sip of her drink. "Yeah, well, I didn't know who Eldritch Hayes was and didn't want to be stuck in a study group lead by some boring dude I'd never laid eyes on."

"That's fair."

"But now that I can put a face to the name, I'm sorry I missed it."

Is she...is she flirting with me?

He felt another plastic cup being pushed into his hand and didn't even pause to see who'd provided it before taking a sip.

"So, you've noticed my face then," he quipped, leaning back against the couch.

"I have," she admitted, angling herself toward him.

"And?"

"You have a nice smile."

The buzz from the alcohol warmed his body, putting him at ease, and he was surprised at how easily the conversation with Michelle flowed. He took another swig from his plastic cup and the room began to spin, every detail melding into one giant blur. Placing the cup on the table beside the couch, he blinked a few times in an attempt to reorient himself. Michelle must have noticed and patted him on the shoulder.

"Hey, pace yourself. No need to down it all at once," she smiled, and any embarrassment Eldritch felt at her words evaporated.

"Sorry. I'm not really a drinker," he admitted.

"Don't worry. Your secret's safe with me." She shot him an over-exaggerated wink as she combed her fingers through her long, dark hair and pulled it over one shoulder.

"Looks like y'all could use a refill!" called a voice behind the couch.

Eldritch turned and saw Todd smirking at them with more drinks in hand. He handed one to both Eldritch and Michelle, and Eldritch realized he hadn't finished his second one—not completely. He went to tell Todd as such, but the boy had disappeared. Eldritch scanned the room for him, but when he did, his eyes fell on the young woman from the hallway. She had moved out into the common area and was staring straight at Eldritch—the shadow creeping around her edges, blurring the lines between Eldritch's reality and that of everyone else at this party. Turning back around in his seat, he grabbed his half empty cup from the table next to him, drained the rest of it in one go, and started in on the drink he was just handed.

By the end of the night, Eldritch was unable to walk on his own, and Jonathan and Todd were kind enough to help him back to his dorm room—stopping a few times so Eldritch could vomit into the bushes. They deposited him in his room, having the decency to place a trashcan beside his bed should he need to throw up again during the night.

When morning came, Eldritch didn't remember much about the party following his third drink. His head was splitting, and his mouth felt fuzzy and dry. He looked down at the trash can at his bedside and saw the contents were covered in vomit. The sight made him sick again, and he ran to the communal bathroom down the hall, purging the remainder of last night's festivities into the first open toilet he could find.

He sat, back pressed against the stall wall, and contemplated the events of the night before. He remembered Michelle, how nice she had been, how much he had enjoyed talking to her. He remembered downing drinks like there was no tomorrow. But there was something else, some important detail he was forgetting. Rising from his seat on the floor, he exited the stall and stumbled over to the sink to wash his face and rinse out his mouth. Thoughts raced through his mind as he fought to remember all that had transpired before he blacked out. Then, as he stared at the dark circles under his eyes, it came to him.

The girl. The demon. Halphas.

He'd forgotten. For a few short hours, he'd forgotten the demon entirely; and even as the image of came back to him, it was fuzzy and fractured. The alcohol had dulled his sixth sense and reduced the demon to a fragmented impression of a memory. Sure, he felt like absolute garbage now, but the lack of awareness—the lack of fear—was something to consider. He shuffled back to his dorm and grabbed his toothbrush, toothpaste, and shower gel. After brushing his teeth and ridding his mouth of the stale, acrid taste of vomit and booze, he let the warm spray of the shower wash away the aftermath of the party. As he dressed for the day, the idea that he may have found a way to handle his sensitivity to spirits refused to leave his mind.

"What's wrong, darlin'?" Gran-Gran's voice was hoarse and weak as she called to Eldritch, pulling him from his thoughts.

"Oh, nothing," he sighed with a shrug and a half-hearted smile.

She shook her head. *She always knows when I'm lying.* Eldritch looked over at the woman who had been a sort of sage and spiritual guide for much of his life and hardly recognized her. It made Eldritch ache, a deep sadness taking root at the knowledge that she wasn't long for this world.

For years, Eldritch had thought Gran-Gran incapable of aging—that she would outlive them all. The last few years, however, saw an end to that line of thought. She was nearing ninety now, and her body could no longer do what her mind and spirit wanted it to. She couldn't stand without the help of a walker, and she had a live-in caretaker named Lindy, a kindhearted Black lady who had worked as a nurse for over forty years. Eldritch felt bad for not visiting more. He was closer to her than he was to his own grandmother—a grandmother he never saw given her strained relationship with Louise.

"You can't fool me, honey," she said in that sugary-sweet tone of hers, "you forget: Gran-Gran knows all."

Eldritch lowered his head and nodded. *She's right. She's always right.*

Something moved on the other side of the room, and cutting his eyes in that direction, Eldritch wasn't surprised to see Papa Reuben, rocking back and forth.

"You see him, don't you?" Gran-Gran asked. "Reuben Sholly. You see him."

"Yes, ma'am," he admitted, turning to face her.

"He built this house, you know. Centuries ago. Do you know who he was?"

Eldritch shook his head.

"He was my husband's great-great-grandfather. You were named after my husband, but you know that. It's a shame you two never got to meet."

"Mama's told me stories," Eldritch replied, "what she could remember. She said he died when she was very little."

"He did, he did. He was only fifty-four. You were named after my Eldritch—your great-grandfather—and he was named after *his* great-grandfather."

"Another Eldritch?"

"Another Eldritch. The veil, you see…" Gran-Gran nodded, her eyes glazing over as her voice dropped to a low mumble.

Eldritch wasn't sure why she'd brought up the veil; probably because he was seeing ghosts in her living room again, but he worried time was beginning to take the same toll on her mind as it had her body.

"Gran-Gran?"

"Yes?" she asked, snapping out of whatever daze she had falling into. "Oh, yes! Another Eldritch; and *that* Eldritch's father was Reuben Sholly, who built this house. He died in that chair, you know. Eighty-two years old."

Eldritch looked in Papa Reuben's direction, but the spirit had vanished, and the chair was still.

Gran-Gran fell silent and turned over into a more comfortable position on her hospice bed; eyes closing and breath evening out. Eldritch was afraid he'd tired her out and, deciding it best to get going, planted a kiss on her forehead and whispered a quick, "I love you," into her hair.

Lindy was seated at the desk in his great-grandfather's study, working on a crossword puzzle, when Eldritch found her.

"Ms. Lindy, she's asleep now. I'm just going to head out," he said, keeping his voice down so as not to startle her.

"Thank you, sweetie," she smiled, putting her puzzle book down and rising from her seat. "I'll just go check on her real quick. I'm glad you came by. I know seeing you did her a world of good." She squeezed his arm as she passed by and headed down the hall.

Eldritch stood alone and let his eyes drift across the expanse of the room. His great-grandfather's study was a window to the past, a glimpse into a bygone era, untouched by the marching of time. Gran-Gran had refused to change it after he died, keeping it as a shrine to her late husband's memory. This was where he'd spent most of his time, according to Eldritch's mother—his refuge, his sanctuary.

A glass cabinet to the right of the desk caught his eye, and Eldritch approached it, curious as to what lay inside. It was full of bottles: whisky, gin, and other liquors Eldritch wasn't familiar with. He pulled on the handle of the glass door, and it opened with ease. After a quick glance over his shoulder to make sure Lindy hadn't returned, Eldritch grabbed one of the bottles and stashed it away inside his coat. Then, shutting the cabinet door, he fled the house and sped away in the new Toyota Celica his parents had bought him for graduation.

Back on campus, Eldritch made a pit stop to grab his mail, face lighting up when he saw the package from home. He could hear the phone ringing as he approached the door to his room and fumbled with the key, managing to make it inside before the answering machine clicked on.

"Hello?" he answered in a rush.

"Hey, baby boy!"

Relief washed over him at the sound of his mother's voice. "Hey, Mama."

"I've been calling all day. I was getting worried."

"Oh, my bad. I was visiting Gran-Gran."

"How is she doing? Your daddy and I have to get down there and visit her soon—maybe next weekend. Does she look bad?"

"A little," Eldritch admitted, "she looks tired and skinny, and they've got her in one of those hospital beds in the living room."

He could hear the sadness in her sigh—could hear the tears threatening to fall.

"But she was in good spirits. Still has her wits about her," he assured his mother. "We talked for a long time."

"Well, we'll be down there soon. Then we can all go visit her together. Did you get the care package I sent you?"

"Yeah, I just picked it up. I haven't opened it yet."

"It's just a little something to remind you of home. You been doing okay?"

"Yes ma'am, I'm good. Made some friends," he added, for her benefit. Eldritch wasn't sure these new acquaintances counted as friends, but he was okay with bending the truth a little for her.

"That's great, baby! I knew this was going to be good for you!"

She updated him on recent happenings back home in Sommerset, and he told her about his classes and new "friends," leaving out the bit where he'd drunk himself unconscious and thrown up in the bushes.

They said their goodbyes, but Eldritch didn't want to hang up, longing for home with a desperation he couldn't put into worlds. He missed his parents and his own bed. One night of partying was a poor substitute for what he really wanted. Even after hearing the click of the other line and the dial tone that followed, he stood, unmoving, hand still clutching the receiver. Seconds passed—maybe minutes, maybe hours—before he gave in and hung up.

Turning his attention to the care package he'd tossed on his bed, Eldritch had the packing tape off in seconds, revealing a pack of Slim Jims, some saltine crackers, Big Red chewing gum, Gushers, Hershey's kisses—on which his mother had placed a sticky note that said "since I can't be there to give you any in person, here are a bunch of kisses from Mama"—and assorted school supplies; but when he came to the bottom of the box, he fought back a sob, more homesick than ever before.

Nestled beneath the snacks and school supplies, were three CDs: *Carpenters The Singles: 1969-1973*, *The Eagles: Their Greatest Hits*, and *The Best of Bread*. His mother had mailed him a piece of home. Eldritch grabbed the Carpenters CD, ripped off the plastic, slid the disc into his boom box, and clicked through until he came to track twelve. As the piano intro of "(They Long to Be) Close to You" filled his tiny dorm room, Eldritch sank to the floor and began to weep. He wept for Gran-Gran, he wept for home.

I don't want to be here anymore. I don't want to deal with this. I just want to forget this whole college thing ever happened.

I just want to forget…

Eldritch remembered the bottle he'd filched from great-grandfather Eldritch's liquor cabinet. He pulled it from his coat pocket and inspected the label and glass. The label was faded—yellowed with age—and the right corner had come unglued from the bottle and was folding over half of the name. He smoothed it back with his fingers and read the words, "Jim Beam Kentucky Straight Bourbon Whiskey." It was old—older than him, maybe older than his mother—but it had never been opened. Eldritch made quick work of the cap and, without hesitation, took his first drink of whiskey.

It burned his throat, and the intensity took his breath, choking him, and sending him into a coughing fit. Once he recovered, he tried again, and this time he was prepared; and the time after that, and the time after that. Eldritch remained there for the rest of the night, slumped against the side of his bed, singing along with Karen Carpenter as he nursed his great-grandfather's bottle of Jim Beam.

CHAPTER TWENTY

The missing Bible is a paradox, and Eldritch spends the majority of the next day scouring the house for it. His search begins in the back den, where he checks every shelf in the glass-front bookcase. The bookcase appears untouched, with every title in its right place. Although he finds two Bibles there—his mother's and the first Bible ever gifted to him as a small child—his father's is not among them.

The end tables and their drawers are next; but still, he comes up empty-handed. He goes as far as to look under the couch and behind the record player. When that proves fruitless, he moves to the living room, then to the sitting room, then to the kitchen, scouring every possible surface and nook before taking the search upstairs. Every bedroom is left ransacked in his wake, but the Bible is nowhere to be found.

Finding himself by the bedside table in his room, Eldritch pulls open the drawer once more—just to make sure he isn't losing his mind—and again finds himself staring at nothing. The Bible has vanished. He sits on his bed, trying to put the pieces of this puzzle together in his mind, confounded by the book's sudden and inexplicable disappearance. The buzz of his cellphone interrupts his train of thought, and he fishes it out of his pocket.

> *11:57 a.m. – I have to go to my dad's church after work. They have their Christmas music service and the children's pageant tonight. I got voluntold to help wrangle children and do makeup. Otherwise, I'd be there with you. You wanna come with me?*

The invitation is tempting, but Eldritch isn't ready to set foot in a church again just yet.

> *11:58 a.m. – I'll take a rain check. Someday soon, just not tonight.*

He hopes his honesty doesn't put her off, and he stares at the screen until her reply comes.

> *12:01 p.m. – No worries, love. I get it. I may pop over for a minute or so after work, is that ok? Tomorrow, I have to head to Georgia right after closing up. Big Walsh family Christmas and all that. I won't be back until the 26th. I really want to see you before I go though.*

> *12:02 p.m. – I'll be here.*

The sadness he felt when she first informed him of her Christmas plans a week ago returns, and he tells himself to get a grip. *We've barely been dating for a week—if you can call it that. She's not spending Christmas with you, idiot.*

Wait…Christmas.

The thought strikes like lightning, and he's out of the bedroom in a flash, his hope at finding the missing Bible renewed. *It's possible it got packed up and put away somewhere when we were decorating for Christmas last week. We did move a lot of things around.* Once he's down the stairs and in the living room, he opens the door to the small half bath in the hall. The entrance to the basement has always been the home's most enigmatic feature. Beside the toilet there is a shower curtain. Move the shower curtain aside, and you find yourself at the top of the stairs that lead to the depths of the house. The stairs are steep and treacherous, and Eldritch is very careful as he descends.

He pulls the chain to the lone lightbulb as he hits the bottom of the stairs. Last week—when Kelly insisted they make the house more festive—was the first time Eldritch had set foot in the basement in years. It's always had a strong, distinct smell: earthy and damp, like standing water in a rock bed. It doesn't matter what time of year it is; the basement is always cold. Eldritch rubs his hands together to warm them against the chill as he locates the bins he and Kelly deposited down here after decorating.

He searches for over half an hour, pilfering through plastic storage containers, pulling out all the contents, leaving no tote unturned; but there is no sign of his father's Bible. He huffs in frustrated confusion and begins repacking the bins, replacing the lids as he goes, when his ears pick up a sound coming from above. Eldritch pauses and angles his head toward the ceiling of the basement. For a while, nothing follows, but then he hears it again: soft dings, musical notes ringing out from the floor above.

The piano.

Eldritch makes for the stairs weaving between the bins in his path. With light, gentle steps, he climbs—up, up, slowly up—making as little noise as possible. When he reaches the top, and steps into the bathroom, he feels it: the chills, the anxiety, the weight of evil pressing in on him.

Oh great.

The floorboards in the living room creak under the weight of him as Eldritch enters the living room. The piano stops, and Eldritch follows suit, unsure why he's frozen in place. It knows he's there, and it's not like the element of surprise would do him any good; yet still he stands and waits. Waits for what, he isn't sure; for the demon to make a move, for it to do something—*anything*—to put an end to this impasse.

His wish is granted as the piano playing resumes; but this time, it's a series of notes—a melody all too familiar. Eldritch doesn't know what the entity thinks it's doing playing *that* particular song on his mother's piano, but he doesn't appreciate it one bit. The playing stops again, and Eldritch takes another step in the direction of the piano. It's just outside his field of vision, but he hears with perfect clarity as the intro to "Close to You" starts up again. Eldritch feels the anger welling up within him, feels this blood begin to boil as the demonic spirit continues to bang out the beginning of the song that Eldritch will forever associate with his mother. It's trying to taint the song, pervert it, defile it, and Eldritch can't have that. He storms across the living room and into the sitting room where the piano sits, lid open, bench pulled out. He slams the lid down over the keys and shoves the bench back where it belongs.

"I thought I told you to leave," he addresses the entity. "You are not welcome here." He stresses each word with all the authority he can marshal.

A noise from behind draws his attention—the scraping of wood against wood, something heavy being moved in the dining room. He turns to face the dining room head-on and stumbles backward at the sight, a weight settling in his stomach. Three of the four dining chairs are turned upside down, feet sticking straight up in the air, seat cushions resting on the tabletop. One chair remains on the floor, pulled out and waiting for him—beckoning him to take a seat.

Eldritch walks around the table, keeping to the edges of the room, eyeing the handiwork of the dark spirit. The stench of rotting meat assaults his senses as a slight movement across the table catches his eye. Looking up, he can make out the shape of the shadow—the demon—lurking in the corner of the room. Its presence reaches out to him, causing the nausea to return and his fight or flight reflex to kick in; yet, Eldritch stands his ground.

His eyes drift to the lone chair still in its rightful place at the end of the table, but something *out* of place—or rather, there is something *in* a place it shouldn't be. On the table in front of the chair, sits a glass and a bottle. The glass is short—one of the tumblers he keeps at the back of the highest kitchen cabinet; one of the tumblers he no longer has any use for. His eyes shift to the bottle, and he takes note of the label. It's a faded tan, aged and worn. The label reads "Jim Beam Kentucky Straight Bourbon Whiskey," but the logo and lettering aren't just outdated and weathered—they're vintage, dating back to the '50s or '60s, and the corner of the label has peeled away from the glass, folding over the "Beam."

Eldritch knows this bottle—not just the brand—he knows this *exact* bottle. This is the same bottle he stole from Gran-Gran's house that day—Eldritch Sholly's Jim Beam—and the revelation makes him tremble. Before his eyes, the bottle moves, lifts off the table, and pours a few fingers of whiskey into the glass; then the chair is shifting, pulling itself further away from the table—inviting Eldritch to sit, take a load off, *have a drink*. He watches the shadow drift out of the dining room and disappear from sight, leaving him to his own devices.

Eldritch can't tear his eyes away from the glass of whiskey before him. How easy it would be—how simple—to reach out and grab it. He knows how it would taste, remembers the burn, and the smoothness—like honey—as it drains down his throat. He knows what would follow if he drank enough: the looseness, the evaporation of his fears and inhibitions. He's been sober for *so long*—hasn't touched a drop of the stuff in *so long*—it wouldn't take much. A few fingers and he'd feel free as a bird…

Maybe if I…
No. Not today.

Eldritch purges the thought from his mind, grabs the tumbler of whiskey and takes it straight into the kitchen, dumping the contents into the sink. He watches the amber liquid slide toward the center and trickle down the drain. His hand shakes at his side, and the part of his brain he's learned to silence over the years whispers to him, *what a waste.*

The demon has made this personal, that much is clear to Eldritch. It knows where to hit him, what buttons to push. The significance of the alcohol, the vintage bottle, the song on the piano, are not lost on Eldritch; with a shudder, he is forced to recognize the specter knows his very mind: what dark secrets lurk there, what fears hide in the shadows. Eldritch knows he isn't dealing with some run-of-the-mill demon. This entity is something else entirely. *But what? Tell me your name!*

Turning from the sink, he walks back over to the doorway leading to the dining room and is surprised by what he finds:

nothing. The chairs are back to normal—all four feet on the ground, pushed in, under the table in their designated spots; but more importantly, the bottle of whiskey has vanished.

He walks back over to the sink and picks up the tumbler. Bringing it to his nose, he sniffs once, twice, and pulls it away as his mouth begins to water. It still smells of Jim Beam. He hadn't imagined it. Returning to the dining room, he inspects the area further, looks for any sign of the whiskey bottle, but like the Bible from his bedside table, it is nowhere to be found.

As he stands there, mystified and disturbed by the blatant attack on his sobriety, the intro to "Close to You" rings out again, only this time it's blaring from the record player.

"Are you kidding me?" He grits out under his breath and makes a beeline for the Magnavox. He shuts it off and, closing the lid, shouts in voice full of indignation, "You don't get to touch this anymore, you hear me?! No more!!!"

The nativity set on the mantel begins to shift and shake, and Eldritch catches sight of it just in time to dodge the figure of baby Jesus as it flies across the room and crashes into the wall. Deciding he's had enough, he flees the den with every intention of heading for the front door, but as soon as he passes the kitchen, the landline rings.

Eldritch stops in the hallway, jaw clenched, and nostrils flared. The phone rings again and again, the sound reducing the whirlwind in his mind to one single thought: his parents. It could be them on the other end of the call. Turning on his heel, Eldritch sprints into the kitchen and grabs the phone from the hook.

"Hello?!" he cries into the receiver.

There is no immediate answer, just the familiar crackle of static like before; but the longer he waits, the more he can make out a voice struggling to be heard through the noise.

"Eldritch!" his mother's voice is distraught, frantic in the way she yells his name.

"Mama?!" he shouts back.

"Eldritch!"

He tries again, voice even louder this time, "Mama! Mama, I'm here! Can you hear me?"

"Eldritch! Honey, look at me!" she begs, and Eldritch can tell she's crying now.

Look at you? How—?

"Mama, I can't see you, but I can hear you!"

"Baby, what happened?!"

Finally!

"Are you okay?!" his mother continues.

"Yes, yes, I'm okay!" He's the one crying now. *She knows something's wrong. Even from the other side, she knows something is messing with me.* "It's in the house, Mama. I don't know why it's after me like this."

"Don't scare me like that!"

"I'm not trying to scare you, Mama, but I don't really know what to do here. I told it to leave, and I thought it did, but now it's back. It's the same demon that was in Mark, I know it is."

His mother is here now, even if it's just her voice on the disconnected landline, she's here and she will know what to do. All these years of trying to find his parents has led to this moment, Eldritch is sure of it. But now, the phone is silent. His mother's voice is gone.

"Mama? Mama, are you there?!"

Again, there is nothing. Panic sets in, and Eldritch calls for his mother over and over, but she does not answer. Instead, high-pitched feedback shoots through the phone, and Eldritch jerks the receiver away from his ear. When the feedback dies, and the piercing screech has faded, he brings the receiver back to his ear and listens. Through the hiss of static, another voice comes through—the voice of a young boy.

"Don't you hear him?" the child asks, and what follows is all too familiar and horrible; a cry of terror, agony, and despair, and Eldritch recoils at the sound of the hangman's wail.

He clutches the phone in an iron grip, eyes squeezed shut and teeth clenched. He's so angry, and that anger in conjunction with the oppressive evil of the entity, is beginning to overwhelm him in a way he hasn't the words for. Part of him wants to grip the receiver so tightly that it breaks, but then the calls may stop. If the calls stop, his parents won't be able to reach him; and despite the demon trying to disrupt their attempts at contacting him, his mother and father are still trying to be heard. Resolved not to smash the phone to bits or hammer it into the drywall beside the base mount, he hangs it up.

As he storms into the back den, The Hollies album catches his eye, still lodged in the wall from the night before. In a fury, he grabs it with both hands and pulls until it is wrenched free, bringing with it a spattering of drywall and dust. Eldritch winces at the thought of one of his father's favorite albums being ruined and brings it closer to his face to check for any scratches and signs of damage.

"I told you to leave this alone!" he rails on the entity for having the audacity to touch his father's things." Now, get out of my house! And stay out! I don't want to have to tell you again!" Eldritch is shouting at the top of his lungs; his throat burning by the time he finishes.

The back door opens and shuts—just as it did the night before—and as the echoes of the slamming wood reverberate through the house, the intense feeling of oppression evaporates. Before Eldritch can allow himself a moment to relax, an unexpected knock at the front door has him crying out in surprise. He hurries toward the front of the house and, taking a quick peek out the window, pulls open the door in a hurry.

"Kelly!"

"Hey, what are you up to?" She smiles ear to ear, all perfect teeth and shining eyes. *She's beautiful.*

"Umm...nothing much," he lies. He knows he should tell her about the demon, but he can't bring himself to say the words. *She'll think I'm losing it.* Despite the winter chill, he steps out onto the front porch—without coat or shoes—and pulls the door shut behind him. "What are you doing here? Did you close up early?"

"Yeah," she sighs, "I had to. It was dead anyways. Apparently, there's been a set emergency at the church. There was a leaky pipe somewhere, and all the backdrops are pretty much ruined. Daddy's called in a favor, and I'm about to go over there to help them throw something together."

"Oh." Eldritch understands what this means, and part of him is relieved. *She doesn't need to be anywhere near this until I figure out what's going on. It's for her own safety.*

"I know I said we'd have some time together this afternoon, but they're really in a bind. I have like...five hours to basically create an entire set."

"No, no, I get it. It's totally fine."

"I feel like I'm letting you down."

"Kelly, you could never let me down," he assures her, stepping closer. "You've done more for me in the last week than anyone has in a long time."

She wraps her arms around him and gives him a tight squeeze before standing on her tiptoes and planting a kiss on his lips.

"Oh, I meant to tell you, I'm closing the café for a few days after New Year's, and I want to spend all my time with you," she says, kissing him again.

"*All* your time?"

"*ALL*. My. Time." she repeats.

Eldritch is about to ask exactly what she means by that, but his attempt is thwarted by a sound from inside the house.

Ring.

"Well, I definitely understand you got to go help your church out, so I'll let you get to it," he says in a rush.

Ring.

He sees the confusion on Kelly's face, and he hates rushing her along like this; but the phone is ringing, and he isn't ready to share what that means with anyone just yet. Eldritch pulls away from her and inches toward the door. "I know they're probably freaking out over there with their set all messed up. But I'm sure you're gonna do great and save the day!"

Ring.

"Eldritch, is everything okay? Are you mad at me?"

Ring.

"Of course, I'm not mad at you. You can't help this. I'm just afraid I'm holding you up!"

Ring.

For a second, he's worried she's about to call his bluff—afraid she can hear the phone ringing.

"Okay. But you would tell me if something were wrong, right?" she asks, and Eldritch breathes a sigh of relief.

Ring.

"Absolutely. You'd be the first person I'd tell."

Ring.

He's not certain she's convinced, but she turns to leave all the same. He watches until her car has turned out of his driveway before he slams the door and races through the house to pick up the phone before the ringing stops.

"Hello?!" he yells into the receiver.

He can hear them—his parents—and they're talking in the background like they hadn't heard him answer the phone.

"He saw a demon today, Louise. Inside a man. He saw it and he knew its name," comes the voice of his father.

"Dad?!" he shouts, trying to get his father's attention, to let him know he's listening.

His father continues talking, "He's my little boy, and he's seeing demons."

"Dad, can you hear me?!" he tries again. The static is heavy, distorting the connection on the phone line between their worlds.

"I don't want that for him. I don't want him to see things like that—to see evil like that—and to be scared." Gene is still speaking to Louise, as if oblivious to Eldritch's cries.

Eldritch is hit with a sense of déjà vu; the words are familiar, but he can't quite place them.

"I'm supposed to protect him, but I don't know how to do that anymore. How can I protect him from something I can't even see?"

He knows about the demon and he's trying to protect me. That's all.

"Dad, the demon—!"

The strident feedback returns, and the line goes dead—no voices, no static, no dial tone. Eldritch spends the rest of the day seated in the den, where he has quick and easy access to the kitchen phone should his parents try to reach out again. The phone doesn't ring for the rest of the day, but the demon does not return either.

Eldritch doesn't know if the two are related.

But if they are—if the demon's presence is what prompts my parents to call—maybe I shouldn't be so hasty to send it away.

CHAPTER TWENTY-ONE

Eldritch slammed the door to his room as he stumbled inside. The anger and frustration surging within him refused to be caged any longer, and he grabbed a pillow from his bed, held it up to his face, and screamed at the top of his lungs. The pillow muffled the scream just enough to where he wasn't worried about the sound being reported by a nosy RA or well-meaning neighbor. After giving the overwhelming rage a quick release, he threw the pillow against the wall above his bed and paced the floor of his room—the anger reduced to a low simmer in his veins.

The number of drinks he'd had tonight would have put the guys over on fraternity row to shame, but the shock of what he'd seen in Berry Hall had hit him like a bucket of ice water, sobering him in an instant. Eldritch knew going to that party was a mistake, knew that Berry Hall was one of the main places he needed to stay away from; but Michelle had asked him to go, and he'd wanted to do everything he could to save the budding relationship.

Berry Hall had a reputation as the most haunted place on campus. While the dorm itself was just shy of a decade old, the site on which it was built had a long, disturbing history. Nearly one hundred years ago, it was the location of an orphanage where multiple children had died during the Spanish flu epidemic of 1918. The building itself was accidentally set on fire during that time. Four orphans died in that fire, and there, their spirits had remained. Sometimes the fire alarms would go off with no one having pulled them. At other times, you could hear the sound of children laughing and playing games—at least, that's what campus legend said. So far, Eldritch had done a decent job of avoiding the spiritual hot spots, Berry Hall included.

I'm such an idiot, he thought to himself, walking back and forth across the small living space. *I should have known it was doomed. I can't have anything I want.*

Things with Michelle had started so well. After their initial meeting back in October, it had taken Eldritch a few more months to ask her to dinner, and much to his surprise, she'd jumped at the invitation. Since then, they'd been on a few dates, had seen *Hannibal* and *Monkeybone* together, and one night, Eldritch had made his move and kissed her.

What had started as an innocent peck on the lips, grew deeper, and Eldritch could feel his body warm and his heart race as she clutched his back. Michelle had broken the kiss first, leaving Eldritch breathless and dazed.

"You know, you can come inside if you want," she'd said, biting her lip.

His body had screamed at him—insisted he take her up on the offer and lose himself in the feel of her lips and body, but his head and his heart gave him pause.

"I'm sorry, I can't," he'd said instead, with an apologetic smile.

"Eldritch," he could see the mischief in her eyes as she addressed him, "are you a virgin?"

Eldritch had been afraid to answer, worried he would be ridiculed for his innocence; but he nodded—his eyes focused on the wall behind her, refusing to meet her gaze.

"You don't have to stay that way you know," she'd teased, running a hand down the center of his chest.

Eldritch reached up and grabbed her palm, halting her movement before her hand drifted any lower. "I can't, Michelle. I'm sorry."

He'd known she was hurt, but she'd kissed him on the cheek anyways and disappeared into her dorm room. That exchange worried Eldritch for several days. So, when she'd come to him with the news about the party at Berry Hall and how she wanted him to join, he'd agreed without hesitation. Eldritch had put on a brave face and gave no indication that he was nearly on the verge of a panic attack at the idea of setting foot inside that building. He'd seen many ghosts over the years; but the thought of seeing children, orphans who had succumbed to a horrible illness or perished in a fire, made him anxious.

After agreeing to meet Michelle at her dorm at eight o'clock that night, he'd locked himself away in his room and started drinking. Eldritch found this form of self-medication necessary before engaging in social activities, especially ones involving large crowds of people. Once he'd learned the effects of alcohol could numb his awareness of activity beyond the veil—his alcohol consumption had increased exponentially.

Anytime he was invited to a party, Eldritch would pregame in his room before going out. It started with the whiskey he'd stolen from his great-grandfather's study. After that, he'd asked his new friends how he could get his hands on some while still underage. They'd contacted their friend, Derrick, and he'd hooked Eldritch up with a shiny, new fake ID. After that "Edward Haynes" was a frequent patron of the liquor store on King Street. Eldritch had quite the stash hidden in the closet of his room now, mostly whiskey—he'd learned that he preferred Jack Daniel's to Jim Beam early on—but there was also a bottle of rum and some cheap tequila.

By the time he and Michelle had reached the party, he was already three sheets to the wind and had continued to drink as the night drew on. With his mind clouded and his inhibitions well on their way out the window, he'd allowed himself to be pulled into an empty bedroom somewhere within the halls of the haunted dorm.

They'd been on someone's bed, making out. Michelle was in his lap, pushing his shoulders trying to get him to lie back. Eldritch hadn't gotten the hint, so her hands had shifted lower, pulling at his belt buckle. He'd felt her hand between his legs, and his eyes flew open at the unexpected touch. As his gaze drifted to the space just over Michelle's bare shoulder, Eldritch had realized they were no longer alone. The sight of four children—two of them badly burned—sent him clambering backward on the bed, dropping Michelle onto the bedroom floor.

"Eldritch, wha—?!" she'd shouted, but he was babbling, cutting her protest short.

"I-I-I can't do th-this! I can't do this!" he'd insisted, back flush against the wall as he tried to tear his eyes away from the dead orphans. "I can't do this in front of the kids, Michelle!"

She'd noticed Eldritch wasn't looking at her and followed his line of sight to an empty space behind her. "Oh, ha-ha, very funny." She turned and walked toward the door, passing through one of the spirits. "There are easier ways to tell a girl you're not interested, Eldritch," she said with her hand on the knob.

"Michelle, no, that's not—"

"Save it. You and I clearly want different things. I'm done with this," and she'd walked out, leaving Eldritch reeling on a stranger's bed.

With the effects of the alcohol waning in the wake of the scare, Eldritch had made his way through the throng of partiers, out of Berry Hall, and all the way back to his room without any trouble. And that was where he found himself now—pacing, fidgeting, running the events of the night through his head over and over again.

It never fails. The second I think I can have a fraction of a normal life...

Eldritch resolved that things had to go back to the way they had been—before Michelle, before the parties full of people. Those days were over. The touch of another person—the feel of a woman in his arms—was something he would always want, but tonight showed that in the end, his *curse* would always get in the way.

Tonight, it had ruined the one chance he'd ever had at a normal love life. Part of him considered calling Michelle and telling her the truth, explaining the events in the bedroom through the lens of his ability. But that came with a severe risk: the risk of ridicule, misunderstanding, and stubborn skepticism. That thought alone convinced him that no one, apart from his parents and a handful of others, could be trusted with his deepest, darkest secret. There would be no phone call to Michelle. They were done—she had made that clear—and Eldritch was done trying.

His legs, tired from his sprint home and the incessant pacing, buckled beneath him, and he fell to his knees, burying his head in his hands and pulling at his hair in frustration. There, on the floor of his dorm room at four in the morning, an eighteen-year-old Eldritch Hayes decided if this life had taught him anything, it was that in the end, he would always be alone.

After the mishap at Berry Hall saw the end of his relationship with Michelle, Eldritch stopped going out. There were no more parties, no more study sessions. He confined himself to his dorm room when he didn't have classes and, after a while, he stopped attending those. Most days would find him lying in bed, sipping on Jack while the sounds of home drifted from the speakers of his boom box.

Weeks turned to months, and when he failed to show up for his second semester midterms, Eldritch was informed by his advisor he was failing. He didn't care. In his mind, he didn't need a college education. It wasn't like he could hold down a regular job at some fancy company where one was expected to function like a normal person. Wanting nothing more than to pack up his belongs and return to Sommerset, Eldritch gave up and decided college wasn't for him. A life spent stocking shelves at Hayes Hardware didn't sound so bad. After all, anything was better than being away from the people and places that made him feel safe. Anything was better than this.

It was a Thursday afternoon when he got the call. Eldritch had skipped music theory—a course he'd signed up for when he'd needed an extra elective—and was tipsy, languishing away on the floor of his room when the phone rang. It took all his effort to pull himself up onto his hands and knees and crawl over to the table where the phone sat.

"Hello?" he croaked into the receiver, the rough crack of his voice making him cringe.

"Eldritch? Baby?" His mother was crying.

Eldritch shook his head in an attempt to focus. "Mama, what's wrong? Is everything okay?" He tried his best to keep his voice even, his consonants crisp and pronounced, to counteract his tendency to slur under the influence of the rum he'd been nursing.

"Baby, I just got a call from Lindy. Gran-Gran's gone."

Eldritch's world came to a halt. Guilt crept in, invading the parts of his mind that weren't drenched in rum. He hadn't been to see Gran-Gran in several months—too preoccupied with locking himself away from the world.

"Eldritch? Are you there?" his mother asked, between sobs.

He got his wits about him enough to respond, "Yeah, I'm here."

"I'm so sorry, baby," Louise said before losing herself to uncontrollable grief.

Oil on troubled waters.

But his mother was lost at sea, tossed about by waters neither of them could calm.

Once she'd composed herself enough to speak, Louise informed him she and his father were heading to Charleston that evening and would be staying at Gran-Gran's house if he wanted to join them. Eldritch assured her he would be there and hung up the phone. The news of Gran-Gran's passing was still processing in his addled mind, but still, he could feel a hole growing deep within his chest. Gran-Gran was gone, and odds were, she died alone.

In the end, that's how we all go: alone.

His parents arrived just before six o'clock that evening. Eldritch was seated on the front porch of Gran-Gran's house—the house that Reuben Sholly built—when they drove up, and he sprinted down the steps, falling into the open arms of his mother. He hadn't seen her since Christmas break, and the reunion was long past due. When they broke apart, his father was there, pulling him into another firm embrace.

"Hey, bud. How you been?" Gene asked, stepping back to look his son in the eye.

"I'm okay," Eldritch lied, finding it difficult to hold his father's gaze. The last thing he wanted was for them to know, to know about the alcohol and the fact that he was flunking out of college. He'd stopped drinking following his mother's phone call earlier that day, and one long shower and several cups of coffee later, he was still trying to sober up. They walked inside together, Eldritch casting a look up to the windows at the faces he knew would be staring back. He searched for Gran-Gran. She wasn't among them.

For the majority of the day, Gene and Louise dealt with the practicalities of the funeral and burial. Louise's mother was supposed to be there, but she was a no-show, just as expected.

"I don't know why I'm upset. I knew she wouldn't be here, but you'd think with it being her own mother—" she paused upon seeing Eldritch standing in the doorway to the living room. Louise never liked to talk about her mother in front of him. She would answer questions if he asked, but the subject wasn't a pleasant one, and talking about it seemed to upset her, so Eldritch never pushed for more details. Over the years, he'd gathered the basics: Louise didn't know who her father was, and her mother resented Louise for being born and taking her mother's "best years" from her. More often than not, Louise had been dropped off at Gran-Gran's for weeks on end without knowing where her mother was. Gran-Gran became the true mother figure in Louise's life until Louise had turned eighteen and moved to Lexington to stay with a friend. Not long after, she'd met Gene and moved to Sommerset once they'd been married. Louise's mother did not attend the wedding.

Eldritch had never met the woman who was supposed to be his grandmother. There was only Gran-Gran, and he'd been perfectly content with that; and now, Gran-Gran was gone, and he was struggling to put the grief he felt into words. While his parents worked on logistics to keep Louise from collapsing into a pool of tears, Eldritch walked the grounds of the old Charleston home.

He began outside, circling the house, taking in the flowers which were already in full bloom. The gardens were no longer as pristine as they once were. As Gran-Gran's health failed, the flowerbeds grew more and more unkempt. Louise would come down whenever she could and try to tidy them up, but many of them were a lost cause; weeds running wild, the flowers and bushes growing and spreading out of control.

He made a point to avoid the giant old oak tree. Now that he was older, the reality of what had happened in that tree a century and a half ago tinged his fear with a deep sadness and shame. As the sun began to set, Eldritch ventured back inside, to the living room where he encountered Reuben Sholly in his usual spot, rocking back and forth. The old man smiled as Eldritch entered the room.

"Hey, Papa Reuben," Eldritch returned his smile, "do you remember me?"

The spirit nodded. "Eldritch," he said. "My boy, Eldritch."

Eldritch laughed at the old ghost's sentimentality. *"My boy." He's only seen me a handful of times these last few years.*

"You grew so fast, but then you were gone so soon," Reuben continued.

"Well, I don't live here. I live in Sommerset, a couple hours away," Eldritch explained.

Reuben Sholly did not respond, rocking four or five more times before disappearing, and Eldritch placed his hand on the empty chair to still its movement before leaving the room. His wandering led him across the hall and into his great-grandfather's study—the study Gran-Gran had refused to change after her husband's death in 1963. Eldritch wondered if his great-grandfather knew how much she had loved him and how she'd refused to change his sacred space. *Maybe, if I wait awhile, he'll show up. If he were to haunt anything, it would be this room, right?*

Eldritch sat in the large leather chair behind the solid, oak desk and waited for any sign of his namesake, but after an hour passed, he grew restless and decided to continue his inspection of the room. As he rounded the desk, something moved just out the corner of his left eye: a man walking, step for step, in time with Eldritch. A slow turn in the direction of the figure had Eldritch face to face with his own reflection. He stared at the faint image of himself reflected in the glass of the liquor cabinet, and through it he could see the bottles full of amber liquid: Eldritch Sholly's stash.

Eldritch walked over to the cabinet and opened it, sifting through the bottles on display. He found a few that were still unopened—like the bottle of Jim Beam he had nicked months prior—and pulled one of them out. It was a brandy. Eldritch had never tried brandy before and began thinking of ways to smuggle it out of the house without his parents seeing, curious to give it a try. It wasn't a small bottle by any means, so he would have to be careful. If they were preoccupied with funeral arrangements in the kitchen, it was possible he could slip out and hide it in his car, but that was risky.

As he worked through possible exit strategies, the steady beat of footsteps sounded in the hall. Eldritch set the bottle back on its shelf and shut the cabinet door before his father popped his head into the study.

"Hey, bud. You alright?"

"Yessir," he responded, inching away from the cabinet.

"I was looking all over for you, didn't know where you'd gotten off to."

"I've just been walking around," Eldritch said, "Did you know Gran-Gran never changed anything about this study after great-grandpa Eldritch died?"

"It's come up before," Gene nodded, walking into the study.

"She must have loved him a lot to keep it exactly as he left it for almost forty years."

"She did," his father said, "but I don't know how healthy it is."

Eldritch raised an eyebrow, inviting his father to elaborate.

"When you cling to something like that—refusing to change a room, refusing to move on—it doesn't seem healthy. You can honor a person's memory and cherish something of theirs, sure. But this—" he gestured around them at the room in question, "it's obsessive, don't you think? Not touching this room for forty years isn't going to bring him back."

"What if he never left?" Eldritch proposed.

Gene laughed and shrugged, "Well you'd be the one to know. Not me."

Eldritch turned back to the liquor cabinet, staring down his own reflection. How he hated the person staring back at him; hated the sad eyes, the pale skin, the downturned mouth. He was so tired; too tired to care anymore, too tired to fight, too tired to try. Eldritch began to shake from the pressure of everything he'd bottled up: his drinking, the state of his grades, the end of his relationship, the grief over Gran-Gran's passing. The strain was too much, and he couldn't take it anymore. Something had to change.

"I want to come home."

CHAPTER TWENTY-TWO

Eldritch rubs his eyes and grunts. He doesn't know how long he slept this time. Without the routine of work to keep him on a regular schedule, the distinction between day and night is no longer there. Time is now measured by moments when the phone is ringing and when it is not; moments when the record player is playing on its own and when the house is silent; moments when Eldritch is tempted by the bottle on the table and when it is removed from his sight; moments when he feels he can tolerate the demonic presence in his home and when he blacks out in a puddle of tears, overwhelmed by its malevolence.

He's exhausted—exhausted from the irregular sleep schedule and the emotional rollercoaster he's found himself riding over and over again. Dragging a calloused hand over his face, his palm rakes over the stubble that has grown into a full beard without him realizing. He doesn't feel like shaving anymore; hasn't in days.

Eldritch tries to throw the covers aside, but there is nothing to grab. Sitting up and peering down at the lower half of his body, he sees there are no covers because he is not in his bed. He is still on the couch in the den. Eldritch reaches for his cell phone, but it's nowhere to be found. He thinks he remembers walking upstairs to charge it after the battery died during his latest attempt to call Kelly. *How long ago was that?*

He misses her—misses the smell of her perfume, the warmth of her body leaning against him on the couch, the sound of her voice—and wonders what could have unfolded between them if his unexpected houseguest hadn't shown up. *I should have known. I can never have that—never have what I want. Does she miss me? Would she still want to be around me in this state?* He has tried to call her many times, but the demon won't allow it. It returned to him some time ago, and here it remains. No more slamming doors and instant relief after one of Eldritch's tirades. It lives here now, alongside a dazed and weary Eldritch who has found he doesn't want it to leave. As long as it's here, his parents will phone and warn him, protect him, call his name through the static on the line. He hates it, but he's letting it stay. *They would be ashamed of you. Kelly would be ashamed of you.*

Throwing his legs over the side of the couch, Eldritch forces his tired and aching body to stand. He has no idea what time it is—doesn't really care, if he's honest—but decides he needs coffee, nonetheless. Opening the cabinet in the kitchen, he is shocked to find the coffee has run out. *That doesn't make sense.* Kelly just brought over a bag a few days ago. Like so many other items in this house as of late, it too has gone missing. He presses a hand to his temple, feeling a headache coming on. If he doesn't get some caffeine in him soon, he worries he'll end up with a full-blown migraine.

With a groan and a slam of the cabinet door, he turns to leave the kitchen, but is stopped by a familiar sound in the dining room. Eldritch tenses, clenching his jaw and fists in frustration, as he approaches the doorway between the two rooms. As he suspected, the chairs have moved again—no longer in their normal positions but inverted, seats flat on the table, legs straight up in the air—except for the one chair which is pulled out for him. The demon is there, in the far corner of the room, lingering in the shadows. Eldritch stares it down and notices its presence is having less of an effect on him. The oppressive heaviness in the atmosphere remains, the constant knot in the pit of his stomach and the accompanying chills that dance across his skin; but he no longer has to fight the urge to throw up—no longer wants to sprint from the room. The shadow shifts, tilts what Eldritch assumes is its head, as if considering him and his thoughts. Eldritch wonders if it can hear them, read them. *You can, can't you?* It drifts out of the dining room, and Eldritch decides he hates watching it move about. He hates it when it floats around, dark mist and spectral limbs ever-moving, ever-reaching. He hates it when it moves like a man, a shadow man on two legs walking around in a perverse imitation of the human form.

When it's left the room, Eldritch's returns his attention to the table and spies another glass and bottle, but this time, the bottle is different. Gone is the vintage Jim Beam from Gran-Gran's house. Now, Jack Daniel's Tennessee Whiskey— Eldritch's drink of choice—is eyeing him down from across the threshold of the dining room. *The same thing I was drinking when I…*

It would be lying to say he isn't tempted. Seven years is a long time but not long enough to erase the taste—the comfort—from his memory. His hands shake at his sides, and he forces them to still before they do something drastic; before they reach out and take the glass of their own volition.

He wants it—*God*, does he want it—tongue slipping out to wet his bottom lip. *What if I just took a sip? One sip couldn't possibly*—

"No," he says, putting an end to that line of thought, "we're not doing this again." He grabs the glass off the table, takes it into the kitchen, and pours the whiskey down the drain. Walking back to the dining room, he looks at the table, expecting the mysterious bottle to have vanished just as it does every other time it appears. But this time, the bottle remains. Eldritch stares at it, waiting for it to move, waiting for it to disappear, but it doesn't. After several minutes of futile observation, Eldritch gives up and decides he'll have to dispose of the bottle himself, but as he steps toward the table, music kicks up in the den.

The soulful whine of an electric guitar blasts through the old Magnavox speakers—that melancholy drag of notes he identifies immediately as "The Air That I Breathe" by The Hollies. The meaning behind this particular song choice not lost on him. It's a ballad, a ballad where the singer describes how he needs nothing more in life than the air that he breathes and loving the woman next to him. They're both sleepy and at peace after making love—something Eldritch has never experienced, and this entity knows that. It knows what he wants—*who* he wants—and knows she was on his mind only moments ago.

"You think you're funny, don't you?" he asks it, walking over to the record player and shutting if off. "I told you to leave this alone. You don't touch it." Eldritch slams the lid shut and heads upstairs to see if his cell phone ever managed to charge. When he grabs it from his bedside table, it lights up, battery at one hundred percent, *Friday, December 22, 3:07 PM*. *I've lost a whole day?*

He has three missed calls from Calvin, two missed calls from Kelly, thirteen text messages between the two of them, and one from Amir. All the texts from his uncle are variations of the same message. He wants to know how Eldritch is doing and is wondering if he'll be joining him and Amy for Christmas. Sometimes Eldritch does, sometimes he doesn't. His attendance is usually dependent upon how well he's handling himself after the blow December nineteenth always delivers. This year, it looks like Calvin and Amy are going to Raleigh to visit her parents, and Eldritch is more than welcome to come with them. The last text earns an eye roll from Eldritch.

12:54 p.m. – Don't make me come over there, you little punk.

Deep down, he knows he should go—*needs* to go, to get out of this house—but he doesn't want to run the risk of missing any attempted communications from his parents. He knows the entity doesn't want them speaking and is corrupting the landline when they call, which is why Eldritch must make sure every effort to contact him is answered. If he were to join Calvin and Amy in Raleigh for Christmas, he'd spend the entire time wondering if the phone was ringing back at home. He fires off a message to Cal, resolved in his decision.

3:10 p.m. – Hey, sorry. My phone's been acting weird. Probably have to get a new one. I think I'm just going to

> spend Christmas here this year. Not really up to going anywhere.

Within seconds, he has a response.

> 3:10 p.m. – Boy, you had me worried. I was about to get in the car and come check on you. You know you can't go radio silent on me like that. You just CAN'T.

They don't talk about it, but Eldritch knows why he can't. Another text comes through from Cal.

> 3:11 p.m. – You sure you're ok? I haven't heard from you since Tuesday.

> 3:12 p.m. – I'm fine. Just enjoying my time off. You don't have to keep checking on me. Enjoy your Christmas. We'll talk when you're back.

It's a lie. He isn't anywhere close to fine, but he needs Uncle Cal off his back. The last thing he wants is his uncle showing up at his house, figuring out something's amiss, and calling Pastor Mike. If Pastor Mike shows up, the phone calls may stop. The demon is a necessary evil Eldritch is determined to deal with if it means being able to hear his parents speak to him again. He *needs* them to speak to him, he *needs* to know he isn't alone, and that he's going to be okay again.

They always made everything okay.

He wraps up his conversation with Calvin, assuring him he'll be fine on his own for Christmas and he'll see him in a few days. The text from Amir is short and to the point.

> 8:55 a.m. – Dude. You still alive?

CALLING ELDRITCH HAYES

Eldritch's response is the same.

3:13 p.m. – I'm fine. Thanks for checking.

He scrolls down to his conversation with Kelly. She's been texting him for the last two days with no response. The first couple are from Wednesday night.

9:46 p.m. – Hey, finally done over here, you still up?

10:02 p.m. – Guess not. I have to head to GA early tomorrow, so I'll text you when I get there.

9:57 a.m. – Hey, just got to my Nana's house. Text me when you get a chance. Or call. Whichever. I miss you already.

12:08 p.m. – Everything ok?

12:46 p.m. – Eldritch?

2:17 p.m. – I'm getting a little worried here. I'm not trying to blow your phone up, but we haven't gone this long without talking, and it's kinda freaking me out.

The first missed call from Kelly rang in at 2:49 p.m. on Thursday. The texts that followed were her expressing further concern and begging him to respond. The last text makes his heart drop. It was sent this morning after her last attempt to call him.

8:43 a.m. – I'm not sure what's going on, but you obviously don't want to speak to me. I don't know what I did wrong. My heart is breaking right now, and I don't know how to

311

fix it. I thought things were going great with us. I don't understand what changed. I won't bother you again. Merry Christmas, Eldritch.

"No, no, no, no, no. Kelly, no," Eldritch can feel himself on the verge of a panic attack. The knowledge that he, in this very moment, is losing the one thing he's cared about in years, causes his chest to tighten. He can't breathe, he can't think, not about anything but Kelly and how much she means to him.

He fumbles with his phone, pulling it from the charger, preparing to push the button to connect the call, when a noise from downstairs halts his movements. He hears static—different from the static on the phone line—and a myriad of voices and music coming and going, as if they were being cut off by one another, like the rapid changing of channels.

Is that the TV?

Eldritch hurries from his room and down the stairs. The television, mounted just above the mantle in the living room, has been turned on, and the channels are flipping by in quick succession. Eldritch searches for the remote—on end tables, on the mantle, in drawers, under cushions—but it too, has vanished. The screen continues to flip, every second a new channel: the news, then a football game, then a Christmas movie, then a game show, infomercial, concert, over and over, they cycle through. Something about the picture and sound is off. The images displayed are grainy and filled with lines. The sound is similar; distorted, buried underneath the pop and hum of static. If this were the old, console television set from his youth, the crackling sound and fuzzy picture would make sense, but this is an LED smart TV; and Eldritch doesn't have regular channels anymore, he streams.

He's frozen in the middle of the room, transfixed by this new development, when the flipping stops—as if the entity controlling the missing remote has settled on something to watch. The blurry picture becomes crystal clear, and Eldritch chokes on a gasp at the image of the hardware store plastered across the screen.

It's as if he's seeing through the eyes of someone crossing Main Street and approaching the building. He sees the old, brick structure; sees its black roof, its white, metal annex, and the words *Hayes Hardware*—displayed in their giant, red lettering. Eldritch is speechless, confounded by what he's watching. Wherever this footage came from, it was taken on a bright, sunny day, and given the position of the shadows, he would guess mid to late morning. He can see the breath of whoever is walking—whoever is *filming*—materialize in the foreground, signifying it was recorded in the last month or two when the temperatures dropped.

What is this? Where did this come from?

The footage continues across the parking lot and through the front door. Eldritch hears the bell, sees the inside of the empty store; then, to his horror, Eldritch watches as he himself walks around the corner of an aisle and faces whoever this point of view belongs to. His stomach drops as he sees his own body go rigid with fear before turning and sprinting in the opposite direction. The viewer gives chase, and Eldritch hears the slamming of the bathroom door, sees the fists of the pursuer stretch out and bang against it. It takes a moment for his brain to process what he's seeing, but the inhuman laugh that follows the knocking brings the realization home. He isn't watching video footage; this isn't some recording. Eldritch is watching the demon as it watches him—as it uses Mark as a puppet—the morning of their first encounter.

The screen shifts once more, the "channel" changing. Now, he sees The Grind. The demon within Mark is walking from the back of the café to the front counter, and Eldritch sees himself come into view. He's talking to Kelly. The sight of her triggers a tightness in his chest. They're arguing about Eldritch taking coffee without paying. Kelly is insisting he's fine, but Eldritch is adamant about running home and grabbing his wallet. Mark speaks. The Eldritch on the screen launches into a full-blown panic attack. Eldritch remembers this day.

The screen flips to another scene: Mark watching Eldritch walk past the Birch-Rainey house on a Friday night. It switches again: Mark confronting Eldritch in the lumberyard at Hayes Hardware. Again: the night of the tree lighting, the full manifestation on the second floor of the old house. Once more: the day of the exorcism. He watches as the demon comes charging toward him after shedding Mark's host body. He sees himself pass out and lie unconscious on the weathered, hardwood floor, Kelly rushing to his side. Then, the screen goes black.

Before he has a second to collect his thoughts, the record player roars to life in the den, volume on full blast. "Just One Look" blares from the back of the house, but it begins to skip, caught on a scratch. Eldritch remembers this isn't the same Hollies album it played earlier. This is the one from the other night—the one the demon threw into the wall.

You scratched it!

The thought of the demon damaging his father's record stokes the burning ember of fury resting deep down in his core. Eldritch charges into the den and shuts the Magnavox off for the second time today. Glancing down, he sees the other Hollies album from earlier discarded, haphazardly, on the floor. He picks it up, locates the sleeve, and puts it back in its rightful place in the cabinet.

Pacing the den, Eldritch tries to formulate a plan. He needs to get a handle on this situation, but he's afraid the phone calls will stop if his actions prove too rash. If he can hold the demon at bay long enough to have a full conversation with his parents, he might be able to expel it afterwards.

His cell phone buzzes in his pocket, and it dawns on him that he never responded to Kelly. He pulls out his phone, hoping to see her name flash across the screen, but all he finds is a spam email. Refusing to run the risk of losing Kelly forever, Eldritch finds her name in his contacts; but before he can press the "call" button, the battery drains, and the phone shuts off. The rage he feels in this moment is unlike anything he's ever felt before. His muscles contract, sending a violent tremor through his frame, and he screams—anger and frustration bubbling up from within and boiling over. He screams until he's out of breath, until his throat is sore and his lungs are empty. He takes the dead cell phone in his hand and hurls it, as hard as he can, across the room. It hits the wall opposite him with a loud thud and falls to the ground behind the record player. He can't reach it without moving the giant Magnavox console, and now there's a hole in the drywall where one of his mother's favorite prints hung many years ago.

Eldritch closes his eyes and focuses on his breathing, counting to ten in his head, when the kitchen phone rings. He turns his head, listening for a second ring, before sprinting into the kitchen and grabbing the phone from the wall mount.

"Hello? Mama? Dad?" he yells into the receiver.

The usual crackle from the other side is there, but soon, he hears it: the voice of his father, cutting through the white noise in a fury.

"That is what I was talking about when I said I didn't want my son in any danger!" Gene is yelling, ranting on the other end of the call.

He knows it's after me.

The static returns, and Gene's voice cuts in and out, fighting to be heard through the bad connection.

"Dad? Dad, can you hear me?!" Eldritch is desperate for an answer, desperate for a direct response from his father.

"I'm not finished!" his father shouts, amid faults in the line.

"Dad, please! It's me! Let me know if you can hear my voice! You're cutting in and out!"

His father's voice filters through the interference once more, "It went for him! You saw that, didn't you? If I had been a second slower, it could have grabbed him…"

What is he talking about? Eldritch knew the demon was in his home, but so far, it hadn't tried to attack him directly. It certainly hadn't gone for him or tried to grab him. *Unless he's seeing something I'm not. Unless he can see what's coming…*

Eldritch tries to ask what his father means by that statement, but the feedback returns and drowns out both of their voices before the line goes dead. His father had been right there, yelling through the phone; but once again, his attempt to reach him had failed. Eldritch feels the sting of tears in his eyes, braces himself against the wall as his legs threaten to give way, overcome by an unspeakable despair. Heavy is the weight on his shoulders, on his heart.

He sees the demon move, the shadow creeping along the length of the den and into the stairwell. Eldritch is tired of watching it lurk about, and deciding it'd be better to not see it at all, he goes room to room, drawing the curtains and dousing every light. He wants the house dark, wants to make it more difficult to see the demon as it moves around—as it makes

Eldritch think he isn't alone in this world when he knows that's the one thing he is.

Once the house is shrouded in darkness, Eldritch ambles into the den, and despite having just woken up an hour ago, he's exhausted. His body is drained, his spirit beaten down. What he wants to do more than anything is curl up on the couch and wait for the phone to ring. He has to keep trying, keep listening, keep calling out to them.

Pretty soon they'll hear. They have to. It's only a matter of time.

Even with the den black as pitch, Eldritch can sense the entity drift into the room with him. He knows it's headed for the record player, refusing to obey Eldritch's commands to leave it alone; but Eldritch finds it difficult to care right now and closes his eyes as the sound of The Hollies permeates the room. He's teetering on the edge of sleep when the unmistakable feel of phantom arms closes in around his body. It's not his parents. It's not Kelly. He knows what it is: evil, and it's wrapping its crooked limbs around him in an unholy embrace. He should rebuke it; he should rise from the couch, retrieve his phone, and run out the door, screaming for help.

Eldritch does none of these things; his desire to be held and comforted outweighing the truth of the situation. He wishes the demonic spirit still made him sick, still made it difficult to breathe. *Maybe I'm getting stronger, and that's why it has less of an effect on me*, he thinks to himself, but at the back of his mind, Eldritch knows that isn't true.

CHAPTER TWENTY-THREE

After expressing his desire to drop out of college and move back home, Eldritch had a long conversation with both Gene and Louise about his struggles. He explained to them how difficult things had been—how he was failing his classes, how he was afraid to leave his dorm room—conveniently leaving out specific details pertaining to his excessive drinking. The decision wasn't easy, but they had agreed. Eldritch withdrew from the College of Charleston and returned home to Sommerset, under the condition that he begin working at the hardware store.

Although relieved to be done with the brief, but trying, collegiate chapter of his life, Eldritch was faced with a new problem: concealing his alcohol habit from his parents. Neither Gene nor Louise were drinkers, nor were they big on the idea of their son partaking—especially at his age—so hiding it was the only option. Whenever the opportunity presented itself—usually when his parents were out—Eldritch would hop in his Celica and drive over to the liquor store in Newberry, fake ID in hand. His bottles of whiskey and rum were wrapped in old sweatpants and stuffed in an old gym bag, which was placed at the back of his closet. Eldritch thought them safe there, but one Saturday, the urge to clean and purge the house of unwanted stuff struck Louise. While helping her son clean out his closet, she grabbed the gym bag and nearly opened it, but Eldritch was quick and told her it was full of college stuff he wasn't prepared to part with just yet. It was a close call, and Eldritch realized he needed to find a better hiding place.

It wasn't until September, six months after he'd returned home, that the idea struck him. His mother, preparing to decorate the house for fall, was complaining about the basement.

"If it weren't for the storage space, I'd have your daddy wall that thing up. I hate going down there."

His mother wasn't exaggerating. None of them cared for the damp and poorly lit room, and unless there was a holiday approaching for which Louise felt the need to decorate, it was rare anyone came down to the basement at all. When the time *did* come for the decorations to be brought up from the basement, that job was almost always delegated to Eldritch or his father, and his father never stayed down there longer than he had to, hating the way it smelled.

The basement…now there's a thought.

He waited until his parents went to dinner one Friday night. They'd invited Eldritch, but he was never in the mood to go out anymore—except on the odd occasion he felt like "going for a drive" through Newberry.

"You sure?" his father asked one last time, hand on the front door before they walked out. "Kitty's Place. Your favorite."

Eldritch shook his head and assured them he wasn't hungry. He told them to make it a date night and to grab a movie or something after dinner. He'd be fine on his own.

"Date night? What's that?" Louise nudged her husband.

Gene rolled his eyes. "Oh, please. I take you anywhere you want to go, and I buy you everything you ask for, woman," he said with mock indignation and a wink.

They left, discussing their viewing options for the night as his father pulled the front door closed behind them. From the sound of it, *Space Cowboys* was winning out. Eldritch knew they'd be gone for a while, leaving him on his own in the house for hours. He took this opportunity to relocate his stash, hauling the gym bag down to the basement and searching for the most out-of-the-way spot he could find. Pushing past the plastic bins full of Christmas, Easter, and Fourth of July decorations, Eldritch ventured to the far left of the basement where it turned a sharp corner into an unused nook with low clearance. He had to stoop down and crawl on his hands and knees to reach it. It was perfect.

The bottles were removed from the maroon gym bag, still wrapped in the old, gray sweats, and Eldritch stuffed them as far into the nook as he could reach. Crawling out of the corner, he fought his way back through the sea of bins and boxes with every intention of putting on a movie and crashing on the couch, but when he reached the foot of the steep, wooden stairs, he paused. His parents were gone—would be gone for the majority of the night. He was alone in the house, and his hand twitched at the thought of what he'd just hidden away. Turning around, he returned to the nook, crouched down, and fished the bottles back out from where he had just stashed them.

The bathroom door shut behind him as he made his way up from the basement and back out into the living room. Eldritch looked down at the bottle in his grasp, shifting it from one hand to the other, watching the amber liquid slosh back and forth as it was jostled. He was hesitant to open it, standing there in the middle of his parents' house—his parents who never drank anymore, despite what they may have done in their younger years; his parents who would have a fit if they came home and found him drunk again. They had been furious that night a year and a half ago, and if they knew how much Eldritch had been drinking this last year—how most of his time at college was spent in a drunken stupor, sprawled out on the floor of his dorm room—they wouldn't be able to handle it.

He had no *reason* to grab the bottle. He wasn't facing an unfamiliar social situation, there were no ghosts or demons hanging around. He was safe, in his house, in his hometown he had so desperately longed for while away. His parents had been understanding of his decisions to leave school, and all things considered, he no longer had a *reason* to drink himself numb, but he had a need—a desire. He craved the taste of the whiskey, longed to fall into that state of intoxication, longed to silence his mind for a bit and drown out the words that bounced around in there, day after day.

Freak. Failure. Cursed. Alone.

Eldritch *was* alone, and as far as he was concerned, he would stay as such; hidden away in his parents' house forever. It was a depressing thought, and Eldritch ruminated on it as he stood in the living room by himself.

I am alone. Always alone. I don't want to feel it anymore.

He unscrewed the metal top, determined to numb the emptiness inside, and took a long drag from the bottle. There it was again, the familiar burn, the smoothness of honey at the end. The flavor danced across his tongue, and he took another swig, losing himself to the whiskey.

He nursed the bottle for a solid hour and a half, ambling about the house, going room to room, and fiddling with tchotchkes and trinkets displayed on tables and shelves.

No purpose. Walking around with no purpose and no plan. Wasting time.

"Wasting time because I *am* a waste," he snorted.

Coward. Scared, little boy. Hiding away at Mommy and Daddy's.

Eldritch laughed, taking another sip of whiskey, and shook his head, "I don't belong anywhere else. I barely belong here." He strolled into the den, feet feeling heavier by the minute. "Let's see what's spinning today," he drawled, speech beginning to slur, as he stumbled over to the record player. Lifting the lid, he noticed his dad had recently been listening to The Hollies. He dropped the needle in a random spot on the vintage vinyl, and from the speakers erupted "Bus Stop" about halfway into the first verse.

"Geez, Dad, get some new music already," he said, listening to a young man from the sixties sing about sharing his umbrella with the girl he loved.

No one will ever share my umbrella.

"I don't even have an umbrella."

No. No umbrella, only rain. There's no protection for me. No protection from the rain.

"That's why I stay here. I go to work, and I come home, and I stay."

All alone.

"All alone."

It didn't occur to Eldritch that he was having a conversation with himself. He did that every once in a while, when he'd had too much to drink. The thoughts were always there, but the drink encouraged him to respond. It didn't matter; no one was there to listen.

When the song ended, he flipped the record player off, returned the needle to its proper resting position, and closed the lid, making a hazy, mental note to encourage his parents to invest in some music from this decade.

'60s and '70s, that's all they ever listen to.

He glanced up at the wall above the record player and eyed the picture hanging there—some print his mother had bought years ago at a Home Interiors party. The faux, wooden frame wrapped around a burgundy background with lilies and another flower Eldritch couldn't identify. In the center of the picture was a scripture, printed on a beige oval. Eldritch read the words out loud, eyes squinting in an attempt to focus, his vision getting blurrier with every drag from the bottle.

"My grace is suffish—suffishten—sufficient for thee, for My strength is made perfect in weakness." It was from the second book of Corinthians, chapter 12, verse 9. He'd seen this picture his entire life. Eldritch knew many scriptures by heart, was always attentive in Sunday school and read his Bible like his parents encouraged. He knew the Word. He knew the promises of God; but right now, they felt so far away.

"My strength is made perfect in weakness," he whispered, staggering away from the picture. "Weakness." A familiar tune and lyrics he'd sang countless times over the years surfaced from the recesses of his mind, and Eldritch began to sing.

"Little ones to Him belong. They are weak, but He is strong."

They are weak, but He is strong.

They are weak.
I am weak.

Eldritch stood there in the den, bottle in hand, feeling weaker than ever. Time after time, he had managed to convince himself that he would feel better once he was drunk. The bottle called to him day and night, from sunup to sundown, and every time he succumbed, he would tell himself that it would all seem better through the haze of alcohol. It had seemed that way at first, back at college when he would party with Michelle and the guys from psychology; but somewhere along the way, things changed. The alcohol only plunged him into a more depressive state, but even that wasn't enough to make him put it down; and now, it seemed he no longer had the ability to do so.

"I am weak," he said to the empty room, affirming the thoughts in his head. He fumbled with the metal top, struggling to screw it back onto the bottle. He needed to get to bed before his parents came home. Climbing the stairs to his bedroom on the second floor proved to be a challenge for Eldritch, having drunk more than he realized—the half empty bottle in his hand proof of that. As he brought his foot up to the final step, he caught the edge of it and his sock made contact with the smooth, rounded wood, causing him to slip.

Eldritch pitched forward, feet flying backward, out from underneath him. He reached out with his empty hand to brace himself, but the liquor in his system caused a delay in his reaction time. He heard the bottle of Jack hit the floor of the second story and slide down the hall, just before his chin made contact with the top of the stairs. Then, there was only darkness.

When he regained consciousness, it was to the sharp, metallic tang of blood in his mouth. Eldritch hauled himself up and climbed the rest of the stairs on all fours, taking a moment to sit and clear his head when he reached the landing. He had to figure out what part of his mouth was bleeding. There was a flash of panic at the possibility of him losing a tooth or breaking his jaw—more so over the thought of having to explain the situation to his parents in his current state. To his left, he saw the bottle of whiskey inches away and reached for it, relieved it hadn't shattered where it landed. Unscrewing the top again, and undoing all his hard work from earlier, Eldritch took a swig. A stinging pain shot through his mouth as the alcohol made contact with his tongue, pinpointing the source of the injury. He had bitten his tongue when his face hit the hardwood—no breaks, no missing teeth. Eldritch breathed a sigh of relief, sending up a quick prayer of thanks that there would be no emergency room visit tonight.

Shuffling to his room, he looked for a place to hide his whiskey—fortunate he hadn't attempted to brave the steep and treacherous stairs of the basement. He decided no one would be rifling through his underwear drawer for the rest of the night, and pulled it open, shoving the bottle under several pairs of boxer briefs before pushing it shut.

Eldritch shed his jeans and socks, electing to sleep in his t-shirt and underwear, and climbed into bed. When he heard the sound of keys in the front door, he flipped over onto his side, turning his back to the door of his bedroom. There were footsteps on the stairs minutes later, and the sound of his father peeking into his room before whispering down the hall to Louise, "He's already asleep," as he pulled the door closed.

Somewhere in the distance, he could hear his parents laughing as they prepared for bed; but he was too tired and too drunk to pay attention to anything they were saying. Eldritch's mind drifted back to the picture downstairs—*My strength is made perfect in weakness*—and he began to sing that old, familiar tune as the warm embrace of sleep closed in around him.

>Little ones to Him belong.
>They are weak, but He is strong.
>Yes, Jesus loves me...
>Yes, Jesus loves... me...
>Yes... Jesus... loves... me...

For the Bible tells me so.

CHAPTER TWENTY-FOUR

Days have passed. Eldritch has made himself a fixture in the den, no longer bothering to go upstairs when it's time for bed. With the curtains drawn and all the lights off, he has no idea what time of day it is anyway. The clock on the mantle no longer works—both hands stuck on the six and refusing to budge—and his cell phone was dead by the time he fished out from behind the record player. He would charge it, but every charger in the house has gone missing—like the Bible, the remote, the coffee. He could leave and buy another one, he could leave and drive to his uncle's house, but he won't—not when his parents could call at any given time.

They have called several times over the last few days, but the connection is always poor. He can hear them speak, but no matter how he shouts and calls out to them, it's as if they can't hear his voice at all. Eldritch spends the time between phone calls languishing on the couch, staring at the ceiling, staring at the walls. He focuses on the spot above the record player, focuses on the hole he made with his phone. His mother used to have a picture hanging there—a picture with scripture—but after she left, Eldritch didn't want to look at it anymore, so he got rid of it. The wall has been bare ever since, and the longer he stares at it, the emptier he feels; so Eldritch rolls over and presses his face into the back of the couch.

Maybe, if I bury my face into the cushions, they'll suffocate me.

It's a morbid thought. Eldritch has been having a lot of those as of late. At first, he was shocked and mortified when they crossed his mind; but now, he can hardly tell the difference between the dark thoughts and his normal ones. All his thoughts are dark now. Eldritch can't remember the last time he ate. He thinks he choked down a piece of stale bread at some point—knows entered the kitchen because he remembers the microwave blinking at him: all eights. It had given up, just like the clock on the mantle, just like Eldritch.

He doesn't bother turning on the Christmas lights anymore. This is not a house of light, and they have no place here. With his face wedged into the back of the couch, he closes his eyes and tries to think of happy times, times when the light was welcome here, when it streamed in through open windows and poured from fixtures in the ceiling. Those times seem so long ago, and as the years have passed, some memories have begun to fade. Eldritch doesn't want to lose those memories. He wants to always be able to call to mind the sound of his father singing along to The Eagles and Bread, he must always remember his mother's laughter and gentle tone. The way she would push his hair back from his forehead when drying his tears. He has no one to dry his tears anymore. Sometimes they flow so freely, he feels as though he will drown in them, and no one is here to save him, to pull him up for air.

He thinks back to the times his father would hoist him up in his arms and carry him to safety. A deep sadness overtakes him as he realizes he can no longer remember the feel of those arms; can no longer remember their strength as they held him close and away from danger. As if springing up from the deep well of his memory, he feels himself being enveloped, wrapped in a phantom embrace. These are not the arms of his father but a mockery of them. It should make him sick, but he leans into them all the same, telling himself he can pretend—he can pretend he is being held by someone who loves him.

His thoughts drift to Kelly. They had been happy here, and despite how brief that interlude may have been, he believes they had loved each other. Eldritch loves her still, but he understands love and light and happiness are all beyond his reach. He longs to hold her, to feel her body close and warm against his own; but to hold her is to drag her down—down into the pit with him—and Eldritch can't do that to her. Kelly is all things beautiful and good. She is fire and light and passion that he so desperately wants to bask in, but he can't.

I am darkness. I always have been. This is what I deserve.

A sound from the kitchen causes him to lift his head. "If you're going through my cabinets, you better be putting the coffee back," he calls to the demon. It's been so long since he's had any coffee—any caffeine whatsoever—since it was taken. The resulting headaches have been murder on him, but he has to struggle through. There is no other alternative. *Or is there?*

He listens for the noise to continue, but only silence follows. Eldritch shrugs and is about to lie back down on the couch, when he hears it again; but this time, it's several sounds at once, loud and violent: cabinets slamming, the clanging of metal, multiple objects hitting the floor. Eldritch groans in annoyance and rises from the couch, head pounding, limbs stiff and weak from lack of use.

He lumbers into the kitchen, but once his eyes take in the scene before him, he stops. Every cabinet door is flung open, and the floor is covered with pots, pans, and the contents of his pantry. Eldritch can't shake the familiarity of the scene as he takes a cautious step into the kitchen, astonished at the mess at his feet. He wants to be angry, wants to rage at the dark spirit for causing such disarray, but he hasn't the energy for that.

Eldritch stares at the floor, trying to force himself to pick something up, but he's too tired and starts to realize he doesn't care if the kitchen is in shambles.

I'll clean it later. If I feel like it. What does it matter?

He longs for the comfort of the couch, needs it to take the weight off his weary bones and aching muscles. There is something else he longs for—something that never vanished from the dining room table. Eldritch knows he's treading into dangerous territory, but he walks over to the to take a quick peek. The chairs are in their normal positions, pushed under the table, but the bottle remains—a constant temptation just within reach. This is why he was in the kitchen earlier; he was passing through—he remembers now. He ambled to the doorway of the dining room a stupor—staring, longing—but so far, he has resisted. *I can't. It's the one thing I can't do*, he reminds himself. *Not this time.*

As he tears himself away from the dining room and turns back toward the den, another sound pricks his ears: the sound of plastic or rubber clicking against something. Without turning around, Eldritch tries to determine the source of the noise behind him.

It's something on the counter. Something is hitting the countertop.

The sound continues for a few seconds before he makes the connection.

A cord. It's fiddling with a cord. The microwave?

He turns in time to see the microwave as it is pulled free from the wall and launched in his direction. Eldritch steps out of the way at the last second, dodging the appliance as it is thrown at him. It crashes into the wall, creating a substantial hole and breaking apart—bits of metal, plastic, and glass joining the mess on the floor. His heart is pounding, startled by the unexpected attack.

"So that's how it's going to be then? A little cuddling on the couch and now you want me dead, huh?"

The entity gives no response, but something moves past the doorway of the dining room. The glimpse Eldritch catches is brief, but it's enough for him to determine the figure is a woman.

Mama?

He hurries into the dining room, his hope renewed by the woman he is certain he saw pass by. But the room is empty when he enters, so he follows the only path she could have taken: through the sitting room to the living room. When he turns the final corner, he comes to an abrupt halt. She's there, and she's staring right at him, green eyes burning bright. It is not his mother, but he knows her face all the same; and just as he watched her do thirty years ago, the spirit raises the sawed off shut gun in her hand, and fires. The first shot is fired at the wall; and even though he knows it's coming—even though his brain screams at him to look away—Eldritch is frozen in place with no choice but to watch as the second shot blows off her head. Blood, brains, and hair splatter all across the ceiling, the walls, the television, and furniture. Only after is he able to force his eyes closed, the shotgun blast still ringing in his ears.

When Eldritch opens his eyes, the room is back to normal. There is no blood, no bone, no body. Everything is as it should be—dark and empty. The ringing in his ears persists, and Eldritch curses the gunshot before realizing… it's not in his ears at all.

The landline.

Eldritch rushes back to the kitchen, the sound giving him a sudden burst of energy. He jerks the phone from the wall and calls out for his parents.

"Mama? Dad? Can you hear me?"

His father's voice comes through the speaker against his ear, loud and clear.

"Get your hands off him!"

"Dad! Dad, I'm fine!" Eldritch shouts, clutching the receiver against his head with both hands.

He must know about the demon holding me. Or maybe the spirit with the shotgun.

"I said get your hands off my son!"

"Dad, I'm okay, I promise," he tries to assure his father, to put his fears to rest. He sounds so angry, and Eldritch is hit once again with a feeling of déjà vu. This, like so many of the other calls, sounds familiar. He hasn't the time to think on it any further because now his mother is speaking.

"It's okay, baby boy, it's okay."

"Mama!" He chokes back tears at the sound of her sweet voice calling him her baby boy after all these years.

"Never again. We're going home."

Home? What did she mean by that? Are they coming back to me?

Static creeps into the line, and Eldritch grows desperate, trying to stave off the impending end of the call.

"Mama, Daddy, wait! Please don't go!"

But the line goes dead.

Eldritch hangs up the receiver and lets the tears fall. He was so close, so close. He knows they heard him. They are trying so hard to keep him safe, but there's only so much they can do from the other side. Yet, through all this, he finds a glimmer of hope.

"We're going home."

Home.

They're coming back to me.

He smiles through the tears and decides it best to start cleaning the kitchen. He doesn't want his mother to be upset with the state of the place.

More time passes, another day, maybe two—Eldritch isn't sure. The kitchen is back to normal, save for the microwave which will need to be thrown away. He still hasn't taken it outside. The large trash can is all the way near the sheds at the back of the yard. It's a long walk and if the phone rings while he's out, he could miss it. *The broken pieces are fine where they are*, Eldritch decides. He swept them into a neat pile in the corner of the kitchen, out of the way where no one can trip over them. His parents will understand.

There has been no sign of them since the last call, but Eldritch knows things like this must take time. He keeps the house dark. The demon is still present, and he hates seeing it slink around from room to room, as if it belongs here. He has to endure it a little while longer, until his parents return. *They'll know what to do. They always know what to do.*

Sometimes, when he falls asleep, Eldritch knows it's holding him. The mixed signals make his head spin. First it holds him, then it tries to hit him with a microwave, then it wants to hold him again.

"I wish you'd just make up your mind," he says to it, drifting in and out of consciousness. "I wish I knew what you wanted from me."

He dozes off for about five minutes when there comes a pounding at the door. Eldritch's eyes fly open.

They're here! They've made it!

He shoots up from the sofa and sprints through the house. The knocking grows louder and louder, and now there's a voice calling his name in desperation.

"Eldritch! Eldritch, open up! Eldritch!"

He knows that voice. *Dad!*

"I'm coming!" he shouts, his voice raw and weak, "I'm coming! Hold on! Please don't go!"

He pulls open the door, unable to contain the joy bubbling up within him. The glare of sunlight hits him square in the face, and his eyes take some time to adjust to the brightness. But when the person before him comes into focus, Eldritch can't hide his disappointment.

"Uncle Cal." The smile disappears from his face, and Eldritch wants to crumble as the excitement drains from his body.

"Do you know how close I was to calling the cops?!" his uncle rails on him, "Where have you been?! What have you been doing?!"

Eldritch doesn't like being yelled at, and the tone his uncle is taking does not sit well with him. "Here. Where else would I go?" he snaps back, wrapping his arms around himself against the cold.

Calvin's eyebrows shoot up to his hair line, then his face changes—brow furrowing, eyes narrowing in anger, "Do you know how long I've been calling you? Do you know how many days it's been since anyone has seen or heard from you? Do you even know what day it is?"

Eldritch doesn't know what today is and he couldn't care less. Calvin needs to leave. The phone could ring any second. He shrugs and moves to shut the door. Calvin reaches out and pushes against it, stopping it from closing.

"It's the day after Christmas, Eldritch! Did you miss it?"

Eldritch blinks, unaffected by the news.

"I haven't heard from you in days! *Days*, Eldritch! You know you can't do that! You can't do that to me, not after—" Calvin stops, but Eldritch knows what he means to say, sees the tears in his uncle's eyes.

"My phone is broken. It doesn't work anymore. I haven't had a chance to get a new one." It isn't a total lie. "I've just been catching up on some much-needed rest."

"Oh, is that all? What rest? You look awful, Eldritch. Like you haven't slept in weeks."

"Well, I have. I'm fine. I'll be fine, Uncle Cal."

Eldritch knows his uncle isn't buying it.

"Kelly's been trying to get in touch with you too. You know that? She called me in a panic yesterday—on *Christmas*—said she had been trying and trying but couldn't get a hold of you. So, she called me."

Kelly. Kelly spent her Christmas worrying about me.

He feels a pang of guilt at the thought of causing her any distress or heartache.

She doesn't deserve this, and I don't deserve her. I have to cut her loose or I'll just drag her down with me.

"Yeah, well, maybe I don't like being smothered." Each word is a knife against his flesh as he says them, but they are necessary. "I need some space, okay? This is a difficult time of year for me, and I'm tired of all the coddling. Kelly wants something I can't give her. So why don't you pass that along next time she calls?"

Kelly, I'm so sorry. I'm so sorry. I'm so sorry.

The words are on a loop in his mind, and he's never hated himself more than he does in this moment.

"I don't understand you, Eldritch." Calvin's voice is quieter, but the anger and confusion are still there, written all over his face. "You have something good like that, a good woman like that…and you're just going to toss her aside? Because what? You're upset?"

Eldritch doesn't want to hear this. He knows his uncle is concerned for him and means well, but there are things happening in this house that he could never understand.

"The coddling goes for you too," Eldritch says with an undeniable sharpness. "I don't need you breaking down my door or letting yourself inside every time I don't pick up the phone. Maybe you need to back off." The words are ice water on a heated conversation. Eldritch feels like a monster as he closes the door on his uncle's shocked expression. Calvin doesn't knock again.

Leaning against the front door, Eldritch throws his head back against the wood. It hurts—a quick jolt of pain that radiates outward. He does it again and again, hands clutching the fabric of his shirt as he carries out his punishment. He knows this will only exacerbate his headache—that he'll probably end up with a migraine—but he doesn't stop. What he wouldn't do for his headache medication right about now.

It would definitely be useful—in more ways than one, he thinks as he continues to ram the back of his head into the wooden door until he becomes lightheaded and drops to the floor. Sitting with his back against the door, Eldritch fights to silence the voice in his mind—the whisper he cannot allow himself to believe—as his head falls forward and he's rendered unconscious by the continued abuse.

They aren't coming.

Hours later, he is awakened by a cold, wet sensation moving against the palm of his right hand. The pain in his head is worse, and he struggles to open his eyes. When he does, he's shocked to find a dog—not just any dog; a muscular, white greyhound with gray, brindle ears—sniffing around his hand.

"Topper?" he asks in amazement. The greyhound looks up at him before trotting down the hallway toward the den. Eldritch staggers to his feet, bracing himself against the solid door behind him, and follows after. When he enters the den, Topper is standing by the back door, and he's not alone. Beside him, with her hand on the doorknob, is the lady from the painting, bedecked in her Victorian garb. She opens the door, and she and Topper walk outside together. The door shuts behind them, and Eldritch is left gaping, speechless in their wake.

"There's no way," he says, pulling the door open in pursuit. "There's absolutely no way."

The daylight is fading as the sun sinks into the horizon, and Eldritch flips on the floodlights, illuminating the backyard; but Topper and the lady are nowhere to be found. To get a better look, he pulls open the screen door and walks out into the yard. The ground is cold and damp, and moisture seeps into the soles of his socks from the frosty, dead grass. Eldritch shivers in the cold, the temperature having plummeted since he'd first opened the door for Uncle Cal.

He does a sweep of the area, scanning the visible expanse of the yard, but finds nothing. The ghost lady and her dog have vanished. The area near the sheds, at the very back of the yard, is black as pitch, shaded by the thick grove of trees on the property line. Eldritch squints, trying to get a better look from his position near the house, but it's impossible in the dwindling light. For a second, he thinks he sees movement.

That could be anything. Raccoons in the trash. Squirrels hopping around in the pecan tree, moving the branches about.

But there is a problem with the pecan tree: it isn't a pecan tree anymore. His feet move of their own accord, walking forward, taking him closer to the tree. He sees it, looming over his father's sheds. It's still a large, towering presence in the backyard, but it's…wrong. The branches are different, the leaves are different. It shouldn't even *have* leaves, not in December, but there they are: bright green as if this were a midsummer's day. He's standing under it now, and it's massive and so very familiar.

Tall, strong, and green. It reminds me of Gran-Gran's house—

It hits him like a punch to the gut, his stomach dropping when he realizes he's staring at the oak tree from one of his most harrowing childhood memories.

"No," he whispers to the wind as it blows past, carrying with it a sound—dreaded and disturbing.

Creak.

"No. It's just the tire swing from back when I was little."

But the tire swing has been gone for decades.

Creak.

"No, no, no," Eldritch repeats over and over, closing his eyes.

Creak.

"No. Not again. Never again."

Creak.

"Just don't look. Don't look at it."

But his eyes fly open against his own volition, and there before him is the hanged man. He swings back and forth, eyes wide and bulging out of their sockets. Eldritch's mouth opens on a silent scream, limbs locking in unbridled terror, reduced to his terrified, four-year-old self; and just as he fears, the hanged man opens his mouth and lets out the blood-curdling wail, the wail that has echoed in Eldritch's mind for decades.

Then, Eldritch is moving—running—as fast as he can back to the house. He makes it onto the porch, then into the den, slamming the door behind him. Eldritch struggles to catch his breath as the panic attack threatens to overtake him. Willing himself to calm down and get a grip, he focuses on his breathing—steady, intentional, measured breaths. After the initial wave of anxiety passes, he chances a look out the back door. The oak tree is gone, and the pecan tree is standing in its rightful place, leafless and bare, lying dormant in the cold of winter.

Eldritch steps away from the door and walks into the kitchen to stand by the phone. He knows it's coming, so he waits. This time, when it rings, he is hesitant to answer. He wants to hear his parents' voices more than anything, but something is off. Eldritch isn't an idiot. He knows there is something very wrong here, but he answers anyway.

"Hello?"

"I said I would protect you, and I failed," his father's voice is quiet, and Eldritch can tell he's crying. "Please forgive me, Eldritch. I'm so sorry."

"Dad, is it really you?" Eldritch doesn't expect an answer, putting it all together at last.

"You did nothing wrong, love," comes his mother's voice. "You are my brave, brave boy."

"It's not you, is it?" The tears flow as Eldritch finally voices what he has feared in secret throughout this entire ordeal. He's heard these words before; he's lived them. He's been listening to his own memories. "It's not them, is it?" he cries into the receiver.

"Eldritch," another voice comes through, one that has him balling his hands into fists. "I don't think you understand how delicate your situation is."

Holland.

Eldritch remembers this conversation, remembers the threat the minister made that night. With the sound of Holland's sanctimonious tone in his ear, he grips the receiver, squeezing it as hard as he can. Even after all this time, nothing makes his blood boil more than Len Holland. Eldritch clenches his jaw and grits his teeth as the reverend's voice slithers through the line.

"You have a powerful gift, and the enemy is going to try to sway you to his side. The more you go around talking about ghosts, the more you're letting Satan win. If Satan wins, I fear for you and your soul."

Holland's words carry a different meaning as he hears them a second time—as the events of his life play across his mind's eye. His rage begins to ebb, giving way to something else: shame. He hasn't exactly been doing God's work in recent years, and his past is riddled with heartache, failure, addiction, and cowardice.

"I fear for you and your soul." Son of Satan. Isn't that what Ryan said they called me? Maybe they were right…

The sharp, dissonant squeal of feedback penetrates his ear, but Eldritch doesn't pull away. When the sound has reached its zenith, and he is certain it can't get any louder, the feedback transforms into an inhuman growl. The growl becomes a voice—deep, demonic—and the hairs on the back of his neck stand on end once again.

CALLING ELDRITCH HAYES

"Careful what you wish for, Eldritch Hayes!" the entity bellows through the phone, repeating the threat it uttered weeks ago in the Birch-Rainey house.

The audacity this spirit has; the way it has manipulated him, made him think his parents were reaching out. The thought stokes the dying embers of rage in his belly, and it returns in full force. Eldritch has had enough of these games and screams into the phone, "Tell me your name!"

No name comes, only numbers. "Sixty-six, twelve, seven, eight, nine. Sixty-six, twelve, seven, eight, nine!"

"What's does that mean?!" he yells at the top of his lungs, grips the bottom of the receiver, and begins slamming it into the wall over and over, tearing through the paint and drywall until the receiver breaks apart. When he can't hammer it anymore, Eldritch grabs the base of the phone and rips it off the wall, throwing it across the kitchen.

He hears movement in the dining room and knows what he will find once he rounds the corner. Just as he suspects, three chairs are upended on the table and one is pulled out, offering him a seat. Eldritch stares at the demon across the room. Even in the dark, he knows it's there; he can feel its eyes on him. The glass has returned to the table, and the bottle of Jack Daniel's rises from its spot and pours three fingers. He's never wanted it more, but he won't cave—not now. Eldritch knows the demon's game and he laughs, the sound bitter and forced, and walks the other way, back into the den. He grabs his phone off the end table, screen cracked from where he'd thrown it at the wall. He has no idea if it even works anymore, but he pockets it anyway. Finding his shoes beside the couch, he pulls them on, marches into the living room, and grabs his coat from the closet. Then, Eldritch is out the front door, keys in hand. He has no idea where he's going, but anywhere is better than here.

CHAPTER TWENTY-FIVE

"So, I've been meaning to talk to you about something," his father said as their laughter died down.

They'd been joking around in the lumberyard while Eldritch checked the inventory, but now it seemed his father had something serious on his mind. Eldritch stopped counting two by four's and turned to face his dad.

"Yeah? What's up?" he asked, worried he was about to find himself in the middle of a conversation he'd been dreading for the last decade.

Gene looked around, making sure they were alone before speaking. "Well, you know, I'm not getting any younger, and you've been working here steadily for what? Eleven years now? You'll be thirty soon, and it's got me thinking. What are your thoughts on taking over?"

That was the last thing Eldritch expected to hear. Although glad this hadn't turned into a discussion about his drinking habits—a constant fear that plagued his mind—Eldritch wasn't sure how he felt about the future of Hayes Hardware resting on his shoulders.

"But I work in the back," he responded, dumbfounded by the offer. "I do inventory, I stock shelves. I don't deal with people."

Eldritch was confused as to why his father would ever think him taking over the family business was an option. Yes, it was tradition for the store to be passed down, generation to generation, but that was before Eldritch the Anomaly popped up in the bloodline. Over the last eleven years, Eldritch had become more withdrawn and isolated. When he first started working at the store, they had tried placing him up front at the register, but after a few unexpected incidents involving customers who walked in with more than met the eye, Eldritch had decided he didn't want to deal with strangers anymore.

Gene had understood and found other ways for him to help out and contribute to the Hayes Hardware legacy. Eldritch was good at his job. He kept the place neat and orderly, was always on top of inventory, and he was good to have around when something heavy needed lifting. No one ever complained about his contribution, and Eldritch was content with his role. The thought of having to step into a more managerial position made him uneasy, certain he wouldn't be able to handle it.

"Eldritch, I know you're happy doing what you do around here," his father countered, "but I think you are capable of so much more. If you're interested, I can start training you in some of the more administrative responsibilities. If you don't think it's something you want to try, I'm fine with that. Calvin can take over."

In all honesty, Eldritch believed his Uncle Cal would do a much better job than he would. Calvin had great ideas and big plans for the place. It was no secret everyone else expected Eldritch to keep to the shadows, stay in the back, and not take ownership of the business. Everyone—Eldritch included—assumed Calvin was next in line when Gene retired. Which was why Eldritch was struggling to process what his father was telling him.

"You…think I'm capable of running this place? You have that much faith in me?"

"Eldritch, I have all the faith in the world in you."

Eldritch doesn't know why. He never understood what his parents saw in him, yet they continued to believe he was worth something, that he was made for something. He often wished he could see himself through their eyes; maybe then he'd feel a little better about his place in the world.

"Look, I don't want you to stress about this." His father came closer, placing a hand on each of Eldritch's shoulders. "We can start small. I'll show you a thing or two here and there. It's not like I'm retiring any time soon."

That sounded doable to Eldritch, and he nodded in agreement, "Okay, that doesn't sound too bad." He gave his dad a sheepish smile, lowering his head and looking down at the dirt and gravel near his feet.

"Hey, hey. None of that. Head up, son. Head up." Eldritch did as he was told and lifted his head to meet his father's gaze. He wished he could be more like his dad. Gene was everything in this world Eldritch wanted to be. As corny as it sounded, he was Eldritch's hero—the one who kept him safe from countless horrors.

I don't know what I'd do without you.

"We'll talk more about it later," Gene said, patting his son's shoulder and walking back toward the main building to start closing up for the day.

That evening, Eldritch and his father walked home together, complaining about the heat and how so many of the businesses on Main Street were struggling and closing their doors.

"The recession hit a lot of folks hard," Gene sighed, "I just thank the good Lord we were able to keep the lights on and recover."

"Small towns are dying everywhere, people leaving left and right. More jobs in the city," added Eldritch.

"Yep," said Gene with a snort, "guess we'll just have to pack up and move then."

"To the city? Isn't that where they keep all the people?"

"You know, I think so."

"Yeah, no thanks," Eldritch shook his head with a laugh.

Walking inside, they were greeted by the sound of Louise talking away on the kitchen phone.

"Well, I did not appreciate the way he did my son, so I most definitely will not be in attendance."

Eldritch and Gene shot each other a look, both trying to figure out who she was talking to and what about. *She does not sound happy. And why is she talking about* me*?*

"No. No, Cheryl," she continued, "he is most certainly *not* a Godly man, and I don't care who knows it."

"Holland," both men said in tandem, with no shortage of disdain.

Eldritch heard the slamming of the phone on the hook, and seconds later, Louise stormed down the hall in a flurry of frustration. When she noticed her husband and son standing in the living room, she cocked a hip, bringing her right hand to rest on it, and with a shake of her head said, "You will not believe who I just got off the phone with."

"Don't tell me," said Gene, "was it Cheryl?" Normally, his father's antics would have Eldritch stifling a laugh, but thoughts of Reverend Holland were clouding his mind and souring his mood.

"Yes!" shouted Louise, tone sharp and eyes ablaze. "The little pot stirrer! I haven't spoken to her in ages!"

"Which Cheryl are we talking about here?" asked Gene.

"Cheryl Bickley!"

Gene shrugged.

"You remember Cheryl Bickley!"

"I have no idea who that is."

Eldritch could see his mom growing agitated, needing her husband to put a face to a name so she could continue with her story. "Gene. Cheryl Bickley. From the PH church. Her husband was always making change in the offering plate."

"Oh! *That* Cheryl," exclaimed Gene. "The one with the laugh."

"Yes! The hyena laugh. Anyways, guess what she just called to tell me because she was '*so* sure I'd want to know!'" Louise emphasized the last statement, adopting her best impression of the woman in question. "Apparently Len Holland is retiring and moving to Beaufort."

Eldritch was shocked by the news but far from disappointed. He hadn't laid eyes on Holland in nearly twenty years, but the man's shadow was inescapable, his presence in the town a tangible thing. The poison and lies Holland spewed about him had followed Eldritch around for decades. Deep down, he wondered if things would have been different for him if Holland hadn't turned on him—if he had just lied and said the name of some random demon when he realized Jessie wasn't possessed; but that would have been wrong, and

Eldritch couldn't have lived with himself after that—not that he did much living with himself now.

He had been ostracized, condemned, scorned, and made the butt of so many jokes over the years. *The Son of Satan.* That title had bounced around the back of his mind ever since the night Ryan had brought the nickname to light. No one would ever understand the damage Holland had done, even before *The Incident.*

"And get this," his mother's tirade pulled him from the spiral of thoughts Holland's name always sent him down, "they're throwing a special recognition service for him Sunday night along with a banquet. *That's* what Cheryl thought I'd want to know. She even had the audacity to extend an invitation."

His mom never got this angry about anything. Even in her dealings with Holland when Eldritch was a child, she was firm, yes, but always calm and collected. Now, she was full on ranting and rolling her eyes—something that was usually reserved for conversations about her mother.

"Well, there's another reason to disconnect that stupid landline," his father snorted.

"This Sunday night?" Eldritch asked, causing both parents to look at him, and he realized it was the first time he'd spoken throughout the entire exchange. "The day after my birthday?"

Louise nodded, and Gene huffed a laugh, "Well, happy birthday to you, right? Ugh. Good riddance if you ask me."

Eldritch didn't respond, his mind too busy replaying memory after memory of his time spent crushed under Holland's thumb; memory after memory of him being used as a puppet for Holland's own glory. This man was the reason he was an outcast in his hometown. Sure, it wasn't Holland's fault that Eldritch could see spirits; but as a religious leader, Eldritch felt the man could have done more to help him deal with the ability during his formative years. He should have been a mentor, someone Eldritch could count on and turn to for guidance; but instead, he'd used Eldritch as a show pony, a performing monkey. Maybe if Holland had been there to help him—a struggling, scared little boy—years ago, Eldritch's parents wouldn't have had to shoulder the burden on their own—shoulder the burden of *Eldritch* all on their own.

Amidst the racing of his mind, Eldritch noticed his parents had moved toward the kitchen, the subject of their conversation changing. Their words became little more than white noise as he headed to the basement—to what he kept hidden in his secret nook. With each step down the stairs, his thoughts continued to churn until they boiled down to one single conviction:

Len Holland is to blame for what I have become.

The church was crowded—Eldritch had known it would be—so he'd waited until most of the attendees had filed into the sanctuary before slinking up the stone steps and through the heavy wooden doors of his youth. He'd neglected to shave over the last few days, allowing his beard to grow as much as possible. Despite the oppressive July heat, he'd thrown on a jacket and pulled up the hood, snagging a pair of his father's reading glasses on his way out the door. It wasn't much of a disguise, but it was all he'd had to work with, and Eldritch believed if he kept his head down, he just might pass by unnoticed.

As he entered the church, the greeters welcomed him, and to his relief, seemed to have no idea who he was. He said nothing, for fear they would smell the whiskey on his breath, but he forced a smile and grabbed a seat in the back pew.

Eldritch hadn't set foot inside this church—in any church—since *The Incident* back in the mid-nineties. Being back was strange, unsettling, and Eldritch felt he was reliving a nightmare from a lifetime ago. His hands dug into the fabric of his jeans, and he let his head fall back, trying to catch his breath.

This room held so many memories, and even with a few drinks under his belt, Eldritch was able to call some of them to mind: Charlie Haskell and Amaymon, countless other demonic spirits that Eldritch had called out by name and Holland had cast out. He closed his eyes and remembered the cries of the afflicted, the growls of the demons, the shouts and sermonizing of Reverend Holland. If he hadn't lived it, Eldritch wouldn't believe any of it actually happened. It seemed surreal to him now, the situations this man had placed him in, and Eldritch and his parents had trusted him. His parents thought they were doing the right thing—the Godly thing—by encouraging their son to help others under the tutelage of the minister, but they had been deceived. Holland was never in the business of helping others; what happened with Miss Jessie was a testament to that.

A sudden blast from the organ refocused his attention on the task at hand. The congregation stood as the piano joined in, and the first hymn of the evening began. Eldritch started laughing as soon as he recognized it. *Of course*, he thought, refusing to believe it a coincidence, *of all the songs in all the hymnals in all the world*. He didn't even bother hiding his amusement as the people around him began to sing.

> Stand up, stand up for Jesus,
> The strife will not be long;
> This day the noise of battle,
> The next the victor's song.

To Those who vanquish evil
A crown of life shall be;
They with the King of Glory
Shall reign eternally!

As the song went on, Eldritch could only picture that prayer meeting—Miss Jessie's oblivious smile, and Holland's ominous whisper in his ear: *"Let's go get our crowns."* It still made his skin crawl.

When the hymn came to a close, the congregation was instructed to sit by a short, round, bald man with glasses. Eldritch thought he looked familiar, but was having difficulty placing him, until he spoke. *Lamont. Holland's number one stooge.*

"Good evening!" Lamont welcomed the congregation from the pulpit, and they answered in turn. He continued with the pleasantries, and Eldritch took that time to scan the rest of the sanctuary for familiar faces. Although aged over the last seventeen years, Eldritch recognized many of them—the same people who praised and cried and shouted during the spectacle of the deliverance services; the same people who turned on him after guzzling Holland's special brand of Kool-Aid about Eldritch's sinful nature.

"And that, brothers and sisters, is why we are here tonight: to celebrate and honor this true man of God!" Applause erupted from the pews in front of him, and Eldritch turned his attention back to Lamont. "To begin, we have a few people who would like to share a few words about Reverend Holland, and then we will open the floor up to anyone who wants to speak; then maybe, if we're all still awake, we'll let the man of the hour talk."

The congregation laughed at his lackluster joke, and Eldritch scoffed. *Spare me.* He struggled through speaker after speaker, flatterer after flatterer, going on and on about how selfless and holy Reverend Len Holland was—a true example of Christ, a helper to those in need, a teacher, a counselor, a friend. Eldritch wanted to throw up. Finally, Lamont stepped back up to the microphone. "Is there anyone else who would like to share? Anyone at all?"

Since half the congregation had already taken the stage to sing Holland's praises, there were no more volunteers. Eldritch had every intention of confronting Len Holland tonight. He knew exactly what he was going to say, had rehearsed it several times throughout the day. The plan was to catch him in private, after the service; but as Lamont opened the floor to any and every one present, Eldritch's whiskey drenched brain had a better idea.

Eldritch slid from the pew and started down the center aisle—the same path he'd watched others take on their way down to the altar; on their way down to him and Holland for deliverance. It was the longest walk of his life, and he felt every set of eyes on him, heard them turning in their seats, whispering amongst themselves. He saw Lamont's face, scrunched up in confusion, mouth opening and closing, as Eldritch ascended the stairs.

Only when he reached the pulpit, did Lamont finally step aside, his furrowed brow smoothing and eyebrows raising in recognition as Eldritch removed his hood, then the glasses. He turned, sliding the glasses into his pocket before bracing both hands on either side of the pulpit, and faced the congregation. His vision was a little blurry, eyes taking a second to catch up with the rest of his head as he surveyed the crowd, eyeing them all as best he could, until his gaze fell on the one face he'd come to stare down.

Though the once brown hair was streaked with grey and white, though there were more lines around the mouth and eyes—eyes which now sat behind a pair of large glasses—Holland was unchanged. He sat in the front row, looking up at Eldritch, eyes narrowed, the corner of his mouth curling upward in a smirk. As brazen as Eldritch had felt when the idea to take the stage had first entered his mind, now, he was reduced to the six-year-old child who once stood in this very spot. Except this time, he wasn't staring into the eyes of demon, he was staring into the eyes of something far worse.

If I'd known I was going to do this, I'd have had another drink.

His hands trembled against the smooth wood of the pulpit, and he could feel droplets of sweat sliding down his back as the jacket trapped the sweltering heat against his already fevered skin. He cleared his throat, flinching as the sound echoed through the sanctuary, amplified by the microphone in front of him.

"G-g-good evening," he said, tearing his eyes away from Holland for a moment. Internally, he cursed himself for stuttering, cursed himself for his weakness.

A hushed murmuring filled the sanctuary as the parishioners came to realize who had taken the stage. Eldritch tried to speak again, but his eyes darted back to Holland's smug face, and he was overcome—feeling so many emotions at once he could scarcely name them all. Anger, hurt, rage, shame, hatred, fear. He gazed into Holland's eyes, eyes which showed no remorse for what had been done to Eldritch. Then, the minister's expression shifted; as he looked up at the broken man Eldritch had become, his smirk spread and broke into a wide, satisfied grin.

The entire speech Eldritch had planned, all the words he'd carefully selected and rehearsed, left his mind in an instant as Holland bared his teeth. The hammering of his heart and the rush of blood in his ears were all he could hear, and the combination was deafening, filling his head until he thought it would explode. When the hammering and the rushing ceased, the minister's rebuke roared to life in his mind.

"Devil! Get thee behind me!"

He remembered the force of Holland shaking him, those large hands holding him in an iron grip. Eldritch's throat seemed to close up, and his mouth trembled as he tried to speak.

"I'm…I'm…I'm sorry." He turned from the pulpit, stumbled down the steps, and with one last glance at Holland's face, he was down the aisle and pushing on the heavy wooden doors that led outside. He cried all the way home.

Throwing open the front door, Eldritch startled his mother who was sitting on the couch in the living room, writing in a notebook. He moved past her and into the kitchen, head pounding and throat dry, in desperate need of a glass of water and his headache meds.

Louise followed after, calling his name. "Eldritch! What in the world?" she shouted as he filled a glass with water from the tap and chugged it.

He polished off the entire glass and, gasping, choked out, "I went to the service. I saw him. I saw Holland."

"Oh, Eldritch…"

"I looked him dead in the eye, and-and there were so many things I wanted to say. I was going to tell him what I thought of him, tell him how I really felt. He was right there! *I* was right there! I had a mic and everything, but-but I couldn't do it. I ran."

His mother's hand rested on his shoulder as he braced himself against the sink, head bowed, sobs wracking his body. "You couldn't do it because that's not who you are. That's not how we raised you. You're better than that." She placed her notebook on the counter beside them and turned Eldritch around to face her, her hands cradling his face. "That man doesn't deserve your tears, but if you need to cry for *you*—to get it all out—you do that."

Eldritch leaned forward and buried his face in his mother's shoulder as she wrapped her arms around him. "I'm weak. Scared and weak. That's all I've ever been," he sobbed into her fluffy robe.

"Never. You have never been weak." She pulled back a fraction, and Eldritch lifted his head. "Not many people could live with this gift of yours. You are stronger than you know, baby boy," she smiled, pushing his hair back from his forehead.

"I'm a thirty-year-old man now," he laughed.

"Doesn't matter. You'll always be my baby boy."

Eldritch felt himself calming down, felt himself coming back from the edge. His heart rate was returning to normal, and the tears had begun to dry. He set his glass in the sink and glanced over at the notebook to his left. The design on the cover was a mix of flowers—*of course*—and green and gold swirls. He'd never seen it before.

"What you writing?" he asked. His mom didn't have a habit of journaling, so he was curious if she'd taken up a new hobby.

Louise grabbed the notebook off the counter, "Oh, nothing. Just jotting some stuff down." She walked off in the direction of the den, and Eldritch watched her file the notebook away in the glass front bookshelf. "Why don't you take a shower? Might make you feel better."

He nodded, knowing a hot shower would probably help his head some. "Yeah, and I think I'm going to turn in early tonight. I'm exhausted," he said as he walked past her, heading up the stairs.

"Good idea. A shave might make you feel better too!" she called after him. Eldritch chuckled in response, closing the bathroom door behind him.

As he stood there under the spray of scalding water, he thought back to the church and his disastrous attempt to confront Holland. He was angry with himself for not speaking, for not saying everything he'd planned. That was his only chance, and he'd blown it.

"You couldn't do it because that's not who you are. That's not how we raised you. You're better than that."

Eldritch slammed his fist into the tile in front of him, felt the skin on his knuckles split, saw the blood pour out and mix with the water as it flowed down the drain.

But what if I'm not?

CHAPTER TWENTY-SIX

Eldritch has no idea where he's going. He has no plan, just throws the car in reverse and peels out of the driveway, taking off down Main Street. He drives for hours with no destination in mind, his thoughts consumed by recent events. He was desperate to see his parents again and foolish enough to believe that after eight long years, he'd finally found them. The entity knew that; it knew what Eldritch wanted more than anything, and it played him. It moved in, and he barely batted an eye. It held him like a loved one—with an intimacy that should have repulsed him—and he leaned into it. It couldn't possess him, but it used every trick in the book to break him. If Eldritch hadn't fled when he did, he wasn't sure what would have happened.

He pulls into a deserted landing at Lake Murray and parks the car in a gravel lot near the water's edge. Leaning across the center console of his Celica, he pops open the glove box and finds a phone charger, plugging one end into the cigarette lighter and the other into his dead cell phone. He leaves the car running for the phone to charge, climbs out, and walks down to the lake.

Eldritch paces along the shoreline, his pounding head buzzing as he replays every phone call, every trick, every temptation. God, how he'd wanted to take that drink. He felt his resolve cracking with every glass that was offered. His hands tremble at the thought of how close he'd come, so he balls them into fists at his sides, clenching them with all his might. His fingernails dig into the flesh of his palm, and he feels they may break the skin if he doesn't relent. When he can no longer contain the flood of emotions within, he cries out, screaming at the top of his lungs. His throat stings from the force of it. It hurts, but he wants to do it over and over again, wants to purge the rage and despair from his tired body, wants to scream until his throat bleeds and he leaves this world choking on his own blood.

He's not at their graves, he's not at the crash site, but he knows it doesn't matter—he's always known—as he cries out to the night sky.

"I need you to tell me what to do! I'm completely lost here! I messed up!" The desperation in his voice is palpable. "There's something in the house. It's after me, and I can't name it. It's so strong, and I let it get too close. It made me think—" he's almost embarrassed to tell them, ashamed that he fell for the ruse, that he mistook the manipulated echoes of memories long passed for the voices of his parents reaching out from the other side. "It made me think you were still here, that you were trying to talk to me. But you're not…you're gone. You're both gone, and you're so far away, and I have no one!"

His face is a mess of tears and snot as he pours his heart out to his parents, unsure if they're listening, if they're even able to hear him. "It doesn't matter how many times I walk around this town; it doesn't matter how many times I visit your graves or the spot where you—you're not there!" He pauses, eyes glazing over, gaze caught somewhere in the strip of moonlight reflecting on the water.

"…You died."

It's the first time Eldritch has said those words. He's skirted around them with expert precision, mentioned the accident, said they were "gone." But to say they are dead—to acknowledge the finality of it—that is something new.

"You died," he says again, as if it's dawning on him for the first time. "You died, and I can't get you back, as much as I wish I could."

He's weeping, his body shaking as grief comes to collect its due. There is no one around to see, no one around to hear as he chokes on a violent sob and whispers, "You can't even hear me, can you?"

The night is still and quiet. Eldritch hears nothing—no wind, no birds, no gentle lapping of waves at the water's edge. *I really am all alone.*

The thought infuriates him, and he looks up at the sky again. "And *You*!" he yells, railing on his Creator, "where have *You* been?! What about all that 'I will never leave you nor forsake you' crap?! I guess that didn't extend to me. You drop this 'gift' on me, and what? You dip out?!"

He laughs—a dour sound, grave and devoid of hope—the laugh of a man at the end of his rope with nothing else to cling to. He surprises himself, finally giving voice to the resentment that has lurked in the darkest corners of his mind—the resentment he was too afraid to express for fear of God's judgement and wrath—but now, he has nothing to lose. If God were to strike him down this very moment, Eldritch would thank Him for taking the initiative.

His knees buckle—legs giving way under the weight on his shoulders—and sink into the mud. It seeps into the fabric, staining his jeans, but Eldritch doesn't care. *I belong in the dirt*, he thinks to himself, digging his fingers into the wet earth.

"I tried so hard to be good, to follow You like You said, and it wasn't easy." His voice is quiet now, the energy and fight draining from him as he collapses, bowed in surrender before the God of the universe, the God he feels rejected him long ago. "I struggled for so long. I dealt with so much. Most days I barely got by…and then You go and take the only two people in this world who understood, who made my life bearable. You took them from me. You took them, and You left too, and I have never been angrier with anyone in my whole life!" He raises his voice at the last few words, the sound bouncing off the flat surface of the placid water in front of him.

"I am so angry at You. You. Left. Me. 'My strength is made perfect in weakness.' That's what You said. It's in the Book, it was on the picture in the den, so it must be true, right? What about *my* weakness? Where was Your strength when I was broken—when I was a sobbing, drunken mess on the floor?" Thoughts of his addiction flash before his eyes—the nights where he was blitzed out of his mind, crying out to God in the dark of night.

"I never stopped believing in You—in spite of everything, but that wasn't good enough. *I'm* not good enough. I never was."

Eldritch sits back on his heels, muddy hands resting on his thighs, head bowed and breathing labored. "I have nothing left," he sighs. "I can't do this anymore. If You don't step in, if You don't do something, I won't last much longer…maybe I don't want to." He thinks of a night, seven years ago—a night he doesn't like to talk about but can never forget. "You should have taken me years ago."

Eldritch goes quiet and his sobs subside as he rests in the still of the night, allowing himself a moment to breathe—to breathe and to simply *be*. A soft breeze cuts across the water, breaking the silence with the rustle of leaves. Eldritch closes his eyes and lets the gentle gust surround him. It fills his lungs, combs through his tousled hair, and dries the tears on his face.

He finds the strength to stand and trudges back to the running car, turning the ignition off and checking to see if his phone managed to charge. When he holds the side button, to his relief, the phone lights up, battery over fifty percent. The phone erupts in a flurry of notifications—countless texts and missed calls from Uncle Calvin, Amir, and Kelly.

Kelly.

He closes his eyes, clutching the phone in his hand, the thought of how he treated her making him sick to his stomach. They need to talk, but in person. He checks the time; it will be dawn soon. She should be back in town, reopening The Grind in about three hours. Eldritch is resolved to fix things with her. That is step one.

With his phone operational once more, Eldritch knows there is something he needs to look into. Opening the internet browser, he types into the search bar: "66 12 7 8 9."

The first result is a cluster of coordinates on a map, pinpointing a spot in the middle of the ocean. *Irrelevant.* Scrolling down, he sees several results related to math problems—equations, multiplication tables, fractions—but he doubts the demonic spirit is trying to give him an algebra lesson, so he keeps scrolling. Eldritch is halfway down the second page of results when he realizes he's found it.

He clicks the link, and the entire twelfth chapter of the book of Revelation appears, with verses seven, eight, and nine highlighted. Eldritch reads the passage to himself and takes a deep breath. The sun will be rising soon, and Kelly will be opening The Grind in about two and half hours. He can't go home, not yet, so he decides to return to the water's edge to sit and wait—wait for the sun to rise; wait for the dawn of a new day.

"Kelly!" he shouts as he jerks open the door to The Grind. The joy he feels when he lays eyes on her—dark blonde hair thrown up on her head in a messy bun, apron already covered in flour—is indescribable.

Kelly looks up from the register, shocked to see Eldritch rushing toward her, pushing past the patrons filed inside.

"Eldritch, what—?" Her question dies on her tongue when she spots him, and Eldritch can't imagine what a sight he must be. His hair is a disheveled mess, unwashed and windblown from his night outdoors. His clothes are dirty with large mud stains on the knees of his jeans and elbows of his jacket. His face is gaunt—pale and tired—and he's sporting a full beard and dark circles under his eyes.

"I need to talk to you," he insists, approaching the counter.

The line of customers he breezed past are shooting a mixture of worried and disapproving looks his way, but he doesn't care. *Let them think I'm crazy.* Kelly gapes at him, and Eldritch knows she's torn. He sees the relief in her eyes—relief that he's alive, up and walking around—but there's something else there: apprehension and hurt. Eldritch doesn't blame her, understands her being guarded and confused by his sudden appearance after days of silence.

"I'm working. We're slammed if you didn't notice."

"I need to talk to you," he repeats. "It's important, I swear." In desperation, he reaches out for her, but she does not reciprocate the motion. She remains fixed, eyes unblinking, expression unreadable, and Eldritch fears it's too late.

"Let me help these customers first. Go wait in the back dining room, and I'll be with you in a few minutes."

Eldritch breathes a sigh of relief, grateful for a chance to explain himself, "Thank you. Thank you, Kelly." He steps away from the counter, moving through the crowd of people toward the entrance of the dining area.

As he passes into the dining area, he hears Kelly call out after him, voice shrill and panicked, "Wait! Eldritch, don't—! I forgot—!" but it's too late.

Eldritch steps into the back room and finds he isn't alone. A long table is set up, off to one side, and seated around it are several men from the community—a sea of white hair and white skin in their Sunday best. Many of them look his way as he enters, eyeing this curious individual who just interrupted their breakfast meeting. Some of their faces he recognizes, some are unfamiliar to him. The man seated at the head of the table, with his back to Eldritch, sees his colleagues have become distracted by something, and he turns in his seat to look behind him.

Time stands still when Eldritch's eyes fall on the aged but undeniable face of Len Holland. He is rendered speechless, standing there with all eyes focused on him, a cruel reminder of that night he took the stage at the farewell service.

Kelly rushes in behind him, "I'm sorry, I forgot. I tried to warn you."

Eldritch doesn't respond, doesn't even acknowledge her at first. He stares straight ahead, unable to tear his eyes away from the old man sitting not twenty feet away from him.

Kelly tries to convince Eldritch to leave, to walk back out front with her, but he is a stone, immovable and unrelenting.

Well, hello there!" Holland pipes up from his seat at the table, voice cheerier and friendlier than Eldritch ever remembers it being. "Can we help you, son?"

Son?

"Come on. Let's go," Kelly urges again, pulling on his arm, but Eldritch wrenches it free, eyes never leaving Holland.

"You…you don't recognize me?" Eldritch asks, half insulted, half curious if old age has chipped away at the man's memory.

Holland looks Eldritch up and down, and shakes his head, "I'm sorry, son. I don't, but I have been away for a long time. Just in town visiting for Christmas."

Eldritch isn't convinced, not yet, so he takes a step forward. "I'm Eldritch Hayes."

That gets a reaction from several men at the table—shocked faces and whispers of his name—but Holland appears unaffected by the information. He brings a hand to his chin and strokes it while looking up at Eldritch, eyes squinted in concentration. "Eldritch Hayes… Eldritch Hayes," he repeats the name over and over, as if searching his memory bank.

Eldritch's blood simmers in his veins. "Oh, come on," he says with a dangerous smile, "of all the names you got stored away up there, I know that one's got to ring a bell. Eldritch Hayes."

"I'm sorry, but I just don't remember you," Holland says with a shrug.

Eldritch doesn't know what to think. As much as he hates to admit it, the man's forgetfulness seems genuine.

"Eldritch, please. We can talk outside." Kelly is back at his side, hand squeezing his upper arm.

He yields and nods at Kelly. "It's not important. Sorry to interrupt," he says, turning from the table of white-haired men—turning from Holland.

"Uh-huh. Just run along, like you did last time."

The words strike like the crack of a whip, and Eldritch spins back around to face the old man. Holland's back is already turned, so Eldritch pulls away from Kelly and marches over to the table. He stands inches from the old minister, looming over him where he sits, and the irony of their reversed positions is not lost on Eldritch.

"See? I knew there was no way you forgot me!" Eldritch spits in Holland's direction. "How could you? After what you did to me."

Holland laughs, "What I did? What are—"

But Eldritch is seething and refuses to let him finish. The audacity of this man, to pretend he'd forgotten all about Eldritch after what he'd done. "You know good and well what I'm talking about, *Len*." He hears his father's voice bleed into his own, the way it would when Gene had enough of Holland's patronizing, holier-than-thou behavior.

The other men at the table are stunned into silence, and Kelly is frozen behind him. Eldritch doesn't care. He's waited decades for this moment; and this time, he isn't running.

"You used me. You ruined my childhood, my life. You took advantage of my ability and tried to make yourself look good. So you could, what? Be the holiest of holy men in this tiny little town? Well, congratulations, Reverend Holland! You win!" His voice grows louder and louder, but no one dares interrupt his tirade, all too shocked to respond; except for Holland, who seems unbothered by the barbs Eldritch throws his way. He sits still, listening to every word with an air of stoicism.

"You're so smug. So righteous. But you know what? It's all fake—a fake righteousness because there is *nothing* holy or Godly about you! You kept me under your thumb for so long! I was afraid to do anything—to say anything without your approval! I was terrified! Terrified of disappointing you—terrified of *you*! And you loved it! You ate it up!"

Eldritch leans down and speaks directly into the old man's ear. "And poor Miss Jessie. What y'all did to her…that was assault, and you turned on me the second I contradicted you. You put your hands on me and called me the devil! She wasn't possessed, and you knew it! I *told* you, but you refused to be embarrassed, refused to be made a fool, refused to let people see you for what you are: a sad, selfish, self-important, little man." He emphasizes each word with a venomous bite before he stands to his full height and waits—waits for a response, or an apology, whichever the man chooses to give.

Holland turns to face Eldritch, removing his glasses and looking up to meet his eyes. "And what are you, Eldritch?" he asks.

Eldritch says nothing.

"Because," continues Holland, "I think I know exactly what you are."

"Is that so?"

"You were the boy who had a gift, but chose not to honor God with that gift, so He turned it into a curse. You are the boy who grew up, never accomplishing anything, and refused to take responsibility for that. You are the man who entertained evil, with all this talk of ghosts, and ended up corrupted by the devil and all alone in the world." Holland's face grows red and soon, he's rising from his chair and standing to face Eldritch. "The town drunk, the lunatic, the hermit, the nobody who decided to come here today and cut down a man of God! Boy, I have seen evil, and I have made it my life's work to rip it up by the root!"

Eldritch steps back, looking up at Holland and cowering—the tables turning a second time, casting him, once again, in the long shadow of the imposing minister. He tries with all his might not to crumble, but it's too much. As Holland shouts at him, berates him, demeans him, all the fire Eldritch felt when confronting the man is extinguished.

"It doesn't bother you?" His voice is small and broken. "How you treated me, what you did?"

"No," Holland says with a shrug, "but then again, you never even cross my mind."

Eldritch feels lost, humiliated—a child scolded in public—and he can't help but wonder if Holland has been right all along. *What if I am the wicked one? The man who "entertained evil"?*

"That is *enough!*" The anger in Kelly's voice startles Eldritch, and he jumps at the sound. "This is my café, and I'm thirty seconds from throwing you out, Reverend!"

"Oh, I believe we're done here," Holland sneers, flashing her a phony smile before sitting down. Eldritch is trembling, fighting the urge to cry.

I wish my dad were here.

He feels Kelly's hands on his arm, pulling him toward the front of the store, but before they turn the corner, Reverend Holland calls out over his shoulder, "Tell your mama and daddy I said hi."

Something within Eldritch shatters as the comment strikes its intended mark—the devastation from the blow spreading outward from the center of his aching chest—because Holland *knows* his parents are dead. Eldritch trips over his own feet as he runs from the room, pushing past the people at the front of the café as he makes a beeline for the front door. He knows he's causing a scene, but he needs to get out of there, he needs air, he needs…home.

Kelly is hot on his trail, following him out the door and running after him down the sidewalk. She catches up to him in his front yard.

"Hey, hey! Wait, Eldritch!" She grabs his arm, spinning him around to face her, but he's not interested in anything she has to say.

What glimmer of strength he may have felt, what semblance of peace he found at the water's edge, was stamped out by Len Holland. Kelly grabs his left hand with both of hers, and brings it up to her chest, cradling it and rubbing her thumb across the scar in his palm.

"Don't listen to him. We both know he is a wicked man. It's okay. Let's just talk about this."

Eldritch jerks his hand away, face twisting in anger. "What's there to talk about, Kelly? I can't *not* listen to him. Everything he said in there is true. I am nothing. I am no one. I am corrupt, and I'm alone."

"But you're not alone, Eldritch," Kelly shouts, tears spilling over her cheeks, "I'm right here!"

"For now. I don't know what you think this is," he snaps, motioning between them, "but it can't last. It won't last. I always end up alone, abandoned, tossed aside. God has tossed me aside, just like that man in there, and I'm not fool enough to think everyone else won't do the same. And *this,*" he holds up his left hand and points to the scar, "this doesn't mean whatever you think it means."

"Eldritch, stop this. Stop this, please," her voice cracks, and the sound cuts him to the core, but he can't do this anymore. It was folly to believe he could have this, that he deserved this—that he deserved her.

Despite every fiber of his being rebelling against the act—rebelling against the thought of breaking her heart—he makes his voice as cold and unfeeling as possible.

"Goodbye, Kelly," he says with finality, schooling his face into an expression that lets her know the subject is no longer up for discussion, and stalks down the walkway toward his front porch.

Kelly chases after, her sobs echoing off the concrete of the front porch, "Eldritch, please!"

He doesn't respond, doesn't look back as he shuts the front door in her face.

The demon within has been waiting for him—he can feel it—and Eldritch isn't the least bit surprised to find he is no longer affected by its presence. The putrid smell of death and rotting flesh does not revile him. There are no chills, no nausea. He has fallen so far these last few weeks, these last few years.

Holland was right about me, about what I am.

He collapses against the door and buries his face in his hands, hating himself for what he has become. *This is what I deserve. I'm a monster.*

His feet carry him to the dining room, and on the table, still sitting there from the night before, is the bottle of Jack Daniel's and the glass of whiskey. He has resisted for so long, fought it for so long, even before this entity set up shop in his house. Eldritch has fought it for seven years, and he just can't fight it any longer.

With a trembling hand, he reaches for the glass and holds it in front of him. The smell of the liquor drifts up to his nose, and he breathes deep, letting the scent fill his nostrils—fill his senses. He laughs once, twice; then, as the tears begin to fall, he brings the glass to his lips and drinks. The flavor explodes across his tongue—the burn, the oaky, caramel taste. Oh, how he's missed this. He drinks and drinks, and soon, the glass is drained. Everything in him breaks apart, like flotsam on the rocks, and he's unable to stop the salt of his tears from mixing with the smooth whiskey as he tosses back another glass.

He has lost everything: his childhood, his parents, his girl, his sanity, his faith. All the horrible memories, all the terrible things whispered about him, all his trials and hardships have led to this one moment: the final destruction of Eldritch Hayes.

Eldritch watches the shadow move from the dining room and into the kitchen. He hears it in the den, fiddling with the record player; and seconds later, the rich, ethereal voice of Karen Carpenter is there to serenade his ruin. "Solitaire."

A full-bodied laugh erupts from Eldritch as he listens to the words of the song; the story of a sad man who lived the rest of his days alone, a pathetic card game his only companion as he wastes away. He foregoes the glass and grabs the bottle, drinking straight from the source. The music fills the air, flowing from room to room, and Eldritch laments the tragedy of it all—how something that used to bring him so much joy—something that was so synonymous with his parents and brighter days—is now being used against him; an instrument of torture to drive him mad.

The volume increases, the song playing at full blast, a reminder of just how alone Eldritch is and always will be. The spirit is goading him, insulting him, making sure he's aware that it knows every thought, every fear—that it knows him better than anyone else ever could.

Eldritch takes another swig from the bottle—the alcohol wreaking havoc on his senses after seven years of sobriety—and staggers into the living room. The room spins around him, and he has to steady himself against the couch before shuffling over to the fireplace and grabbing the iron poker from the rack.

The song is still blaring when he reaches the den, and Eldritch decides he's had enough. After taking another long drag from the bottle and setting it aside, he approaches the old Magnavox. There is a moment of hesitation where his attention is drawn to the hypnotic movement of the record on the turntable, but it's short-lived as Eldritch raises the poker over his head and brings it crashing down in front of him. The first hit destroys the turntable and the album, sending it flying up in pieces. He swings again, and again, breaking the wood of the console, bashing in the dials and knobs. As he destroys this symbol from his childhood, he breaks apart alongside it—the shattered pieces of his heart and soul joining the slivers of wood, plastic, and metal with every destructive blow that is dealt.

When he feels he has done enough damage to the front of the player, he moves to the side, determined to smash the entire console to bits. He rears back with the poker, and glass shatters behind him as the front of the bookcase is destroyed. Eldritch is undeterred. He strikes it over and over again, screaming and sobbing with every swing. The cabinet doors are smashed, along with the treasured records inside. Nothing is safe from his attack. He swings and strikes until his arms are tired, until he no longer has the strength to clutch the poker. Only when it slips from his hands does Eldritch collapse, falling, unconscious, into the wreckage.

CHAPTER TWENTY-SEVEN

As the credits for *Scrooged* began to roll, Eldritch switched off the television and looked down at his phone: 9:36 p.m. *Where are they?* His parents had taken a day trip down to Charleston to visit Gran-Gran's grave—a tradition they honored every holiday since she passed. Eldritch, who seldom left the house for anything other than work, drained the rest of his whiskey and called his dad's cell phone. The second the call connected to his parents' car he could hear Gene fussing in the background.

"Daggumit! I swear, no one around here knows how to drive!"

"Hey, Dad?" Eldritch tried to talk over him, concentrating on every syllable, trying to mask just how drunk he was before ten o'clock on a Saturday night.

"Gene, watch that guy, he's going to try to jump over in front of you. Look at him! Didn't even use a signal."

Eldritch rolled his eyes and raised his voice. "Hello? Dad? Mama?"

"Oh, yeah—hey son," Gene began, "Sorry, just a bunch of idiots on the road today."

"Everything okay, Eldritch?" Louise called from the passenger seat.

"Yeah, I was just expecting you home a little earlier. I was getting worried."

His dad grunted, "There's a huge back up on I-26. I don't know what's going on. I'm about to get off at the Little Mountain exit and take backroads, I'm not fighting this anymore. We should be home in about twenty minutes."

"Okay, sounds good. I'll see you in a bit. You missed *Scrooged*, by the way."

"Ugh! See? I just can't win for losing today!" his father huffed. "Twenty minutes! Time me!"

The call was disconnected, and Eldritch decided twenty minutes was plenty of time for another drink, so he poured himself a few more fingers of whiskey. When the glass was drained, he looked down at his phone again: 10:01 p.m. *Well, he didn't beat that goal.* He laughed to himself, thinking how his dad was probably just shy of cussing right about now for not making that twenty-minute deadline; but as more time passed, Eldritch began to find less humor in the situation. At ten after, he called his father again. There was no answer. Trying his best not to panic, he tried his mother's cell. The phone rang and rang before going to voicemail.

Something's wrong.

No sooner had the thought entered his mind than the sound of sirens filled his ears. Eldritch jumped from his seat and ran to look out the front window of the house. Two—no three—highway patrol and Sommerset PD cars flew by, headed down Main Street as fast as they could go. Eldritch's heart began to pound.

No, no, no. I don't know anything yet. Calm down.

Again, he tried both their phones, and again neither Gene nor Louise answered his calls. In desperation, he called again, his shaking hands struggling to press the button.

"Mama, pick up!" he whispered to the ringing phone, "Mama, please pick up."

"Hey, this is Louise, leave a message!" His mother's voicemail, so cheerful and bubbly, chilled him in a way he couldn't explain. He hung up and tried his dad again.

"Come on, Dad."

Ring.

"Dad please. Please, God."

Ring.

"Dad..."

Ring.

"Please pick up...Daddy, come on."

"Hi, you've reached Gene Hayes of Hayes Hardware—" Eldritch hit the red button to end the call and began to spiral. He tried to talk himself down, convince himself that he was jumping to the worst-case scenario and there were hundreds of reasons why his parents weren't home or answering their phones. The cop cars were just a coincidence that his brain, fuzzy from the whiskey, had linked to his parents' delay.

He went into the kitchen and poured a glass of water, chugging it in an attempt to clear his head. He paced the house for another half hour and waited—waited for their car to pull into the drive, waited for the phone to ring, waited for the panic to subside—but the waiting proved in vain. Unable to silence the maelstrom of spiraling thoughts and fears in his anxious mind, Eldritch found himself running up the stairs, stumbling along the way on clumsy feet. He made it to his bedroom, shed his pajama pants, and threw on a pair of jeans and boots before racing back down to the living room. He tripped at the foot of the stairs, misjudging the last step, and nearly fell into the coat closet as he tried to open it.

Taking a minute to collect himself and breathe, he grabbed his coat, and tried once more to convince himself everything was fine.

Chances are there was another wreck on the backroads, and they got held up in traffic because of it. They're not answering because they're too busy fussing about how nobody can drive.

The thought was a short-lived comfort, and Eldritch shook his head, not wanting to delay any longer. Grabbing his keys from the table by the window, he headed out the front door, slamming it behind him with more force than intended. He stumbled down the steps on the side of the porch, cursing his eyes for refusing to focus, and struggled to find the right key to unlock the car. It wasn't until he pulled open the driver's side door and sat behind that wheel that the realization hit him:

I can't drive like this.

Pouring himself from the seat, he shut the door and leaned against it, legs unsteady and head spinning.

Where was I even gonna go? Follow the sirens?

As the idea settled in his mind, an ambulance blew past him, taking the same path the police cars had earlier.

Follow the sirens…

Eldritch pushed himself off the car and lumbered toward the sidewalk as quickly as he could in his current state. He decided the easiest way to calm his nerves and prove his paranoia wrong was to follow the ambulance and lights to whatever scene they were called to. As soon as he saw it didn't involve his parents, everything would be okay. It was possible they'd even drive past and see him walking down the road. The thought spurred him on, and soon his walk became a wobbly, shambling jog.

He passed The Grind and the general store and was approaching the Sommerset Drug Company when he saw blue lights cut around the corner, turning from McLeary Street onto Main at the stoplight. Eldritch froze, fear gluing his feet to the pavement. The highway patrol car sped down Main Street in the opposite direction Eldritch was traveling. As it passed, he turned to watch—had to make sure it kept going, kept going, kept going, past his house and out of town. When it passed the town square, Eldritch saw the red of its brake lights, and his stomach dropped. Then, the car made a left—a left into the Hayes's driveway.

"No, no, no, no—"

The fear that had held him in place now pushed him to move, to run. Eldritch sprinted as fast as he could, faster than he'd ever moved in his life—faster than that day at Gran-Gran's when he fled the hanging tree; but the terror he felt in this moment was a thousand times more profound than what he had he felt all those years ago.

He saw the car come to a stop, saw a highway patrol officer and a man in street clothes climb out and walk toward the front porch. Eldritch tried to catch up to them, but they seemed so far away, and no matter how fast he ran, he felt he was moving in slow motion. He heard the knock on his front door. The two men were speaking to each other, but he couldn't make out the words.

Then, it seemed time had sped up, and he found himself at the foot of the steps, looking up at the men at his door. The officer spotted him, tapped the other man on the arm, and nodded at Eldritch. The other man, donning jeans, a black jacket, and a ball cap, turned and walked to the edge of the porch, toward Eldritch, who had yet to move from his spot at the foot of the steps, and that's when Eldritch saw it: the writing on the man's jacket: CORONER. He knew the man was about to speak—knew he was about to say something Eldritch couldn't bear to hear. The need for the man to just say it—to deliver the news and get it over with—warred with his desire to never hear the words spoken aloud.

Removing his hat, the coroner opened his mouth to speak, and in the fraction of a second it took him to draw a breath, Eldritch's world began to crumble.

"Eldritch Hayes?"

―――――――――

Following the funeral, a wake had been held at the Hayes's home, and Eldritch found himself caught in a loop of handshakes, attempted hugs—which he resisted more often than not—hollow condolences, and platitude after platitude—which he had no desire to hear. It hadn't taken long for him to retreat to the basement, where he could find solace from the noise and the crowd of people whose names he didn't know—where he could find solace in what lay hidden away down there. Eldritch sat with his back against the cold, stone wall, legs bent, and feet planted on the floor in front of him. He still wore his black suit, but his tie had been discarded the second he descended the stairs, and it hung loosely off the top of a plastic tub of fall decorations. He'd had a few sips of whiskey and was letting it settle into his body, warming him up despite the chill of the damp room and concrete floor.

"*You missed* Scrooged, *by the way.*"

That was the last thing he had said to them. He'd been drunk, and that was the last thing his mother and father ever heard him say.

So stupid.

"Twenty minutes. Time me!"

Eldritch *had* timed him. He had timed him, but the car never pulled back into the drive. His father's last words to him were etched into his mind, but no matter how hard he tried, Eldritch couldn't remember the last thing his mother had said. The conversation had been brief, trivial, and he'd been far from sober. He cursed himself for not remembering. His mother was the most important person in the world to him, and he couldn't even remember the last thing he'd heard her say.

Oh, to hear her voice just one last time—to hear her call him "baby boy," to hear her make everything okay again, with just a few words, whenever he felt the world closing in on him.

Oil on troubled waters.

But now the world wasn't just closing in on him, it was crashing down around him, and she wasn't there to put it back together. She was gone, they both were. Never again would he hear that sweet, southern drawl of hers point out the irises and daylilies by name as they bloomed in the spring. Never again would he hear his father's terrible jokes and sarcastic comments or the sound of his warm, infectious laughter.

His entire existence had boiled down to a series of *never agains*, and Eldritch didn't know how to keep the list from growing. So, he took another swig, and another, and another, but the pain persisted no matter how empty the bottle became.

"Eldritch, you down here?" Uncle Cal called from the top of the stairs.

Eldritch wasn't surprised to hear his uncle searching for him, knew it would only be a matter of time before his absence was noticed. There was no point in hiding anymore.

"Yeah, I'm here," he rasped, voice raw from crying for the last three days.

The sound of Calvin's footsteps on the stairs prompted Eldritch to move, and he tucked the bottle away, before standing and shuffling to meet his uncle halfway.

"If I'd have known you were down here, I would have joined you." Calvin paused on the last step and gave him a weak smile as Eldritch emerged from the shadows. "I've had about as much of this as I can stand."

Eldritch nodded, still finding it difficult to talk about the ordeal. In fact, it was Calvin who had ended up making the arrangements and planning the funeral. Eldritch had been little more than catatonic—in the moments where he wasn't sobbing uncontrollably or drinking himself unconscious.

"Everyone's pretty much gone if you want to come back upstairs. Amy is tidying things up in the kitchen. You got enough food up there to feed an army."

Eldritch remained silent, eyes cataloguing the imperfections in the wall just over his uncle's shoulder.

"Eldritch, please talk to me," Calvin pleaded with his nephew.

"I don't know what to say. I don't have words anymore," Eldritch finally spoke, every syllable slurring into the next as they left his lips, carried across the room on shaky breaths made warm by the whiskey.

"I'm not going to insult you by asking if you've been drinking," Calvin sighed, stepping off the last step and onto the concrete floor of the basement, "but I don't like the idea of you drinking alone with everything that's happened. You sure you don't want to come and stay with me and Amy for a few days? The offer still stands."

Eldritch shook his head. The only thing he dreaded more than sleeping alone in this house tonight was leaving it. Tonight would be the first on his own since the accident. Calvin and Amy had slept here the last few nights taking care of the practicalities and forcing Eldritch to eat, but it was time for them to return to their own home. It was time for Eldritch to face this alone.

There were tears in Calvin's eyes when he moved toward Eldritch and pulled him into a tight embrace. Eldritch wrapped his arms around his uncle and listened to him weep into Eldritch's shoulder. Calvin had lost his brother, his best friend, and he was the only one who could understand a fraction of the pain Eldritch was feeling inside. Eldritch wanted to comfort the man, wished he had the capacity to, but he had nothing left.

Calvin pulled back, gripping Eldritch's shoulders, and looked him in the eye, "If you need anything, you call me, okay?"

Eldritch nodded and followed him up the stairs.

The closing of the front door behind his aunt and uncle rang through the house, and Eldritch was struck by the significance of it. That moment marked the end of the liminal space that seemed to exist between time of death and post-wake cleanup. The closing of the door signaled a return to real life—a life Eldritch was unprepared to face alone.

He had no idea what to do—had no idea what was expected of him—so, he retrieved his whiskey bottle from the basement and walked from room to room, imagining his parents in each setting. Both of them rushing around their bedroom, dressing before work. His mother hemming a pair of pants at the sewing machine in the spare room upstairs. His father shaving at the sink in the bathroom. The two of them watching television in the living room and reading in the sitting room. Gene reenacting that one Venkman moment from *Ghostbusters* at the piano, like he always did when he passed it. Both parents setting the table for a big Christmas dinner. Louise on the phone in the kitchen—the one they'd had disconnected a few years ago—chitchatting while she made dinner.

Eldritch moved from the kitchen to the den and faced the record player. He imagined his parents arguing over which record to put on, and it almost always ended up being one of four bands: The Eagles, Bread, The Hollies, or the Carpenters. He used to tease his parents about their taste in music; said they needed to get with the times, try out something new, invest in a CD player or something, but they never did. Both of them were content with their favorites from the late sixties and seventies, and in their minds, vinyl was the only way to listen to it.

Eldritch lifted the lid of the old Magnavox console, and his breath caught in his throat when he saw *Carpenters The Singles: 1969-1973* still sitting on the turntable, side two facing up. No one had touched this thing in days and the last record his parents had listened to was still sitting there, waiting for them to return. He thought back to five days ago. His mother had been blaring the Carpenters' Christmas album for a week straight, and his father had gotten sick of it, so they had compromised: the Carpenters could stay, but Gene needed a break from holiday music.

Switching on the console, Eldritch lifted the needle and placed it on the edge of the album. The opening line of "Yesterday Once More" wrapped around him, and Eldritch's head was filled with memories. Just when he thought he had nothing left—that he had long since cried himself to the point of emptiness—the tears returned, streaming down his face and dripping onto his shoes. He took a seat on the floor, leaned back against the console, and replayed memory after memory in his mind. When one album ended, it was replaced with another, and another; and it was almost as if his parents were there, listening to their favorite records while Eldritch watched the happiest moments of his life play out behind closed eyes.

As the sun rose over Sommerset, and sunlight began to stream through the windows, Eldritch remained where he was, content to stay there forever and never let the music end. As long as he had this—these records, this old Magnavox—he had something to cling to. And whenever the need arose, he could switch it on and be transported back to a time when he wasn't alone in this room; a piece of his parents would be there, and everything would be okay again.

CHAPTER TWENTY-EIGHT

When his eyes open, the first thing Eldritch sees is the ceiling above him. The fan is whirling around at high speed, and he stares at it for a while as his eyes begin to focus. The fan reminds him of something—a circle spinning, spinning, spinning.

Like a record.

The pain in his head is immense, reminding him of his worst hangovers from years ago.

Why do I feel like this? And why am I on the floor?

With his eyes still trained on the ceiling fan, he searches his memory for clues as to what led him here. He takes a deep breath in through his mouth and notices how fuzzy and dry it feels. Moving his tongue around and sucking on his cheeks to make himself salivate, Eldritch attempts to rid his mouth of the sensation. When he does, he can't ignore the familiar taste swirling around his tongue. It's acrid, bitter, and sets off alarm bells in his mind.

Oh, God, no.

He tries to lift his head, but the pain is too great, and Eldritch fears he had far more than one drink. His head drops back down, and he braces himself, expecting the back of his skull to hit the hardwood floor...but it doesn't. It lands on something else—in a pile of something else—that shifts and crunches beneath him, and he has no idea what it is. Closing his eyes, Eldritch thinks back to earlier.

He remembers the lake, remembers screaming at God at the top of his lungs; then there was the coffee shop and Kelly and—

Holland.

There was a fight, an argument, and Eldritch struggles to call the words of their altercation to mind. He knows Holland insulted him, berated him, and Eldritch started believing the words he spoke were true. If only he could remember specifics. Most of it is a blur, except for one comment that slithers its way to the forefront of his mind:

"Tell your mama and daddy I said hi."

That did it. That sent Eldritch running home, that set him off and made him turn on Kelly.

Kelly.

Eldritch remembers being cruel, remembers her face as she cried and begged him to stop, to stay and talk to her, but he didn't.

I don't deserve her. I'll only drag her down.

He follows his train of thought through the front door. He recalls how he felt, recalls the spirit waiting for him, and then...

The whiskey.

Eldritch curses himself for his weakness, the darkest slurs of self-deprecation emerging as he berates himself for throwing away seven years of sobriety; yet, as he lies there, amidst the whirlwind of self-flagellation, another thought creeps in.

Why does it matter? I've already sunk so low. Why does it matter if I have a drink?

He moves his arms, reaching out, searching for the bottle, but his hands continue to make contact with something else. He feels around with his right hand to determine what he's lying in—his head still hurting too much to raise it up and take a look. He grasps a piece of the curious pile, and rolls it around in his hand, sliding his fingers over it. The edges are rough, and instinct warns him of the prospect of splinters.

It's wood. Why am I lying in a pile of wood?

With his left hand, he does the same: feels around to grab another piece, but when he does, the object slices his flesh. Eldritch releases it with a gasp and feels the blood seep into his palm; feels the pain as it radiates from the gash. It reminds him of a night many years ago.

Glass.

He breathes in and out through his nose, trying to push the pain aside and figure out why he's surrounded by wood and glass after blacking out. His right hand moves again and grabs something thin and smooth—smooth with small ridges carved into it. As he rubs his fingers along it, he can tell it isn't wood, but the texture is familiar. One edge is curved, another is sharp and rough, as if it were broken on one end.

What is this? I know this.

His curiosity wins out, and Eldritch lifts his right hand, bringing the object within his field of vision. He squints and sees it's a fragment of something black.

Like a record.
Like a record...oh, God.

Eldritch drops the shard of vinyl and turns his head to the right, catching a glimpse of the wreckage around him at last...and he remembers. Panic sets in, and despite the pounding in his skull, he forces himself up, surveying the scene he was afraid he would find. The old Magnavox has been destroyed, smashed to bits—the records too, every last one of them—and Eldritch had done it.

"No. No, no, no, no, no!" He pushes himself onto his knees and starts grabbing at the shattered pieces of the record player, attempting to put them back together. Breathing is impossible—he tries but chokes on every sob that forces its way out of him.

"Oh, God, please no," his speech is reduced to a series of pleas and denials, unable to think of anything other than the damage he caused in a moment of drunken rage and anguish. He sees the broken albums, scattered all around, and lying on the floor, in the midst of the carnage, is the iron poker.

Eldritch crosses the line of panic and devolves into absolute hysteria. He's sobbing, scrambling, gathering every piece he can and trying to undo what cannot be undone. With a scream, he lets himself fall back into the wreckage, accepting the record player's fate.

He wallows in the debris until all his strength is gone—until he is exhausted and empty again; and that's when he feels it. The dark entity is there, encircling him, wrapping him in its sinister embrace. He feels the presence of evil stroke his cheek; it holds him close, and Eldritch hates himself for leaning into it.

His mind is filled with thoughts of how far he's fallen, how much has changed since his first encounter with the demon.

The days of running and panic attacks feel so far away as he lets it cradle him—as he welcomes the lie it offers. For a second, Eldritch imagines what it would whisper to him, what it would tell him, if he could hear its voice.

"Don't worry. Don't cry. It will all be over soon. I'm here. I've got you. After all, you're mine."

He doesn't know if the words come from his own mind, or if he's somehow connecting to the demon's thoughts. Either way, the shame it induces is all-consuming. He can't do this anymore, can't go on like this. All his life, he has tried so hard to stay in the light, no matter how difficult; and yes, he has failed on more than one occasion, but he never stopped believing. At a young age, he tried to help others, tried to use his "gift" for good, and look where he ended up. He identified countless demons, called them out by name; yet here he is, spirit broken, and unable to name the entity in whose embrace he lies. It had all been for nothing. He clenches his fists at the thought, and a sharp pain shoots through his left hand, reminding him of the cut. *The glass.*

It's subtle—the way the idea slips into his mind, but soon it grows and grows until the glass and the escape it offers are all he can think about. Seven years ago, Eldritch had tried to end it all, and his attempt proved unsuccessful. This time will be different; this time, it has to be quick with no interruptions. Turning onto his front and rising to his knees, he shuffles over to the left, in search of the broken glass. He remembers hitting the bookcase during the attack on the record player and sees its destruction has contributed to the mess on the den floor with bits of glass and wood, as well as several books that were knocked free.

Eldritch reaches out, right hand trembling with the knowledge of what he's about to do, and grabs a large, jagged shard of glass. He doesn't want to think about it, he just wants to get it over with. With a labored breath in, and a shaky exhale, he brings the shard to his left wrist and presses. The edge of the glass breaks through the skin, and Eldritch can feel a trickle of blood escape the puncture, but he hasn't hit the vein, not yet.

God, forgive me. I'm just too weak.

He goes to shut his eyes, not wanting to watch the glass sever the vein, but before he does, one of the books on the floor catches his attention. He pauses and cocks his head to the side, observing the cover as it lies there, open, spine up, pages down. It's not a novel or cookbook or devotional, but he recognizes the floral pattern with its swirls of green and gold. It's his mother's notebook—the notebook he saw her writing in the night he came home from Holland's farewell service. She placed it in the bookcase, and Eldritch never saw her touch it again. He'd always thought it a curious thing—to come home to her journaling when he'd never seen her do it before. Curiosity gets the better of him, and he sets the glass aside and picks up the notebook. There is only one entry, on the very first page. Eldritch feels his heart skip a beat as he begins to read.

My Dearest Eldritch,

I know things haven't been easy for you. In truth, I never wished any of this on you, but if I have learned anything in this life, it's that things actually do happen for a reason, and God does have a plan, even though we may not understand what that plan is.

He hears her voice, clear as day, as it eases through beautiful scrawl of her handwriting; hears the sweet timbre of her drawl as if she were standing there speaking the words aloud.

> *The day you were born—a day I will remember and treasure as long as I live—was not without its complications. I bled a lot. For a while, the doctor and nurses were concerned that you and I weren't going to make it. But we did, baby boy. We did because we are fighters. Both of us.*

How he wishes it were true. His mother had always seen him as a fighter, but he couldn't, for the life of him, understand why.

> *I'll never forget the moment they brought you to me. I didn't get to see you right away because I was rushed into surgery, but when they brought you to me, and I held you in my arms for the first time, I knew: you were perfect. You are perfect, my love. When they broke the news to me that I wasn't allowed to have another child because the risk was too great, I wasn't even upset. I wasn't upset because I had you.*

Eldritch has heard the story of his birth so many times, but this is new. He had no idea his mother was advised against trying for another child, and the thought makes him ache for her. *I was all she got. What a disappointment I turned out to be.*

> *I heard the whispers, seconds after they laid you in my arms. You were born with a veil over your face. I knew what that meant.*

Eldritch can't imagine what a shock that must have been to his mother. Having the birth of her baby overshadowed by the horrible knowledge of the life that newborn child was destined to lead.

TORI LEWIS

> You see, my grandfather, Eldritch Sholly, was also born with a veil over his face. His great-grandfather was too. It goes back for generations, and each and every Eldritch has had the gift. That's how you got your name, my love. I know it's a funny name. I know kids picked on you for it, and I'm sorry I never explained the meaning behind it. I don't know if we ever told you this, but you were originally going to be named after your father, and his father, and his father before him. Robert Eugene Hayes, IV. A Hayes family tradition. But I heard the whispers. I heard the whispers and changed it, right there in my hospital bed. You are Eldritch Sholly Hayes. That's just who you are, and I knew it the second I saw you, the second I heard the whispers about the veil.

Eldritch can't believe what he's reading. *"His great-grandfather was too. It goes back for generations."* As he reads those words, he is reminded of his conversation with Gran-Gran during his final visit with her. She mentioned the other Eldritches before him, but nothing about the gift. *Or did she? "The veil, you see.."* He remembers wondering why Gran-Gran had said that, but his mother's words fill in the blanks. Eldritch knows the truth now. He is one of many.

> When you were very little, I hoped and prayed that the gift had skipped you, and for years I even pretended it was a fluke. Up until that weekend at Gran-Gran's. I know you haven't had an easy life. As a child, you saw and experienced things no child should ever have to face. And now as a man, I see the effect it has had on you. I see the sadness, the fear, the exhaustion in your face, and it breaks my heart. Because darling, this is not what I wanted for you. But I do know that you are strong. You are strong, my son—stronger than you know.

He clutches the notebook and his blood stains the corner of the page in his grasp. *If only you knew the truth, Mama.*

> *I'm sitting here in the living room, writing this letter to you, and I don't even know why. I just can't get this out of my head, so I thought maybe writing it all down would help. Baby boy, I see you. I see you struggling, even though you try to hide it. I see your pain, and I just wish I could take it away. I know you've been hurt, my love. I know the church has used and abused you, but that was the work of men. Of imperfect men who were looking out for their own gain. That wasn't God. Please don't lose faith. Please, Eldritch. You know what verse I'm going to quote, so I don't know why I'm even bothering to write it down:*

And there it is: the verse he will forever associate with his mother; the verse she insisted on quoting at the end of every prayer. The one he had inscribed on her tombstone—that cold, hard reminder of her departure.

> *"Be on your guard; stand firm in the faith; be courageous, be strong."*
> 1 Corinthians 16:13.
> *Be courageous, be strong, Baby Boy.*
>
> *Oceans of Love,*
> *Mama*

She never gave it to him. The letter has been shut away in the bookcase for eleven years, and Eldritch never knew. The tears return as he reads his mother's words, as he hears her voice in his head, telling him to be courageous, to be strong. How he wishes he could, how he wishes he could be the man she thought he was, the man she always hoped he would be.

The weight of her words on his shoulders is crushing as he thinks about how he's let her down.

"Be courageous. Be strong."

But I'm not strong. I'm weak.

He doesn't know where the thought comes from, or why his brain conjures it up, but Eldritch's mind is filled with the picture that once hung over the record player.

"My grace is sufficient for thee. My strength is made perfect in weakness."

And though the sound is labored and hoarse, Eldritch begins to sing.

> "Little ones… to Him… belong…
> They… are weak… but He… is… strong.
> Yes… Jesus… loves me…"

He feels the entity recoil as he sings the line, and it strikes Eldritch as curious, so he continues.

"Yes… Jesus loves… me…"

It does it again—loosens its hold on him and withdraws even more.

"Yes, Jesus loves me…"

It releases him and moves away, retreating to the other side of the room. Eldritch's voice trails off as he comes to understand, and he speaks the final line, putting the pieces of this maddening puzzle together at last.

"For the Bible tells me so."

Eldritch stands. It isn't easy—his legs are unsteady, and they tremble as he rises—but he rises nonetheless, and in spite of everything that's happened, Eldritch smiles.

"You're strong. I'll give you that. You've been hiding your name from me since day one, and it always baffled me, but here's the thing," he says, turning to face the shadow hovering in the corner of the den, "I don't need to know your name."

He spins around and rushes toward the battered bookshelf, scanning the titles until he finds a Bible. It's not his father's, but one of the many others his parents collected over the years. He pulls it out and flips through the books and chapters until he finds the scripture he's looking for—the scripture he remembers Pastor Mike reciting during Mark's exorcism. Then, with his finger planted at the beginning of the verse, he turns to face the demon, and begins to read from the book of Mark.

"'And these signs will accompany those who believe: In my name they will drive out demons; they will speak in new tongues;'"

"In my name."

"Yes, Jesus loves me."

"See, I don't need to know your name because there's only *one* name I *need* to know."

The entity shifts, changing its form, losing the shape of a shadow-man. It pulses outward, tendrils reaching for Eldritch, but finding they are no longer able to touch him. It makes itself larger, doubling—tripling—in size, and Eldritch feels the floor beneath his feet begin to quake; sees the tremor run up the walls, knocking down pictures and Christmas décor. Eldritch is undeterred and flips through the Bible again, page after page, until he lands on the passage from Philippians he's searching for.

"'Therefore, God exalted him to the highest place and gave him the name that is above every name, that at the name of *Jesus*—'"

The room shakes, rocked by the force of the demonic spirit displaying its power in a moment of distress.

"'—every knee should bow, in heaven and on earth and under the earth, and every tongue acknowledge that Jesus Christ is Lord to the glory of God the Father!'"

The whole house is shaking, and Eldritch has to catch himself to keep from falling. The entity is lashing out, the scripture having struck a chord within it. Cracks appear in the walls of the den—paint and dry wall splintering from the force of the spirit's manifestation of power—and Eldritch looks into the kitchen and sees the same thing happening there.

Filled with a strength which surpasses his understanding, Eldritch is determined to see this through to the end. The anger he felt—the bitterness, the loneliness—are pouring from him like the blood from the gash in his hand. He lets it go; facing down this evil, he lets go of everything that has held him back—everything that has held him down—and for the first time in his life, Eldritch Hayes decides to fight. There is only one way to win this battle, and he has failed too many times to try it on his own again. He turns to the last book, Revelation, and reads in a loud voice, emboldened by the Word in his hands.

"'I saw heaven standing open, and there before me was a white horse, whose rider is called Faithful and True. With justices He judges and wages war. His eyes are like blazing fire, and on His head are many crowns. He has a name written on Him that no one knows but He himself. He is dressed in a robe dipped in blood, and His name is the Word of God.'"

The cracks travel up the walls and onto the ceiling, spiderwebbing along the plaster. The ceiling fan comes crashing down in the middle of the room, but Eldritch steps to the side as it falls and continues heralding the passage. All thoughts of running, all thoughts of slashing his wrists, all thoughts of letting this unholy spirit overtake him are gone.

"'The armies of heaven were following him, riding on white horses and dressed in fine linen, white and clean. Coming out of his mouth is a sharp sword with which to strike down the nations. He will rule them with an iron scepter. He treads the wine press of the fury of the wrath of God Almighty. On His robe and on His thigh, He has this name written: King of Kings and Lord of Lords!'"

From the living room, comes a resounding bang, and Eldritch runs to see what havoc is being wreaked in there. Turning the corner, he finds the TV has exploded, sparks and hard plastic flying everywhere. The cushions of the couch are being ripped to shreds by unseen claws, and the keys of the piano are pounded upon—a dissonant cacophony of notes bleeding from it as the bench seat is hurled toward Eldritch from the sitting room. He tries to dodge it, but he isn't quick enough, and it slams into knees, knocking him to the ground. The Bible slides from his hands as his face smashes into the floor. He smells blood—can taste it, feels it dripping from his nose—and he brings his right sleeve up to wipe it, smearing it across his face.

Scrambling to his feet, Eldritch searches for the Bible amidst the wreckage in the den. He spots it near the fireplace, among the shattered ruins of the television. The house continues to rock on its foundation, and Eldritch fights to maintain his balance as he pulls the Bible free. He stands firm, he stands strong, in the knowledge of who he is and *whose* he is.

"I'm not afraid of you anymore! You have no power over me! You wanted me so badly, but you knew you couldn't possess me! You couldn't have me because I already belonged to someone else! So, instead, you try to get me to take my own life! Not this time! Not again—*never* again! Now, get out of my house!"

As he gives the command, the sound of scratching fills the room, and Eldritch looks around to see numbers being carved into the walls. *66 12 7 8 9;* over and over again, like it had at the Birch-Rainey house, but this time, Eldritch isn't in the dark. This time, he knows the meaning of those numbers and, lifting the Bible one more time, he turns to the sixty-sixth book of the bible, the twelfth chapter, verses seven, eight, and nine.

"Yeah, yeah, I get it now! Do you hear me?! I understand!"

The numbers continue to appear, etched in the walls and ceiling in an unholy scrawl, and Eldritch recites the passage.

"'Then war broke out in heaven. Michael and his angels fought against the dragon, and the dragon and his angels fought back. But he was not strong enough, and they lost their place in heaven. The great dragon was hurled down—that ancient serpent called the devil, or Satan, who leads the whole world astray. He was hurled to the earth and his angels with him!' See? You weren't strong enough—none of you were! You lost then and you're losing now!!"

Eldritch is screaming at the top of his lungs, his voice rising above the scratching, above the slamming of keys on the piano. There is a sound like a hurricane, and a phantom draft blows through the room, nearly taking Eldritch down, but he manages to remain upright. The supernatural wind swirls about him, knocking over everything else standing in the room: end tables, décor, potted plants, the Christmas tree. It threatens to tear the Bible from his hands, but he holds it in an iron grip—his right hand keeping the pages from flipping while his left hand paints the cover scarlet as he clutches it.

"Sixty-six, twelve, seven, eight, nine! That's what you were trying to tell me!" he shouts amidst the turmoil unfolding in his house, "but why did you stop there?!"

Eldritch looks down at the Bible and locates the next verse—verse ten—and picks up where the dark entity's numerical reference stopped.

"'Then I heard a loud voice in heaven say: "Now have come the salvation and the owner and the kingdom of our God, and the authority of his Messiah. For the accuser of our brothers and sisters, who accuses them before our God day and night, has been hurled down. They triumphed over him by the blood of the Lamb and by the word of their testimony!"'"

He can feel the demon's desperation as it lashes out with the full force of its fury, shaking the house with a violent intensity. Every light fixture falls to the floor and shatters on impact. Beneath his feet, the planks of hardwood are pried up and apart, breaking and snapping to ruin, causing Eldritch to lose his footing and fall.

His right shoulder takes the brunt of the impact as he pulls the Bible to his chest, hand still marking his place, refusing to relinquish his grip on the book. To his left, something large begins to move, and Eldritch turns just in time to see the sofa being hurled across the shifting floor at him. He scrambles to his feet and lunges out of the way as it goes hurtling past him and crashes into the piano in the sitting room. The piano's destruction is loud and grating—the instrument breaking apart at the impact, wires and keys torn from the wood and flung about the room.

As his childhood home crumbles around him, Eldritch stands his ground, lifting the Bible one last time.

"'Therefore rejoice, you heavens and you who dwell in them! But woe to the earth and the sea, because the devil has gone down to you! He is filled with fury, because he knows that his time is short!'"

Eldritch slams the Bible closed and shouts at the demon, squaring off with it as it undulates and jerks about in a furious, wounded rage across the living room. "Did you hear that?! His time is short!! You and your boss have already lost this war!!!" And mustering all the strength he has left, Eldritch commands, at the top of his lungs, "By the power and the might of the Holy Name of Jesus Christ, I bind you and cast you out by the blood of the lamb! Get out of my house!!!"

An ear-piercing shriek erupts from the demon, and Eldritch is unsure whether he's hearing it in this reality or through the veil, but his hands come up to cover his ears, and he drops to his knees as the scream transforms into an explosion. Glass flies across the room from every direction—slicing Eldritch's face and hands—as, all at once, every window in every room is shattered, every door is blown from its hinges, and every wall splinters and cracks. The house shakes one last time before stilling and silence descends.

Eldritch lifts his head and looks around, taking in the absolute destruction the demon rained down upon his home. The house is broken, but Eldritch feels as though he has been knit back together by expert and loving hands. Unable to stop the laughter welling up from within him, he lets it out, along with tears of joy and release. The demon has fled, and it has taken with him all the darkness—all the anger, the doubt, the despair—Eldritch has harbored over the years.

His laughter continues as he rises and walks toward the front door, which has been ripped from the frame and blown out into the yard. The sun is still up when Eldritch steps outside, into the light.

He is bleeding and exhausted, barely able to stand, but he is free.

CHAPTER TWENTY-NINE

The thought first entered his mind at the cemetery. Eldritch collapsed in a pile, weeping between his parents' headstones, begging God to take him too, to take him from a world without them. But God didn't; so Eldritch tore himself away from the tombstones, and rose from the dead grass that covered their graves. With a dark notion taking root in his brain, he walked from the cemetery to the site of the crash and waited, like he always did. When he found nothing there, the dark root grew and grew, and soon became a full-fledged idea—a decision, a choice—and Eldritch had made his.

The sun began to rise on his way home, but the sky was overcast and dark, matching Eldritch's mood. Shutting the front door behind him and turning the lock, he felt the inescapable emptiness of the house as the sound echoed around him, bouncing off the walls with nothing to drown it out—no music, no talking, no laughter, no one within. He'd been out all night, searching for the spirits of his parents, like he did every Friday night—a sort of ritual he'd started following the funeral. But last night was not Friday, it was Monday—Monday, December nineteenth. They had been gone for a year; one year yesterday.

He pushed himself away from the door, unable to ignore the trembling in his hands any longer. Eldritch always made a point to resist the bottle before he went out in search of his parents—he needed to be of sober mind when he found them—it was difficult, but somehow, he managed it every time. In the early hours of the morning when he would return, the first thing his shaking hands would find would be the nearest bottle of whiskey. They littered the house these days, one always within reach.

But this time, things were different. Eldritch didn't grab the bottle just yet. Instead, he walked to the large window to his left, knelt in the window seat, and drew the curtains closed. With half the living room cast in shadow, Eldritch moved over to the sitting room, drawing every curtain on every window as he went. Soon, the entire front of the house was dark, and Eldritch continued into the dining room, where he did the same to the curtains there. There were no curtains to close in the kitchen, only valances hung over the windows, so Eldritch swiped a half empty whiskey bottle off the counter and continued into the den, where he locked the back door and pulled the thick blue curtains shut.

He stood in the center of the room, darkness closing in from all sides, and brought the bottle to his lips. After several drinks, he felt the shaking in his hands subside, and decided now was as good a time as ever. Taking another long drag from the bottle, he climbed the stairs, feet heavy—weighed down by gravity of his decision. Without the curtains drawn on the second floor, the gray, morning light was streaming in through the windows of every room, spilling into the hallway. He squinted and shielded his eyes against the brightness. Eldritch hated the light; he wanted all things to be dark—dark like the gaping hole within him.

He turned into the bathroom and went straight for the cabinet beside the sink, grabbing his bottle of migraine medication before heading back downstairs—back to the den shrouded in darkness.

Setting the pills and Jack Daniel's on the flat top of the Magnavox console, Eldritch opened the lid section over the turntable, flipped it on, and moved the tone arm over the record. He'd been listening to Bread before he'd left last night, and their 1972 album, *Baby I'm-a Want You*, was ready and waiting for him. He'd listened to this album so much over the last year that, even in the darkened room, he was able to drop the needle in the middle of the record, catching the tail end of "Down On My Knees" just in time to hear Jimmy Griffin go up on the last note and the music fade to nothing.

There was a beat of crackling white noise before the next song began. Eldritch knew what was coming; his placement of the needle was intentional. His dad had loved to tell him trivia about his favorite bands and songs. Gene had told him long ago the story behind "Everything I Own." David Gates had written it about his dad who had died in 1963 and never got the chance to see his rise to fame—never got to see him become who he was meant to be.

The opening line eased through the speakers, and Eldritch braced his hands against the console and closed his eyes, grief washing over him in an all-consuming wave. David Gates continued to sing, and Eldritch's tears fell atop the old

Magnavox. What *he* wouldn't have given to have them back here with him again—back here to tell him it was all okay, that he was loved and understood. He was the boy who could see the dead, the boy who could see spirits; yet no matter how hard he tried, how often he searched, the souls of his parents eluded him. Eldritch was alone.

Taking the prescription bottle in hand, he popped the top and poured the remaining pills into his left palm. Eldritch stared at his handful of little, white tablets; noticed the way they filled his palm all the way up to his scar. He had carried that scar for years, and not a day went by that he didn't think back to the night he got it, but even that memory isn't enough to pull him back from the brink. Closing his hand into a tight fist, Eldritch squeezed the pills, fighting the urge to pour them back into the bottle and pretend none of this ever happened.

Lifting his eyes, his gaze fell on the picture on the wall above the record player, and he read the words written there.

"My strength is made perfect in weakness…"

They made him angry. Eldritch had been nothing but weak this last year, and nothing—no one—had stepped in with their own strength to lift him up. God had abandoned him. God had taken his parents, ripped them from this world, and abandoned him. He couldn't go on like this.

Resolved on the matter, Eldritch threw his head back and tossed the cluster of pills in his mouth. The taste was bitter on his tongue, but it was short lived as he followed it up with a long swig of whiskey. He swallowed and felt the combination slide down his throat. Now, he need only wait. Eldritch stretched out on his back in the middle of the den and closed his eyes, accepting his fate and letting the mellow sounds of Bread carry him to his eternal rest.

Mama, Daddy…I'll be there soon.

Eldritch opened his eyes expecting to find the waiting arms of his mother and father. Instead, he found a white ceiling and a rectangular fluorescent light—his first indication this was *not* the afterlife. This wasn't heaven, this was a hospital. He could hear the beeping of the machines to his right, he could smell the sterility of the environment, he could feel the cheap sheets and hospital gown against this skin, the oxygen meter on his finger and the tube in his nose. Turning his head to the left, he was greeted by a weary Uncle Cal who clutched the side of Eldritch's bed, waiting to see if his nephew was waking up.

"He's awake!" his uncle shouted, excitement springing forth from under the haze of exhaustion and worry. "He's awake!"

Over the next several hours, Eldritch got acclimated to the real world again and was informed he had been sedated for over a week following the overdose. He learned that Calvin had stopped by the house and found him, called 9-1-1, and started CPR. Eldritch was furious with him and screamed as much as his abused throat—sore after several days of intubation—would let him. Calvin remained calm and collected and let his nephew unleash his anger. When Eldritch calmed down, exhausted from his bitter rant, Calvin spoke.

"It's a miracle you're alive, and I don't use the word 'miracle' lightly."

Eldritch scoffed, "You call it a miracle. I call it bad luck. Par for the course." His voice was hoarse, his body tired from fighting to stay alive against his will.

Calvin shook his head, and Eldritch feared his uncle was seconds away from breaking down, "Eldritch, I don't think you understand. The meds you took…they should have killed you—"

"Yeah, well, that was the plan."

"Shut up!" The seriousness of Calvin's tone silenced any rebuttal Eldritch had prepared to fire off. "That medication for your headaches was a tricyclic antidepressant. The doctor told me it is extremely—*extremely*—rare for someone to come back from an OD with something like that."

Eldritch had known that, which was why he knew his headache meds in combination with the whiskey should have been a full-proof plan. "So why didn't I die?" he asked, more resentful than confused.

"They don't know," Calvin answered with a huff. "They have absolutely no idea. They didn't even have to do…oh, Lord, what did they call it? Dialysis. Emergent dialysis. For your kidneys. Usually, drugs like that destroy them, but somehow, they're functioning just fine. Someone was looking out for you, boy."

"No one was looking out for me!" Eldritch spat, tired eyes blazing as much as they could. "I just happen to have a nosy uncle that comes by unannounced!"

Calvin's face dropped, and he brought his hands to his temples. He took several deep breaths before fixing Eldritch with a look of stone. "I'm not going to sit here and tell you that you're an idiot for doing what you did."

Eldritch rolled his eyes.

"But I *will* tell you, I am not the least bit sorry for calling 9-1-1 and helping to save your life. You are the only blood I have left, Eldritch. Don't you get that? Don't you know how losing you would absolutely destroy me? Maybe that makes me selfish, but I don't care. What you did was selfish too, and I will not sit here and feel guilty over the fact that you're not dead!"

Eldritch had no response to that. To be honest, he hadn't thought about how his death would affect his uncle. His only thought had been putting an end to the pain.

When Calvin spoke again, his tone was tender, his stern expression softening, "Eldritch, I love you. I don't say it enough, but I do…and God knows, I have no idea what you're feeling right now—the pain you must be in, but I miss them too. God, I miss them." Calvin lowered his head to hide his tears from Eldritch, but it was no use. Eldritch knew they were there, heard the way his voice cracked and how his breath quivered on the exhale.

"I can't do this without them," Eldritch whispered.

"You got me, pal," Calvin squeezed his hand, "I know I'm a poor substitute, but I'm here."

Eldritch closed his eyes and let his head fall back into the pillows. His anger hadn't subsided, but he was far too weary to fight; and though he didn't say it out loud, Eldritch agreed with his uncle.

You are *a poor substitute.*

The next few weeks crept by, and Eldritch spent most of them in a psychiatric facility. A few days after he'd awoken in the hospital, a counselor from behavioral health had stopped by for an evaluation, and once the hospital had deemed him healthy enough to leave, Eldritch was discharged into the care of Midland Rivers Behavioral Health.

Eldritch was growing tired of hearing the words "miracle" and "miraculous" thrown around every time he spoke to someone. He didn't want to think about the implications such words carried, nor did he want to talk about it. His regular sessions with the doctor—a lady named Dr. Blanch—eventually landed on the subject of his drinking. After finding himself in the throes of withdrawal, there was no denying his addiction. The headaches, nausea, confusion, shakiness, fever, and sweats wreaked havoc on his mind and body, and Eldritch found himself begging for a drink—*"just a little something to take the edge off"*—several times. After an excruciating week of withdrawals, Eldritch's symptoms began to subside, and his alcoholism was addressed by the psychiatrist.

Despite his initial reservations, he ended up discussing his addiction with her—when his drinking began, how often he drank at such-and-such age, and how often he drank now—even if he skirted around the supernatural truth behind it. Eldritch may have been admitted to a psychiatric hospital following his overdose, but he wasn't planning on becoming a permanent resident, and informing the doctor of his ability to see spirits seemed a surefire way to achieve just that. After several weeks in her care, Eldritch convinced Dr. Blanch that he wanted to recover and was no longer a threat to himself, and he was discharged from the facility.

Returning home was a struggle at first. Calvin and Amy had raided the house in his absence and removed every bottle of alcohol they could find. He was no longer allowed his headache medication and was given a list of safe, holistic ways to battle his migraines. He returned to work, stocking shelves, managing inventory, tidying up. After the accident, Eldritch insisted Calvin take over the store, convinced he was incapable and unfit to run it himself. Calvin had agreed to do so, but only because Eldritch had seemed adamant about refusing the responsibility. He tried attending AA meetings in Newberry, but his ability—and his resistance to reciting the Serenity

Prayer every time he got the urge to drink—put an end to that. Eldritch stopped attending after three weeks, resolved to fight the battle for sobriety on his own.

Slowly, he began changing things around the house. Some of the décor was removed, including the picture above the record player. Eldritch wasn't sure why it bothered him so, but he wanted nothing more than to see it gone. It was sent to a thrift store along with the rest of the inspirational, downstairs decor. It took longer for him to part with his parents' clothes, but three years after the accident, he deemed it necessary, and they were donated as well.

Another two years passed, and one Sunday morning found Eldritch standing in the doorway of his parents' bedroom. Despite having donated all their clothes years prior, the room itself was untouched; just as his parents had left it. As he stood in the doorway, looking in on a room which seemed frozen in time, he recalled a conversation he'd had with his father many years ago.

"She must have loved him a lot to keep it exactly as he left it for almost forty years."

"She did, but I don't know how healthy it is. When you cling to something like that—refusing to change a room, refusing to move on—it doesn't seem healthy. You can honor a person's memory and cherish something of theirs, sure. But this—it's obsessive, don't you think? Not touching this room for forty years isn't going to bring him back."

Eldritch moved himself into the master bedroom that night, swapping their décor for his. He didn't want to disappoint his father—and he liked the extra space and the fireplace—but it would take a long time for him to get over the guilt of acknowledging the fact that his parents no longer had any need for that room. Actions like this had Eldritch convinced he was dealing, letting go, moving on; yet his Friday night rituals continued, and every week would find him walking the same path in the wee hours of the morning, searching for two souls who could not be found.

Time continued its relentless march, and Eldritch's life remained the same—predictable, stable. He would wake up early and go to work, stopping by The Grind, on occasion, for a cup of coffee and to see Kelly—which he refused to admit was a factor. He would spend his day working at the hardware store with Calvin, Lanny-Ray, and the new hire, Amir, who he liked despite many attempts to ward off the younger man's attempts at friendship. When closing time rolled around, Eldritch would walk home, pop a TV dinner in the microwave, and fall asleep to the sounds of his parents' records spinning on the turntable, and every Friday, he would venture out in search of them.

Nearly eight years after the accident—seven after he'd attempted to take his own life—Eldritch had fallen into a normal, steady routine. This was his life now. He had a job, he was sober, and spiritual encounters were a rarity. He couldn't even remember the last time he saw a demon. The suicide attempt was never discussed again, as neither he nor Calvin knew how to deal with the emotions surrounding the traumatic event. All in all, Eldritch recognized that life could be worse and, at times, fooled himself into thinking he wasn't angry or depressed. He wasn't happy, but he was no longer to the point of self-destruction; content to continue in his routine, going from point A to point B, head down and alone.

When his alarm went off one November morning, Eldritch dressed and headed downstairs to make a cup of coffee, but to his dismay, he found the cupboard bare. He'd run out the morning prior and had forgotten to go by The Grind to buy a new bag of grounds. *Guess I'll be making a stop before work.* After checking the weather and seeing the temperature had dropped below freezing—quite unusual for early November—Eldritch grabbed his coat from the closet and headed out the door, prepared to face what he thought would be another uneventful day at Hayes Hardware.

CHAPTER THIRTY

Eldritch falls to his knees in the front yard, bracing his hands against the cold ground to keep from toppling face first into the stiff grass. Drawing in a deep breath, he lets the crisp air of the December afternoon fill his lungs. It's chilly and burns in the best way.

Purifying.

From the right, he hears the sound of rapid footfalls on the pavement, then the grass.

"Eldritch?!" the voice calls out when it's still several yards away.

Kelly.

She hits the ground in front of him, her knees pressing against his as she brings her hands to his face, lifting his head. "Oh, God!" she exclaims when she takes in the sight of him. His face is bleeding, his eyes are bloodshot with dark circles resting beneath them; yet in spite of this, Eldritch is smiling.

"Hey, Kelly," he says, voice a hoarse murmur. The look on her face tells him she is on the verge of full-blown panic, so he reaches out and touches his right hand to her cheek.

"Eldritch, what happened?"

"It's okay. I'm okay, I promise," he leans forward, and Kelly mirrors the action, bringing her forehead to rest against his.

They sit like that while Eldritch catches his breath, and when he pulls back, he sees a crowd of people gathered on the sidewalk. The blare of sirens in the distance confuses him at first, until he remembers the sound—the explosion of sonic proportions—the demon made when cast from the house.

Of course, someone called 9-1-1.

First responders arrive on the scene, bombarding Eldritch with questions he knows he can't answer, certain they all would have difficulty believing he'd spent the better part of the day battling with a powerful demon, and that the house was an unfortunate casualty. The chief of police pulls up in his patrol car just as Calvin comes racing down the sidewalk and toward his nephew.

"Eldritch?! What the heck happened?!" Calvin shouts, pushing aside the EMTs who are failing to convince Eldritch to accept medical treatment.

Eldritch hugs him, using the embrace as a chance to whisper in his uncle's ear, "I'm fine. It was here, but everything's okay now."

They pull back as they hear the police chief approaching—a man Calvin played high school baseball with and knows very well—and Eldritch doesn't have to ask his uncle to intervene; Calvin is already moving to intercept his old teammate in the driveway. Eldritch continues to fend off the paramedics, insisting he's fine and can tend to his own wounds until they relent and let him be. Moments later, the chief begins dispersing the crowd and sends his officers on their way, assuring them everything is fine, and the situation will be handled.

Eldritch sends up a silent prayer of gratitude for his uncle's community connections as the crowd thins and the emergency vehicles drive off. Calvin gave his friend just enough information to convince him there was no rational explanation for the event, and the police chief—familiar with Eldritch Hayes and his ability—decided the official report would attribute the damage to a gas leak in the home; but Eldritch knows rumors will spread. He laughs, excited to hear how the story will evolve as it travels through the grapevine.

"Now, what are we going to do about this?" Calvin says, turning to the house.

"I have no idea. I'm too tired to do anything tonight," Eldritch answers as his uncle heads inside to assess the damage. "I owe you an apology," he tells Kelly once they're alone again.

"I think you mean an explanation."

Kelly helps him up the front steps, letting him lean against her for support. As they cross the threshold into the living room, he turns and sees her gaping at the destruction the demon caused.

"Eldritch, what happened here?!"

"Seriously, pal," he hears Calvin shout from the kitchen, "this place is trashed!"

"I beat it," he says to Kelly, with a smile on his face. "I won."

With the light fixtures destroyed and the power knocked out by the force of the entity's departure, the house is plunged into darkness with the setting of the sun.

"You can't stay here. You can't sleep in this, Eldritch." Kelly's hands are on her hips, and Eldritch knows better than to argue.

Eldritch has never been to Kelly's house before, but now, he's standing in her shower, watching his blood trickle down her drain. Looking around, he takes in the tiny space, sees her shampoo and conditioner in the shower caddy, a bar of soap—fancy soap, the handmade kind you get at a special boutique or craft festival—and a hair mask in the back right corner. He's struck by how intimate this feels, to be naked and bleeding in Kelly's shower, surrounded by her things, with the water she pays for washing over his body.

When he steps out, dressed in pajamas he'd packed before leaving his house, Kelly is waiting with the first aid kit. She starts with his face, sterilizing and treating the tiny cuts scattered there. The bleeding has stopped, but Kelly takes good care of each laceration, no matter how small, covering them with antibiotic cream.

As she moves to his left arm, Eldritch watches her pause, her eyes glued to the puncture on his wrist where he almost ended it all with a shard of glass. She says nothing, giving it the same treatment as the cuts on his face, but her fingers linger a moment in what he interprets as silent understanding.

She continues to his palm and begins tending the gash there. "Well, this is familiar," she says, looking up at him from under her lashes, the corner of her mouth turned upward as she applies the cream.

He thinks back to the terrible things he said to her this morning, the way he lashed out, the way he tried to reduce their connection to nothing.

"And this…this doesn't mean whatever you think it means."

"I'm sorry," he whispers as she begins wrapping his hand. "It's funny how you insisted this scar meant nothing, and then it goes and opens up again. You know I don't believe in coincidences, Eldritch."

"Neither do I," he says, holding her gaze.

When the bandage is secured, Kelly places the first aid kit aside and sits beside him on the couch, feet tucked underneath her.

"Okay, spill," she says, tone shifting from gentle to insistent. "I need to know exactly what happened for three reasons. One: there was obviously no gas leak, and you said you 'beat it.' Two: I need to know why you've been so horrible, particularly to me. Three: you're…different."

Eldritch cocks his head. "Different?" he asks.

"Not bad different, just…different."

Her attempt at clarifying her previous statement makes him chuckle, but Eldritch catches her meaning. He starts from the beginning and tells her what happened from the time he sensed the evil presence in his house to the moment she found him outside in the yard. Kelly is silent for most of it, reaching out with a reassuring touch or stroke along his arm when he chokes up or struggles to recount certain moments; like when he explains how he was certain his parents were reaching out to him, certain they were coming home.

Kelly is crying by the time he gets to the near suicide attempt and the letter from his mother, and she draws closer, holding him in her arms as he finishes.

"And then it was gone, it was over, and I felt like I could breathe again. I feel like a weight has been lifted off me. I came to terms with so many things today, Kelly. I'm still trying to process it all, but I *am* different, like you said…I'm free."

Eldritch turns in his seat to face her. "I can't apologize to you enough for what I did."

"Eldritch, you literally battled the forces of evil today. In your house. I think you get a pass this time."

"No," he shakes his head, "you don't understand. I pushed you away because I was spiraling, and I didn't want to drag you down with me...and I nearly lost you."

"Hey," she says, moving into his space and placing her hand atop his bandaged palm, "I'm still here."

"I love you, Kelly," he says, and it sounds so right, so natural, falling from his lips, that he has to say it again. "I love you."

Kelly surges forward, and Eldritch meets her halfway, kissing her with everything he has, making up for all the time stolen from them—all the time since that night in the closet under the stairs at the Birch-Rainey house. She pulls back and places a hand against his cheek. He winces at the sharp jolt of pain as her hand comes into contact with the cuts littering his skin.

"Oh my gosh, I'm sorry!" Kelly gasps, pulling her hand away.

Eldritch laughs and assures her he's fine, reaching for her hand and placing light kisses across the tops of her knuckles.

"I love you too, you know," she says. "Just so we're clear."

He spends the next two days cleaning his house and repairing as much as possible with the help of Kelly, Uncle Cal, and Amir. The hardwood floors will have to be replaced, along with every light fixture. The windows are a lost cause and, in the end, Eldritch decides to board them up with plywood, for the time being.

CALLING ELDRITCH HAYES

At one point, Calvin and Amir go down to the basement to look for signs of any structural damage, leaving Eldritch and Kelly to pack up his things. He's been staying at her place, and there's an unspoken agreement that their arrangement will continue until Eldritch's housing situation is sorted.

He's carrying down a bag of clothes when he runs into Amir on the stairs.

"Hey, what do you want me to do with this stuff?" Amir asks, motioning to the small cardboard box in his hands. "Cal sent me into that weird little nook at the back of the basement to look for cracks and I found these. They were just stuffed back there."

One by one, Amir holds up the items he found: a remote, two phone chargers, a bag of coffee, and a black, leather-bound Bible with *Robert Eugene Hayes, III* embossed in the corner of the cover.

Eldritch sets the bag of clothes on the floor and takes his father's Bible in hand, "In the nook, you say?"

"Yeah, it was the weirdest thing. Did you put those down there?"

"No, *I* did not," answers Eldritch, equal parts disgusted and amused by the demon's twisted joke. *What a jerk.*

It's Friday night, well after ten, before they come to a stopping point. Nothing further can be done without a contractor but, it just so happens, Eldritch knows a guy. Kelly is already gone, taking a final carful of Eldritch's stuff to her place, and Amir dipped out just before. Calvin and Eldritch are walking down the front steps together when his uncle turns to him and asks, "So, do you want me to come with you?"

"Huh?" The question catches Eldritch off guard. "Come with me where?"

"To the cemetery."

Eldritch is stunned into silence and stares at his uncle.

"Oh, come on, Eldritch," Calvin sighs, "you honestly think I don't know what you do every Friday night?"

Eldritch can only shake his head in disbelief. "Of course, you know."

"Why do you think I made you take Saturdays off? I knew what you were doing the night before, getting in at the crack of dawn."

"But how?"

"It was about six years ago. I noticed how tired you were at work one Saturday and I asked you about it. You brushed it off and said you'd had trouble sleeping, but then it kept happening. Every Saturday morning, you were a zombie. I was worried you had fallen off the wagon, so I watched you," his uncle admits.

"You thought I was drinking again, so you stalked me?" Eldritch asks, trying hard to sound offended but failing.

"Basically," Calvin shrugs. "I hung back so you couldn't see me, and I followed you there. Heard everything you said."

He has no idea what Calvin heard that night, but most of his one-sided cemetery conversations were variations on the same, sad theme.

Eldritch turns and looks at his house—his home, the only home he's known for forty-one years—the home he shared with his parents. Its ramshackle appearance reminds him so much of the Birch-Rainey house back when it sat abandoned and neglected, back before Mark. It's amazing how much has changed since Mark rolled into town—how much Eldritch has changed.

"You know they're not here, Eldritch."

Eldritch shakes his head and turns to his uncle. "I know," he says, looking up to the sky. "They're dead."

It has taken eight years for him to admit that, and since he first forced the words out of his mouth earlier that week, Eldritch has been trying to get used to saying it—to get used to *hearing* himself say it.

"My parents are dead, and their souls are in heaven," he continues, "and no amount of searching will change that."

Calvin steps closer to his nephew. "I never said anything because I figured this was how you were dealing with your grief, but then it kept going and going, and honestly, I had no idea how to tell you I knew. So, I just kept my mouth shut. Especially since you didn't seem like you were on the verge of killing yourself anymore."

They don't talk about it. They never do, never have; yet here his uncle is, bringing it up. Eldritch has had a lot of time to think over the last few days, the subject of his suicide attempt weighing on his mind. Something that sat in the forefront of his mind whenever the subject surfaced was how he had treated his Uncle Cal—how callous and ungrateful he had been in the wake of his survival.

"I've been thinking a lot about that lately," Eldritch says, seeing Calvin's comment as the opening he needs to face his guilt and apologize to his uncle. "I never thanked you."

"For what?" Calvin asks, and Eldritch rolls his eyes at his obliviousness.

"For saving my life! For not giving up on me. I swear, if I'd hid that spare key any better…" Eldritch trails off on a sigh and chances a look at his uncle. Calvin's brow is furrowed, confusion plastered across his face as he stares at his nephew.

"What're you talking about?"

"Really?" *Man, he's getting old.* "The spare key."

Calvin shakes his head, shoulders drawing up and hands lifting in a shrug.

"Uncle Cal, the spare key. The one under the brick in the flower bed!" To prove his point, Eldritch walks over to the steps on the side of the front porch. Lifting a brick at the back of the flower bed there, he finds the key and holds it up to his uncle.

"Eldritch, I didn't know anything about that key."

It's Eldritch's turn to look confused, his expression mirroring that of his uncle's.

"No, you did. You must have. You let yourself in."

"Eldritch, when I got here, the front door was wide open."

The news hits Eldritch square in the chest, knocking the wind from his lungs, and he swears time stands still as his uncle recounts the events of that morning.

"You were late for work, and something told me to go check on you. I walked down here, and the door was wide open—*wide* open. I could see straight inside, down the hall, and into the den. I saw you on the floor, ran in, saw the pill bottle. Then I called 9-1-1 and started CPR like they told me. Eldritch, I told you it was a miracle you were alive. Do you know how rare it is for someone to come back from that kind of overdose with virtually no damage to their brain or their kidneys? But not just that—"

"The door was wide open," Eldritch repeats, stunned, still processing the information.

"Yeah, it was. Guess you were too drunk to shut it, or just weren't thinking clearly, but either way, thank God."

"No, Uncle Cal. You don't understand, I locked that door. I locked *all* the doors."

Calvin lets out a long whistle, "Well, somebody wasn't ready to take you, pal."

Eldritch is rocked to his core. In his darkest moment, when he tried to end it all, *He* had opened the door. Eldritch wasn't alone. He had never been alone.

Calvin clears his throat, "Kind of makes you think, doesn't it."

"Think about what?"

"About why it wasn't your time to go. About why you aren't finished here."

Eldritch ruminates on his uncle's words, forced to contemplate why he wasn't allowed to go, and what he could possibly have to contribute and achieve on this earth. *Why would He want to keep me here?* For the most part, Eldritch felt he had spent most of his time hiding away, closing himself off, avoiding people as much as he could because of his gift—

It strikes like lightening.

Because of my gift.

Eldritch hadn't called it that in a long time. "Ability," "curse," those had become the norm over the years. "Gift" hadn't passed his lips in almost thirty years. His parents had always referred to it as such—his mother especially. Where Eldritch saw darkness, his mother saw the light; where he saw a curse, she saw a gift. Maybe—just maybe—she had been onto something.

He thinks back to the times where his gift didn't seem so bad, the times where he felt he had done some good, helped people.

Nadine. Charlie Haskell. Mark.

Eldritch's gift had made a difference in their lives. *Eldritch* had made a difference, and he hadn't even been trying all that hard. Maybe that was the reason behind all this, the source of all his pain and struggle. He had to endure the fire and emerge a new creature, refined, tested…

Strong.

A verse from Isaiah pops into his head, pulled from vaults of his memory.

"Behold, I have refined you, but not as silver; I have tried you in the furnace of affliction."

Although he is reluctant to admit it, Eldritch knows he has a purpose—he has always had a purpose—but he resisted it after being hurt.

Calvin side-eyes him, and as if reading his mind begins to speak, voice low, testing the waters, "You know, I got this friend in Pomaria. He stopped by the store the other day. Started talking about some weird activity they've been having in the house they just bought. Apparently, it's pretty bad."

A few days ago, such a suggestion would have sent Eldritch into a rage, wondering why his uncle would ever suggest placing him in such a situation, but now…

"Tell him to give me a call."

The Birch-Rainey house is a flurry of commotion as Eldritch is given a tour of the place and the substantial progress that has been made in the last several weeks. Mark has an entire crew working for him these days, trying his best to make up for the time stolen from him. The house is coming along, and Eldritch absorbs every detail in wonder. The floors and windows have been replaced, the exterior is being repainted—a light yellow which will go well with the bright, white gingerbread trim, and the black, tin roof he plans to have installed down the line—and the plumbing is being worked on as they speak. This old house that many people had written off as a lost cause was getting a new life, coming into its own, and Eldritch is moved by the knowledge of it.

"So, when do you expect to finish it?" he asks Mark as they climb the grand staircase to the second floor.

"We still have a long way to go, but I'm hoping mid to late spring. Had to hire some extra workers to hit Harry's 'tentative' deadline, but he's going to love it when it's done."

"Well, I think you're doing a spectacular job," Eldritch says as he surveys the expanse of the second-floor landing. His eyes drift to the French doors and notices they've been replaced. Everything about the house has changed since the last time Eldritch was here. Light pours in from all directions, and the air is crisp and clean, despite the lingering sawdust.

"You going to keep it or sell?" he asks, running his hand along the wall where Mark once carved the numbers—remembering how the man's nails cracked and fingers bled from the effort. The numbers are gone, concealed by a fresh coat of sage green paint.

"Sell it. The whole point of this project was to flip it for a profit," Mark says, giving his back a good stretch, which Eldritch knows must be sore from endless days of hard work. "Why? You interested in buying?"

Eldritch turns away from the wall and faces his friend, "What if I am?"

Mark snorts, but Eldritch's face is a picture of sincerity.

"You serious?"

"Very."

Eldritch has thought about this for a while and, given everything that's happened, he feels starting over in a new house wouldn't be such a bad idea; a new place where he can make new memories, memories that aren't sullied by tears and loss. He remembers his first time setting foot in this old house as a teenager. He'd felt a connection, a kinship with the home;

and now that they have both been given a second chance, it makes sense in Eldritch's mind for them to do it together.

"Let me know when you get close to finishing. We can work out the details then."

Mark smiles and shakes his hand, "Deal. It's the least I can do for you. I have to figure out what I'll do once this baby's done."

"I may have just the project for you," Eldritch laughs as the two men descend the stairs.

Mark walks him outside and is shocked to see Eldritch's Celica. "You drove here? That's new."

"Oh, yeah. Surprisingly enough, I do drive from time to time," he jokes. "I'm actually headed to Pomaria to help a friend of my uncle's with a little problem they're having."

"A demon problem?"

"Demon, ghost, who knows? That's where I come in, I guess," Eldritch shrugs and pulls open the driver's side door.

"It's good of you to help like that. People need it."

Eldritch hears the rest of the sentence, the part Mark doesn't say aloud.

"I needed it."

With a nod to the contractor, he climbs into the car and drives away, staring at the Birch-Rainey house in his rearview mirror until he takes a left at the stoplight.

The drive to Pomaria takes about fifteen minutes. Eldritch pops in his *The Eagles: Their Greatest Hits, Vol. 1* CD, and listens to it along the way. *Old habits die hard*. He reaches his destination, pulling into a long, dirt drive lined by maple trees, as the intro to "One of These Nights" begins. The house in question is large and stately, though a bit weathered and worn—every bit as old as the Birch-Rainey house, but in far better shape.

Shutting the car door behind him, Eldritch steps out into the dusty front yard, taking in the area around him. Based on the style of the house and surrounding acreage—and the fact that Pomaria is mostly rural—he guesses this was once a legitimate farmhouse, not the pseudo interpretations one sees on cable design shows.

"Here goes nothing," he says, climbing the steps to the front porch. He looks for a doorbell but can't seem to find one, so he lifts the heavy knocker and raps it against the wooden door three times. Half a minute passes, and Eldritch is tempted to knock again, but the handle turns, and the front door is pulled open, just far enough for a face to emerge. It's a young girl, no more than sixteen. Her eyes are bloodshot, and the dark circles underneath them stand out against the pale skin of her face. She says nothing, and Eldritch can see the apprehension written across her features. Wanting to assuage her fears, he tries for his friendliest smile and speaks first.

"Hi, I'm Eldritch Hayes."

EPILOGUE

It starts small—it always does.
Then it progresses.
At this point, we have two choices: push the truth back down and live in denial or come to terms with the phenomenon and seek a solution. For those who choose the latter, the first step seems an obvious one: identify the presence in question. In the town of Sommerset, South Carolina, a name will be spoken, a number given, from one person who has previously taken this first step to the next person in need.

Step one: call Eldritch Hayes.

ACKNOWLEDGEMENTS

There are many people to thank—many people, without whom, this book would not exist—and I have agonized for hours over how to start this section. See, the trouble is, there is nothing I can say that could possibly convey just how grateful I am for each and every individual who has played a part in the creation of this book. I guess I have to settle for the only words available to me at this moment, but please know, they do my level of gratitude no justice.

To my best friends, Sammi and Cathy: thank you for believing in me, believing in this book, and being two of my biggest cheerleaders from start to finish and beyond. You are the best friends anyone could ever ask for, and I owe you both so much.

To my work family: thank you for your excitement and continued support throughout this journey.

To my beta readers, Cathy, Kristy, Jane, Janice, Ruth, and Sammi: Thank you for sacrificing your time to read this book and provide feedback. You played such an important role in this process, and you helped me realize there really was something to this story.

To my editors, Holly and Taneet: Thank you for taking care of my book-baby and treating it as if it were your own.

Taneet, your developmental edits provided insight and clarity. Holly, your line edits helped turn this book into the best version of itself and made it shine. Eldritch belongs to all of us, and I am so thankful to have had your expertise and advice during this process. I am beyond honored to call you my editors, but more importantly, my friends.

To Monica Hay: Without your program, these pages would have never seen the light of day. Your boot camp changed the trajectory of my life and helped me achieve my dream. Not only that, but through you, I found the most amazing community of writers who I now count among my closest and dearest friends. And, on that note…

To my discord family: What would I have done without you? You saw me through the entire process. From chapter 1 to chapter 30 and all the edits thereafter, you were there to read my ramblings during sprints, help me brainstorm when I was stuck, and support me when I faced some of the most difficult moments in my life. Even though we were hundreds—thousands—of miles apart, you lifted me up when I wanted to crumble. You held my hand as I cut myself and bled these words out onto the page. I love each and every one of you more than you know. Thank you for showing me the true meaning of "found family."

To Kalayna: Girl, you saw it all. The extreme highs, the depressing lows. You saw me at my best and my worst over the last year and a half, and I owe so much to you. All those times I wanted to give up and forget this whole writing thing, you were there with a giant "NOPE" to get me back on track. Thank you for being my constant companion on this journey.

To Mama and Daddy: The real-life Gene and Louise Hayes. My rocks. My anchors in the storm. The reason I have even the slightest bit of belief in myself. Everything I am, everything I have accomplished, is all because of you. I know how blessed I am to have the greatest parents in the world—parents who encouraged me to chase my dreams, who never tried to shove me in a box or snuff out my weirdness. Eldritch's love and attachment to his parents was born out of my relationship with the two of you. This book is as much a part of you as it is me. You are my inspiration. It also helps that you raised me right and made sure I was listening to the good stuff: The Eagles, The Carpenters, and Bread. Every song in this book found its way there because of you. I love you so much—with oceans of love.

And to my Heavenly Father: I *am* nothing without You. I can *do* nothing without You. I *have* nothing without You. You have ordained every step of this journey, and I hope I made You proud. Thank You for implanting this story in my soul and allowing me to be the one to tell it.

Jori

ABOUT THE AUTHOR

Image courtesy of Ruth Cain Photography

Tori Lewis resides in the town of Lexington, South Carolina with her three cats, Webster, Abby, and Bones, and her rough collie, Jamie. She is the first-place winner of the Seventh Writer's Playground Challenge, and Calling Eldritch Hayes is her debut novel. A lover of all things gothic, spooky, nerdy, and weird, she can usually be found bingeing Daredevil, Downton Abbey, or Buffy the Vampire Slayer, or having a horror movie marathon (when she isn't writing, of course). Tori is active in her church and serves as the contemporary worship director, where she puts that music degree she received from The University of South Carolina to good use.

Printed in the USA
CPSIA information can be obtained
at www.ICGtesting.com
LVHW041937040424
776453LV00001B/1

9 798218 385194